He knew he should have thought this through beforehand. "Well," he said, "at the end of it you have me. The person who got the power of the gods. I'll work for you."

Gratt snorted through his malformed nose. "An easy promise to make," he said.

"Well, you do have in your possession some people who are pretty important to me," he said. The gears of his mind were starting to smoke now.

"Hostages," Gratt said. Of all the things Will had said, Gratt did seem to like this the most.

"I'll need some of them," Will said quickly. "You couldn't have all of them. If I'm going to pull this off, I'd need my team."

"Your team?" Gratt said.

"Yes." Will nodded enthusiastically. "The humans. You keep the gods, I go with the humans and get the Deep Ones' power, and I bring it back to you, and then I make the world burn, or whatever you want, but I get to live. Sound good?"

He didn't mention that he'd have the power of a god, and would do whatever in the Hallows he wanted, and that Gratt could go hang. However, he figured that Gratt would probably figure that out on his own.

And yet, somehow, Gratt didn't. Because Gratt said, "All right."

"What?" Will asked.

"A bargain. A deal. You have it." Gratt reached down and seized one of Will's bound arms. His fist was so large it enclosed both forearm and bicep. It would take only a slight squeeze for multiple bones to be broken. "We shake on it." Gratt shook Will's entire body.

By Jon Hollins

The Dragon Lords

THE
DRAGON LORDS
BAD FAITH

JON HOLLINS

Orbit
An imprint of
Little, Brown Book Group
Carmelite House
50 Victoria Embankment
London EC4Y 0DZ

An Hachette UK Company
www.hachette.co.uk

www.orbitbooks.net

ORBIT

First published in Great Britain in 2018 by Orbit

1 3 5 7 9 10 8 6 4 2

Copyright © 2018 by Jonathan Wood

Map by Tim Paul

Excerpt from *You Die When You Die* by Angus Watson
Copyright © 2017 by Angus Watson

A CIP catalogue record for this book
is available from the British Library.

ISBN 978-0-356-50768-2

Printed and bound by CPI Group (UK) Ltd, Croydon CR0 4YY

Papers used by Orbit are from well-managed forests
and other responsible sources.

MIX
Paper from

For Tami, Charlie, and Emma.
Their faith got me here.

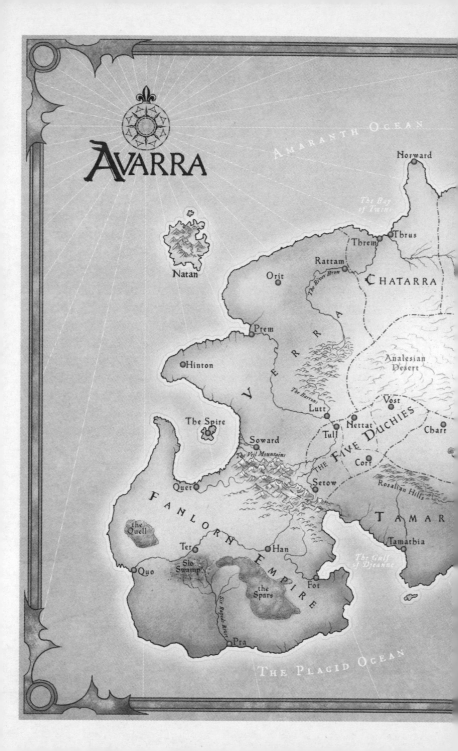

"I'll never pause again, never stand still,
Till either death hath closed these eyes of mine
Or fortune given me measure of revenge."

—*Henry VI, Part 3*,
William Shakespeare

PART 1:
BAD LUCK

1

Death and Other Minor Inconveniences

Klink. A god named for the sound of two coins striking each other. A god of that very sound. A god of all things mercantile and profitable. The catalyst for coin moving from one man's hand to another's purse, where it could join its fellows and . . . clink.

Klink. A god. A being who had been old when the world was young. Worshipped by millions. Even loved by some of them. A being who had inspired hymn, and poem, and myth.

Klink. A god.

Will Fallows watched as Klink's dirty, broken body was hoisted before the crowd and the weakly struggling deity's throat was slit broad as a smile.

Things were definitely not going to plan.

To be fair, that was a statement that could be applied to quite a lot of Will's life recently.

Six months ago, Will had died.

Actually, technically speaking—and Will was definitely willing to get technical over this particular point—he had been murdered. He had been on the verge of liberating the whole world of Avarra from tyrannical dragons—and, incidentally, tyrannical gods like Klink as well—when he had been metaphorically stabbed in the back, and literally stabbed in the throat, by Barph.

Barph was another of the gods, and one whom Will had

previously judged to lack such despotic tendencies. It had been, Will was willing to concede, a fairly big miss on his part.

As was typical when such things occurred, Will subsequently found himself in the Hallows, the lands of the dead. Many of his friends arrived along with him. Barph, it turned out, was pretty liberal when it came to the whole murder thing. He was a god, after all. In fact, after this little coup d'état, Barph was the only god, because all the other gods had previously headed to the Hallows. They had been there under the impression that Will and his friends were going to rescue them. The whole overthrowing-their-tyranny thing hadn't really been discussed with them at that point.

Anyway, as was also typical with such things, Will was pretty pissed about the whole affair. There had been a lot of clenched fists and passionately proclaiming revenge on Barph. Lette—a woman more poetic with her blades than most bards were with words, and therefore someone Will trusted on such issues—had informed him that it felt very epic. There had even been a ledge and wind-tousled hair involved.

Balur—a giant, mercenary lizard man and Lette's usual traveling companion (although Balur had conceded that "into the Hallows" was further than he had intended to take things)—had possessed a differing opinion. As he put it, "Passionate words are being okay for getting bards laid, but they are killing about as many gods as my prick."

Afrit—a former university professor, and therefore someone who Will actually thought might produce an intelligent thought once in a while—had disappointed him by agreeing "with the sentiment, if not the specific phrasing," as she sanctimoniously put it.

Will had not been in the mood for his friends' snark, and had immediately set about trying to prove the lizard man wrong by escaping the Hallows.

That had been six months ago.

To be fair, Will's efforts had been hampered by a number of things. First, his friends' snark. Second, in the wake of Barph's takeover of the heavens, things in the Hallows had—not to put too fine a point on it—gone to utter shit. Previously the domain of Lawl, king of the gods and head cheerleader of rules and regulations, the Hallows had been a highly ordered domain. Tallies of sanctity and sin had been taken for each of the arriving dead, and appropriate afterlives delivered. Massive guardians—all muscles and no personality—had enforced these highly scripted hierarchies, and everything had been in its correct place. Barph, though, was not such a god. Barph was the god of revelry and anarchy and pissing in Lawl's eye. Now he ruled the Hallows, and Lawl was in them, and so Barph was going to have fun.

All rules in the Hallows had been canceled. Anarchy reigned. And then, shortly after that, warlords did. All the guardians—all the massive, powerful enforcers Lawl had put in place—had nothing to hold them in check. And so they made armies of the dead, and went to war on each other.

That sort of thing tended to get in the way of one's revenge, Will had found. And when you explained that to a massive undead general three times your height and weight, things tended to go badly. As Klink could attest.

Well…he could have about ten seconds ago.

The gods were another epic pain in Will's arse. There were six of them. Five now. Lawl, the former ruler of the heavens. Betra, his wife, former goddess of hearth and home, and utter pissing harpy as far as Will was concerned. Klink's twin brother, Toil, god of fields and farmers, and one of the biggest disappointments in a series of fairly massive disappointments in Will's life. Will thought maybe he should be reconciled to them now, but it was still a hard thing to know that you had sacrificed a fatted calf to someone you had subsequently watched cry while he pissed.

After that there was Knole, who was reportedly the goddess of wisdom, although her primary field of expertise seemed to be being an absentminded stain in the britches of Will's life.

Finally there was Cois. Oh, Cois. Will had slept with Cois. It was before either of them had been killed, back when zhe was the hermaphroditic god(dess) of love and lust. If Will were a bragging man and not hopelessly in love (in a more literal sense than normal) with Lette, then it would have been quite the conquest. However, the reasons for their union had been more rational than romantic, and the whole thing had been rather undercut by the fact that Balur had been in the Hallows only about three seconds when he hooked up with hir. What made it even worse was that they were a revolting couple. Will was fairly sure that that level of face licking was decidedly unhygienic.

Will and his friends had met the gods immediately upon their arrival in the Hallows. It turned out the gods had been waiting for them, full of expectations and eagerness, because they had been, at the time, still under the impression that Will was attempting to save them and deliver Avarra back into their greedy little hands. A rather uncomfortable conversation had followed, but Will had figured that would be the end of it. But oh no, instead they had decided to tag along until he fixed things, as if he had any intention of doing that. Still, to a former deity, killing Barph in an inventive and painful way apparently sounded close enough.

And despite all of this, despite the nagging and the bickering and the delays and his companions' endemic lack of urgency, Will had come up with a plan. Will had figured a way out and back to Avarra.

It had been Cois who had told them about the Deep Ones.

They'd been in the Hallows about a month. The initial scrabble to survive, and to escape the collapsing power structures that had come with Barph's rise to power, finally seemed to be over. They had scavenged enough food, wood, and clothing to be comfortable for the night. They had made a fire, roasted meat.

Will had been pacing in circles. It was his default setting at the time. Plans for revenge seethed beneath his skin.

Balur's mind was elsewhere, though, because apparently Will was the only one of them who could focus.

"Who would be thinking," Balur had said, pointing at Lawl, who'd been curled up in a corner muttering angrily to himself, "that that prick built the Hallows?"

"No, he didn't!" Cois had sounded scandalized. "It existed long before he did."

"What?" Afrit, sagging by the fire, had come alive with such ferocity, Will could almost believe she'd actually... well, come alive. "Before?" she'd said with wonder in her voice.

"Lawl repurposed this space," Cois had said patiently.

"Silence, harlot!" Lawl had snapped. Though, to be fair, that was about 90 percent of what he'd said even when he was a god.

"Fine," Cois had acknowledged. "Yes, he did expand upon it. And restructure it. And put in place a lot of the hierarchy you see now. But he didn't build it from scratch."

"But..." Afrit had pushed her hand through her growing nest of hair. "Before?"

"Is this being the first time you have been hearing that word?" Balur asked. "It is being to do with chronology."

"I know what pissing *before* means, Balur," Afrit had snapped. "The issue is that there isn't meant to be a before. When it comes to Lawl, he and Betra are ground zero for divinity. They are the beginning."

Cois had looked over at Lawl and squinted. "Is that what you've been telling people all these years?"

"Silence, harlot!" Lawl had said, taking his cue.

"Well then," Cois had said, looking directly at Lawl while zhe spoke. "Let me dispense some truth. There was a before. There were the Deep Ones."

"The who?" Afrit's voice had scraped for octaves higher than the cavern ceiling above them.

"Seriously?" Cois had looked about at the surrounding mortals.

"Don't be looking at me," Balur had said. "Analesian religious education is stopping at, 'And the gods were inventing punching people in the face.'"

Cois had shaken hir head minutely. "The Deep Ones. Our former masters. Vast, horrifying beasts beyond human ken. The infinite unknowable made flesh. Well...almost flesh. Or... something a lot like flesh, although also exactly the opposite of flesh. They're hard to explain. Just assume they're sort of like the inverse of sanity made into giant monsters, and you're probably close enough. Total pricks.

"Anyway, they ruled the Hallows before we did. They also created Lawl and Betra. Who then birthed the rest of us one way or another. But we were all their slaves. And then Lawl led us in rebellion against them. And we defeated them. We condemned them to eternal sleep. We stole their divinity. Lawl reshaped this place, then got into the whole 'divine ruler' thing, and created the heavens and the mortal plane. Then humanity, and eons later...this mess."

There had been silence then, except for the sound of Afrit hyperventilating.

And in that silence it had felt as if tiny slivers of glass were falling through Will's mind—slashing through confusion and frustration and carving a shape.

Stole their divinity.

"The Deep Ones?" he had said. "They're still down here?"

"I didn't condemn them to be eternal sleepwalkers," Lawl had barked.

Stole their divinity.

And for the first time since he had entered the Hallows, Will had smiled.

*   *   *

Will didn't know much about how to escape the Hallows, but he did know that divinity sounded a lot like a way to achieve it. And apparently some of it had been left lying around. And so all he had to do was get to it. And as he had the very architect of the Hallows with him, that hadn't seemed like too much of a problem.

Except Will Fallows was also the punch line of life's little comedy.

"How should I know?" Lawl had said when Will had asked him where the Deep Ones lay.

"For all the obvious reasons," Will had pointed out, while trying to ignore all the obvious reasons for punching Lawl in his obnoxious face.

"There is so much," Lawl had told him, apparently relishing the rare opportunity to be a condescending dick, "that you don't understand. I constructed reality. I created law. I made order. That is not a simple thing. I hid the Deep Ones. I sealed them from memory and discovery. They are a hidden thing. That is a rule. I did not tuck them under a rock. I created a rule of reality that they be hidden. They are hidden from everyone. Even me."

Will had checked his companions' faces just to make sure it wasn't just him. It wasn't. "Yeah," he'd said. "That's a stupid rule."

Lawl had shrugged. "The Hallows were a first attempt."

Lette had cleared her throat. It had sounded a lot like the word *bullshit*. Lawl and Will checked to confirm this.

"What?" Lette said. And then, off their continued arched eyebrows, she said, "Oh, come on. Even if that is true, what? He just threw that much power away? Nobody does that. Not even someone who comes up with a rule that stupid. If he doesn't know, someone knows. Someone he had access to. There is Someone Who Knows Hidden Things or some such portentous bullshit."

Lawl had a terrible poker face.

* * *

The name of Someone Who Knows Hidden Things was Gratt. He was one of the massive guardians, all muscle and no personality, three times Will's height and weight. A creature to make even Balur's eight feet look small. Gratt was also one of the generals in the civil war that was churning the eternal plains of the Hallows to mud.

Still, Gratt also knew what Will needed to know, and so Will had traipsed across the eternal plains, dragging his sorry crew of companions with him, and finally, after months of searching and haranguing, and dodging combat, and not dodging combat and subsequently washing a surprising amount of blood off himself, he had arrived here.

Klink's body spasmed once, twice, lay still. The god's blood steamed in the early morning.

Here wasn't as good a place as Will had hoped.

Once one was already dead, Will had figured, that was pretty much the last stop on life's journey. There were no places to go from here. Yet again, reality had found a way to disappoint him. "There is the Void," Cois had told him after their first real fight in the underworld, while Lette had been picking throwing knives out of the corpses and Balur had been licking the blood off his claws. "There is the utter unmaking of one's self. The dissolution of personality and identity into the abyss."

"At least it would mean not listening to you," Lawl had called.

Well, now Klink never had to listen to Cois or Lawl or even Will ever again.

Gratt was holding Klink by the feet. In his other hand he held a vast sword, at least as long as Will was tall. One edge was sharp and bloody as a butcher's cleaver, the other was a ragged assembly of rough spikes.

"That is being an impractical weapon," Balur muttered next to Will.

"Seriously," Lette whispered. "That's just going to get stuck on a lot of armor. Someone's going to stab you in the kidneys while you're trying to unhook it."

"Well," Will said, "why don't you go up there and tell him?" Will was never at his best, he knew, when he was bound hand and foot.

"Silence!" barked one of their guards. He put a boot in Will's back and kicked him face-first into the mud.

The guard was a member of Gratt's army. One of the many, many dead who had found their way down to the Hallows however many millennia ago, who now had found his way into Gratt's employ. He seemed to enjoy kicking people bound hand and foot. Will hoped he'd had some pretty shitty millennia down here.

In all honesty, that was probably the truth of things. Many of the members of Gratt's army, now all arrayed before the general and Klink's limp corpse, seemed to have had a rough go of things in the Hallows. Enough that they felt more than a little resentful toward the gods who had established the system of rewards and punishments within the Hallows. Enough that should, say, some unsuspecting idiot march into the middle of that army asking for favors, with all those gods in tow at his back, then negotiations would take a distinct downward turn for said unsuspecting idiot.

And then said unsuspecting idiot would find himself tied hand and foot in a cage at the back of an army, while a despotic warlord stood at the front of it, slitting the throats of one of those gods for his army's amusement.

The army was cheering. The other former gods—also enjoying the hospitality offered by the cage—were in more of a wailing-and-gnashing-of-teeth mood. Toil, Klink's twin, was crying and had apparently pissed himself. Will couldn't help but think of all the meals he could have enjoyed if he just hadn't bothered sacrificing that fatted calf.

The morning's entertainment over, the army dispersed and

went back to...doing army things. Will wasn't entirely sure what that involved. He had been a farmer before he had been... several other things. A false prophet. A figurehead of a popular uprising. A farmer again. A resistance fighter. A man with divine power in his blood. A dead man. None of them had given him any insight into what armies did in their off-hours.

What one small detachment of soldiers was doing, though, was approaching the cage where Will and his companions were all being held. They exchanged words with the enthusiastic back kicker. He went over and kicked Lawl in the back. "Get up," he said, somewhat paradoxically.

In the end, several large and energetic soldiers got tired of kicking Lawl over, and carried him away like so much bundled meat. Lawl screamed a lot, which was rather unbecoming for someone who had once styled himself "the king of the gods," but on the other hand this was exactly what had happened to Klink shortly before his all-too-brief appearance onstage with Gratt.

"Well," Lette said to Will, "if you're all done observing people we know being killed, now seems like a good moment for a plan out of here."

This was an entirely accurate statement. However, it didn't help Will come up with a plan any faster.

From the direction of Gratt's tent, the screaming intensified.

"Bones are being useful," Balur contributed. "I have been using them as all sorts of tools for escaping jails. Clubs. Shivs. Picks for locks."

Will looked over the bare iron floor of the cage they were in. "There aren't any bones here," he pointed out in the vague hope it might get Balur to stop.

"Toil is being full of bones," Balur pointed out. "And it is only being a matter of time before he is being murdered anyway. Why are we letting Gratt have all the fun?"

This didn't help Will plan either.

Eventually Lawl was brought back to them. He wasn't screaming anymore. He was barely even breathing.

"See you bright and early tomorrow," said one of the guards with a cruel laugh. Another drew his finger over his neck and rolled his eyes back. His compatriots laughed. Toil let out another sob.

Will still did not have a plan. Will did, perhaps, have the idea of what his plan might be. But he supposed that was as much as he usually had. And it wasn't as if his plans ever seemed to work out anyway.

"Take me to Gratt," he said with as much force as he could.

The soldiers stopped laughing. They eyed him cautiously. Which was what sensible people did when they were in a room with a crazy man, and that was what Will was announcing himself to be.

"Will," Lette said, "let's talk about this."

"You got a death wish, little man?" said one of the guards, ignoring Lette.

Will ignored her too: "Yes," he told the guard. Because that, in the end, was his plan.

There was a lot of kicking involved, of course. The guards took great pains to ensure Will knew where his kidneys were and exactly how much they could hurt before they took him to see Gratt. It seemed to be a point of pride with them.

They dragged Will across what was left of a field of wheat. There wasn't much left of it. Mostly it was mud and trenches and poorly dug latrines. There had been a lot of wheat fields when Will had first arrived in the Hallows. In one of his less truculent moods, Lawl had described them as a "motif." Lette had interpreted that as "a pretentious way to describe a lack of imagination." Even Afrit had laughed at that.

The Hallows themselves consisted of a seemingly endless chain of massive, country-size caverns. Each one could take weeks to traverse. Some were tall enough for clouds to form. They were interconnected by narrow channels of rock that formed natural choke points and had served as most of the battlegrounds in the sprawling civil war that had consumed the past six months.

Gratt's tent—complete with its surrounding army—was near the entrance of one of these tunnels. It was, Will suspected, supposed to be imposing. In all honesty, it mostly resembled a filthy circus tent, but based on how Will's last conversation with Gratt had gone, he wasn't going to point that shortcoming out.

Will had been unceremoniously flung at the feet of many people in his time. More than most people, he suspected. Still, Gratt's feet were by far the most imposing.

Gratt himself was perhaps twenty feet tall, and squat despite his height. His skin was the dull angry red of yesterday's violence, covered in whorls and knobs of hardened gray horn. Tattoos in a myriad of styles, colors, and skill levels had been scrawled across his arms. Slabs of metal were strapped haphazardly across his vast muscles, which seemed to have been built on an industrial scale.

Atop this mountain of angry flesh was a head that looked as if it had been abandoned halfway through its construction. It probably had been. One evening, Lawl—in an oddly confessional mood—had told Will the creatures here had been among his first creations. He had, he'd said, still been figuring out how to do faces.

"Getting the eyes even...," he'd said. Then Lawl had just shaken his head.

Gratt sat in a chair built on the same scale and with the same skill as himself. A lot of skulls were tied to it.

"He wanted to see you," one of the guards said by way of an explanation for Will's abrupt appearance. He kicked Will in the kidneys again just in case Will had forgotten where they were.

"So?" Gratt asked.

"What?" asked the soldier.

"So what if he wanted to see me?" Gratt asked around massive jutting jaws. His grating voice made Balur's baritone sound almost melodious.

"Erm," the soldier managed.

"He's a prisoner," Gratt said slowly. "We don't take requests from him."

"But...," the soldier said, "I thought...perhaps...some sort of valuable information...or...something? Like...a bargain?"

Gratt stood from his chair. He paced toward the soldier. He peered down at him. He was three times the soldier's height. The soldier gulped. Then Gratt backhanded him. Gratt's hand was so big, he actually backhanded most of the man's torso. Large parts of the man's body lost their structural integrity. A bloody, ragged, pulp-filled sack that used to be a soldier flew through the tent flap and outside.

Will begin to think he should have waited until he had slightly more of a plan.

Gratt then looked down at where Will was, in the dirt at his feet. He smiled. His tusks were very prominent. "So," he said, still smiling, "what was it you wanted?"

"Okay," Will managed, "this probably isn't the smartest thing to do, but I'm going to ask you to bear with me here for just a moment."

Gratt cracked massive knuckles.

"So," Will said, because, really, talking was all he could think to do now, "I've been thinking. For, well, millennia, you have known where the Deep Ones are. The very beings that gave the gods themselves power. For millennia you've had the possibility of going down and taking that power for yourself, of ascending to godhood. And you've not done it."

Gratt stooped. His face was monumental. His breath smelled of meat. "You have come here," he said, "to tell me things I know?"

"Oh no," Will said. "Sorry, I should have been clear. I'm negotiating."

"And what," Gratt asked, "do you have to offer beside a fast mouth?"

Which was a fair question, although in Will's opinion it underestimated the value of a fast mouth. His had gotten him this far, at least. Though this was the Hallows, so perhaps that wasn't that far after all.

"Well," Will said, "I do have a death wish."

This seemed to give Gratt pause, which was good because it was supposed to.

"You see," Will went on into the gap, "the only reason I can think that you haven't taken that power for yourself is because you're afraid."

Gratt straightened. He licked his tusks. "Not so fast a mouth after all," he said.

"Oh!" Will would have held his hands up in protest if they weren't bound together. "I'm not calling you a coward. Not at all. That's sort of my point. If you're afraid of it, then going to the Deep Ones and taking their power must be some pretty messed-up shit. Something really awful, and almost certainly involving being condemned to the Void. And I have to figure you don't have a death wish. So you don't want to go and get it. But you see, I do, and I'm willing to give it a go."

Gratt thought about this. "So I let you go and get the power of the gods, because . . . you are suicidal? That is your bargain?"

Which on the face of it, Will had to admit, probably didn't sound that attractive. He knew he should have thought this through beforehand. "Well," he said, "at the end of it you have me. The person who got the power of the gods. I'll work for you."

Gratt snorted through his malformed nose. "An easy promise to make," he said.

"Well, you do have in your possession some people who are

pretty important to me," he said. The gears of his mind were starting to smoke now.

"Hostages," Gratt said. Of all the things Will had said, Gratt did seem to like this the most.

"I'll need some of them," Will said quickly. "You couldn't have all of them. If I'm going to pull this off, I'd need my team."

"Your team?" Gratt said.

"Yes." Will nodded enthusiastically. "The humans. You keep the gods, I go with the humans and get the Deep Ones' power, and I bring it back to you, and then I make the world burn, or whatever you want, but I get to live. Sound good?"

He didn't mention that he'd have the power of a god, and would do whatever in the Hallows he wanted, and that Gratt could go hang. However, he figured that Gratt would probably figure that out on his own.

And yet, somehow, Gratt didn't. Because Gratt said, "All right."

"What?" Will asked.

"A bargain. A deal. You have it." Gratt reached down and seized one of Will's bound arms. His fist was so large it enclosed both forearm and bicep. It would take only a slight squeeze for multiple bones to be broken. "We shake on it." Gratt shook Will's entire body.

Gratt went back to the cage with Will. The others watched openmouthed as Gratt commanded the soldiers to free Will's arms.

"Sold us out, did you?" Lawl asked.

Will ignored Lawl. He looked to Gratt. "And the other humans," he said.

Gratt nodded, and Lette's and Afrit's arms were freed. Will realized his mistake. "Oh, and the Analesian," he said, pointing to Balur.

Gratt arched what might have been intended to be an eyebrow.

Lawl really had done a terrible job on his face. "That was not what we agreed."

"I need him," Will said, and then tried to think why on earth that might be true. "For muscle."

Gratt considered. "You will need it," he said.

Will began to think he should probably have checked exactly how difficult it was to get to the Deep Ones before he started embroiling his friends in these dangers.

Limbs freed, Balur stood and growled at a lot of people. Then he pointed to Cois. "And hir," he said. "We will be needing hir."

"Cois?" Gratt said. He sounded amused.

"For muscle," Balur said, somehow keeping a straight face.

Gratt looked to Will. "Zhe has..."—Will tried to kill that little pause—"important information about this place. And zhe's Cois. Zhe's unimportant. You have Lawl and Betra. The king and queen of the gods. You have Toil, the god I worshipped my whole life." It was hard to keep a straight face when he said that. "I will come back for them."

And he would. He really did mean it. They might be arseholes. They might have been tyrants. But they had been the gods of his childhood. And they had somehow become his responsibility as well. He would come back, and he would bring the power of a god with him, and he would free them, and he would scrape Gratt from the landscape as if he were scraping pig shit off his shoe.

They all assembled in front of Gratt. "So," Will asked, "where are we going?"

"The Killing Plains," Gratt told them.

"That doesn't sound great," Afrit said.

"It sounds bad," Lette agreed.

"It is bad," Cois said.

"What?" Balur shook his head. "It is sounding amazing." But then again he said things like that.

"It is where we send the worst who come to the Hallows,"

Gratt told them. "It is where we send the psychotics, those who kill for pleasure and who cannot stop killing. It is where we send them so that they may kill each other and condemn each other to the Void. It is where only the strongest, and fastest, and most deadly of us survive. It is certain death to go there. In the Killing Plains—if you live long enough—you will find a gorge. Go down into the gorge. At its base is a tunnel. That will take you to the Deep Ones. To something worse than simple death."

He smiled at Will. It was not a pretty smile. "What is left of you will return to me, or these gods will die." He nodded. "A good bargain, I think."

Will's companions did not seem to agree with Gratt on this point. But they, in Will's opinion, were still having a lot of trouble focusing on the end goal here, which was getting out of here and beating the ever-living shit out of Barph. As far as he was concerned, this was a step forward.

And so he stepped forward, and he led the others toward the Killing Plains, and toward certain death.

2

First in the Heavens,
Last in Our Hearts

Gratt watched Will and the others leave. When they were out of earshot, he signaled to his guards and headed back to his tent. A few minutes later, they deposited what was left of Lawl in front of him.

Gratt hated Lawl. He hated him with all the passion of a spurned child. Of a malformed creation ignored by his maker, abandoned for his ugliness, and left down here for millennia to fulfill rote duties over and over and over again.

However, Gratt was also practical.

Lawl looked up at Gratt and grinned. "See," he said. "What did I tell you? He knows nothing. He thinks going to the Deep Ones will make him a god as well."

Gratt shrugged. "You have bought yourself a week of life at best. When he doesn't return, I will kill you then."

"I promise you, he is surprisingly effective."

There was a gleam of hope in Lawl's eyes, which was the only reason Gratt had agreed to this bargain. He didn't give the human much longer than two minutes in the Killing Plains. And then he would get to pull all that hope away from Lawl, and it would be so sweet.

For a moment the idea crossed his mind that the human would be successful. He dismissed it quickly, but not before he shuddered. Gratt wouldn't wish that upon anyone. Not even Lawl.

3

Fiery Zeal

Far, far above Will and Lette and all their terrible, terrible mistakes, Quirkelle Bal Tehrin was getting ready to make her own.

Her belly was pressed into long grass. The smell of dirt and animal shit was ripe in her nostrils. The sheath for her hunting knife was pressed painfully into her hip. Mud was smeared over her hands and clothes. And she was grinning like a fool.

Five men and women were scattered in the grass around her, armed with a variety of weapons. Gartrand clutched his grandfather's short sword, sharpened so many times that its blade was almost as narrow as a rapier's. Ellabet had a wooden staff, its tips encased in cold, hard steel. Poll held a club he had carved himself from the limb of a heavy oak. Tarryl had his old yew bow, an arrow fletched with goose feathers clutched between his teeth. And Salette... well, Salette had a sock weighted with sand. But Salette brought a lot of enthusiasm with her, and that made up for a lot.

There were eight others scattered farther afield, all with their own makeshift and homespun weapons. Thirteen men and women. Thirteen fighters. Thirteen people fueled by anger, outrage, and an unshakable sense of justice. Thirteen who refused to simply lie down and accept the world as it was. And all of them were waiting for her signal.

The Barphian temple lay below them like a throat waiting to be slit.

Quirk's rage was almost a palpable thing in her gut. She could swear that she could feel it crawling around inside her. Its barbs and hooks caught at her, inflamed her.

It was almost a year that she had been at war now. It had started in her hometown of Tamathia, long before Barph's rise, back when the dragons started to threaten dominance over Avarra. And she had been a reluctant fighter. She had resisted violence for as long as she could. But in the end her opponents only understood the language of force. So, slowly, she had learned the grammar of bloodshed. It came easily to her now.

But this creature of rage. This thing that mewled and spit and tore inside her...that was Barph's creation. That was his own thing. His gift to her.

She had owned it once before. A long time ago. It had been forced upon her. When she was seven, Hethren, the demigod horseman, had plucked her from her parents' cold, dead hands and taken her to be part of his war band raging through the north. He had cultivated her rage like a royal gardener in his hothouse. He had broken her until her only concept of human-ity was viscera and bone. Things to be broken. Breaths to be taken. Blood to be burst from the sack of skin that contained it.

And then...then there had been rescue. There had been kindness. Concepts she had forgotten or had believed were only myths. Eight years. Eight years it had taken the kind men and women of Tamathia to bring her back to herself, to teach her how to be human again, to slay that beast of rage.

She had liked being the person those Tamathians made her. A professor at a university. A creature of logic. An educator. She helped the world. She broadened its horizons. She was so very, very close to being whole.

And then, somewhere, somehow...Afrit.

Afrit had been a professor too. And at first she had just been that. Just a face in the corridors of the university. But then she had been... what? A nuisance. That thought almost made Quirk smile now. Someone nipping at her heels with questions. Someone waiting at her door at odd hours. Afrit had believed herself Quirk's fan, enamored with Quirk's early adventuring and her academic vigor. Such an idea had been foreign to Quirk's view of herself. But then events had forced things to a head. The dragons' attempt to overthrow the gods had thrown the pair of them into partnership as unlikely leaders of a resistance movement. Everything had come clear.

And then everything had become less clear... Emotions had become entangled. Afrit, it became apparent, was enamored with more than Quirk's mind. But that part of Quirk was broken, a casualty of Hethren's brutality. She was a creature of intellect now. She had left physicality behind. That was who she was.

And then Afrit had broken Quirk's idea of herself utterly. She had destroyed all Quirk's ideas. All her promises to herself.

Afrit had made Quirk love.

Afrit had made her love by sacrificing herself.

Barph had come for Quirk, to kill her, to take away the divinity that Quirk held nestled in her heart, thinking she was keeping it safe for Knole's return. And in the confusion and desperation of the fight, Afrit had sacrificed herself. She had let Quirk live. And she had made Quirk love her.

But then she was dead. And so Quirk's love was born a useless, pointless thing. And then, just as Afrit's death had breathed life into Quirk's love, Quirk's love breathed life into her rage.

Barph had done this to her. Barph had taken Afrit from her. And so Quirk would take everything from Barph.

Slowly she began to crawl forward on her belly. The thick grass she lay in continued for another ten yards before it was interrupted by the pebble-strewn pathway that surrounded the temple's forecourt. She could just make out a guard strolling back and forth through the space right before her, swinging his arms and working out a crick in his shoulder. He would pause from time to time, adjust the crotch of his britches, yawn.

It was easy, in some ways, to think of him as just a man. A little hungover, a little tired, waiting for his shift to end so he could shuffle back to his barracks or dormitory room to polish his armor and play dice with his friends. His only crime his utter banality.

Easy. And a lie.

This man was a monster. An oppressor. This man's simple existence condoned a dictator, a killer, a peddler of hate and lies. This man didn't just accept Barph's hegemony, he defended it. When Barph told him to tear something down, he obeyed. He ripped and tore at the foundations of culture and learning and hope, all at his master's will, all without any care for the consequences. There was nothing banal about this man, just as there was nothing banal about the god who commanded him.

Six months ago, with Lawl's carefully ordered world laid out before him, Barph had begun to kick at the anthill like an angry toddler. He had manifested in palaces and castles. He had plucked the heads from kings and queens as if they were grapes upon the vine. He had slain generals and dukes and ambassadors. He had torn down the walls of courthouses and set alight cities' guards. He had systematically and comprehensively destroyed every individual and institution involved in maintaining order in every city in the world.

It had taken him a month to bring Avarra to its knees. A totalitarian insistence on anarchy. It was a concept so hypocritical it would have made Quirk laugh if she had still been capable of laughter. If she hadn't been trying to mend the broken bodies that always seemed to be thick around her. If she hadn't been stabbing his priests over and over and over again in their stupid, ugly, dumb fucking faces.

Quirk crept forward another yard. The guard stopped,

squinted out over the scrubland where she was hiding. The others were lying flat and still. She was leaving them behind. She could feel Tarryl's eyes boring into her, trying to act like hooks to hold her back.

Tarryl was a pussy who needed to remember to bring his balls to these affairs, as far as Quirk was concerned.

Furtively but furiously she signaled him to come forward. He hesitated, then wriggled up on his belly.

"There's too many of them," he said. "There's thirty guards plus the priests. Surprise isn't enough." There was more passion in his voice than she'd expected from the old man. He was a phenomenal shot, but for a resistance fighter he was usually surprisingly reluctant to either resist or fight.

There were words that Quirk could say now. She had reams and reams of words. For so long, in her life after Hethren, she had worked on always having the right words. She had so firmly believed that all problems could be talked out, be reasoned out, if everyone just came with an open mind. That deep down, everyone was reasonable, if you just gave them a chance.

For an intellectual, she had been shockingly foolish.

Quirk didn't say a word. Quirk just stood up.

She heard Tarryl gasp.

She saw the guard cock his head, turn around. She saw his eyes go wide.

And she smiled once more.

There was a reason Hethren had taken her to be part of his war band. There was a reason others followed her. There was a reason she had been able to stand against the dragons, and against Barph.

When she had been in her mother's womb, one of the gods had touched Quirk, and she had been given a gift.

Quirk stretched out her hands toward the guard, and gave birth to fire.

*　　*　　*

When Quirk had first set the world aflame, it had scared her so badly she had pissed herself. She was six years old. She had been thinking about how her brother, Andatte, had stolen the licorice root that she had hidden in her bedroll, and that she liked to chew at night when everyone else was asleep. She had been thinking about how unfair it was, and how she didn't want to cry, but it made her feel like crying. She had been alone, dodging the other children and trying to avoid her mother's giving her a chore to do. She was hidden in a woodshed, empty during the hot summer months. And as she raged silently at her brother and fought vainly against tears, the heat of the shed had seemed to rise and rise, scalding her. And she had almost screamed, she was getting so hot, almost gone to look for her mother. Almost.

And then...

Then her hands were on fire. And then the woodshed was on fire. And she had screamed for real and true then. And she had gone running for her mother. And she had been so scared she would get in trouble, she hadn't told anyone how the fire had really happened. And every time she remembered what had happened, hot tears would spill down her face, and the other children would point and laugh, as long as Andatte wasn't around.

But even in that first moment, in that unbearable crescendo of heat, in the terror that had gripped her, there had been a sense of ecstasy too. A sense of release. Something chained within her broke free, and it rejoiced in that freedom.

And now, here, burning the guard of a Barphian temple dressed in bronze armor and gripping a steel-tipped spear, she felt it again. She understood it now, she thought. She didn't long for it as she had once, when she was wild and blunted to almost every other pleasure in life. She didn't think of it as a curse either, as she'd been taught to. It was simply part of her. And she had to be careful, yes, but that didn't mean she had to be fearful. Magic and flame—they were tools and had their uses.

Like burning this living shit of a guard at a Barphian temple, dressed in his preposterous armor and gripping his useless bloody spear.

In the crackle of the flames and the screams of the dying guard and the shouts of shock and horror from the others, she missed the twang of Tarryl's bow. But then an arrow fletched with goose feathers was jutting from the throat of another guard, who was gurgling and collapsing. Another arrow glanced off the curve of a bronze helmet.

From Quirk's right there was a whirring sound, and then a rock the size of a hen's egg smashed into another guard's cheek, and bone crunched and blood sprayed, and the man was dropping howling to the ground.

Her signal, it seemed, had been universally clear. Around her the last resistance force she knew of in Avarra tore into battle.

It was not an efficient fighting force. It was not well disciplined. There was no uniform charge. No attempt to pick off particular weaker-looking members of this tribe. But there was passion. And watching Salette smash her weighted sock into the side of a priest's head brought a genuine smile to Quirk's lips.

She marched into the chaos her plans had created. Into the screams and the shouts, the blood and the fury. A guard came at her, spear clutched in both hands above his head. She made a pyre of him, pushed him casually away.

The majority of the priests had retreated back to the body of the temple. They were pushing the heavy wooden doors closed. She could see others already wrestling with the bar to hold them closed and leave their comrades trapped outside.

Wooden doors. She would have laughed if she laughed anymore these days.

A blade whistled past her ear, buried itself in the smoking wood. A bronze-clad temple guard howled, wrenched the blade free. The guard recovered, came at her again, blade held low. She closed the distance, feinted left, darted right, put her hand into his face. Her hand was wreathed in fire.

Teeth gritted, Quirk burned down the temple doors, filled the room beyond the doors with fire, and marched inside.

Smoke roiled around her head as she strode through an elegant stone arch carved with vines and lifelike clusters of grapes.

The soldier waiting behind the arch missed his chance to kill her by a split second. His blow came just a fraction of a moment too late. She caught the slightest glimpse of movement, and her hair-trigger nerves sent her skittering sideways, ensuring his blade bit into her shoulder and not her neck.

Howling in pain, staggering away, she kept the wherewithal to clamp a flaming hand to the wound, stanching the bleeding. But the guard was already trying to make up for his poor timing, and Quirk didn't have moments to spare in preventing herself from bleeding out.

The guard was rushing her, sword held above his head. She staggered back, tripped over her own feet, sprawled.

The guard stood over her, started to swing the sword down at her stomach.

Afrit. She would find Afrit in the Hallows.

Afrit.

There was a gurgling sound and a clank of metal. She opened an eye. An arrow sprouted from the guard's neck. He keeled over backward.

She blinked. Smoke was everywhere and she didn't...

Tarryl appeared, looked down at her.

"Gods." He spat. "The fuck is wrong with you?" He reached down, grabbed her wrist. It was the injured arm. She screamed as he hauled her to her feet. The man blanched. "Fuck's sake."

"Leave me." Quirk was panting through the pain. "We've got the element of—"

"Would you shut up." Tarryl shook his head. "Crazy bitch. We've got two dead outside and five wounded. The only reason they haven't retreated is because they wanted to get you out of here in one piece, and I was stupid enough to volunteer."

Shouts from the other end of the room cut off Quirk's objections. Shadows moved through the smoke of her fires. Tarryl pulled her backward down the corridor. Her arm protested. She didn't.

They made it outside, and three others closed around them. Gartrand had a gash in his skull above one eye, and half his pale face was sheeted in blood. Poll was holding his club in his off hand, the other arm clutched protectively to his ribs.

"Salette," Quirk managed to say. "Where's Salette?"

Tarryl didn't look back at her, instead launching an arrow at the temple doorway. "Two dead," he said.

They retreated up the hill, back toward the safety of the trees. Smoke poured out of the windows of the temple as Quirk's fires took hold. Temple guards attempted to rally. Priests tried to smother flames with wineskins. And supported by the arms of others, Quirk felt like nothing but a failure.

4

Did I Stutter?

Up, far above Quirk, and impossibly far above Will, Barph rose and so did the sun. The exact relationship between the pair was hazy to Barph. Did the sun rise because he did? Or did he rise because the idiotic ball of fire was shining directly into his eyes through the bedroom window? He could probably figure it out if he concentrated, but he was trying to avoid concentrating, especially with a hangover like this one.

After a while he attempted to get out of bed. His red silk sheets had apparently launched a sneak attack in the night and mired his legs. As he tried to rise, they flung him murderously off the edge of the four-poster and onto the floor, where he fell and rolled through discarded wine bottles, stained chalices, and plates of grapes. He flung the sheets away, picked himself up, and stumbled blearily through the room, searching for the door. He couldn't find it, so he waved his hand at a wall and had one appear there.

He staggered through the Summer Palace, rearranging corridors as necessary to allow for a more rapid journey to some fresh air. Then, bored of that, he rearranged the palace so that most of it was behind him instead. The architecture rumbled and rattled, marble sliding over granite, as plaster ran and moldings folded and unfolded in and out of reality.

Only the font stayed in place. The font at the heart of the

palace. The font full of his blood, which marked him as owner of this place. Its one true owner. Him alone.

When it was done, there were double doors before Barph, and he opened them onto the gardens. The sun saw its opportunity to make a fresh assault on his eyes, so he rearranged some clouds, and then grew a few trees for shade and sent the clouds skittering away. The sun glowered at him, but could do no harm. Nothing could.

Barph was a god.

No. Not just *a* god. *The* god. Barph was it. The solo deity. Numero uno. The heavens, and Avarra, and all of creation were his and his alone.

He pulled a chair into existence, and a table, and a large carafe of something red and exquisite. Then he reinvented the chair four or five times until he got the volume and consistency of the cushions just right.

Yes. It was good to be god.

Just because he was the only god did not mean he was alone, of course. Under Lawl's rule the heavens had been populated with servants and guards and butlers and valets and kitchen maids and all sorts of creatures who had roles too obscure for anyone but them and Lawl to know. Barph had done away with all that. That wasn't him. In fact, Barph was the exact opposite of what Lawl was. Now there were no longer servants or guards or butlers or valets or fucking kitchen maids. Now there were just very drunk, very happy people, most of whom would wake up with no idea of where they were because he'd just rearranged the architecture again. Ah well. Hopefully no one was trapped in a doorless room this time.

Barph could see at least one of the heavens' former guards lying unconscious in the middle of a gravel path. He thought about it and then reshaped the creature's feet so that they were massive and splayed and waved in the breeze. He thought about the noise they would make slapping about as the thing walked, and giggled to himself.

Yes, it was good to be a god. He could run things the way he wanted. And what he wanted was to make sure nothing really ran at all.

One edict, that was all. He had issued just one command: Let there be disorder. No more hierarchies. No more rules. No more enslavement of the self to artificial strictures. He had freed all of Avarra.

There had been a lot of bloodshed after that edict, but... omelet, eggs, and so forth.

He emptied the carafe down his throat, felt the hangover retreat in fear of what else he might do to it. Reenergized, he decided to go and survey his kingdom. The world he'd liberated.

He swayed through the gardens—once formal, now a riot of color and bramble that he remade just frequently enough to keep the former servants on their toes. He had half a memory of creating something vile and grisly and mostly made of mouths to wander around here at some point, but maybe that had just been a dream. Without Toil here, he couldn't be sure. Toil had always been good for reminding him what he'd gotten up to the night before, mostly because he wouldn't shut up complaining about it.

But Toil, of course, wasn't here. Toil was in the Hallows, whining and wallowing in misery. Because he fucking deserved to be. All the gods did. All the useless, worthless pricks who had made him suffer for eight hundred years. Piss on them. Piss on them all.

Which, in fact, Barph now did, standing on the edge of the heavens and emptying his straining bladder onto the Avarrans below, who were free from everything except getting splattered by their only god's urine.

Satisfied, Barph stared contentedly at the world below.

And then he stared less contentedly. Because...seriously...

one edict. One. That was it. Was it confusing somehow? He had explained it very carefully. He had told his priests—who were now all the priests in Avarra—to take care of this, and yet still... still the mortals kept doing this. To themselves. To him.

A trial. They were holding a pissing trial. They had a jury and lawyers and a bailiff.

It was like they were openly mocking him.

Barph was sick of this shit.

Gathering himself, he leapt off the edge of the heavens and rocketed toward Avarra. He tore through the air with such ferocity that the air around him flamed and roiled, and a thin sheet of flickering plasma formed a corona around his body, and when he landed in the center of the jury-rigged court— assembled by some Saleran villagers disgruntled by their youths' newfound freedom to steal and burglarize now that rules such as those governing ownership had been abolished by divine decree—most of the men and women gathered there were atomized instantly. Half the village blew apart, bodies and buildings flying about in a homogenized mass of debris.

Barph straightened, stood in the smoking crater, and worked a crick out of his neck.

He could hear a lot of screaming.

He decided to go and see what he could do about it.

"What did I tell you?" he asked as he strode up and out of the crater. "What did I explain? No rules! Two words! That's it. Could I have made it simpler? I don't know how, but I'm open to options!"

Nobody offered up an option. Most of the surviving villagers were just crawling around, clinging to whatever limbs remained on them or trying to stem the bleeding on others who lost theirs.

"Who did this?" he yelled at them. "Did I do this?" He was shouting at such a volume that he could see the survivors' ear- drums bursting with enough force to expel blood from their ears in a fine spray, but he couldn't help himself. "Cause and effect, you idiots!" he bellowed. "You are the cause. I am the effect. You did this. All of you. And yet somehow, I'm the arsehole!"

He spat at a woman who was wailing and flailing at him with one and a half arms. The phlegm blew a hole through her chest, and she collapsed backward.

"Here," he said, finally finding it within himself to lower his voice. "Let me explain it one more time."

Then he concentrated and wove his hands through the air and gathered up what was left of the village and its inhabitants and wrote in words of rubble and mud and stone and broken bodies that stood fifty yards tall: NO RULES.

"A monument to your gods-hexed stupidity," he told one of the screaming women, who was jutting out halfway up the edifice. "Maybe you'll pay attention next time."

He walked away, out across the misty Saleran morning, waiting until the screams faded. As they did, so did his anger. Had that been too much? This was normally the point at which Cois would appear and tell him that it was too much.

But zhe didn't. Of course zhe didn't. No one could spoil his fun anymore.

It was good to be god.

5

Party Planning

Quirk pushed back the ragged curtain that served as her door and hobbled out into the angry glare of the early-morning sun.

These days she made her bed in a burned-out servant's house. It was part of a small cluster of similar buildings on an abandoned estate perched on the dusty plains of southwestern Batarra. In its heyday the estate had belonged to a local magistrate. How much his particular brand of justice had depended upon the law, and how much had depended on hefty bribes, Quirk wasn't sure, but given the extent of his estate, she was willing to guess that he had favored the latter. Still, the magistrate had been symbolic enough of law and order for Barph to manifest and reduce his life and his entire holdings to a large scorch mark.

And that was why Quirk had picked the estate as the base camp for her resistance force. Not only was it isolated and quiet—the city of Tarramon, gateway to the Analesian Desert, was fifteen leagues north of them, and they had seen little evidence of its existence since arriving—but there was also symmetry to their occupation. Barph had cleared this place, as if preparing the field where the seeds of his own destruction would be sown. Every moment she spent here, planning Barph's end, was a moment spent spitting in his eye.

The encampment's other inhabitants were milling about in the small courtyard formed by the old servants' buildings.

Tarryl, the reluctant archer, was in one corner distributing fist-fuls of corn among a clucking mass of chickens and geese. Svet-son, their Chatarran blacksmith, was busy hammering away, beating horseshoes into submission. Next to him Norvard, the blacksmith's thickset son, held one of their horses steady using a makeshift bridle of rope. Poll was lying on a wooden pallet, a bandage around his ribs, a hand shading his eyes. Ellabet was sitting with a gaggle of younger children at her feet, spinning a yarn about the old gods.

One of the children had her hand raised. "What's an orgy?" she was saying. "My momma is always talking about the old gods and orgies."

Others were out in the nearby fields trying to coax life back to the land. Quirk still felt ambiguous about that. It was good for them to be self-sufficient, to not need to go begging for food from the people they were trying to liberate. But it also meant putting down roots. It meant that this place would be harder to leave. And Quirk was certain that a time would come when how many of them lived would be directly proportional to how fast they fled this place.

She started to hobble toward Ellabet. The wound in her arm throbbed angrily at her. She showed it the size of her own rage, and it backed off a little.

"You shouldn't be up."

She turned to see Gartrand coming up behind her holding a pail of water. The gash on his forehead had been inexpertly stitched. Still he seemed in good enough cheer.

She scowled at him.

"Those wounds need another day or two of rest," he said without any trace of rancor. "Unless you have some healing magic you never mentioned before. Because if you do, then you and I need to have words." He tapped his hand an inch below his head wound.

Gartrand had been a grocer in his former life. His wife had

been part of the Tarramon city guard. Then Barph had decided to step on the guard barracks when Gartrand's wife was in them.

"Barph doesn't rest," Quirk pointed out. She had spent four days on her back after the temple mission went so far awry.

"Well," said Gartrand, setting down his pail, "Barph is a divine being powered by the worship of millions. You're..." He shrugged. "Well, you're a whole lot more driven and powerful than I am, I suppose. But if you start stomping around today, I'm going to come and tell you I told you so when you're laid up on your back again this afternoon."

"Aren't you supposed to be doing something with that pail?" Quirk didn't see how this conversation was helping her get her revenge.

Gartrand shrugged. "Nothing urgent." There was the slightest hint of insolence to his smile.

She understood, of course. The attempt to bring levity. Gartrand knew how bleak life could be. He knew the importance of being able to glimpse the sun between the clouds.

But she still couldn't quite appreciate the gesture.

"Are we free, Gartrand?" she asked. "Have we liberated people from Barph's rule? Have we avenged our loved ones?"

A cloud crossed Gartrand's face for a moment, if only a moment.

"No," he said. "But we're still alive, aren't we, Quirk?"

She didn't answer. And she saw the point he was angling at, perhaps. But as well as she had come to know Gartrand, she did not know him well enough to discuss her own ambivalence toward life.

"Anyway," he went on in the face of her frosty silence. "You're wrong. Barph does rest. In fact, he is mostly a god of leisure these days, it seems."

Confusion plowed a furrow in Quirk's brow.

"You ain't heard?" Gartrand looked faintly amused. "Word is that for the past two days Barph's been manifested in a suburb of Tarramon drinking his way through all of last summer's vintages."

He smiled at her, an amused twist of his lips, a sparkle in his eyes. And he was utterly oblivious to the bomb he had just detonated in her mind.

Barph. Fifteen leagues away. Barph, sitting in Tarramon, waiting for her. For her blade. For her revenge.

"Quirk?" said Gartrand. He seemed to realize that he'd miscalculated somewhere along the way. "Are you—"

"Get everyone ready to ride," she said. "Now."

"What?" He just stared at her. Because for all his good heart and insurrectionist tendencies, he was apparently a complete fucking fool who wouldn't recognize a golden opportunity should it sidle up to him in a bar and offer to fondle his manhood.

"Everyone!" she snapped. "Everyone who can wield a blade, raise a club, form a fucking fist. Get them. Get them on a horse. We are riding to Tarramon!"

She was vaguely aware that she was shouting. The others were gathering around.

"Tarramon?" Gartrand stared at her stupidly.

"A city. Near here. Containing our mortal enemy." She turned to the gathering crowd. "Move!" she yelled.

"Containing *a god*." Gartrand was not moving. "Containing a being of unlimited divine power."

She stalked forward, grabbed him by the lapel. He looked at her, caught between surprise and bewilderment.

"Six months," she spat at him. "Six fucking months, waiting for this."

"What are you going to do?" He was almost laughing at her, and gods she wanted to roast the skin right off his face right then. She wouldn't. But she wanted to.

"He's a god," Gartrand repeated.

"He's Barph. And we are dedicated to ending him."

Gartrand shook his head as best he was able. "You're serious?" He let out a huff of something that was not quite mirth. "I'm a resistance fighter, Quirk," he said. She opened her mouth to answer, but he cut her off. "That's what I signed up for. What we all signed up for. Because we saw your passion, and we saw a world gone to shit. And we wanted to fight against the tide. And we wanted to fight for something better than what we have."

"Then saddle the fuck up," she hissed.

"Shut up," he snapped. And she suddenly saw how close to the edge she'd pushed Gartrand. She let go of his shirt. For all that she could melt him alive, the man had four inches and fifty pounds on her.

"I signed up to fight back. But I never expected to win. He's a god, Quirk. A god. We can't kill a god. We can slow him down. We can make pockets of the world where he doesn't crush us. But that's it. That's all. We're resistance fighters. Not suicidal fuckwits."

And there was still heart in his words. Still that decent goodness. He was, he thought, trying to save her, to save them all.

"Gods can die," she hissed. "I was there. I saw it. It will happen again. I will make it happen again."

Gartrand's anger seemed to ebb out of him. "I know you're hurting," he said. "We're all hurting. We're all a little broken. We wouldn't be here if we weren't, but...gods, Quirk. We all lost people. Ellabet lost her gods-hexed kids. This is worth fighting for, yes. But it's not worth dying for."

"She was." It was out of Quirk before she caught the words. And may the gods piss on the man for making her say it. For even bringing Afrit up. She wasn't his to talk about. And this wasn't about Afrit. This wasn't. This wasn't.

"This is about Barph," she managed. Her voice wasn't quite steady, but she tried to mask all the hurt under her anger. "This is about all the horror he has rained down upon this world." She turned away from Gartrand. She turned to the crowd. She could play to them, even if she couldn't play to him. She was the glue that had bound them all together.

"Barph lies within hand's reach. He is fat and exposed. He sits, ignorant and uncaring of all the pain and suffering he has wrought upon the world. Upon us. He flaunts his callousness. He celebrates this pain everyone feels."

They stared at her. Some chewed their lips. Some ducked their heads. Some had the same look of shock that she knew was on Gartrand's face. Some even looked disgusted.

But not all of them.

Ellabet stepped out of the crowd. She had a hand raised. "I'm in," she said. "That's why I'm here."

"Ell...," Gartrand said. He was sweet on her, Quirk thought. She wondered if that would sway him.

"I'll come." It was Norvard, the blacksmith's son. She smiled at him, finding herself grateful.

"And me." Poll already had his club ready.

There were five of them in all. Five who would ride with her. Five who would fight at her side. Five of them who were actually worth her time.

"Good," she said to them, when it was clear no one else had the balls for this fight. "Now we ride."

Quirk had spent an inordinate amount of time over the past six months thinking about death. Afrit's primarily. Barph's second. Her own close behind that. She had spent a long night staring at a knife and wondering if she could be reunited with Afrit that way. In the end she simply could not take that plunge before she knew she had taken every step possible to stop Barph and his endless reign of bullshit.

Right now all those deaths felt very close. Lying on her belly, creeping down an alleyway, approaching Barph.

Unfortunately the waste matter of Tarramon also felt very

close. Apparently Tarramon lacked a functioning sewage system, and its populace used the streets as public latrines.

She set her jaw. She could take this. She could take whatever Avarra handed out. She had nothing left that could break.

"I don't know how we'll get in." Norvard was squatting on his haunches deeper in the alley's shadows. "That crowd."

Barph was in a whorehouse. His presence was sending people mad, so the city was awash in stories of people dancing and drinking and screwing to death. And the square outside the whorehouse was so full of people, even the sane citizens were in danger of being crushed to death by the throng.

"Crowds scatter," Ellabet said. "They panic." She was down on her belly beside Quirk. She tapped the steel tip of her staff against the ground. She was smiling.

"That crowd," said Quirk, "is perfect."

"It's funny," Norvard said, shaking his head. "The berserkers back home were normally much bigger than you."

Norvard had a hammer in each hand, both with heavy, well-worn heads. His father had pressed them into his hands, tears in the older man's eyes. Now he worked them back and forth, as if practicing battles in miniature.

"You don't stab a god to death," she told him.

It was Ellabet's turn to look confused, and more than a little angry. "Why are we here?"

"Gods thrive on belief," Quirk said. "We have to kill belief."

"Kill belief?" Poll, standing well back with the other recruits, looked as if someone had just punched him in the frontal lobes.

Quirk took a breath. This was why they attacked the temples. They understood that, didn't they? "We undermine his authority," she said. "We make him look weak and stupid. And that makes him become weak and stupid."

"How do we do that?" Norvard had borrowed Poll's look.

"Don't worry," Quirk said. "This I have done before."

*   *   *

The flame was small at first. It sat in her palm and glowed. She felt the warmth of it in her chest. Something deep and profound. She felt possessive of it. This was her creation. It was from her body, her will. She wondered if this was how the mothers of murderers felt.

She released the flame, watched it become a ribbon stretching across the ground of the square. Even this effort pushed at the walls of her control, so she kept the line small. Just a whisper of flame, enough to fight the breeze. And she pushed it out, around the edge of the crowd.

A handful of people noticed it, shouted, jumped back. One tried to stamp it out. She felt the pounding of his foot as if it were beating against the inside of her skull. She redoubled her efforts.

"Is she okay?" she heard Norvard ask.

"Let her focus." Ellabet had seen Quirk work before.

"Looks like she's going to shit."

Quirk wasn't sure she would bring Norvard out on any missions again. Should it come up. Maybe, just maybe, if she controlled this fire correctly, there wouldn't be a need.

She pushed the fire farther, faster. It reached the wall of the brothel where Barph lurked. A swaying sign announced its name as the Parting Curtains.

Letting the flame go was almost a relief, feeling it bloom and blossom and consume. Feeling the old paint and timber of the brothel wall feed it.

But there was only so much freedom she could allow it to have. And now that the flame had broken free once, it fought harder and harder against her. And the limits she placed on it and herself became harder and harder to keep in place.

More saw the flames now. More and more. She heard the gasps from the crowd, even as she closed her eyes, as she felt out the shapes the fire had to occupy with her will alone. It felt as if something were chafing inside her mind. Thoughts bent out of shape.

Barph had taught her this, of course. And there was some justice in using the lessons against him.

Sweat beading her brow, she made the fire obey her.

"The fuck?" breathed Norvard.

And this time she smiled. Because she heard the words on the lips of a hundred others gathered in the square.

Written on the walls in fifty-foot flaming letters was a single three-word message:

"Barph blows goats."

6

Look, Dragons Are in the Series Name, Okay?

"Are you kidding me?"

Ellabet's reaction was not, to be fair, the one Quirk had been hoping for.

"Trust me," she said through gritted teeth as the fire fought against her confining will. "This was how it was in Vinter. The dragons were poised to ascend to the heavens. I...We...we mocked the dragons mercilessly. We turned the people against them. You can't worship someone you ridicule."

"We've come all this way to tell dirty jokes about him?" Ellabet was practically spitting. "We could do the same thing by painting graffiti on temple walls! I came here to make a god bleed!"

Quirk so didn't have time for this, as the fire desperately tried to consume the rest of the whorehouse and dissolve into nothing but chaos.

"If he's to bleed," she managed, "the people have to see him as someone who can bleed. They have to see him as someone laughable. We have to make them laugh at him."

She forced the fiery words to twist and change.

"Barph likes fat moms."

It was crude and stupid, but if life had taught Quirk anything, it was that belief, faith, and life itself were crude and stupid.

"Then why aren't you being funny?" Poll asked. He sounded genuinely confused.

"I'm open," Quirk hissed, "to suggestions."

She forced the flaming words to change: "Barph is so fat..."

"This is not how anybody dies," said Norvard, standing up. He was clutching the two hammers his father had given him, white-knuckled. "This is how someone is left with a bloody nose in a schoolyard."

How fat was Barph? She could feel the sweat steaming off her skin.

"...he can't fit back out of this whorehouse."

Even Quirk knew that was weak.

"We're going to die," said Poll.

But then, suddenly, there was laughter. Booming, riotous, and filling the square. And for a moment Quirk's spirits lifted and raced for the sky. But there was something wrong with the laughter too. It was laughter at a volume that assaulted ears. It was laughter that could be felt rippling over the skin.

It was not the crowd's laughter.

It was Barph's.

Quirk opened her narrowed eyes, and she saw him.

Barph emerged from the whorehouse. Barph laughing. Barph laughing at *her*.

He still looked a lot like the old man he had pretended to be for so much of their acquaintance. The village drunk. His beard was still a wild, untamed mat of hair that flapped and slapped at his bare pigeon chest. His hair was still gray and long, though now it was slicked close to his skull and plaited down his back. And the strange, magnetic energy was still there, though now it was amplified a thousandfold. Her eyes could not help but be drawn to him, track his every movement. His laughter, deafening as it was, was also somehow fascinating. She didn't want to miss a moment of it. When he spoke, she would hang on his words.

The crowd were on their knees. Some were prostrated, mumbling prayers, shouting their sins. Some had flung themselves to the ground so they could lie there quaking, slowly marinating in their own piss puddles. Others were running. Others standing bewildered, paralyzed.

The fire tore free of Quirk's control. Behind Barph the flames roared lasciviously, rushing up and over the whorehouse's walls.

"Quirk!" boomed Barph. "Quirk? Is that you?"

"Oh gods." Ellabet's voice quavered. "We are so fucked."

"What do we do?" asked Norvard. His hammers hung slackly by his sides, and his eyes searched for exits.

"I don't know about you"—Poll stood up—"but I'm dying on my feet."

"Yes." Barph's voiced boomed out in answer. "Yes you are."

There was a flash of light, a crack of sound. It was so fast and so...absolute...so big and loud, it seemed to fill the world around Quirk utterly. And then it was over almost before it had begun, and Poll wasn't there. There was just a wet red smear on the ground.

"Am I not a bountiful god?" And there was still laughter in Barph's voice. He was slurring noticeably. "Do I not give my people what they ask for?"

He hiccupped.

"Fuck you." Quirk didn't say it loud enough, she thought, for him to hear. But it wasn't for him. It was for her. It was so she could hear her defiance. So she could know who she was, and why she was here, and what she was doing. It was to remind herself that he couldn't break her anymore. That was already done.

"Fuck you!" she screamed to the world, to the absent heavens, to the crowd who would not abandon their faith in this monster. "Fuck you!"

Ellabet and Norvard and the others were staring at her. Which

part of her knew was better than them staring at the mess that
had been Poll.

"Oh," Barph said, "this is boring. He waved a hand at the
alleyway where they were crouched. "They're over there."

It took the crowd a moment. It took Quirk a moment. But then
the crowd turned and looked.

"Come on," said Barph. "Your god commands you and all
that shit."

The first to pick himself up was a man in his fifties. He came
charging at them, face contorted with hatred. "Unbelievers!" he
screamed at them. "Filth! Deviants!" Anger and disgust poured
out of him.

He was also unarmed. And he was the sort of person they
were meant to be liberating from Barph's rule. Quirk pulled herself up out of the dirt, held up an arm to defend herself. But she
didn't set fire to him.

The man plunged into her, fists slamming against her ribs. He
drove her back against the alley wall as she fought for air. His
hand found her throat. He pinned her there while she gasped.

Ellabet was the first to recover. She cracked her steel-tipped
staff over the man's skull. There was a sound like a ripe water-
melon being split open. Then the man's fingers fell nervelessly
away from Quirk's throat, and he dropped bonelessly to the
ground.

And then a thousand of his friends seemed to arrive all at
once.

The alleyway was a bottleneck. It forced the screaming,
gnashing horde to pile into each other, to push and heave,
straining against its walls. The alleyway saved their lives.

Yet still the weight of people bore down. Ellabet stood with
her feet planted, whirling her staff in tight arcs, smashing at
limbs and skulls. Norvard was beside her, swinging his hammers in wild, clumsy arcs. One of the women who had accompanied them had strung her bow and was firing arrows over the

first few ranks, desperately trying to sow fear in their attackers. The other had a long polearm and was jabbing it to either side of Norvard and Ellabet, trying to keep the crowd at bay.

And it was not enough.

Men and women dropped to earth under the resistance fighters' blows. But they were simply trampled by more and more and more and more people desperate to get at them. Even those still on their feet had people desperately clambering and leaping past them. The bottleneck would burst.

"Help us!" Ellabet risked a look backward at Quirk. A dagger glanced against her cheekbone. Blood sprayed down her face in a red sheet. "Fucking help us."

Quirk was here to save these people.

If she didn't kill these people, they would kill her.

And then fire. Great gushing sheets of fire. Fire that fell like rain. And the crowds screamed and flailed and finally thrashed back and away. And still fire roared at them, and consumed them.

Quirk stood openmouthed. Because it was not her flame.

A shadow in the sky. A flicker of swift wings. A roar, throaty and deep. The whistle of wind as the thing, the shape, the terror sped overhead. Fire fell from it as if it were some inverted cloud.

People were on fire. Ellabet was flinching back from scorching heat. The wall of murderous people scrambling toward them was falling apart.

Quirk looked up, wished she could will the walls of the alleyway farther apart so she could make out what in the Hallows was happening. Then she saw it again. Saw the shape of it clearly, its silhouette framed against the summer sky. The faint impression of color—blue flanks and a white underbelly blurring together. She saw its long neck. She saw its leathery wings. She saw its jaws open.

She saw fire.

"A dragon," she breathed. "It's a gods-pissing dragon."

No one else was looking. No one else cared. They just wanted to get away, to run screaming from this new and unexpected source of death. Norvard was cheering. He thought it was her.

But the dragons are dead, thought the academic.

Barph killed them, thought the realist.

He's fallible, thought the optimist.

He's going to kill this one, thought the pragmatist.

And there Barph was. Still laughing, still smiling. He was growing, physically growing before her eyes. He was becoming larger and larger, a giant of a man, ten feet tall and growing.

The dragon came round at him again, focusing its fire now. Barph was engulfed in an endless stream of destruction. Behind him the whorehouse, already trembling under the assault of Quirk's flames, let out tortured cracking sounds as beams split and splintered. Walls started to collapse.

And still Barph laughed. And still Barph grew.

The dragon howled, slashed at Barph's face as it danced past him.

"Attack!" Quirk screamed to the others, shedding paralysis. They had to take advantage of this. "Now!"

The crowd was scattering, fleeing from this apocalyptic newcomer to their party. And Quirk didn't understand this dragon. She didn't know what its motives were or its goals. But she recognized an opportunity when she saw one. She hurled herself forward.

Norvard was the first to join her, whirling his hammers, punching a woman out of the way, making space for her. Ellabet was staring at them. But another resistance fighter had accompanied them, blood streaming from her face and from the two daggers she held in her hands as she charged after them.

Barph was almost three stories now. Massive. His face contorted by insincere merriment.

The dragon raced overhead. Quirk felt the heat of its lance of flame reaching out, lunging toward Barph's face. She heard the dragon's roar.

Maybe. Maybe. With this unexpected ally on their side... maybe...

Barph swept out a hand and backhanded the dragon. Its whole body crumpled around the blow. Its wings were fluttering rags. There was an audible crack as its tail flicked around the massive palm and slammed into its own skull. And then it was sailing away, a broken crumpled thing that smashed into the northern wall of the square like a catapult stone before falling limply to the ground.

And even as Quirk skidded to a horrified halt, still Barph laughed.

Quirk looked from the stunned, broken dragon twitching on the ground to Barph's massive grinning head. His shirt was on fire, but his skin and hair were unmarked by the brutal assault.

For a moment Barph focused solely on her. He ignored all the madness around him, the unfathomable dragon, all the people who worshipped him, all the other people caught midstride in a race to kill him. She felt the weight of his attention. His massive eyes met hers.

"For you to be able to insult me, Quirk," he said in a voice laden with disdain, "I actually have to give a shit about your opinion."

Then he shrugged. Then he was gone.

Quirk blinked. And stared. And blinked. But he was...He had left. He had ascended to the heavens. As if this was...was...

This was meaningless to him. This was nothing.

She looked again at the dragon. At the crowds. All of it. All of it was nothing to him.

Gartrand was right. This had never had a chance.

What other choice had she had, though? What option had Barph left her with?

The crowds were staring too. At the empty space where their god had been. At the broken dragon. At the collapsing whorehouse. At their friends and family, broken and charred on the ground.

The crowd worked out what to do before Quirk did. They worked out that they were going to beat the ever-living shit out of the handful of surviving jackasses who had broken up their party.

A man standing not five feet from Norvard leapt at the young man, clotheslining him around the neck and sending them both tumbling to the ground. He was howling, an animal sound. The man's fists came down again and again. Norvard had his arms up trying to protect his face.

The woman with the bloody knives lunged at Norvard's attacker but never made it. A gaggle of three more Barphists intercepted her, and suddenly she was the nucleus of her own circle of violence, hacking and yelling, as more and more people closed in.

"Ellabet!" Quirk yelled. She glanced back at the alleyway. Ellabet and two others were still there. And Ellabet was shaking her head.

Shit. Shit and piss and fire. She turned back to the crowd. She didn't want to burn them.

She didn't—

A stone, flung from the crowd, smashed into her temple. She staggered. Black spots exploded across her vision. The pain was like a needle in her thoughts.

And her fire would not be extinguished.

Fire raced out of her, smashed into the crowd in a wall. Women and men reeled back, screaming, arms pinwheeling.

Forgive me, she thought, but she didn't know whom she was praying to. Not anymore.

Then something crashed into the back of her head. Pain exploded through her skull, drove her to her knees. She tried to get up, but her arm was made of rubber. She collapsed rolling. A woman stood over her, kerchief tied around her head, clutching a rolling pin. Flour and blood mixed on her smock.

"Fuck you!" the woman screamed.

A roar. A flash of light and heat. The woman staggered away. She was on fire.

I didn't ..., Quirk thought. Because she hadn't set the woman on fire.

The dragon had. It wasn't dead. It was down, but it was still fighting. It roared like thunder. People scattered. Fire raced over Quirk's head. Half of the woman holding the rolling pin turned to ash. Her legs tumbled down, smashed into Quirk still smoldering.

Quirk yelled, kicked spastically, still trying to get her body to work, still fighting through pain and confusion. She staggered to her feet. Someone came at her. She couldn't see if he had a knife or a clenched fist. She reached out a hand to ward him off, and then she was burning him alive, melting the muscle from his bones. She was out of control. She was scared. And the dragon roared. And the crowds pulsed. And flame poured out of her. And she was struck. And she was bleeding. And she was struggling to her feet once more. And...and...and...

Nothing made sense. There was just a string of moments before her. Brief scenes of horror and violence lit by the flicker of a guttering flame. She tripped over a body, and it took her a moment to realize the mess of meat had been Norvard just a few minutes before.

The whole square was on fire now. The dragon was lunging and thrashing. One wing was broken, twisted beneath its body, and it howled every time it had to turn. But still it killed and killed. Bodies piled up around it.

And then suddenly the crowds were gone. They had either fled or died. And Quirk was on her knees in a field of bodies, staring a barking, braying dragon in the face.

It was half-buried by the wall it had collapsed into. Blood ran down its sides. And it was small, she saw, by a dragon's standards. Only twenty feet, perhaps, from snout to tail.

A dragon. A tyrannical, megalomaniac beast. Intelligent, but inhuman also. A creature driven to dominate and kill. A relation somehow of the creatures that had tried to take over Avarra, that had opened the door to Barph and all his ills.

She reached out a hand toward it.

It was small, it was young, it was injured. She could kill it. She could and should end it.

It turned baleful eyes upon her. Fathomless pools of yellow. It opened its jaw. Teeth that went on forever glinted at her. Flame flickered in the back of its throat.

It could and should end her.

They stayed there, frozen in that tableau of death.

"You attacked Barph," the dragon said. Its voice was a rough rasp, like a body dragged over sharp rocks.

"So did you," she said, and each word felt like a lead weight she was heaving up from her lungs.

"Yes," agreed the dragon.

"He has to die," she said. She couldn't quite make the words into a question. It was a fact stamped too deeply into her heart.

"Yes," the dragon said again.

Quirk let her arm drop. She sighed. "Fuck it then," she said, and she lay down to rest.

7

In Which Lette Is Full of Shit

Down in the Hallows, Will had just discovered the mouth of a tunnel decorated with skulls. Given that it led to a place called the Killing Plains, this struck him as gilding the lily a little bit.

"I just want to check one more time," Afrit said as they walked beneath the leering arch of bone. "The Killing Plains. We're all totally on board with that?"

Will aimed for stoic silence. He missed wildly.

"I don't know," he found himself saying. "Did you negotiate a better deal for our freedom when I wasn't listening?"

"I am thinking," Balur rumbled, "that it is sounding like quite an exciting place. The sort of place where one can really get into one's hobbies."

"It's good to keep busy," Cois concurred.

This, Will thought, *is why one day I will call myself a murderer.*

"Look," he said, "I was under the impression that Lette and Balur were pretty good at this whole killing thing. They talk about it a lot, at least."

"We *talk*?" Lette's expression suggested Will's words were unlikely to change the status of their off-again, off-again relationship.

"And there are five of us, whereas I have to assume psychotic killers generally have trouble binding together in groups. So we'll outnumber them."

"So Lette and I are doing all the work," Balur concluded. "As is being usual."

"Again," Will said, "what freedom did you negotiate? I've done my part."

They pushed farther into the darkness of the tunnel. Will tried to keep the pace up. Water dripped around them. Puddles splashed beneath their feet. Everything smelled slightly of copper. Will started to wonder if the puddles weren't filled with water. He didn't stop and examine the situation.

Finally the cloacal darkness receded. The end of the tunnel came into sight. The light beyond was a bright, bold yellow, with hues of orange and red splashed across the sharp stones of the tunnel mouth. Well... the sharp stones and the skulls. The endless, endless procession of skulls.

"Honestly," said Balur as they entered the gallery of bald craniums, "I am always finding this sort of thing a bit played out." He picked up a skull. "If you are going to do it..." He pointed the skull at Lette. "Are you remembering that place... the necromancer's tower? He was having the whole skull thing going on, but he had also been filling the place with snakes. Now, that I could be appreciating. Making a classic feel new."

"We talked about doing the Summer Palace in skulls," Cois said, as if this were a rational conversation starter.

"The what now?" Will probably shouldn't ask, but at this point in life he was pretty much resigned to that feeling.

"Your religious education was truly shocking," Lette told him. Which added shades of inadequacy to Will's emotional palette—creating yet another feeling he was resigned to.

"Yes," he agreed.

"The Summer Palace," Afrit said, because it was an opportunity to be a know-it-all. "The palace of the gods. Their home within the heavens. The home of the font of Lawl's blood."

"It's not Lawl's blood," Cois objected.

"I am not thinking," Balur cut in, "that skulls are suiting somewhere called the Summer Palace."

"Whose blood is it?" Afrit looked genuinely puzzled.

"Honestly." Cois shook hir head. "The bullshit Lawl was spouting. We all have our blood in the font."

"Skulls and the name *the Summer Palace* is an aesthetic dissonance in my opinion," Balur went on.

"Yes, love." Cois patted his arm.

"All your blood?" Afrit wasn't willing to let that go.

"Why does this even matter?" Will wanted to know. "We are a few days away from a way out of here."

"It matters because Lawl is a lying, self-aggrandizing bastard." Cois didn't seem interested in Will's priorities.

"It matters because Lawl's blood in the font is what establishes him as the de facto ruler of the heavens." Afrit seemed to be of a different opinion. "It's the basis of a lot of theology."

Cois threw up hir hands. "The font doesn't do that!"

"It doesn't?" Afrit somehow managed to sound just as affronted as Cois.

"Why do we care?" Will was pretty close behind them.

"The font is the defense mechanism of the heavens," Cois said. "That's all. If your blood isn't in the font—or if someone whose blood is in the font hasn't given you permission to be there—the Summer Palace itself attacks you. The very fabric of it. You have to understand, the whole 'overthrow of the Deep Ones' thing was pretty recent back then. We were still feeling a bit skittish."

"A font of blood too?" Balur shook his head. "You should have been keeping the skull theme and calling it the Winter Palace. That would have made sense. Your scheme is being all over the place."

Nobody seemed to have much to add after that.

Beyond its macabre entrance, the Killing Plains cheered up considerably. Lawl's ever-present wheat fields were actually in surprisingly good shape. War, it seemed, had decided it honestly didn't have the balls to come here, and had left them to grow in peace, free of an army's trampling feet.

After half a mile or so, Afrit stopped and held up a hand. "Shouldn't we find some way to get to higher ground?" she asked. She batted at the chest-high stalks of wheat. "I know I'm not the one who knows about fighting, but it feels like anyone could come stalking up to us in this mess. And this is the sort of place where stalking seems like it might be a problem."

Lette shook her head dismissively. "In my experience wheat is crap for stalking in. It rustles too much. You can't get near anyone without them hearing you coming half a mile off. Now, grasslands are perfect, but wheat is just a pain in a hunter's arse."

"You know," Cois said from behind them, "you sound very confident, but have you ever considered that you could be as full of shit as a midden heap?"

Cois's voice sounded unusually strained. Will turned around. A massive soldier held a knife to Cois's delicate throat.

"Okay," Lette said. "I'll concede that. I'm full of shit."

8

This Ain't Your Father's
Negotiation Tactic

Balur saw Cois with a knife to hir throat and smiled.

He was going to get to kill someone.

"Now then," said the man with the knife, "you're a lovely piece of lovely, aren't you?" His voice was rough, drawn out like the jagged scar that marred his own neck. He pressed a broad nose against Cois's pale cheek, inhaled deeply.

Two more men lifted themselves out of the wheat. Balur's smile grew, and he moved his hand slowly toward the sword at his waist.

"Ah-ah!" One of the new men pointed his sword straight at Balur. He was roped thickly with muscle and crosshatched with little white scars. Balur would kill him second, he decided. After the one threatening Cois. His hand kept moving toward the sword hilt.

"I don't need this one to be breathing to have fun with her," said the one holding Cois, looking at Balur.

A thin line of red started to trickle down from where he pressed the blade against Cois's neck.

"Perhaps, lover," Cois said, and hir eyes were large and round, "I might beg a boon of you. Because I know how much you want to kill these men." Zhe flinched as a muscle twitched in hir captor's arm and a second trickle of blood appeared. "But"—zhe swallowed—"perhaps, just this one time, you could wait just a second and see if there's a way to resolve this in a way that doesn't end with me dead on the floor?"

There was no sarcasm in hir voice. Zhe was as genuine and open with him now as zhe was in his arms at night. And for just a moment he hesitated.

"Lette?" Balur called.

Lette hesitated. A hesitation wasn't fantastic. "Perhaps," she said eventually.

"Perhaps?" Balur said. "That is being a pretty pathetic answer."

"Well, it's not a great angle."

Balur looked at Cois again, standing there, not shaking, just meeting his eye and waiting. And rage was in him, yes, but there was something else there too, something unfamiliar and hollow in the base of his gut.

"What's your name?" Will cut into the proceedings. "Let's get to know each other."

Cois's captor grinned. "I'm Chev," he said. He looked at the knife. "And this is my friend Pigsticker."

Will kept a surprisingly straight face. "Nice to meet you," he said. "So, Chev, what do you want? Let's negotiate."

Balur's rage was thundering now, beating and thrashing at this stupid, pointless leash he had put upon it. These men should be being dead already.

And yet. Still his gut fluttered.

Fear. It was fear there.

Not for himself. Not over Lette's aim.

For Cois's life.

"I want," said Chev, grinning with his lopsided mouth, "to eat the big ones. To fuck the pretty ones. And to turn you"—he nodded at Will—"into a pair of shoes."

"Hmm." Will sighed. "Okay, well, let's see where we can bargain to from there."

Chev's tongue snuck out from between his lips and licked Cois's cheek. "Tasty," he said.

Chev had to die. That was a certainty in Balur's mind. He needed to feel the man's organs bursting over his fingers. He needed to feel the man's skin grinding to paste between his molars.

But...how?

And then the solution occurred to him. And...oh, may all the gods piss on it.

"Will?" Balur said. And gods, he was never going to live this down.

"I'm working on it," said Will. He was walking toward Chev very slowly, arms open wide, hands empty, fingers splayed.

Balur spat.

The sword pointer seemed unsure whom to point his sword at. "Working on what?" he asked. He sounded suspicious.

"This," Will said, still slowly pacing toward Chev.

And then he wasn't. Then he vanished, and there was just empty air where Will had been.

Everyone stared. Everyone except Balur. He was rolling his eyes. Will Fallows. Always being with the trickery and bullshit.

Once he was done with the eye roll, Balur focused on the space behind Chev's back where Will was reappearing and pressing a blade into Chev's own throat.

"Put the knife down," Will said conversationally.

The other two men twitched.

So Balur killed them. When the red mist lifted, he appeared to have made mittens from two men's innards. Afrit looked mildly unwell.

Chev pulled the knife away from Cois's throat. But when zhe turned around, the person zhe was staring at was Will.

"Oh," zhe said, "my magic."

9

How to Make Friends and Influence Psychopaths

Magic. It was in the blood, Will had discovered. Or rather, it was in the bodily fluids. But blood was usually the easiest to lay one's hands upon.

Personally, Will had first obtained magical powers after his night of passion with Cois. Or...after his fifteen minutes of awkward, half-hearted romping. He had been meant to act as a repository for them, a place of safekeeping until after the threat of draconic tyranny had been dealt with. But then there had been the whole murder thing, and Barph had slit his throat and drained the magic from him and drunk it for himself.

Barph had done it to all of them, to Afrit and Lette and Balur. And yet with Will he had been, what? Hasty, perhaps? No matter the specifics of it, the fact was that a drop of blood had remained. Not enough to sustain organs, or keep the beat in Will's chest. But enough for the magic to cling to. A little piece of the divine.

It didn't let Will do much, but it did let him do this. Disappear. Reappear. Cast his appearance elsewhere. A simple illusion. A pickpocket's, perhaps. But right here and now, it was enough.

"There's a big man," Will said. "Someone in charge down here, isn't there?"

"I'm going to fucking wear you," said Chev.

Will pressed the knife harder to Chev's throat. "Three of you," he said. "Three of you psychopaths. That didn't just happen. Someone told you to hunt together. Someone you're scared of—"

"I ain't scared of shit," Chev shouted, though the stain he'd created on his pants when Balur had gone to town on his two friends suggested otherwise.

"Someone told you to go hunting," Will said. It had to be that. He was sure of it. For there to be any semblance of social order down here, someone had to be enforcing it. "Who was it?"

Chev spat.

"Look," said Will, "I know you're into the whole drooling psychotic thing, but it's either give me a name or go to the Void. Is that decision really that hard?"

"You ain't got it in you," Chev said. "Not in cold blood. I seen your eyes, man."

Will thought about that. He thought perhaps he'd surprise Chev. Still, that wouldn't get him many places.

"Maybe," he said. "But my friend Balur definitely has it in him."

Chev considered this. "Turuck," he said finally. "Big man's name is Turuck."

"He's in charge here?" Will asked.

Chev gave an ill-advised nod and almost ended the conversation there. Will sighed. Knifepoint conversations were impractical.

"Okay," he said, and pulled his knife away from Chev's throat.

"Noooo!" The bellow came not from Chev, but from behind Will's shoulder. He turned to see Balur charging at full speed toward him, a blade in each hand. Before Will could even put a hand up to ward the lizard man off, both blades punctured Chev, smashing through his ribs and tearing through his lungs. With a massive flexing of back and shoulders, Balur tore his arms apart, ripping both swords out of the man's chest. Chev virtually exploded. Bones and organs and blood flew. His head, neck, shoulders, and arms burst free from his torso and flopped to the ground six feet away.

"Holy shit, Balur!" Will managed, spraying another man's blood from his lips as he spoke.

Balur pointed a dripping sword at Will. "You will not be stealing my kill," he thundered.

Will blinked Chev's blood from his eyes. "I was going," he said, voice as cold as he could make it, "to have him lead us to Turuck."

Balur hesitated. "Oh," he said. He looked at his swords. "Well…" He wiped one blade on the back of his calf. "Then that was being a stupid idea, and I am glad I made sure I was killing him." He nodded.

"My hero!" Cois called from where zhe was bending to work a stone out of hir shoe. Which really wasn't helping.

"Why do you even want to find Turuck?" Afrit asked. "Shouldn't we be avoiding the head psychopath?"

"Where is being the fun in that?" Balur asked, still licking gore from his snout.

"This cavern," Will pointed out, "is as big as all Kondorra. We can wander aimlessly looking for a hidden gorge, and hope none of the other nutjobs in here are good enough to sneak up on us, or we can go find the big man and kill him and scare everyone else into submission. Then they might even tell us where to find the stupid gorge."

"Fine," Balur shrugged. "I'll do it."

"Put it back in your pants already," Lette told him.

"Actually," Will told him, bracing himself slightly, "I think I have to do it."

Balur looked at him coldly. "Were we not just having a lengthy discussion about not stealing my kills?"

Will thought back. "You mean when you just killed Chev."

"Was there any other lengthy discussion?"

Will wasn't entirely sure how to answer that. He decided to

just sidestep the issue and head as directly toward rationality as he could manage. "For us to cow these people," he said, "we need to demoralize them. You heard Chev. He didn't think I could kill him. If I kill Turuck, then it will devastate these people."

"So . . . ," Balur said. "Your logic is being that I'm already scary, and therefore . . . stupid shit you were just saying?"

"I'm saying," Will said as patiently as possible, "that as scary as you are now, it's not enough to stop people from continuing to attack us. We need to surprise them somehow. Make them think twice."

"This is a stupid plan," Balur said.

"I don't know." Lette came to Will's defense with surprising speed. "I think that logic sort of holds."

Balur spat. "Just screw already." He stomped away.

It took two more ambushes for them to get the directions they needed to Turuck's camp, but by the end Cois seemed to be taking the position of hostage as one of high esteem.

"Some of us have it," zhe told Lette and Afrit, "and some of us don't."

When they finally got to it, Turuck's camp was larger and better established than Will had expected. Some people lived in their own filth, for certain, but others had attempted to build solid structures, and many of the tents were relatively elaborate. Yes, the skull theme was hit a little too hard—Will could see Balur's point there—but considering half the people he could see were dribbling on themselves and carving into their arms with knives, it was fairly impressive.

"Well, this should be fun," Will lied as he led the group down the hill toward them.

"Not for me, apparently," said Balur, who was still sulking.

Will had half suspected that they would be attacked on sight, but the inhabitants of Turuck's settlement were apparently civil enough to just stare balefully at them all. However, their social skills seem to falter and die when it came to answering Will's questions. "Where's Turuck?" just resulted in people laughing manically, or in a few cases physically attacking him. He tried going with something he thought might be more in their parlance, but "Where's Turuck, arsehole?" just got fewer laughs and slightly more violence. "I am here to kill Turuck," got blank stares, as if what he was saying were utterly unfathomable.

Finally he went with, "I, Willett Fallows, do hereby call Turuck a coward, a weakling, and a monkey fucker who couldn't battle his way out of his nursemaid's arms, and I am here to swaddle his berry-bright arse so that the kicking I give it won't damage his delicate feelings so badly that he goes crying to his mommy." He even did it from astride a pile of three corpses that Balur had dropped at his feet. And that seemed to do it.

A hush fell over the crowd of figures that had gathered around them. They were almost universally big men, some lean, some bulky, some bright-eyed, some peering from beneath hulking brows. They were all armed, though sword care did not seem to be a common practice among them. The blades on display were rusty and crusted with blood. Some had resorted to carrying clubs. One or two just held large pieces of rock. And yet, in this crowd of psychopaths and killers, it seemed Will had found a subject that was taboo: Calling Turuck names was apparently not something you did, even if you were stone-cold crazy.

At the back of the crowd, a tent flap stirred. The tent was low, dirty, and generally to be considered a significant step down from a hovel. Will hadn't paid it much heed. But then a man pushed back the tent flap and emerged. And emerged. It seemed to go on forever.

Muscles bulged off the man in a way that Will could hardly make sense of. He seemed a parody of anatomy. There was something deeply wrong with the man's physiology. Some tumor planted deep within him, twisting him further and further out of true. As he moved, his skin rippled uncomfortably, veins pushing up against it from beneath the skin. He was perhaps even bigger than Balur. Will hadn't realized that people came in that size.

"I am what?" he called. Turuck's voice was pitched so low, Will almost had trouble picking out the words.

Will hesitated. He knew he was here to start a fight, but gods...just the sheer size of him.

He wanted to look at Lette, to run to her so she could tell him reassuring clichés about how the bigger they came the harder they fell.

He took a breath and looked Turuck in the eye.

"You're my bitch," he said. "My sniveling little bitch."

Turuck grinned. "Many come to me to die, little man," he said. "I shall not turn you away." He reached over his shoulder and pulled out...Will tried to work out what it might have been in another man's hands. Some sort of forge equipment, perhaps? Something trawled up from a dwarven mine?

It resembled a cleaver, but was surely almost six feet long. A massive chunk of sharpened metal streaked brown with blood and rust, but with an edge that still gleamed. There was no guard on the handle, just a ragged steel pipe roughly welded on and wrapped with rags. Turuck didn't even hold it in both hands. He used his spare one to beckon to Will.

"Come on, little man. It will be over soon."

The psychotics stepped back, made an oval in the mud. Turuck hulked at the apex of one curve. Will stood at the other, trying to remember where someone's kidneys were.

"I was always saying this was a stupid plan," he heard Balur mutter, which really didn't help.

You're cheating, Will said to himself. *It's going to be okay, because you're cheating.*

He fumbled for the tiny scrap of magical power still flickering in his belly.

He remembered what true power felt like. He remembered the days after he had slept with Cois, feeling hir power unfurling through his body, the slow realization that the world could be bent to his will. When anything seemed possible. He remembered standing in Vinter, watching the dragons fall, watching his dreams become reality.

This scrap of power was a mockery of that. A pittance. He had come to this fight as a magical pauper.

But it had to be enough.

See me elsewhere. He pushed the thought out into the world. Forced it into existence, hefting all his weight behind it. Just as he had done with Chev. And it had worked then, hadn't it?

He stepped away, around the edge of the circle, focusing on maintaining the illusion that he was standing back where he had started, playing with his dagger, smiling at Turuck, utterly unconcerned.

The big man kept walking toward the spot Will had occupied, didn't look away for a moment, and Will's heart leapt. It was working. It was actually bloody working.

"Do not be shy, little man," Turuck said. "It is too late for regrets now, you know."

Turuck wasn't in a rush either. Which was good considering the ground Will had to cover. He scampered as quickly and quietly as he could. His palm felt sweaty as it gripped the dagger. He'd scavenged it from a battlefield early in their stay down in the Hallows. It was nothing special. Just six inches of sharp metal on the end of an ivory handle. Walrus tusk from the Amaranth Ocean, had been Balur's assessment. Will hadn't given it much thought at the time. It had just seemed better to have something than nothing. Now...Gods, now a great deal depended on the knife.

He'd asked Lette about a sword. She'd told him there wasn't enough time to get him familiar with the weight. "A knife will do all the work you need as long as you get close enough," she'd told him, "and I think that's the whole point of the magic in your plan, right?"

And yes, yes, it was…but now that he saw Turuck, Will wasn't completely sure he wanted to get *that* close.

He took a deep breath, puffed out his cheeks, forced the air to leave him slowly. *This will be quick. This will be quiet. All these people will think I moved too quick for them to see. They will believe. They will fall in line while Turuck bleeds out on the ground. It will be fine.*

His heart thundered back at the preposterousness of his rationalizations.

He let Turuck walk past him. He made himself count another beat. This wouldn't work if Turuck sensed Will behind him and turned.

Turuck's back was like a landscape. Contortions of muscle brutalizing the skin, rising in outlandish hills and valleys. Thick black plaques disrupting forests of hair. The scraps of armor looked pathetic in their attempts to cover that vast expanse, paltry when compared to the natural hide.

You know where the kidneys are. You can mark the spots on his back. And it was true. Higher than he'd ever struck before. But approximately five feet off the ground. Well within reach.

Turuck stopped five yards away from where the illusory Will stood. "Any last words, little man? Anything you want to whisper in my ear?"

Oh shit, thought Will. *This is it.* He concentrated on giving his illusion an insouciant look of indifference and on keeping his bladder from leaking. He was two yards from Turuck's back now, closing slowly.

"It is all right to weep." Turuck's voice had an almost lilting quality. "Many have before you. Some shit themselves. Some laugh. It is all right. It is important in these last moments to simply be yourself. To be honest with yourself and your world. That is what I give people, you see. These moments where pretense is no longer necessary. That is my gift. To lift away the veils so you can reveal yourself."

There was, Will thought, a really special sort of crazy going on in Turuck's head.

Turuck raised his monstrous cleaver. His back arched. Muscles in the small of his back bunched. The straps of his armor creaked. The crowd inhaled.

And Will pigstuck him like a motherfucker.

Again and again he plunged the knife into Turuck's back. A flurry of blows he hadn't thought himself capable of. Again and again, the knife flicked out of Turuck's back, great red spurts spattering his face.

And then Turuck spun round and hit him with a hand that seemed to strike the entirety of Will's torso with the force of a charging bull and sent him flying across the dirt circle and landing with a crash of jangled limbs and senses.

He tried to get his feet under him, failed, sprawled in the dirt. He managed to focus on Turuck. The big man was reaching around, feeling his back. He brought back fingers dripping red.

Will tried to focus, to get his bearings. He had stabbed Turuck. He had stabbed him a lot. Why wasn't the man on his knees, bleeding and weeping and ruing the day he had laid his eyes upon Willett Fallows? Why was he advancing on Will with his quite frankly preposterous sword in his hand?

"Hmmm," said Turuck, licking the blood off his fingers. "You are quick. But you are also making me angry. And that"—he hefted his blade—"is a mistake."

Will focused. On staying alive. On being a horrendous cheat and liar.

He rolled desperately in the earth, while sending another illusion the other way.

Turuck's blade came down and smashed into Will's illusion, which burst apart in a puff of disproven air. Turuck roared.

Will kept on scrambling. Turuck swept the blade back, not

quite able to turn the massive weight, so that the flat of the blade crashed into Will's hip and sent him sailing to eat more mud.

He tried to turn it into a somersault, landed on his injured tailbone, howled, and lay flat on his back. Turuck lumbered around and looked down at him.

"Not quick," he said. "Tricky."

"Yeah," Will huffed out. "Totally." Summoning what little willpower remained to him, Will threw out another illusion, a version of himself standing a little way away. And then another, and another. A ring of illusory selves standing around Turuck.

"But which one am I?" he said.

Turuck looked at him, puzzled. "What? You are the one lying on the ground in front of me." He shook his head. "That's not even...What are you trying...?" He pointed at one of the illusions. "How could you have gotten over there?"

And as his eyes left Will to look at the stupid illusion, Will took his chance. One last illusion. One last scrap of effort, which made his skull throb and his mind feel as if it were being scraped raw. An image of himself lying defeated in the mud, while he himself scrambled away hidden from everyone's eyes.

He went and stood panting in the ring while Turuck looked down at the illusory self still lying in the muck. Will could see the wound he had gouged in the giant's back. He had made a mess of the skin and muscle, but Turuck's immense physiology had rendered Will's concerns about the knife actually relevant. He just had not penetrated the man's hide deeply enough to do the damage required.

Turuck leaned down. "To be tricky, little man," he said in a hushed voice, "you also have to be smart."

Which seemed as good a moment as any for Will to launch himself out of the circle and slam onto Turuck's back. Still yelling, he scrambled upward. The blade was big enough to get to the arteries in the man's neck, at least.

He got a good one or two utterly bewildered seconds from

Turuck, Will's weight throwing the massive warrior off and sending him stumbling one step, then two. Will grabbed at armor straps, hair, trying to haul himself aloft. He used the knife to gouge a bloody purchase on the brute's back.

Turuck howled in anger as around and beneath him illusory Wills vanished, all blowing silent raspberries. Will himself was grunting and cursing, fighting for an angle.

With a roar Turuck flung himself onto his back.

Will had about a nanosecond to appreciate that he was about to be sandwiched between the ground and several hundred pounds, and then he was. The air sprayed out of him. His ribs creaked. He screamed, and lost track of many of his other pains.

After a while he realized that Turuck wasn't getting off him. Also he was wet. And warm.

Bugger, he thought, *I think I'm bleeding.*

Turuck was very still and very quiet. Everyone, Will realized as his awareness slowly grew to expand beyond his immediate body and situation, was being very quiet.

Grunting, cursing, and still in considerable pain, Will squirmed free.

Turuck lay on the ground next to him.

Turuck was very, very dead.

Will wasn't entirely sure what had happened. He didn't think anyone was.

Then Will started to wonder where his knife was...

He'd been holding it when Turuck flung himself backward. He'd had it lodged in the middle of the man's back...

Turuck's weight...Gods, when they landed it must have finally been enough to drive the blade deep enough to do... Gods, what had he hit? There was blood everywhere. The blade must have struck the man's heart.

Everyone was staring at him. Everyone was staring at Turuck lying at his feet.

His feet.

He'd won.

"YES!" Will bellowed. Gods, he suddenly felt remarkably and miraculously alive. "COME ON!" he bellowed at the astonished crowd. "That's what I'm fucking talking about." He kicked Turuck. "Bring it on, you son of a bitch. Bigger they come!" He pounded his own chest with his fist. "Yeah!" He lifted back his head and whooped at the sky.

Everybody kept on just staring silently at him.

"Yeah!" he shouted again.

"Okay," said Lette, stepping out of the circle of onlookers. "I think that's enough now."

"I—" Will started.

"Yes, yes. They know." She was nodding.

Will held out a finger and pointed at every single member of the crowd he could see, circling so they all knew. "You listen to me now. You listen to me!"

"Settle down."

But he couldn't. He wouldn't. He had them in the palm of his hand. They would take him to the gorge. He would steal the Deep Ones' power. He would get out of here and get his revenge. And his revenge was closer than it had ever been before.

10

My Enemy's Enemy

When Quirk came to, she was staring a dragon in the face. It was, it seemed, chewing on a dead body.

She flinched backward. Then she shouted in pain. She had injured her body well beyond the point where she should be flinching.

"What...?" Quirk managed, then ran out of words.

Then it came back to her. The utter and miserable failure of her attack on Barph. Fighting alongside the dragon. Killing alongside the dragon. And then...

Then she had passed out. In Tarramon. In her enemy's stronghold.

The dragon swallowed the body, a flopping leg disappearing obscenely between its leathery lips. It belched. A flicker of flame leapt out of its nostrils. It didn't apologize.

"What happened?" She managed the full sentence this time. She wasn't entirely sure why she was asking the dragon. She supposed it was the only other living thing around.

The beast turned a great yellow eye on her. It had a more aquiline head than most of the creatures she had seen before. The scales around its nostrils and eyes appeared fine and delicate, mottled blue and white. Its neck—almost as wide as its well-muscled jaw—was long, almost snakelike.

She should kill this creature, she thought. She was the leading expert on dragons in all of Avarra, after all. She knew exactly

how beautiful, mesmerizing, and awful they were. To dominate
and to enslave were as necessary to a dragon as breathing was
to her. She knew it coveted all her wealth and could not help but
do so. If human words could be applied to its bestial emotions, it
was cruel, greedy, and more than a bit of a dick.

She should kill it. If she could. It was injured, if she remembered correctly. A broken wing. If she was ever to get an opportunity, this would be it.

But she was not uninjured herself.

"I failed," the dragon said. "Barph lived."

There was something odd about its voice, Quirk thought. It
was not quite the bowel-quivering bass of some of the dragons
she'd faced before.

Quirk tried to focus. "But..." She shook her head, regretted it
as another spike of pain shot through her. "We're still... We're
in Tarramon. No one's killed us."

The dragon looked back at the mostly collapsed archway that
had once led into this courtyard. Burned wooden timbers jutted
like ribs from piles of broken stone.

"Some people came," the dragon said. "I killed them." It
turned its head away, started snuffing against the pile of rubble to its right, farther away from Quirk. "They stopped coming
after that."

The dragon nosed aside a section of wall. Its tongue snaked
out of its mouth and snagged a protruding leg.

"Why didn't you eat me?" she blurted. It was a little blunt perhaps, but Quirk's social skills didn't stand up well to stress, and
that was the next question on her list.

The dragon turned its eye on her again. Then it rolled away
again, went back to the severed leg. "You fought Barph. You can
make fire. You are like a little dragon. A cub thing. You may be
useful again if the humans come back."

Useful. Yes. From what she knew of dragon psychology, that
actually made sense. It felt honest.

And gods, it was talking to her. And if it was not exactly friendly—she wasn't even sure if dragons could do friendly—it was also very far from animosity. The things she could learn from this creature. The questions she could ask.

And then, as the academic in her stirred, she placed what was different about the dragon's voice.

"You're a female," she said.

The dragon turned both of its eyes on her this time. Black cat-like slits in yellow orbs. Forward facing. Predator's eyes. And it was small for a dragon, but it was also so very much larger than she.

"Yes," it said finally. "I am aware."

"I'm sorry. I just..." Quirk was dangerously close to gabbling. She was feeling light-headed. She wondered if she had lost any blood. She looked down. It turned out that she had. Though not so much that she should worry, she thought. And she wasn't losing any more. All her wounds had clotted.

Slowly she tried to haul herself into something closer to a sitting position. Her body shouted at her. Her head pulsed. She remembered being hit repeatedly above the neck. She wished people hadn't done that.

The dragon had found another body. She started to chew.

Quirk lay back, panting at the exertion of movement. "I'm...," she said, took a breath. "I'm Quirk."

The dragon didn't look up. "Yorrax," it said with its mouth full.

"Hello, Yorrax," said Quirk. The dragon ignored her.

She leaned back. At least it was easy to fall asleep.

Sound ripped her out of blackness. She struggled to sit up, almost bellowed at the pain in her head. She stared about wildly. It was evening, the light fading.

"What in the Hallows was that?"

After a long time, a husky dragon voice said, "Nothing."

Very slowly, and very carefully, Quirk rolled her head to look at the dragon. Its whole body seemed hunched around its broken wing. She could feel the tension coming off it in waves.

"I don't know if you know this," she said, "because you're not human. But most of us can pick up on bullshit that obvious."

"You cannot help," the dragon said. The fire in her eyes seemed dull in the thin light.

"Not if you don't want help," Quirk agreed, with a tone balanced between patience and petulance that she strongly associated with a nurse who had cared for her during her early days in Tamathia.

Yorrax didn't answer. The pair of them lay there in silence. Quirk lost track of time until her stomach growled.

"Is there food," she said, "that isn't..." She hesitated, searching for a diplomatic word. "That isn't people?"

Yorrax continued to ignore her. Quirk gathered what strength and willpower she had and bunched her legs. With a grunt that became a shout and then a shriek, she stood. The world spun about her. She put out a hand to steady herself. Then the ground hit the side of her head. Then she threw up.

Gods, she had to get out of here. She couldn't just lie here wasting time. She had to...to...what? What could she honestly do besides lie here and slowly starve to death?

Even if she could overcome the limitations of her flesh, what then? She had come at Barph with every scrap of revenge she had held, and he had simply laughed. He had torn everything apart. It hadn't even been an effort for him.

Despite her best efforts, a sob escaped her. She stuffed her hand into her mouth to try to stop the next one.

She heard the dragon move, ignored it.

Gods, she was a joke. Her whole life was a cosmic joke. Her whole struggle...How long had Barph been laughing at it?

There was a dull scraping sound from behind her. She wanted to glance back, but knew enough now to turn her head slowly.

Yorrax had reached out with her tail and was rooting in the rubble of the whorehouse's walls. Quirk watched curiously, then looked at the dragon's face. Yorrax was looking studiously away, as if her tail was operating entirely of its own volition.

With a wrench the tail pulled free. Several large crates came with it, tumbling toward Quirk and spilling open as they came. Breads, cheeses, and bottles of wine spilled across the ground. Some bottles cracked, leaked their contents into shards of glass, but another came to rest against her thigh. A roll landed in her lap from the small explosion. Quirk stared at it. She stared at Yorrax.

"I...," she said.

Yorrax wasn't looking at her, was instead staring studiously at the stars as they began to appear in the sky.

An unexpected warmth flooded Quirk. A gratitude so profound that it caught her off guard. "Thank you," she said. "This is..."

"Hmm?" Yorrax turned around, eyes wide and innocent. "What?"

And despite everything, despite the fact that this was a dragon, Quirk couldn't help but smile. "You are the worst liar I have ever met."

Yorrax stared at her a little while. "I will eat you tomorrow," she said finally. "Once you have put on enough meat to be tasty."

The Tarramoners came for them in the night.

Quirk was having trouble sleeping. Her head throbbed viciously. The wine had not helped. Moonlight painted the courtyard in a dim chiaroscuro. Jags of rubble seemed to loom out of a surrounding abyss. Yorrax shifted uneasily in her sleep.

At first Quirk thought the noises she heard came from the dragon. Her tail shifting rocks in her sleep. Some scratching of her massive claws over the broken cobbles. But then she heard the whispers.

Quirk tried to lie perfectly still. Tried to hold her breath steady.

Each voice was too low for her to make out the words, but there were a lot of them. They were climbing up over one of the more intact buildings. She could hear metal rattling. Swords, perhaps?

They would reach Yorrax first. And perhaps that was a good thing. Whatever else she was, Yorrax was a dragon. Dragons needed to be killed. Even if they did help feed you, and occasionally saved your life.

She should definitely let these Tarramoners kill Yorrax.

She didn't let the Tarramoners kill Yorrax.

She lit up the night.

Her first swath of flame went over their attackers' heads, a bright signal flare that boiled away the delicate light of moon and stars. She saw them in stark relief, poised with ropes against the wall of the courtyard, eyes suddenly wide with fear and surprise. There were shouts, bellows. Then darkness. She let the fire die, and in the blinking, blinding darkness she moved.

Yorrax was grumbling, stirring, shifting her vast bulk. Quirk crawled, trying to move her head as little as possible. The men were shouting back and forth to each other, panic tearing through them like a plague through a village. Quirk could hear some of them scrambling to get up and away. Those packing more lunch meat in their britches were dropping to the courtyard's uneven flagstones.

Quirk sent out another jet of flame. A man screamed, twisted away, arms flailing. He ran, throwing up leaping shadows, eliciting shrill shouts from his comrades. Then he tripped, fell, lay twitching and screaming. Then he just burned.

"What?" Yorrax's voice was slurred.

"It's awake!" A voice clear in the cacophony of terror.

Quirk flooded the courtyard with flame. She let it wash out of her. A great gout of flame. And it felt like freedom, and it felt like dancing, and it felt like a betrayal of what she had thought she and Afrit could be. But Afrit was no more, and her plans were no more, so maybe there was only this. Maybe there was only scouring the world clean of Barph's infection. Maybe there was only leaving him with no world to rule.

She was vaguely aware of the shouting, the screaming, the men and women running for cover, the gleam of firelight reflected on sharp steel. Of Yorrax rearing up on one leg, body twisted but head held high. Of Yorrax's flame twisting with her own.

And then... then it was over. She was gasping. She felt hollow. She could smell burned meat. She could hear men and women fleeing in panic.

She lay on her back staring up at the stars. They seemed impossibly distant in that moment.

"Well," said Yorrax, settling back down on the ground. There was a strain in her voice. "I suppose it was nice of you to cook them for me."

Then came a meaty crunching sound. Quirk closed her eyes and let exhaustion take her.

The Tarramoners left them alone after that. They had sacrificed enough sons and daughters here, it seemed. No one came and bothered them. They did not go and bother the rest of Tarramon. She could barely move without her head's threatening to detonate. Yorrax simply lay still and ate the dead.

For the most part there was silence between them. Sometimes Quirk tried to plan. She tried to imagine returning to her resistance fighters at the estate. She tried to imagine whether they'd be surprised to see her or horrified. She wondered what they could possibly achieve. She wondered if she would finally give in and simply burn the world.

Other times she meditated. She focused on the surface of the lake. She kept it calm. She held the wind still and silenced its deep currents. She found her head hurt less when she did.

And sometimes, as the days ticked past, they talked.

"Gods, please... That was somebody's grandmother," Quirk said once, as Yorrax slurped and slapped at a body.

"Not mine," said Yorrax.

On another occasion Yorrax asked her why she was making "that irritating noise." Quirk rolled away and tried to keep the keening sense of loss inside her quieter.

And then sometimes they laughed. Yorrax had farted. A barrel, spilled from the whorehouse and caught in the blast, flew halfway across the square and landed in a clatter of spilling wooden uprights and metal hoops, and Quirk simply lost her shit entirely. Yorrax attempted an imperious stare that slowly dissolved into a rumbling, stumbling growl that Quirk had eventually realized was laughter.

In another, more confessional moment, Quirk admitted, "I wrote a book on dragons once. A lot of people read it, actually."

It seemed a lifetime away to her. Before Afrit. Before dragons attempted to take over all of Avarra. Before Barph. It was less than a year. Gods.

Yorrax turned to her. "You wrote about dragons?"

"Yes." Quirk avoided nodding still.

"What did you say about them?"

"Oh." Quirk licked her lips. Now didn't seem like the time to mention that the book had done so well because of her role in liberating Kondorra from the rule of dragons. "Their biology. Their musculature. Their diet. Their mechanisms of flight. Their dominance patterns." She shrugged.

"People liked reading this?" Yorrax's head was cocked on one side.

"Some, yes."

"We were a curiosity," Yorrax said. "Like . . . some sort of bauble." The last word sounded as if it didn't quite fit in her dragon's mouth.

"Well . . . ," Quirk hedged. "Not exactly."

Yorrax didn't seem to be paying attention. "Where I came from," she said, "we didn't have books. We had violence and fire and death." She turned her vast head away from Quirk.

"That...," Quirk started, but realized she honestly didn't have much of a comeback to that. She wasn't sure she was supposed to. There seemed to be a point she was missing.

And then...Gods, the enormity of the whole thing hit her. Because once dragons had terrorized all Avarra. But then, hundreds of years ago, they'd been driven away. And for hundreds of years there hadn't been dragons. They had been a legend. Until thirty years ago, when they had returned and taken over Kondorra. They had come out of myth. And nobody—absolutely nobody—knew where the dragons came from.

"So," she said as casually as she could. "Where *do* you come from?"

"The only place humanity left for us."

Oh...Barph's balls. The dragons had been driven away. And of course that was a wonderful thing for humanity. But if you were a dragon it was a purging. It was genocide.

A genocide committed by humans on dragons.

Quirk decided not to push the subject.

The next day, Quirk's head felt a little clearer. She felt a little steadier on her feet. She scavenged deeper among the whorehouse's spilled cellars and found salted meats, overripe fruit, and an almost innumerable stash of spare chains, leather straps, and whips.

She sat out in the sun, enjoying the trickle of juice down her chin. She set a barrel of cured hams before Yorrax. She almost felt peaceful.

Yorrax broke the silence. "You attacked Barph," she said.

Quirk paused, a tangerine segment halfway to her mouth. Quirk's encounter with Barph was proving the slowest wound to heal. It still felt raw in her mind.

"Yes," she conceded.

"Why?"

Quirk thought hard about how to answer that. "He took

everything from me," she said. "My purpose. My job. My friends. My love. My world. Everything."

Yorrax nodded. "You hate him?"

"With everything I have," she said finally.

Yorrax didn't say anything. Then slowly she nudged a ham toward Quirk with her nose. "It is surprisingly good for human food," she said.

Quirk tried it. It was good. She made a decision. "Are you willing to admit that your wing is broken yet?" she asked.

Yorrax snapped her head around, lips peeling back from fangs.

The fruit in Quirk's belly soured. She held out a placating hand. "I just want to help. I know how to heal it."

"I don't need your help," Yorrax growled.

"I mean…" Quirk closed her eyes. And gods, she wished she knew more about dragon psychology. But…this had to be a pride thing, didn't it? Yorrax hadn't complained, because she couldn't admit weakness. "I didn't mean help," she said. "I meant…I want to repay you."

Slowly Yorrax nodded.

"I'll need to set it with a splint," said Quirk. And then, because she didn't want it to be a surprise later on, "It will hurt."

Yorrax scoffed. "You cannot hurt me, human."

It turned out that Quirk could.

Later, after night had fallen, they both lay in the square, staring up at the stars. The heavens were up there somewhere. Barph was in them. Their mutual enemy.

"You asked me why I attacked Barph," Quirk said. "Why did you do it?"

Slowly Yorrax settled her head down on the rubble of the courtyard. "You asked me about where I came from," she said. "And at first it will seem like I am answering that question. But I am not. I am telling you about my hate."

11

The Backstory I've Spent Three Books Getting Around To

"Once we lived in Avarra," Yorrax began. "Once humans cowered before us and gave us our due, their all. Once this world was right. This is something every dragon knows. It is our legend of ourselves. I doubt your people tell the story this way, but this is how we tell it.

"Times changed, though. Humans banded together. They scurried together like ants. They made cities and alliances. We, though, were complacent. If the humans built their wealth, then they built our wealth. Everything that belonged to them also belonged to us, and was to be taken whenever we desired it. We did not dream things could change.

"But humans dreamt. They are ambitious creatures. They built machines of war. They built skins of steel to wear into battle. They built teeth they could fire from their bows to bite at our wings and throats. They built armies.

"And still we were complacent. Even when they killed us. Even when humans cut us down from the skies. We thought these were anomalies, accidents, twists of misfortune. And by the time we realized the threat for what it was, it was too late. And so the world was turned upside down. The apex was inverted. We were laid low. We became the hunted, the prey. Our birthright was stolen from us.

"The hatred humans harbored in their hearts for us—and for the tried and proper order of the world—knew no boundaries. It could not be satiated. They would hunt us down until the very last of us was dead, and we were no more. Our very race ended.

"So we fled. We took to the skies and flew west. Ever west. Looking for somewhere else to live. A refuge, a shelter, a home.

"And so we found Natan. Our new home. An island in the endless blue of the Amaranth Ocean. But where Avarra had been a lush land of plenty and ease, Natan is a land of rock and hardship. It is jagged spires and hard-won food. Many more died there. We took long strides closer to the brink of extinction.

"But the strong survived. Those with the willpower to cling to the precipice of survival. And those dragons mated, had young, raised the strong of mind and body. Despite all that was done to us, we did not give up. Even as the very land conspired against us, we survived.

"We were few then. Extinction's maw might have retreated, but it still regarded us from the horizon. We longed to return to Avarra, to reclaim our place and set the world to rights. But for century after century, our ambitions were kept in check by the very place we now called home.

"Then from across the sea, for the first time in living memory, a ship came. It was aimed straight toward our shores. And it navigated easily past the rocks that lurk in the waters as if it had made the journey a thousand times before. In it, we knew, must be our hated foes. So we gathered to kill them, to vent a thousand years of pent-up rage upon the humans.

"There was only one man inside the boat, though. And he looked upon us with no shock, no surprise, and no fear. He said he knew what had been done to us, and that he had come to right a great wrong. And I cannot explain why, but we listened.

"He told us we had become legends, almost mystical. He told us that the gods had betrayed Avarra. He told us that man could learn instead to worship us. He told us that man would voluntarily put us back in our rightful place, if only we would follow his advice. We could tear the heavens themselves from the grasp of the gods. We could be gods ourselves. All the wrong done to us set right.

"And so, of course, we argued. And argued. And argued. And the man grew impatient and railed at us, but he was just a man for all his words. And so, in the end, we sent just seven dragons. Seven ambitious dragons. Seven willing to risk their lives. Seven champions to establish a foothold and see how man responded to our rule. And the man called us a fool, and told us that we would see he was right. But he was just a man.

"And so seven dragons captured Kondorra. A nation as far away from Natan as possible. A way to hide the scent of our trail, should anyone seek to follow it. And our champions did not do what the man said. They did not simper. They did not pander. They dominated. They destroyed. The established their right to rule.

"For thirty years they ruled Kondorra. For thirty years men bent their knees to the rule of dragons, as once all Avarra had done. And we laughed at the man for what he had told us. Because we did not need him.

"But then, as we prepared to bring our rule to all of Avarra, things began to go awry. There was an uprising. History was repeating. Men were uniting against us. And in a great battle, the champions of Kondorra were slain.

"Perhaps then we should have stopped. Perhaps then we should have recognized the ruination that our ambition would bring. But we were ready. We were poised for war. And again the words of that visitor to our shores were discussed. And we were so tired of struggling and scrabbling for survival. And the reports our champions had sent back to us...What they had learned mirrored what the man had told us. And so, in a great council, it was decided we would come to Avarra in force. We would become gods.

"It was beautiful. It was magnificent. It was everything we dreamt it could be. We were welcomed with open arms. We were worshipped. We were obeyed. We were elevated. And even the gods trembled in fear at our might. The whole world rang with the sweet sound of perfection once more. We were where we belonged once more. We rejoiced.

"And then betrayal. In our moment of ascension, our moment of victory. Everything torn from us. Our lives. The world cast into chaos and disaster. Our race closer than ever to annihilation.

"Because the man who had come to our shores had lied to us. He had hidden his true intent. He had made us his tools. We were just a stepping stone for his own ambitions."

"Barph," Quirk said. And gods...she saw it now. All of it. Thirty years ago, dragons had returned to Avarra out of legend. Because Barph had told them to. They had taken over Kondorra. They had oppressed it. And in Kondorra, Will had been born. Will who had been nurtured by a man called Firkin. A man who had filled Will's head with dreams of revolution and plans to take down the dragons. A man who was, in the end, just a mask, a sham. A man who was Barph. It had all been his plan. And it had all worked. They had all been deceived. And Barph had won.

"I will kill Barph," said Yorrax, and there was no doubt in her voice. "For everything he has done to my kin. I will have my revenge or die trying."

And Quirk smiled, because in this dragon, this beast, this engine of destruction, she had found a kindred spirit.

"You want to kill Barph," she said.

Yorrax nodded. "I just said that. About ten seconds ago."

"I want to kill Barph." Quirk would not be distracted. Purpose was starting to return to her, slowly at first, but with increasing force.

"But neither of us..." Quirk shook her head. "We don't know how to kill Barph. We don't even know if there is a way to kill him now. He's too...He has the power of seven gods within him. It's too much."

"So you have given up," said Yorrax. She looked away. "I have not."

"He'll kill you." Quirk's vision was still unfolding before her. The present was drifting out of focus. "He'll kill me too. It's inevitable."

"Well, I'm glad you appreciated the tragic history of my people." Yorrax put her head down on the ground. "I'm happy I spent all that time sharing it."

"But it doesn't matter that we'll die." Quirk was barely listening, caught up in the currents of her own logic. "If it's inevitable, it's not even part of the equation. What matters is what we do with the time we have. And what we can do with that time"—Quirk tried to restrain her smile but was unable to do so—"is hurt him like a motherfucker."

Yorrax picked up her head.

"For six months," Quirk went on, pacing now, unable to fully contain her excitement, "Barph has been focused on one thing: reshaping this world. He has a vision for how it should be.

"There's something he wants, Yorrax. And that means there's something we can take away from him. Something we can burn to the ground." Quirk fixed her bright eyes on Yorrax's yellow ones. "We may not be able to win, but we can make sure Barph loses."

Yorrax hesitated, but didn't say anything.

"I have people," Quirk pressed, walking toward Yorrax now. "People who hate Barph." She licked her lips. A vision of the future was beginning to form in her mind. She was beginning to see things clearly. "You can join us." *No, that was wrong.* "We can join you. Together we can bring this world down around Barph's ears." She smiled. Gods, she thought she might even laugh despite the mounting pain in her head. And she should sit down, but she couldn't. She put a hand on Yorrax's flank.

"Together. Think of everything we can do. Think of everything we could burn."

Yorrax's black tongue snaked out, licked a lower lip.

"Humans," she said. That was it.

Quirk understood the objection, though. "If you have a horde of dragons hidden nearby that are poised to rain destruction down on Barph, then I'd be more than happy to join them."

Yorrax was silent for a moment, then she raised her injured wing. "I cannot travel far."

And then Quirk did laugh, because if that was Yorrax's only remaining objection, then her argument was won.

Three days later they climbed up onto what was left of the brothel. Yorrax's claws scrabbled through the rubble. Quirk went mostly on all fours, occasionally steadying herself against Yorrax's flank. The pale-blue scales felt oddly warm, and supple despite their strength.

Upon the mound of broken stone and wood, Yorrax spread her wings. The wood of the splint Quirk had built creaked, and Yorrax grimaced.

"You're sure you're ready?" Quirk tried to force all the impatience out of her voice, to appear nothing but concerned.

"I do not need your concern," rumbled Yorrax. Then she spat three balls of fire into the square. They landed with sharp detonations. "If you tell anyone about this," said Yorrax, as several screams drifted up from the town beyond, "then I shall kill you and everyone dear to you."

"Yes, but that's why I like you," said Quirk, and, grabbing ahold of the spot where Yorrax's wing joined her body, she hauled herself up onto the dragon's back.

"If I drop you," Yorrax said, "then our partnership is over."

And then vast muscles contracted beneath Quirk, almost throwing her free. She clutched desperately at the edges of scales. She gripped the beast's flanks with her thighs and cursed at the top of her lungs.

Yorrax's wings smashed at the air. Small hurricanes whirled past Quirk. She felt her hair pulling painfully at her skull.

Again and again, Yorrax beat at the air, and again and again, Quirk fought for solid purchase on the beast's back. Her heart was hammering in the back of her throat. Her headache felt ready to split the world in two. Her stomach lurched. Her palms were sweaty.

And then the ground dropped away, and everything was worse.

It seemed to her they hovered for a moment, hanging above everything. The world becoming smaller and smaller. But as that happened, the last of her fear and doubts dropped away.

At some unspoken signal both of them let fire loose into the sky, filling the air with heat and fury. Then they were racing forward, ready to scorch the earth clean.

12

The Downward Spiral

Down in the Hallows, Lette stood at the head of a gorge that was like a knife wound in the landscape. A gibbering wreck of a man was pointing to it and saying, "Deep, deep, deep," over and over again while drooling on himself. He'd tried to claw out Lette's eyes earlier, which was why he was bleeding now.

"Okay, Sparrow," Will said to the man. "Thank you for showing us. That'll...Oh gods, Balur."

Balur had just killed the man.

"What?" asked Balur. "Were you not being done with him?" He wiped his hands clean. "Sorry, I was thinking you were done with him."

"Just because I was done with him doesn't mean..." Will broke off and shook his head. "Why is this a concept that needs explaining?"

"But he was being a horrifying psychotic killer," Balur said.

"So are you!" said Lette. Balur looked at her. He was pretending to be wounded.

She rolled her eyes and went walking into the abyss. Eventually the others followed.

Lette would be the first to admit that she had not handled all her time in the Hallows with perfect grace. Things had been... difficult at first. It had been a difficult time for her. She had been morose. She could admit to that. Her efforts to find a way out lackluster. She'd had trouble finding hope.

She wasn't sure how else she could have handled it, though. There had been a moment—a moment just before she was killed—when she had... what? How to put that into words?

They had been about to overthrow the dragons. They had been about to overthrow the gods. They were about to free Avarra from dictators... Will had created a moment. A movement. He had united humanity in a moment of pure rebellious independence.

It had been so beautiful. And she'd been part of it. Everything she'd been doing. It had meant something. Will had created meaning for her.

And then it was gone. Then she was dead, and it was all ash. Who would take that well?

But now, here, stepping into this gorge, stepping toward power... could she believe again? Could she be part of something again?

Will caught up with her, put an unselfconscious hand on her arm. The gorge, it seemed, had had a salutary effect upon the sensibilities that Balur's murder had affronted.

He grinned at her. "We did it!" he said. "We actually did it! We're going to the Deep Ones! We're going to go home!" He grabbed her arm, and for a moment it felt as if lightning were shooting up to her shoulder. "We are going to take this fight all the way, Lette. All the gods-hexed way."

Suddenly she thought that she was going to kiss him. And she wasn't sure it was a good idea. They had been down that path, and it had not ended well for either of them. But right now, gods... she would like to kiss him.

His eyes looked very large and very deep. Her breath came fast. Her heart unloaded a flurry of blows against her sternum.

"So—" Cois said from far too close, and Lette almost gasped, managed to make it simply a sharp inhalation. She whipped around slightly too fast. Trying to hide her movements, she slowly slipped the knife she'd drawn back into her sleeve.

Cois arched an eyebrow at her. "I know, I know, I should have asked this earlier, but you are totally set on this whole Deep Ones plan, are you?"

Lette felt Will's good mood evaporating off him like steam. "Wasn't finding them your plan?" he asked.

Cois looked shocked. "Shit, I hope not. I think I just mentioned them to piss Lawl off and then you went and made all these plans."

"About five months ago," Will checked.

Cois shrugged. "If you say so."

"And you're bringing this up now?"

Cois looked around, a pantomime of innocence. "I appear to be."

"But you said they're where you got your divine powers from, right?"

"I think," Cois said, adding a little of hir own bite to hir words, "that I said they were horror and insanity made into physical nightmares that enslaved me and my brethren. Did you miss that bit?"

"But you took in their blood and you became the gods," Will said.

"You seem very fixated on that part of the story," Cois said.

Lette was still holding her knife. If she'd thought Balur would ever forgive her, she might have considered using it to encourage Cois to be more forthcoming.

"Because it's the bit that gets me out of here."

"Drinking the blood of something so utterly beyond your ken it will use your sanity as a small, squishy plaything."

"You drank it, didn't you?" Will had stopped walking now, was leaning in. Balur was baring his teeth.

"I, Will," Cois said, ever so sweetly, "am not human. I look human. I behave like a human. Admittedly, I have slightly better tits than most humans. But I am not a human. I am of the Deep Ones. I am their creation. I am built upon their designs.

There is compatibility. You...you are Lawl's thing. He made your race. Little batteries of worship to power the gods. That's what you were designed to be, which I know sounds awful and demeaning, but that's because it is awful and demeaning. But the point is, you and I are not of the same design. We are not built by the same minds."

"So it was good for you, but it isn't good for me?" said Will, doing an increasingly poor job of controlling his anger. "Okay for the gods, but not for mortals? Well, guess what you are now."

Cois finally seemed to attempt some conciliation. "This is not simple jealousy, Will. Yes, the gods achieved much by stealing the power of the Deep Ones. But we also lost some things. And some things changed irrevocably. And it was not all to our design, or even our liking. I will not take their power again. I don't think..." Zhe shook hir head.

"You worry about being replaced," Will said.

And that gave Lette pause. She looked at Will. And in her mind this had always been about the power to escape here, to get revenge. But the Deep Ones' magic...Could it really make a god out of Will?

"I worry about you, Will," Cois said.

But Will was already storming deeper into the gorge. He was already refusing to turn away from his goal.

And even though he might well be an idiot, and he might well be making a mistake, one that might even cost her, Lette was warmed by Will's commitment, by his sense of purpose. And she was jealous of it, and wanted to live it through him. And so she followed.

Down the gorge they went. Down. Steep rock walls rose on either side of them. The artificial light of the Hallows dimmed. Loose scree crunched beneath their feet. They didn't come to the end of the gorge on their first day. Nor on the second. The walls stretched up impossibly far. Every moment felt like twilight. A blue phosphorescent fungus started to daub the walls, giving everything an ethereal glow.

Lette thought about what Cois had said. She thought about what hir motives might be. Of all the gods, zhe had been the most amenable, the most sympathetic. Zhe did appear to be genuinely affectionate toward Balur, and as strange as Lette found that idea, she appreciated it all the same.

She wasn't sure Cois was jealous of Will's potential power.

But when zhe had seen him use that last remnant of hir magic...maybe?

She drifted closer to the former god(dess). For a while they walked alongside each other, both trying to avoid contact with the strange fungus.

"If Will..." Lette broke the silence and then realized she wasn't sure what to do with the pieces. She struggled to find the right way to phrase it. "If he drinks the Deep Ones' blood, if he takes their power...what happens then? What is he taking, exactly?"

Cois walked on for ten paces before replying. "Those are two different things," zhe said. "And I think you're asking them in the wrong order."

"How about you just answer both," Lette said, "and I don't have to explain to Balur why you're shitting out your own teeth?"

Cois smiled. "And here I was thinking I knew everything there was to know about sweet talk."

Lette didn't smile back.

Cois sighed. "When...If Will takes the Deep Ones' power into him, then it will take up residence within him. It won't be part of him. You shouldn't think of it like a crown, or an extension of his willpower. It will be something...other to him. A creature, almost, that feeds him, but that also feeds on him. It won't be a creature, but that's the closest word I have. It will be a thought, really. An idea. But not his own thought. Not a thought that will fit in his skull. I tried to explain. I really did. You're not of them, you see. You're made of different stuff. So exactly how this creature, this thought will manifest inside him...I don't know." Zhe looked at Lette's expression. "I really do wish I had better answers."

Zhe sounded genuine, Lette decided. Genuine could be faked, and she could be fooled, but her gut was all she had to go on down here.

"Will it fuck him up?" she asked in the end. It was a bald question, and exposed more of her own fears than perhaps she would like, but perhaps a direct question would beget a direct answer.

"Maybe." Cois shrugged apologetically. "Maybe not. It will change him. Somehow. But power always changes people."

Lette reviewed the answers she'd received. "So you don't know shit?" That seemed like the big takeaway.

Cois gave hir sad smile again. "What I really know about is love, Lette," zhe said. "And I know that the man you pretend not to love is going to be someone else soon. I don't know who, though. And I don't know if you'll still love him. Maybe once I would have, but I'm someone else now too."

Lette considered punching out Cois's teeth after all. What sort of pissing answer was that?

But she had plenty of time to think about it. The descent went on. And on. And she saw the blue light of the fungus reflected in Will's eyes, and she knew that ending Barph was all he cared about. That was his purpose. His goal. And she had taken strength from that.

But now...here...in this dank hole...was his goal still hers?

13

Never Go Full Lovecraft

Will could feel the walls of this place sapping the others' resolve. It was the fifth day of descent. Lette was slipping back into the quiet introspection that had marked her first few months in the Hallows. Afrit was dragging her heels. Even Balur and Cois's lovemaking was muted. In unguarded moments Cois looked scared.

And of course he knew why. He saw this place just as they did. He understood why someone might have reservations. But this was all part of the bigger picture.

He pushed on.

Slowly Will became aware that it was getting colder, that the glow of the fungus was growing dimmer. He was forced to walk more and more slowly. The ground was uneven. He could not afford to break his ankle now. Not down here.

He tried to suppress a shudder.

An hour later the darkness was almost complete. He heard someone approaching him from behind.

"I think—" It was Lette.

"Wait," he cut her off. There was something on the floor ahead of him. Something...

He stepped closer, stooping down to see it.

"Will..."

Will was vaguely aware of Lette's rising anger, but he paid it no heed. In the floor ahead of him...there was...something his mind wanted to call light. Something glowing. But...He cocked his head to one side, trying to see it more clearly, reaching out a hand. And his hand was no more visible in whatever it was that was glowing from...

A hole. There was a hole in the floor.

He held out his hand over it and felt...He felt...the absence of a feeling. That he was somehow *not* feeling something he should be. Something that wasn't heat, or cold, or fear, or dread. Something he wasn't equipped to feel. Something utterly other.

"Oh shit." He glanced back. Cois was grabbing at hir stomach, a queasy expression on hir face. "I can feel them."

A moment of indecision. Then Will hardened his resolve. He turned back to the hole, reached out to feel the edges. It was approximately four feet in diameter, and the walls were far from smooth. He could climb this.

"You want to go down there?" Afrit sounded as if she was trying to avoid simply asking outright if he was crazy.

"I have to," said Will.

"You don't even know what to do when you get down there." Lette sounded as if she wasn't fully reconciled to his dismissive tone.

Will ignored them. He ignored the basic, animal part of his mind that was starting to scream. He lowered himself into the hole.

"I won't go down there." Cois was shaking hir head emphatically. "You can't make me."

"I won't," Will said. "I don't need you from here."

It was a cold thing to say, but he felt cold now. He was close. Power lay below him. So much power.

"I will be staying with you," Balur grunted to Cois.

"No." Cois didn't sound as if zhe meant it.

Will left them behind, went down hand over hand. The hole's

walls felt slimy, and his heart beat faster as he thought his hands would slip. But when he wiped his palms against his thighs, they felt dry.

He heard people lowering themselves into the hole above him. He didn't look up.

Down. Down into darkness, greasy handhold by greasy handhold. The strange not-light swelling around him, becoming not-brighter. His stomach roiled. Strange strands of emotion whispered through his mind. His face contorted into smiles and grimaces without his conscious effort. He could hear Afrit praying to gods that she knew full well were useless, dead bastards.

And then suddenly he found solid ground beneath his feet. His ankle jarred and he swore. But the hole had leveled out, had become a tunnel again. He felt his way forward, crawling as the ceiling became lower and lower.

Still the ceiling descended. He was forced onto his belly.

What if Gratt had betrayed him? What if this had all been an elaborate trick? What if he would be trapped down here in this tunnel...this hole...this ugly dead end of hope that he was crawling through?

Rock seemed to press in on him from every side. The space was too narrow to get a full breath.

And then suddenly he was through. Suddenly he was in space. Vast, cavernous space. Suddenly he could see. The whole world around him was flooded with blue light.

He gasped. He felt as if he were falling into space. He staggered, trying to steady himself even as he crawled up off his knees. He tried to understand everything he was seeing.

A cavern. He was in another cavern. There was a roof. He could...Yes, he could see that. But it was distant. So very distant. Because of all the caverns he had been in in the Hallows, all the enclosed spaces that had taken days or weeks to cross, this was by far the largest. This went on forever.

And it was full. Full of...

His brain struggled. Gears churned.

"Fuck this." Behind him, still in the tunnel, he heard Balur come to the narrow exit.

Then there was scrambling and Lette emerged. Then Afrit.

"I'm not doing it," said Balur. "I won't."

"Oh," breathed Lette, standing beside Will. "Oh. I don't...I can't..."

Then Afrit was there. She kept rubbing her eyes and her head alternately.

It was...They were...

There was something in front of Will. That was for certain. Something vast. Impossibly vast. It was a body in the same way that a country is land. But it was more than just its size that made it hard to grasp. As Will looked from one part of the mass to another, it seemed to shift in the corners of his vision, and when he looked back it was as if he had never seen it before. And yet he couldn't precisely say what had changed. And as he stared at one part, looking for evidence of the motion he'd glimpsed, everything was perfectly still, and more and more things seemed to churn just where he couldn't see them.

"Oh, that is fucked up." Lette turned away. "Gods, I think I'm going to be sick."

"My head." Afrit dropped to her haunches, clutching her temples, and closed her eyes. "I can't look at..."

"What?" called Balur, still inside the tunnel. "What are you talking about? I cannot be seeing anything in here."

Will didn't say anything. He just walked toward it. His goal. His purpose. He didn't know how far away it was. The size of the...being...twisted space around it so that distance no longer had the meaning it used to possess. But still he walked. He had come this far.

"No," said Lette. "I don't think...You shouldn't." But Will ignored her.

"Gods, my head." There was genuine pain in Afrit's voice. "I think it's going to split."

Will ignored her.

"Maybe I shall be going back up," said Balur. "Make sure Cois..."

"You can't, Will." Lette's voice was getting more insistent. "That's not...We shouldn't...That isn't safe. Isn't..."

Will was still walking. He wasn't sure he could do anything else. He'd been walking for so long now. To this place. To this time. It felt as if the creature had its own gravity.

"Wait." Afrit still managed to be shocked through her gritted teeth. "You're still planning on drinking that thing's blood? That's *still* your plan?"

And Will didn't know anymore. He just didn't know. Where did he end and his purpose begin? Or was it the other way around? Who belonged to whom here?

And then it was in front of him. A cliff of flesh that wasn't flesh. A gelatinous, craggy, writhing, static wall of other. He reached out, and then couldn't quite touch it. All the hairs on his arm were standing on end, straining to get away from this thing, this being, this Deep One.

He could feel the strange not-light blasting off it, like not-wind, not-causing his hair to billow.

"You can't, Will." There was desperation in Lette's voice. "You can't. You mustn't. Not even for Barph. It's not worth it. He's not worth it. Whatever it is. Nothing is worth it."

And part of Will knew she was right. That in a life full of spectacularly stupid things, this was by far the stupidest he had ever contemplated.

And part of Will knew she was wrong. Because part of him simply hated Barph too much.

He reached down to his belt, pulled out a knife.

"Oh gods." He thought perhaps Lette was crying.

He wasn't sure the knife would be able to cut the Deep One,

but it sliced through the not-flesh easily. As if it were a thousand whisper-thin sheets of gelatinous membrane, stretched taut and ready to rupture. Clear, gelatinous fluid burst over him, and yet he stayed perfectly dry. And this was not its blood. Somehow he knew that, though he wasn't sure how.

He cut deeper, working his way into the flesh. He was wrist deep, elbow deep, shoulder deep. His cuts became larger and wider, ripping the not-flesh farther and farther apart, trying to get in, to get deep enough. He was leaning his whole face into the Deep One's side. There was no smell to the creature, no taste. And yet still his stomach churned and roiled.

And then his blade met resistance. Something thicker and meatier beneath his blade. He couldn't see it, but he felt it. And he wrestled and jabbed with the knife, forcing it into the creature.

Something convulsed. Nothing physical. The sagging gelatinous walls of not-flesh stayed perfectly still, but suddenly he was staggering back, barely clutching on to his knife.

And standing there in the blue light of this impossibility, he saw violet blood on the blade of his knife.

It was in his hands.

Lette was sobbing. Afrit was retching.

He lifted the blade toward his mouth. All he had to do was lick the blade.

He thought he was going to be sick.

He thought he was about to scream, to laugh, to cry, to run away, to walk straight back into the wound he'd slashed and never come out again.

He thought he'd never been closer to his revenge.

His tongue slipped out between dry lips and touched the blade.

Fish, and metal, and fear, and hate, and endless, endless years of sleep.

It was in his mouth. His mouth was full of...of...

And this was a mistake. Such a stupid fucking mistake. What the fuck was he doing? What was he thinking?

He tried to spit it out. He couldn't. It cloyed to the back of his mouth. He gagged. But he couldn't vomit.

And then *it moved*. He felt it very distinctly in his mouth. Even as his whole being tried to reject it, it clawed into his gullet and down. Down. Down. Down. Deeper than he was. Boring into him. Into his very core. Into the very essence of who he was.

And there it sank its barbs.

14

Cultural Indifferences

Quirk couldn't help but feel that her triumphant return to the estate would have gone better if so many people hadn't screamed and run away. On the one hand, there was a certain sense of imperious potency as she swept in on Yorrax's back and all fled before her. On the other, this probably wasn't giving Yorrax the impression that she was at the head of a band of cutthroat desperados.

"Come back!" she shouted as she slipped from the dragon's back and onto the dry earth of the courtyard. "Find your balls and get out here."

Svetson the blacksmith, Norvard's father, was staring at her slack-jawed, a hammer held loosely in his fist. She thought she caught sight of Gartrand ducking behind a doorway. Children were diving through windows, screaming in absolute terror.

Yorrax preened, clearly enjoying the effect she was having. She snorted blue-white jets of flame from her flaring nostrils.

Svetson dropped his hammer.

Quirk grunted in frustration. "Come out!" she yelled again. She felt impossibly stupid standing in the middle of the courtyard shouting at nobody in particular. "I gathered you together so we could fight Barph. So we could fight alongside each other, protect each other. I'm not just going to have a dragon come here and kill you. And, quite frankly, Tarryl," she said, spotting the old archer where he was hiding, "if Yorrax here wanted to kill you, I'm not sure the pigs' slop trough would stop her."

It still took the old fellow another thirty seconds to sit up, dripping potato peelings and celery stalks.

Quirk tapped her foot as slowly, hesitantly her force of hardcase resistance fighters shuffled out of their various hiding spots.

They still seemed to be trying to hide behind Gartrand, though. The former grocer looked at her with more than a little suspicion.

"Gartrand," she said impatiently. The man had something to say, and the sooner he spat it out so she could step on it, kill it, and kick it away, the better.

He licked his lips, folded and unfolded his hands into each other. "Ellabet told us what happened at Tarramon," he said. "What happened with..." His eyes flicked to the heavens. "When you confronted Barph."

Quirk nodded. "And what did she tell you?"

Gartrand sighed. "She said—"

"Where's my son?" Svetson suddenly shouted. The blacksmith had picked the hammer back up. "Where's my godshexed son?"

Quirk nodded. She would not hide from this. "I am so sorry, Svetson," she said. "Barph killed him."

The blacksmith was not a small man. But he was quivering as he pointed his hammer at her. "*You* killed him."

Quirk weighed that. And in the end, she did not believe that. She would not accept that guilt.

"No," she said. "I took him to fight. And he fought. He fought for what he believed in. He fought for a better world. He died because the forces that would prevent that better world from coming into being killed him. Not me."

"He died"—and suddenly there was Ellabet pushing to the front of the crowd, and finally Quirk saw someone here with a bit of spine—"because you led him into a fool's battle, with a fool's plan. He died because you promised us you knew what you were doing."

Quirk weighed that. And that she could not so easily shrug off. "Yes," she said finally. "Yes, that's true."

Another noise from Yorrax behind her. But she wasn't looking to the dragon for leadership advice. And the crowd was not, it seemed, particularly happy with either of her answers.

She spread her arms. "What did you expect? Did you think that this would be easy? We are trying to defeat a god. He could crush us all without a second thought. That has always been true. I never promised you that it wouldn't be. You are free to delude yourselves, but I won't take the blame for that."

Gods, there was a time when she would have been on her knees begging for their forgiveness. But that was from another life.

Ellabet, though, didn't seem to be coming around. She was shaking her head. "You're a gods-hexed psychopath."

And some of the crowd, it seemed, agreed with Ellabet. Quirk thought that perhaps it was time for some more obvious truths.

"We have a dragon!" she bellowed into their shouts, just in case the giant blue-white beast standing just over her shoulder had slipped their minds.

Yorrax snorted fire again.

"We are more powerful now than we have ever been," she said as their attentions all flicked to the dragon once more. "And yes, I miscalculated when I led people into Tarramon. But the whole point of mistakes is to learn from them. We are too weak to take on Barph head-on. I see that now. But Barph has been trying to build something. He wants something. We can take it away. We can hurt him now. More than ever."

She smiled at them all. Yorrax's head snaked forward to hang beside hers, a wicked grin on the dragon's face.

"So," said Ellabet, "burn the world? That's your plan."

Quirk nodded. Because now they saw. Now they would understand.

"Gods piss on you and your madness," said Ellabet, and she stalked away.

Quirk paced in circles out in the fields, away from the old servants' buildings, as evening fell. The rest of the afternoon had not gone well. There had been shouting, accusations, and threats of violence, and that had just been her part in the proceedings.

They did not want to fight. They had said they did, but they had lied. To themselves mostly, but to her as well. They wanted a different world, yes, but would someone else please go out and do all the hard work of making it happen?

She sat staring out at the fields of wheat her fighting force had been busy cultivating in her absence. She could hear children playing in the courtyard now that all the adults had stopped shouting at each other. Domesticity. That was what these people really wanted. Even domesticity as fragile as an eggshell.

She heard heavy footfalls behind her. The huff of bellows breath.

"I know," she said without turning to look at Yorrax. "You're going to leave." She looked at her hands in her lap. She couldn't blame the dragon. She thought she was going to leave too. What she would do then...the gods knew. Except the gods didn't know. The gods were as dead as her plans.

"They are not how you described them," said Yorrax in her baritone rumble. Which was, Quirk thought, quite diplomatic.

"No," she was forced to agree. "Because I'm pretty sure I didn't describe them as a bunch of pathetic..." Her voice was rising, and she was half turning, ready to shout insults back at the houses. She choked herself off. "I deluded myself about a lot of things," she said finally. "And because I misled myself, I misled you."

"You are a rare human, I think," said Yorrax.

Which was borderline nice. Alarm bells sounded in Quirk's skull. Maybe Yorrax was going to do more than just leave. Maybe she was going to ask forgiveness for eating one of the children.

She turned to face the dragon, eyes narrow. But there were no prepubescent limbs stuck between the dragon's teeth.

"Back in the square," Yorrax said, "you asked..." She hesitated, cocked her head to one side, then the other. "You asked if I had a horde of dragons hidden anywhere who were poised to rain destruction down on Barph."

Quirk knew the hope that leapt in her was ridiculous, but still she couldn't quite stop herself from saying, "Wait...you do?"

"No." Yorrax's head shook on its serpentine neck. "All the dragons are back on Natan."

"So...?" Quirk was still a mental lap behind Yorrax.

"I came from Natan," said Yorrax. "It is not a difficult flight."

The dragon was being irritatingly cryptic. "So you're going back to Natan," she guessed.

Yorrax narrowed her eyes as if confused. "Yes," she said eventually. "That's why I'm bringing it up."

"You could stay," Quirk said. The begging felt half-hearted even to her own ears.

Yorrax's shake of her head was more definitive.

"But think of what you could achieve!" And there was, Quirk found, still a scrap of passion left in her. "You could inspire something bigger than yourself. You could help start the fire that burns Barph down, even if you don't get to see it end."

Yorrax was back to confused, it seemed. "But why," the dragon asked, "achieve so little, when we could achieve so much more with all of Natan at our backs?"

And now Quirk was mirroring Yorrax's look of confusion. "What?" she managed.

"Natan," said Yorrax again, more insistently. "I do not know why you are being so resistant to the idea. I was willing to come here, to see your fighters. That has not worked. Now we go to Natan. We speak to the other dragons. We see what can be done there."

"We...go...to Natan?" Quirk could barely hear herself speak over the roaring of blood in her ears.

"Did you take a blow to the head at some point today?"

"An army of dragons," Quirk breathed. "To burn Barph's world away."

"Yes," said Yorrax, nodding. "That is seeming worth trying, isn't it?"

But Quirk didn't bother answering, she was already running toward Yorrax, ready to mount her back and take to the skies.

Flight, Quirk thought, *explains so much about dragons*. Of course they believed they were superior. Of course they were prideful. Of course they were driven to dominate. They could do *this*.

The Avarran countryside skidded beneath her at murderous speed. It was irrefutably too far away. This was definitely not a human domain, and as exhilarating as it was to invade, it was terrifying too.

The journey from Tarramon back to the estate had been, short, low, and mostly full of the excitement of a sudden lurch into action. But this journey, this new venture... The terror went on and on. Unending hours of it. Numbing her body to adrenaline's tender ministrations and allowing her mind to wander.

First it focused on the distant ground, on the space between her and it. It summoned half-remembered equations for velocity and terminal speeds and the force that had to be applied to bones to break them. But then, when even that began to lose its bite, her mind found a new theme: her destination.

She was rushing toward dragons. An island of dragons. And yes, she had made friends with one now, but...she had been a leading figure in the revolution in Kondorra that had killed seven dragons. She had been part of the party that had thwarted their ambitions in Vinter and paved the path for Barph's victory over the world. And even if the dragons remained ignorant of those points—she certainly wasn't going to raise them—*they were dragons.*

Yorrax was clearly a young dragon. She was small for her kind. She had not been taken as part of the main invasion force. Why should the other dragons listen to her? Why should they not treat Quirk as a particularly tasty canapé?

There was no reason.

No reason except her need. Her ability to get them to see that their paths aligned and their desires were one.

They flew through the day. Yorrax did not complain, despite the presence of the splint on her wing. They landed as night fell, finding shelter at the edge of a wood. Quirk had no sense of where they were, but Yorrax seemed confident of their path, and the sun had set in the right place, at least. They slept on the ground, woke the next day to a meager breakfast, and took to the air once more. Two more days passed this way, sweeping them across the Avarran landscape.

And then the ocean. Vast and blue and unyielding. Even more terrifying than the land racing past. She screamed as Yorrax raced over the cliff's edge of the Verran coast and left the known world behind. She felt unmoored, drifting in a void with only the horizon to define it. They passed out of sight of land. The day stretched on. She felt vaguely nauseous, but couldn't put it into words. Even the wind roaring in her ears canceled itself out through the constancy of its chaos.

And then ... a dark smudge against the horizon, almost like smoke. But it grew thicker and darker, ridges bulging out of it.

"Is that ... ?" she managed to shout against the wind.

"Natan," Yorrax bellowed. She turned her head back, didn't look where she was flying when she spoke to Quirk. It made Quirk's stomach flip. She cut the conversation short.

Natan came closer, came clearer. The sight of land settled

Quirk's queasiness. She tried to dredge up what she knew about the island. Not much. She seemed to recall it was mentioned in a lot of sea shanties. She'd looked at transcripts of them while researching the relationship between kraken migration and merpeople breeding seasons. There had been one report... A barren land, if she remembered rightly: a lot of mountains and not much else. Scrub and very steep rock.

From the saw-toothed silhouette taking shape on the horizon, the tales had been relatively accurate.

Despite watching the vast island approach for the best part of three hours, Quirk still had the impression that it had leapt up suddenly from nowhere. She had become accustomed to its diminutive presence on the horizon, and then suddenly white sand beaches were tearing toward her. Then she was flying over lush forests, their leaves the verdant green of Fanlornian jade. Then rock was a great impassive wall before her, reaching out to bring their rushing flight to an abrupt halt.

Yorrax angled upward, ascending at a terrifying rate. Gravity placed both its hands on Quirk's shoulders, began to pull. She screamed again.

"Quiet!" Yorrax hissed.

Yorrax's ascent became even steeper as she clung close to the abrupt cliff face of rock. Quirk kept her screams to herself, though more from the wind battering her in the face than from any act of will. Then Yorrax's body flexed convulsively, wings angling, and they were hurtling sideways, parallel to the ground hundreds of yards below, hugging the side of the mountain, racing toward a narrow passageway between the peaks.

Quirk thought perhaps she was going to vomit. Trees rushed up beneath them, climbing the valley floor like a fist punching toward them. Then they were in the passage itself, rock all around her, the change in air pressure rattling her skull, and then out, into a labyrinthine territory of peaks and cliffs, trees, and scrubland.

Yorrax flared her wings, extended her talons. Rock loomed. Quirk screamed again, unable to help herself, and then suddenly they were perched on a rocky outcropping, peering at the twisting maze of the island's interior.

"Quiet," Yorrax hissed again. Her neck wove back and forth on its sinuous neck.

Still gathering her breath and her thoughts, Quirk stared about, trying to take it in. The lush fringe of trees gave way quickly inside the mountains into drab brown scrub. The trees in this sheltered interior were little more than brown stalks.

But that was it, Quirk realized. Rock and scrub, and the memory of trees. Nothing else. No mountain goats scurried up and down the escarpments. No rabbits flashed across the valley floors. No eagles wheeled above them. No life stirred here. "Why," she said, managing to keep her voice under control at last, "do I have to be quiet?"

Yorrax ignored her, head still flicking back and forth. Watching for something. Alert.

"You're scared," Quirk said as realization hit her. "Of the other dragons."

"I am not," Yorrax hissed. "Be quiet."

"Be quiet because otherwise I might alert the other dragons to our presence," Quirk said. It wasn't a question.

And gods, it had been so easy to talk herself into this. This glorious suicide.

"It is a question of approach," Yorrax said finally, conceding the power of Quirk's condemning silence. "Of putting ourselves in the best light. And your querulous screaming does little to help with that."

And yes, that made sense. Dragons respected strength, after all, and shrill screaming did not usually represent strength. But it was more than that. Over the past few days, Quirk had grown used to the rhythms of Yorrax's movements. She felt how rigidly the dragon was holding herself now.

"We should wait," Yorrax was saying. "Until dusk. Until they've eaten. They will be more...receptive then."

Sleepier. Sated. Less aggressive. Still, given the new facts, Quirk saw the sense in the proposal.

"Okay," she said. "Where shall we—"

The roar that interrupted her was so loud her vision shook. Quirk almost lost her perilous grasp on Yorrax's back. She only stayed in place because Yorrax was already moving, leaping away from the cliff face, the momentum of her body plastering Quirk's arse in place.

Quirk looked around wildly, saw it. A massive slate-gray brute of a dragon, descending toward them. It must have been on the peak above them. Gods, it might have been part of the peak above them. It was a craggy, crenellated monster of scale and claw. It was a mountain peak of teeth and flame. And it was falling through the sky toward them, mouth open, teeth exposed, the red of its maw the only hint of fleshy softness in all its massive frame.

"Runt!" it bellowed as Yorrax performed aerial maneuvers that slammed Quirk's internal organs about like so many bowling pins on a tavern lawn. "We told you never to return, runt!"

And oh gods, they were going to have words about that. Except they were probably going to have them while dissolving in this newcomer's stomach acid.

And then Quirk discovered that her dismay—which surely had reached its zenith—had peaks yet to climb, as fresh calls rose from deeper within Natan's rocky borders. And even as she and Yorrax raced away, hugging the ground, twisting through impossibly narrow spaces between cliffs, she looked back over her shoulder and saw more vast shapes battering their way into the heavens on blunt wings. The sky was heavy with them, bursting with beasts.

"A question of fucking approach?" Quirk managed, as all around them death began to rain.

15

The High-Stakes Art of Public Speaking

The fireball arced over Quirk's right shoulder, somehow finding the infinitesimal space between her head and Yorrax's snaking neck, and hurtled past them both to detonate among the scrubland below. Quirk felt her mop of hair shorten by a smoldering half inch.

Screaming honestly didn't seem to have much point anymore. There was no way it could extend her life. She could only desperately cling to Yorrax's barrel-rolling frame, gripping scales with knees and fingers stiffened by horror.

A vast shape flashed into her vision, a howling blur of claws and maw. Then Yorrax was twisting away, bucking over this half-glimpsed specter of death, so she could not be sure if it had been real, or if her inability to draw a decent breath was finally causing her to hallucinate.

Fire. She could summon fire. She should be fighting back.

That would mean letting go.

She tried to convince herself to pry a hand free. Her hands remained unconvinced.

A roar so close she could smell the rotten meat breath.

Her thoughts felt too slow against the racing backdrop of Natan's bleak landscape.

Yorrax dived. The ground raced toward them. Quirk braced

for the inevitable punch to her internal organs as Yorrax pulled up at the last moment. More fire spattered the air around them, painting the trees they were about to crash into a violent, flickering orange.

They were so close now, Quirk could see individual leaves blackening.

Yorrax was going to pull up now. Had to now. Yorrax was...

Oh fuck, was Yorrax dead? Had she somehow missed her ride's vitals being left behind somewhere in the sky?

Had she—

Trees closed around her.

Quirk found she could scream again.

"Fuck you."

Quirk stood in a narrow tunnel of rock that hid under a sharp lip of rock. The sharp lip of rock was in turn hidden by trees. Trees that Yorrax had punched a dragon-shaped hole through. Trees that still contained, Quirk was relatively sure, a lot of her residual terror sweat.

She slipped off the dragon's back, leaned against her heaving flank.

"From the bottom of my heart," she said. "Fuck you."

If Lette and Balur had taught her nothing else back when they were both alive and screwing up her life, it was the importance of letting off steam.

Outside, flashes of yellow, orange, and red painted the entrance of the tunnel, while the sounds like thunder shook the stone beneath their feet.

"We will be safe here," Yorrax said. "They have never found this place before." Quirk thought the dragon was attempting to sound dismissive, but she was panting too hard to pull it off.

"Before?" Quirk was feeling her fire rekindle. "So you've needed to hide from the other dragons before?" She pushed herself off Yorrax's flank. It was hard to chastise someone while

you were also using them for support. She staggered to the tunnel's far wall on shaking knees while Yorrax set her jaw.

"I told you," the dragon said, "that we needed to wait for dusk."

"So we would be harder to find?" Quirk managed. "So you'd perform better in that game of hide-and-seek?"

"They're hungry now." Yorrax exposed her teeth. "I'm hungry now."

"And what about later?" Quirk snapped. "What about..." She could see Yorrax's hackles rising. And perhaps she should check her anger just a little bit. "Let's be honest," she said, trying to modify her tone, trying to acknowledge to herself that she was shaken and probably not thinking straight. "You do not enjoy high social standing here on this island. Mine is likely to be worse. Your ability to vouch for me is going to be negligible."

"No!" Yorrax snapped. "They have to listen. They want to listen. Even if they don't know it." She huffed jets of blue fire through her flaring nostrils. "They will listen to me." None of the performance distracted from the desperation in Yorrax's voice.

"What?" Quirk managed. "How delusional are you?" Which was probably the sort of thing she would have known better than to say out loud if she weren't so shaken. "We have to leave."

Yorrax lurched suddenly, thrusting her massive head toward Quirk's gut, teeth exposed. Quirk could feel the furnace heat coming from those flared nostrils.

"You," Yorrax growled, "will listen to me."

Quirk had been close to death before. She recognized the hollowness in her gut.

Dragons were driven to dominate. She should acquiesce, expose her belly, be submissive. Except then Yorrax would wait until nightfall, take her outside, and get her killed by a hundred other dragons.

Which left the other side of dominance.

If the circumstance had allowed it, Quirk would have groaned. Because this honestly didn't do much for her chances of survival. Closing her eyes for only a fraction of a second, she summoned fire. She let it flood out of her and fill her hand. A globe of inferno cupped in her palm. Then she folded her fingers into a fist and brought it crashing down on Yorrax's nose.

Yorrax yelped, reared back, smashed her head into the roof of the tunnel.

"No!" Quirk thundered, while Yorrax was still staring about, wild-eyed. "You will listen to me."

For a moment their eyes locked. Yorrax opened her mouth.

Quirk was ready. Two short sharp blasts of fire aimed at the thin joints where Yorrax's wings joined with her body. They were as delicate as a creature Yorrax's size got. And her aim was true. Yorrax yelped again.

"You will listen to me!" Quirk yelled.

Yorrax hissed, curled back. And there was rage in her eyes, but there was fear too. For a moment the two emotions raged, tearing at each other the same way Quirk's heart was tearing at the confines of her chest, plunging and bucking like a colt new to the saddle.

And then she saw fear win.

Part of her wanted to mourn, because this had been a partnership of equals. This had been two allies in the face of an uncaring world. And in this moment of calculating survival, that had irrevocably changed. Another friendship had died.

But survival depended on this. Her ability to keep fighting against Barph depended on this.

"We will wait here." Quirk spoke slowly and loudly, careful to keep her emotions tamped down, shoved deep in her gut. "We will wait until darkness. And then we shall take to the air, and we shall return to the Verran coast. Is that clear?"

Yorrax let out a noise that was almost a hiss, almost a growl, but not quite either.

"Is that clear?"

Yorrax bucked once, a short spasm as if trying to throw off the yoke of Quirk's will, but then she lowered her head, averted her eyes. "Yes," she hissed.

Quirk felt different astride Yorrax's back. Earlier, during their flight here, she had felt almost a part of Yorrax. She didn't sit astride Yorrax; instead she had been some symbiotic creature, living in a feedback loop of mutual purpose.

Now she sat up above Yorrax, imposing her will. It made her feel tired and lonely.

"Let's get out of here," she said.

Yorrax hesitated. She had been sulking all afternoon. But finally she started to move at Quirk's command, a lumbering run at first, down the length of the tunnel, which then broke into something more graceful and lithe, a rhythmic rising and falling of her long body.

Then the tunnel released them, and Yorrax's wings burst apart, and she beat the air, her muscles an earthquake of pulsing skin and scale beneath Quirk, and then they were up, up, up. And just for a moment Quirk felt again the glory of flight, the easy dismissal of an earthbound existence. This was a sort of magic too, she thought. This escape. No matter that they were fleeing. They were fleeing gloriously.

And then, all of a sudden, they were not.

Something massive fell from the heavens and slammed into Yorrax, snapping the dragon's head and neck sideways and sending her plunging down, down, down to earth.

Quirk didn't have a chance to howl. She was too busy scrambling for a handhold, feeling her legs sliding free, feeling her chance at survival slipping through her nerveless fingers. Her head rang from the impact.

Below them something roared. Something opened a maw bursting with yellow light.

A dragon. Another dragon. One that had been...what? Waiting nearby? Just in the area? It didn't matter. It was there. It had struck them. And now Quirk was plummeting to earth on the back of an unconscious dragon.

And then she ran out of sky to plummet through.

The impact was massive. It replaced the world she lived in with new forces, new geographies. Gravity was suddenly a racking, directionless beast ripping through her one way and then another. The ground was now scale and rock and dirt, hot then cold. The air she breathed was now the taste of blood in her mouth, the grit in her nostrils. Her body was a rag doll of spinning limbs.

And then, by some magic that was utterly beyond her ken, she was lying on her back, staring up at the swirling heavens, transported back to the world she'd always known. She seemed to have brought a lot of pain back with her. She took a breath. It hurt. She wondered if she'd broken a rib. It felt like a strangely abstract thought.

She tried to raise a hand to her face, found she could do so. That was a good sign. Still, the amount of blood on her fingers wasn't. She tried to sit up. She managed it, though she gasped with pain, and her eyes watered.

Then she realized the thrumming she could hear was not the rush of blood in her ears. It was the beating of wings. She turned around very slowly. Everything was done slowly now. Her body had found a lower gear and was insistent about sticking there. She thought about trying to support her weight on one hand and balked. She shifted awkwardly onto her chafed knees.

A dragon looked at her. So did its friends.

Yorrax lay sprawled on the ground, a slack rope of muscle and scale, wings crumpled like discarded drafts of their escape plans. Around her were gathered dragons. And dragons. And dragons.

She hadn't...So many...How could she have imagined? How

could she have believed in this? A sight to give the academic in her chills. A sight to turn the bowels of the pragmatist in her to water.

They were gathered around her in a vast circle. Ranks of yellow eyes and long snouts. Myriad colors, from dark browns and grays to bright vibrant greens and oranges. Some were squat, others were lithe. Some had horns, others rows of sharp scales, and others were as smooth as snakes.

One stood slightly in front of the others, looming over Yorrax like a mountain peak. He was the color of day-old meat, lit by the flickering light of the fire he and his fellows had set among the trees around her.

"So," the dragon said with a voice like the world ending, "the runt has brought a playmate home. She has made friends with our great enemy. She thinks one human enough to defend her."

The dragon twisted its head away to look back at the others. "Perhaps she grows tired of being mocked for her weakness. Now she wants to be mocked for her stupidity instead."

The noise that came next was so loud, so harsh, that Quirk had to close her eyes. Her head was still ringing. Her teeth hurt. She couldn't tell what part of her mouth she'd bitten. All of it? Was that possible? She didn't understand.

And then she did.

The dragons were laughing. They were...they were bullies.

The world was coming to her like shards of broken glass, interrupted by the needs of her aching body. She half collapsed backward, found a rock she could lean against. She spat out a wad of phlegm and blood.

The lead dragon reached out with one of his forelimbs, picked Yorrax's head up off the ground. He was...what, three times her size? Four? Almost as big as the Kondorran dragons, she thought. Not quite as geographically massive, perhaps, but still a vast brute. He leaned his head close to Yorrax's.

"Can you hear me in there?" he roared at Yorrax. Quirk

slammed her hands to her ears unthinkingly, almost howled at the pain that shot through her left shoulder.

"Do you have the brains left to listen to me tell you how pathetic I find you?"

He laughed again. The other gathered dragons laughed again. The sound was like the bones in her ears breaking.

She had to focus. If she was to live through this, she had to get herself together. Yorrax had told her something about these dragons.

Plunging into her memories felt like walking into a swamp. Everything was cloying and slow. The smell of the dead bodies in Tarramon. The sound of Yorrax crunching bones. The accusing stares back at the estate. The almost audible sound of Svetson's heart breaking.

And Afrit. Behind it all, Afrit. Her face. Her calm words. Her...everything.

More dragons were coming, flocking down. The night air was alive with their wings. Their sound like a storm coming.

The lead dragon turned away from Yorrax, brought its attention to Quirk instead.

"Human," it growled.

Quirk had to focus now. Right fucking now. Because Yorrax had said something. About this place. About Natan. About the dragons. About who was here. Who had gone to Avarra.

The dragon was very close. And she could see the jowls on it. The way his skin hung on him, looking loose and baggy, almost as if he was...

Old!

The old. The sick. The weak. The young. They had been left behind. They had not been part of the invasion force. They were not strong enough.

Bullies.

These were the dragons not taken to Avarra. Those judged by the brethren to be unworthy of conquering a world. And this...

this was how they were coping with rejection. They found someone even weaker to dominate...

Which meant there was only one way to deal with them.

Oh gods, this is going to get me so killed...

Standing up hurt. Keeping the pain off her face hurt almost as much. Dragons were gathered all around now. They encircled her. Rank upon rank of rough wedge-shaped heads, row upon row of eyes—yellow orbs of fire and hatred. They were thick in the air above her. Darker slices of night cutting the sky apart. She could feel the heat of them, the fire in their guts radiating out to crowd her further.

But she understood them. And she understood fire.

So very killed.

She reached into herself, found what she needed. Not quite courage. Not quite desperation. Not quite madness. Something born of all three, though.

And then she summoned a fiery whip and crashed it with all her might into the dragon's nose.

It reared back, roaring, bellowing—more shocked, she suspected, than hurt. But she kept at it, slashing again and again with the fiery whip. She pulled another into existence, held it in her left hand, made clumsy strikes with that one as well, scouring at the softer skin beneath its chin, its neck.

Around her was chaos. Other dragons roaring. She was caught in a maelstrom of sound. The force of the sound battered at her. But she did not give an inch. She fought forward. She was screaming defiance. She was hurling her refusal to be cowed in their faces.

Old. Weak. Frail. And these were dragons, so everything was relative, but perhaps—just perhaps—she could find a crack in their self-regard and wedge her chance of survival in there. And so she slashed, and she slashed, and she slashed.

The dragon recovered, spread its wings, beat up at air, rose to hover above her. It opened its maw.

She sent the fireball arcing straight into its gut.

For just a moment, the roaring stopped. There was a collective inhalation as the dragon crumpled and fell to earth.

And for just a moment, nobody killed Quirk.

She seized the chance with both hands. "Do I have your fucking attention?"

They were so bewildered by what was going on, they forgot to kill her for another moment. She thought perhaps some of the dragons farther back found her defiance amusing, but gods, she would take that over fiery doom.

"You are not here because you are strong!" she howled at them. "You are not here because you are wise! You are not here because of your value to your fellows!" She shouted as loudly as she could, punctuated her words with blasts of fire. Nothing capable of killing, or even of injuring. More sparks to dazzle and sting. To keep them focused.

"You are here because you were duped. Because you were made fools of. Because you are scared. You sit here and you hide." Gods, this better be true, or at least close enough to the mark to sting. If she missed her target by even a hair...

"You mock this one." She lit Yorrax up with another fireball. "The runt. The weakest, most pathetic of you all. And yet of all of you, only she had the guts to go to Avarra. Only she had the stones to brave Barph's wrath. She charged him down while you all sat here and cowered like worms. You mock her, and yet you are too scared to do a tenth of what she has done. She has charged down Barph himself, bathed his face in her fire. She has stood by my side as we took the fight to his very feet."

She was exaggerating wildly now, but she thought the circumstances allowed it. Only adrenaline was holding her upright.

But the dragons, she realized, were silent now. They were not roaring. They were not laughing. They were...they were...

Oh gods. They were listening.

For a moment she didn't know what to say. She was caught

utterly off guard by her own success, almost undone by it. And there was a very thin line between a dramatic pause and mumbling like an idiot.

"You are better than this." She made the turn. She had to. There were only so many insults creatures as self-important as dragons could absorb. "You are dragons!" Her throat felt raw. She sent an arcing gush of flame at the heavens. "You ruled Avarra! You had it in your grasp. It was taken from you. Not by strength. Not by force. Not with honor. It was stolen. Through trickery. Through deceit. Barph thinks that he is smarter than you."

Gods, she thought, *I pray that I am smarter than you.*

And she still somehow wasn't dead.

"You are dragons!" When she had heard Barph speak, he had always seemed to have a refrain. Will had too. This might as well be hers. It didn't mean much to her, but it seemed the sort of vacuous platitude that people often liked. In fact, it was probably the sort of thing that she should have said to her rebels more often. But this was not the best moment for hindsight.

"Avarra waits for you!" she howled. "Avarra demands to be saved by you." That felt like a misstep. What did these dragons care about liberating her home? She tried to dance around it. "It begs to bow to your might. Save Avarra from Barph. Burn his world down. Build your own from its ashes. Take your rightful place! You are dragons!"

She was babbling now, and she knew it. She reached for the next sentence, but found it wouldn't come. She had reached the end of her plea for survival.

Shit.

The dragon whose guts she'd made a punching bag of still lay before her, not unconscious, but curled up and cowed around its singed belly. She turned to look at the others, trying to meet as many eyes as possible. She tried to project power and defiance into her gaze. She felt like the most abject of frauds.

"Another has come here before..." At first she couldn't place the voice. She stared around the crowd. Then she realized it was Yorrax. The dragon had picked her head up off the ground, was staring at her. And was this betrayal or collusion? She couldn't tell.

"Another has made promises to us."

Quirk took a breath, thought as fast as she ever had in her life.

"I make you no promises," she spat back. "You could all go to Avarra and die. Barph could laugh in your faces, turn you all to dust. Because perhaps the others were right. Perhaps you are old and weak and frail and pathetic. And perhaps you cannot seize what is there to be taken. Maybe you are not dragons. Maybe you are lizards and worms, skulking through the earth. Maybe you were not weaned from your mother's teats. Maybe dying here pathetic and alone is all you are good for. But I do not know that. Only you do."

She was shamelessly playing on their pride, but she was also well beyond shame.

"Your words," Yorrax said, and Quirk could see now the effort they were costing the dragon, "could kill us all."

Gods piss on it. Quirk was fairly sure that Yorrax wasn't actively trying to undermine her. Their fates were too intertwined to make that likely. Yorrax was probably trying to encourage her to weave a denser fabric of half-truths and platitudes. Unfortunately, Yorrax had significantly overestimated Quirk's inventiveness.

Then a massive claw reached out of the crowd and slammed down on Yorrax's head, plunging it into the dust once more. A dragon the same size and texture as Quirk's nightmares stepped into the center of the crowd.

It leaned a tar-black head down level with Quirk. Its eyes flashed yellow in its skull.

"You mewl for your life," it growled. "Your words smack of desperation."

Well, it was a good run.

"Yes," she said. "Yes, I do. And yes, they do. Look at me. Look at you. I am not a fool. But at least I have the courage to fight." She set her feet. "So let's fucking do this."

She was just tired. And frustrated. And sick of being afraid and outgunned. If this was not going to work, then she might as well get it over with.

The dragon stared at her. And she was so infinitesimal a threat to it. This little stance of defiance was so absurd. It would barely have to chew her.

Its black maw opened. Teeth and a tongue and stretching, stretching fear coming down to consume her.

"What is your name, human?" It was not fire that leapt from the dragon's jaws, or a roar, but a question.

"Quirkelle Bal Tehrin." She didn't know where this was going anymore.

The dragon turned away from her. Quirk tried to suppress a wince as it ground Yorrax's head into the ground. "This human," it roared, "is Quirkelle Bal Tehrin. Let her name be remembered. She is our enemy. She is of the race that stole the world from us. She is of the race that condemned us to this stinking isle of imprisonment. And it is she who reminded us what it is to be a dragon."

What . . . what now?

"It is she who came here, alone, and reminded us of our destiny. Of the wrong that was done to us. It was she who lit the fire of revenge, when we could not do it ourselves."

Quirk suddenly had the feeling she had wandered into this play halfway through, and that she had misunderstood the playwright's intentions utterly. Because what was happening now?

"It is she," the black dragon thundered, "who came here and demanded the vengeance we should have demanded ourselves. Barph has wronged us! Barph has laughed at us! Barph has forgotten how we made the world tremble. He has forgotten how we made the world burn. He has forgotten to fear us. So now we shall remind him. Now we shall make the heavens themselves burn!"

And then every dragon was roaring. Every dragon was launching fire into the sky. And then Quirk realized that, against all the odds, she was not going to die.

Quirk had seen it before. She knew exactly how fickle the mob mind was. How quickly it could turn. She knew it better than most. And yet still it always left her gasping. The madness of it. The idiocy.

But it was idiocy that let her see the sun again. It was idiocy that allowed her to feel the wind tousling her hair again. And it was undoubtedly idiocy that put her again on Yorrax's back, riding at the head of an army of dragons, heading back to Avarra.

16

Anarchy in a Teacup

Barph watched the woman as she crossed the temple square. She was, he thought, quite beautiful. The gentle jade of her eyes and the subtle curves of her body were all picked up and accentuated by the green robe she wore. Her movements were careful and considered, the product of long study and years of practice. She knelt slowly. There was no hint of the effort such movement must cost. Everything remained smooth and graceful. She reached out and took the first teacup from its prescribed place. She leaned forward at a precise angle, whose elegance and suitability had been written about in a legion of texts, and poured the first cup. Liquid splashed happily. The kettle gurgled slightly. Arrayed around the woman, ten others each permitted themselves the slightest of smiles.

It was as if they were openly fucking mocking him.

A tea ceremony? A gods-hexed tea ceremony? Barph looked about for someone who could appreciate his exasperation.

No rules. *No* rituals. *No* imprisoning themselves in the petty constraints of prescribed thinking.

Had he not been clear?

He didn't even bother explaining it to them. He didn't go in there and chastise them.

He reached out his hand. Lightning flooded the temple. Filled it with crackling, screaming white light. He squeezed. A lot of the screaming stopped. The bricks crumbled, fell. He waved his hand. The lightning dissipated. The dust that had been the temple blew away on a sudden wind.

There was no beautiful woman pouring tea now. No appreciative crowd. No perfectly glazed kettle. Barph looked around him again, for someone who could either nod in sympathy or shake his head in disappointment. But there was no one. There were not even any witnesses to learn from this lesson. He was alone in a temple full of corpses.

He shifted his focus, let his mind slip away from this plane of reality, and when he was paying attention once more his body had followed his mind. He was in the heavens, poised above Avarra, impossibly distant from that sad little temple and its sad little scorch mark on the ground.

He looked down on creation. His alone to rule. Yet still the nagging thought was there: Someone somewhere was defying him, refusing to be free. Someone was trying to impose order on his beautiful chaos.

He narrowed his eyes, scoured all of existence. He would find it. He would eradicate it. The last essence of Lawl would be gone from the world. It would be *his* design. *His* turn now. He would unlock the beautiful potential of the world.

But he saw … nothing. No order. No hierarchies. No laws. No justice. No queuing. No rituals. No defiance.

There has to be a mistake.

He concentrated harder. He would find something. He would crush it. He would make the world perfect. And still he could detect nothing.

And he realized: the chaos was … perfect. Unfettered, untainted, and absolute. It was what he had aimed for.

He had won.

No…

But yes. Yes. He had won. He had achieved his goals. All the world. All Avarra. Perfect chaos.

He had won.

He stared at Avarra. At his world. Dominated and subservient. Willing to do whatever he asked.

He had won.

Shouldn't it feel like more than this? Shouldn't there be some beautiful upswelling of emotion in his chest? Shouldn't he be whooping for joy?

Shouldn't this feel like victory?

Slowly, trying not to hesitate—though for whose benefit he still wasn't sure—he turned his back on Avarra and stumbled away.

17

What Passes for Victory
These Days

Lette was dragging Will to safety. She wasn't sure how. The only thing she was certain of right now was that she had been incapable of getting any closer to the Deep Ones. She hadn't been able to follow Will. And yet here he was in her arms. Being saved. By her.

She had been aware of his approaching the Deep One. Although how she had known, she also couldn't say. She had closed her eyes. She had put her fingers in her ears. She had tried to avoid vomiting. She had shouted something. But she had been completely aware of his movements. She knew he had produced a knife. That he had cut the Deep One's flesh. That he…he…

Her mind balked at the next. Glossed over events it did not care to relive. And then…then she was here. Then she had Will in her arms, was dragging him bodily back into the tunnel. He was semiconscious, mumbling and moaning. Afrit was crowding in behind her, babbling words that didn't make sense, that didn't gel together into sentences. Just words.

She thought perhaps she was doing the same.

"What? What? What?" Balur's confusion was a steady bass rhythm, located deeper in the tunnel, echoing around her. She just kept backing farther and farther into the darkness, pulling on Will. He groaned. Or maybe she did.

The journey back up the hole was a sweating, grunting nightmare. Time felt as if it were still slipping back and forth. At some points the dull disk of blue light above her head seemed so close it seemed she would grasp it with her next handhold. Then it was barely a pinprick. Will was deadweight, and Afrit was no help. Balur tried to reach around her, but he mostly impeded her progress. They were all out of sync with each other.

And then finally it was over. Finally they were lying gasping in the thin light of the tunnel above. Lette was flat on her back. She held Will's hand in her own. It felt cold and clammy. And if the bastard had gone and died after everything she'd just done for him...then she'd...she'd...

She found the energy to roll over. To sit up. To slap Will across the face. His head rolled to one side, absorbing the blow without flinching.

She got him with the full backhand.

"Ow," he said. "What in the Hallows is wrong with you?"

Then he opened his eyes, and she was so relieved she laughed out loud. And she bent down. And her hair was hanging all around them, making a curtain of privacy around their faces. And she was looking into the brown depths of his eyes. And he was looking back into hers. And she was losing herself. And then...then...

Then she saw something move.

Something rippled beneath the surface of his skin, and where it moved, his skin seemed to change...No, not just *seemed*. A discoloration spread below the surface, a rash of purple stains the color of spoiled plums that roiled and heaved over his face. And gods, it was in his eyes. She could see the irises changing color. His cheeks taking on a lilac hue. And he was still smiling at her. Even some of his teeth were fucking purple.

"What?" he said, finally picking up on the horror that was spreading through her just as this—gods, what was it?—was spreading over his face.

"Your...your fucking..." She pointed at his face, at his chest, where she could see the...the...rash? She could see it spreading. She leapt off him. What if it was contagious? What if she had it?

Will was looking down at his chest.

"Piss on it," he breathed.

"What in the gods' names is that?" Afrit was beside them now, wiping vomit from her chin but still staring.

Will was silent, just touching the skin.

"That doesn't look right." Afrit shook her head. "Oh gods."

Will looked up at them. It seemed to have stopped now— whatever it had been. The rash was still there, staining his skin with dull purple blotches. It was still on his teeth, in his eyes. When he opened his mouth to speak, she could see it on his tongue.

"I think it's fine," he said.

"Fine?" Afrit and Lette shrieked the word in near-perfect unison.

"I feel fine," he said. His calm was enough to make Lette want to put her fist through his marred face.

"You're fucking purple," she reminded him.

"I'm not all purple."

"You're more purple," Afrit said, the strain audible, "than I think most people would consider normal."

"So he is being purple," said Balur. "Who is giving a shit. He is being alive. He has been getting what he came here for. Aesthetics is seeming like a stupid concern."

"Thank you, Balur." Will smiled.

"Especially," Balur went on, "when we are not knowing where in the Hallows Cois is being." And now Lette heard the urgency behind Balur's feigned frustration. The...Wait...Could Balur be panicked? How deep beneath his skin had Cois gotten?

It was not unknown for Balur to have a long-term relationship. There had been a whore in Leche that he had seen on and off for over a year. He had owned a pet iguana that Lette had held suspicions about for almost two. But Balur had never been anything but cavalier about his romantic partners. He enjoyed being tangled in sheets far more than he enjoyed emotional entanglement. But now, as he strode back and forth, this felt like more than just concern for where his next fuck was coming from.

"Well," she said, "we're in a narrow gorge. There's not many directions zhe could have gone..."

Balur did not seem to appreciate her attempt at levity. "I should not have been leaving hir..."

"I can feel hir."

Lette, who had been moving toward Balur, stopped and turned. Balur stopped and turned. So did Afrit.

Will had his head cocked to one side. "All of them," he said. "All the gods. They're close." He nodded to himself.

"How?" Lette asked, and was impressed by how calm she kept her tongue. "How do you feel them, Will?"

He blinked a few times, and were his pupils larger than usual? Were the irises larger?

Then he straightened and started walking fast and with purpose. "This way," he called as he pushed past them, back in the direction of the gorge's mouth. "They're all this way."

Lette felt a scream trying to rise up in her.

"Is zhe safe?" Balur called after Will, but Will just kept pushing forward.

There wasn't much to do except hurry after him. Well, hurry after him and worry that he had done something irrevocable and awful to himself, that the purple stain went much deeper than his skin, that it was saturating his mind and thoughts, this foreign other, this deep old thing that should have been left long buried.

And then Afrit went and made it worse. She opened her mouth.

"Look up," she said.

"No," Lette said. Her shoulders felt like two iron bars already. She couldn't fit more tension in her life.

"We walked down this gorge for what, two days after the sky disappeared?"

"Do I look like a sundial to you?"

"I can see the sky," Afrit said. "We've been walking for less than an hour and I can see the sky."

Lette considered. Why should she look up? What if Afrit was right? What would that prove? That everything down here was deeply and profoundly messed up? That the Deep Ones were pure evil? That the man she...cared for had taken some vile uncleanness into himself? That Cois's warnings had been true? That Will was on a journey to becoming something other than what he was? That happiness was the grossest of lies?

She looked up.

Oh gods. The sky was there, a sharp splinter of light.

"The others are close," Will called back to them. He sounded like a child excited to be taken on a trip by his parents. He touched his temple. "It's stronger now."

Should she stop this? Was it possible to cut the uncleanness out of Will...or was that just another way to describe caving in his skull? She didn't want to do that. She wanted to get back to Avarra.

She wanted to get out of this gods-hexed chasm. To get to somewhere where she could think.

She walked and tried to ignore the geography slipping past her, moving faster than her feet could explain. And it got easier as the light seeped down, stronger and cleaner every moment, and the blue fungus fled from sight. The rock around them took on brown hues, became something warmer, familiar, reassuring. The ground rose steeply beneath them, far steeper surely than any descent they'd navigated, but they were getting out of here, they were getting closer to the Hallows, as if the earth were eager to reject them.

"Almost there," Will said. He was squinting, though whether in pain at some psychic pressure or just because of the exertion of their climb, Lette wasn't sure.

And then the mouth of the gorge came into view, and the broad wheat-filled plains of the Killing Plains.

And an army.

And Gratt standing at its head.

And held clear off the ground, with Gratt's fist around hir throat, was Cois.

18

Dependency Problems

Will kept on smiling. It was easy to smile. Just twist the muscles on your face, pull up your lips, and look, he was happy. Nothing was wrong. No mistakes had been made. Everything was fine.

Even this. Even Gratt.

The vast general of the underworld strode toward him with a grin as broad and fake as Will's own.

"Reunited," he boomed. "Become one once more." His cheer oozed threat. Will could sense every muscle in Lette's body tightening. He knew without looking that she was holding two knives. Balur was loosening his arms, working his shoulders. Afrit was just cursing.

And he … What did he feel?

There was something inside him. Something foreign curled about his guts and his mind. And that should have been terrifying. That should have scared the shit out of him. He was half fucking purple, for crying out loud. But all he could feel was calm. Even watching the tears roll down Cois's face, all he felt was an odd sense of detachment.

"It is time," said Gratt, savagery sneaking past his tusks and entering his words, "for you to fulfill your end of our bargain. For you to bring me victory."

Members of his army were circling them, were aiming bows at Lette and Balur and Afrit. The cage holding the other gods had been pulled up a few yards behind Gratt.

"Victory," Will said. He felt the word in his mouth. And the thing inside him felt it too. Felt the intent of it, and how Will's idea of what that word meant was so very different from Gratt's.

"Yes," Will agreed. "It's time for something like that."

For just a moment Gratt's smile faltered. Then he shook his head slightly. "You should not have succeeded," he said, almost to himself. "It is too much." He turned to his men. "End this," he said.

And the arrows flew.

And still Will did not feel fear.

He watched the arrows flying toward them. It was not so far for them to have to travel. Ten yards, perhaps, nothing more. But to reach him they had to travel half the distance, and then half that distance, and then half again. He had, he knew somehow, all the time in the world to sort things out.

When he had taken Cois's power into him, it had been about will. It had been about having the strength to want something enough. It had been about bending reality to see things his way. It had been an act of coercion. Even now, when he wanted to be invisible, to be seen as something other, it was still that way.

This... this was different. This was far more violent.

When he focused, he could feel the whole world around him. He felt every stalk of wheat, every grain of dirt. He felt the cells flaking off his own skin. He could feel Gratt's army and its intent and its actions. He could feel the physics of the arrows moving toward him. The tension in Gratt's fingers as they held Cois's throat. And he felt Lawl, and Lawl's hand in its design. And he felt how everything had been put together, and how the pieces of this place fit together. The Killing Plains were the way they were because it was the only way they could be. And Lette and Gratt and Lawl... All of them here, all of their feelings were the feelings they had to be feeling. Because that was how the planes of reality intersected and existed. Those were their rules. Geography intersecting with psychology, interlocking with the spiritual, the physical, the thermodynamics of the air. All the separate hidden pieces of the world laid bare to him. The perfect wholeness of everything.

He felt all of it.

And while everything here and now was the way it had to be, he *could* change it. If he moved this piece of reality this way, then everything else would move with it. It had to. Everything was linked. And all he had to do was push.

So he pushed.

His gut spasmed. His eyes swam. His mouth filled with bile. His knees buckled. The whole world fell away around him. And inside him, in his chest and his arms and his head—oh gods, his head—he felt something flex. Something that was not him, that was becoming him, invading him. He felt jolts of pain burning into his skull. He felt himself convulsing. And then...

Then the arrows that had been coming to kill him and his friends were not there. They were unmade and tumbling. And Gratt's hand was opening, and Cois was falling to the ground. And the archers too, were unmade, were unraveled from reality as Will pulled on those threads too. He could do it all. He could do anything. Everything was his to play with. And yes, yes, he could feel the exit from this place, the great gate that had barred a return to Avarra for all eternity but would no more. And he opened the door.

He turned to Lette. And he smiled. Because he had to smile. Because when he pushed reality this way, it pulled at the corners of his mouth, and he smiled.

But then he felt the horror in Lawl's mind. And he didn't understand it. But that in turn didn't make sense because he understood everything. And so he pushed unthinking into Lawl's mind, through the onion layers of pride and petty jealousies. And then Will reached the horror—exposed and bare—and he examined it, and then... then he understood. Then he felt that same horror grip him. Because now he truly understood.

He understood that while he had seen everything, he had not seen EVERYTHING.

He had seen this world. The Hallows. He had seen how everything in them was connected. How moving one piece moved another within them. But he had not looked beyond them. He had not seen how when he moved one piece, he affected not just it, not just the Killing Plains, not just the Hallows. He affected everything. EVERYTHING.

He saw how Lawl had written the flight path of the arrows into reality. How gravity, wind resistance, torque, potential energy, and acceleration all intersected. How Lawl had built other things upon these concepts. How he had built a world teeter-totter upon idea after idea after idea.

He saw how he had just pulled one idea out from the stack, and how everything else was poised to fall.

19

There's No Place Like Home

Lette was about to die. She saw Will misstep. She saw Gratt make his decision, and she reached for her knife, but it wasn't enough. Not with a whole army in front of her. Not with the fractional delay that came with the thought of what Balur would do when Gratt twitched and crushed Cois's throat.

The archers loosed their arrows, and she was dead.

And then... she wasn't.

Then there were no arrows. There were no archers. Their bodies spiraled out of existence, an unraveling mass of skin and gut that evaporated into the air. Gratt's hand spasmed open, and Cois dropped to the ground.

And then Will turned to them. To her. And he was smiling, but it was not his smile. It was too big, and too broad, and showed far too many teeth. And his eyes... what was wrong with his eyes?

And then Lawl screamed.

She knew it was the king of the gods straightaway. Something about the timbre of the sound was unmistakable. And so she looked directly at him, because the idea of Lawl—king of the gods, lord of law, judge of all the world, narcissistic jackass, and preening lover of his own machismo—screaming was surely absurd. But there Lawl was, trapped in his cage, clutching the bars, his eyes full of horror. Staring and screaming.

Then the wind started.

She looked away from Lawl, looked about, looked up, as if there were a sky to correspond to this weather change. But there was just rock, blank and unassuming. So she looked to Will, because...gods...Will had just evaporated twelve archers. Will had just...Holy shit. He had unmade them. Will had. Her farmer.

And now there was horror in his eyes too.

"What did you do?" she tried to say, but the wind was howling now. The sudden rage of it was astounding. Her clothes flapped, her hair was yanked from side to side, a sharp tug against the back of her head. She staggered a step. Balur was leaning into the wind. And still the wind grew.

Then the ground began to shake. A tremble. Then a quake. More and more. And it felt almost as if the world were making fun of her, because honestly, how was she meant to stay on her feet now?

Then she didn't. She fell, throwing her hands wide for support, for safety.

They didn't strike the ground.

The wind had her. It whipped her around and around. She could see Balur staring up at her with wide, horrified eyes. Something struck her, a rock or a body, she wasn't sure which. But she was flipped over in midair so she was on her back, and her own panic-stricken eyes could see what Balur was looking so cursedly scared about. And maybe she would let him off the hook just this once because the sky was, quite literally, falling.

A chunk of rock the size of a church crashed past her. It smashed into the fallen army. Smashed *through* it. The ground beneath it had become as insubstantial as the ceiling. A gaping chasm howled below them. But still she didn't fall. And still the wind grew. And chunks of the ground were in the air now. Mud rained sideways, spattering her with all the loving tenderness of crossbow bolts.

And Will, oh, Will, what the fuck have you done? Weren't you

meant to get us to the gates out of here? I don't remember the bit in the
plan where you pulled an ocean of rock down on our heads.

She was so going to have to kick his ass for this.

It felt as if the whole Hallows was coming undone. And then
she realized that yes, yes, of course it felt like that, because Will,
her once and maybe future beau, had taken the power of deep,
old, weird-as-fuck gods into himself, and he had unleashed it
without having the slightest clue what he was doing.

She wasn't falling anymore, she realized. She was rising. She
could feel the inverted tug of gravity hauling harder and harder
on her. She could feel the wind pressing into her face. And the
whole world was rising with her, rushing up. And gods, she could
still see Balur, flailing wildly. And massive chunks of rubble, of
earth, of rock. More and more souls. The whole unmade Hallows were rushing up, and up, and up, and up, and up. Forever
they were rising. Forever sledgehammers of stone were crashing
around her. Stone and sticks and wheat and bodies battered at
her. Her friends whirled past her. Her own vomit, because gods
yes, she had been sick, and she made no apologies for that.

Up, and up, and up, and up, and up, and up. A never-ending,
whirling, chaotic ride of fear and horror.

And then suddenly . . . suddenly . . . what?

A sense of rupture. Something bursting and breaking. And
what could there be left to break? But something had. And there
was blue sky above her, instead of the awful white nothingness
of a moment before. And there were clouds and affronted birds
being smashed to pieces by flying bits of another world. And
she was no longer rising, she was falling.

Oh shit! She was falling!

And then she wasn't. She landed. Hard enough to make spots
dance before her eyes, and make her mouth fill with so much
blood she couldn't curse. And pain racked her. And all she
could do was lie there as rock fell around her. And gods, gods,
gods, how was she still alive?

And still as she lay there, full of pain and wonder, the sky stayed obstinately above her. And then it struck her. Sky. There was no sky in the Hallows.

She was in Avarra.

She was home.

PART 2:
BAD DECISIONS

PART II
BAD ELECTIONS

20

What the Hell
Happened to Kansas?

Afrit sat up. She bellowed a little bit. She was in a lot of pain. She had...Gods, she had no idea what she'd done. What had been done to her. She was sitting in what had been almost, but not quite, the exact center of an explosion. It seemed to have been quite a large one. Rubble was strewn about her. Taxonomically, she would have to file it among the monumental variety. Vast building-size chunks of rock were involved. Some of them were representative of quite large buildings, such as museums and universities. All of them terrified her.

Somewhere, Afrit knew, there was an explanation for what in the Hallows was going on. Except she was very afraid that what was going on in the Hallows right now was nothing. She was very afraid, in fact, that Willett Fallows—farmer, false prophet, and all-around psychotic nutjob—had managed to ingest a god, and used the resulting powers to destroy the Hallows utterly.

Which meant there was nowhere for the dead to go in death.

Which meant...

Oh gods...

They were in Avarra.

And gods...it got so much worse.

This...this violent eruption of the Hallows into Avarra, this vomiting up of an entire plane of existence, it couldn't have happened in a desolate plain somewhere. Not high on a mountain peak. Not in the barren desert. Nowhere far from life. At the edges of this crater, between the peaks of the wreckage, she could see buildings, real ones. That were collapsing. That were on fire. A town. Perhaps a city. A thousand or more lives had been ended by this arrival.

And the bodies were everywhere. So many bodies. Bodies to outnumber the broken boulders that used to be the underworld.

She realized she recognized some of the bodies. She could see Lette. Balur's bulk was half-buried but stirring. Others were less familiar, but their colors and armor marked them as part of Gratt's horde.

And yet, of all the things she could see, the one that horrified her the most was the exact center of the crater, and it was about six feet from her own heels.

The crater's heart was perhaps fifteen feet across. Its edges were slightly raised, an upcurling of the earth emphasized by rocky debris. Beyond the lip...

Afrit struggled to find the right words to describe the crater's heart. It was not quite a whirlpool, but neither was it a storm. As she stared at it, liquid clouds of something that was not quite water boiled and whirled. Something black and purple and viscous and crackling like a thunderhead. The central well went down and down and down. Afrit could not see where it ended. She did not want to.

There was a time, she thought, *when I was just a college professor trying to get laid by another, more famous professor. And somehow this has led to the death of most of the gods, and the destruction of the Hallows.*

And then things found a way to get worse.

A hand emerged from the whirling substance at the crater's heart. Massive, red, covered in hair and horn. Vast talons marked the ends of vast fingers. It grasped the lip of the crater, hauled its owner up and out onto the savaged land.

Gratt stood and surveyed the world laid out before him. And then slowly, like the sun breaking through the clouds, a beatific smile spread across his face.

More hands appeared around Gratt. From out of the maelstrom, more people heaved themselves up into Avarra.

Gratt grabbed one by the neck and hoisted him aloft. "Are you with me?" he bellowed.

The man he was holding blinked at him. "Who the piss are you?" he managed.

And that was apparently sufficient excuse for Gratt to grab the man by the ankles as well and rip him in half.

Blood rained and Afrit blanched. Another man, fresh from the crater, stared at the gore and shouted, "I'm with you!"

Around Afrit too the scattered bodies were starting to stir. Some wore the colors of Gratt's army. Some didn't. One of the former came around faster than one of the latter. Gratt's man pulled a sword from a makeshift scabbard and gutted his opponent where he lay. Another man, wearing the colors of yet a third army, saw this, let out a yell, and charged. Gratt's man looked up just in time to receive the charge full in his chest. The pair flipped back over the lip of the crater's heart and were instantly struck by a blast of lightning that reduced them to little more than a red haze.

Gratt laughed. Afrit started scrabbling away.

She struck something. Someone. She screamed. The thing she'd struck lurched to his feet. She screamed again.

It was Balur. He looked down at her, brow creased. "What?" he said to her. "Am I having...?" He brushed at his lips.

Someone ran at the lizard man bearing a jagged rock in one hand. Without really looking Balur reached out, grabbed the man by the face, and then closed his hand. What was left of the man dropped, gurgling. Balur looked at Afrit's wide-eyed, openmouthed horror. "What?" he said again.

"We're..." She tried to get across the magnitude of it. "We're in *Avarra*. We've destroyed the Hallows. Will did. And now the dead are invading Avarra. Gratt's invading Avarra. And he's not dead anymore. Because the Hallows have gone. They've *gone,* Balur. They're not there anymore. So all the dead are pouring into...here. Avarra. Through that." She gesticulated wildly at the maelstrom still boiling a few yards away, still brimming with bodies. Gratt was still there, preoccupied with killing half of them and recruiting the others. She started to back away.

Balur, who had been nodding sagely and licking blood off his fingers, looked at her and paused.

"Oh," he said finally. "Sorry, I was thinking there was being more."

"Is that not enough?" Afrit screamed. Just over the lizard man's shoulder, she could see some ghastly and possibly sanity-damaging acts being carried out on a corpse by two of Gratt's soldiers.

Balur sighed heavily. "I suppose it is being enough for now."

"For now?"

"Secure the area!" Gratt boomed. "We will take this city. We will take this world. Any who are not with us are against us!"

"Well," said Balur, "now there is being that as well."

Some of Gratt's troops were charging them now. Women and men apparently not even waiting to ask for their allegiance. And Afrit thought she was going to scream again.

But then Balur turned his back on her, and he was...he was... graceful. It was awful, yes. It was sickening. It was bloody and brutal and full of inhuman savagery. But it was also graceful. And it was going to keep her alive. And so a part of her—small and to be hated at a later date—admired it too.

Something or someone touched her. She screamed again. She was doing that a lot. She whirled around.

Lette was grinning at her. The mercenary was covered in blood. Afrit bit back another scream.

"He's good at it, isn't he?" said Lette, looking beyond Afrit to where Balur was using other people's body parts as weapons. Then she flicked her gaze back to Afrit. "Tell him I said that, and I'll gut you, of course."

And finally, Afrit was very messily sick. Afterward she felt better. Not much. But at this point she'd take whatever she could get.

"We have to find Will," she said. With the churning in her guts finally subsiding, clarity was starting to return.

"Well, of course," said Lette.

"So he can put it back. So he can fix the world he just broke." Afrit wanted to be sure she and Lette were on the same page.

"Yes," said Lette, though with a lot less certainty this time. Then she turned toward the lizard man and shouted. "Oi! Balur! Heel!" and they took off searching.

Around them more and more of the scattered bodies were regaining consciousness. Some stood around blinking blearily. Some lay screaming at the horrific wounds they had sustained on their journey back to Avarra. Others said nothing. Their bodies were crumpled messes of meat and blood. Their souls burst free of their mortal containers and lost to the Void forever. The gods-hexed Void. Because there was nowhere else for them to go. Because the Hallows were gone. And so these people were unmade. Utterly. Because of Will pissing Fallows.

And yet, what was perhaps even worse than that, most people—far too many people—fought. They fought for Gratt. They fought against Gratt. They fought just because fighting was going on. They fought because the epicenter of the explosion had been in the Killing Plains, which was full of the worst psychotics in history, and those people were scattered all around them.

"Stop it!" Afrit shouted at them, feeling the vastness of her impotence. "Stop it!"

"Shut up," Lette snapped. "Will just spilled a civil war on the world, so this is going to be bad for a while. Please stop attracting attention."

To emphasize her point, three men, bare-chested and painted with other people's blood, had turned around and moved to block their passage. Lette bent and picked up three stones from the ground. She grimaced at them. Then suddenly all three were in the air one after the other. They cracked into the men's foreheads one-two-three, and the men all fell down.

There were more horrors. They built upon each other, as if striving for a crescendo. And yet there were simply too many of them. Nothing coherent could emerge from the whole.

Afrit began to suspect that they weren't looking for Will at all. They were simply fleeing the scene. Lette just didn't want to call it that in front of Balur.

And then there he was. Will stumbling out of the smoke of a fire, looking around dazed and confused. Cois was with him. Balur ran toward the god(dess), picked hir up, and held hir. And gods, Afrit had forgotten about the gods. But she didn't have time to worry about what their fate had been in the chaos and madness of everything because she was too busy hurtling toward Will, hands stretched out before her, fingers curled like talons.

She seized him by the throat. "Fix it!" she screamed full throated into his face. Her voice felt too big for her chest. "Put it back!" She hurled the words like rocks. "Undo this!"

Will mostly gawped and gasped at her. His fingers fumbled at her wrists. She realized she was throttling him. It took a lot of effort to let go.

"Put the Hallows back!" she screamed at him, managing to restrain herself to simply punching him in the ear.

"I..." Will didn't seem capable of meeting her eye. "I can't."

And no. That was unacceptable. Afrit hit him again. She was opposed to violence in general, but in this specific case, she was willing to make an exception.

"Now!" Afrit thought she had damaged something in her neck, because her voice was a feral growl.

Behind them Lette and Balur had picked a fight with a pack of fifteen men armed with other people's legs.

"I can't," Will said. He finally managed to face her. "It's...it's gone."

"What? What?" She spat and frothed monosyllabically at him. "What's gone?"

"The..." Will stared about him. Smoke and fire, murder and horror. Balur tearing a man's head from his shoulders. "The power. The power I used. I took it into me. It became me. We were the same. We were..." He shook his head.

She balled her fists again.

"I spent it." There was desperation in Will's voice. Horror. "I changed something. Something too big. I didn't know what I was doing. And then I did. But only after I'd done it. Only once it was too late. What I'd taken into me, I put it back out into the world. Too much of it. And there's not enough left in me. I can't change things back. If I could, I would have already. But... but..." He trailed off, stared through her as if she weren't there.

"No," she heard herself say again, but it was a small sound now. A defeated one. Because she knew he was accusing himself more vehemently than she ever could. He was telling the truth. The awful, awful truth.

Lette and Balur caved in the skull of the last leg wielder. Then they herded Will and Afrit and Cois away from an oncoming tide of bellowing men with red handprints smeared over their faces.

"How do you get it back?" Her brain was struggling to follow logical lines while her body struggled over rocks. They needed power. They didn't have power. They needed to get the power back.

"I don't...I don't..." Will dissolved into staring. From the look on his face, Afrit didn't want to turn around and see what he was staring at.

And then a voice the size of one of the mountains of rubble boomed out across the land. "Now!" it called. "Now we take this world!"

Gratt's voice. Gratt's voice with glee in it, and an animal energy. But the thing that made it truly stand out from this mire of chaos and blood was the simple confidence of it. Gratt spoke as if there were a natural order here, one he could see if all others could not. There was something even beguiling about it.

The once-dead took note.

Lette came back to them at speed. "It is time to leave," she said. "Now." She grabbed Will by the wrist. "Move. Fret about destroying large chunks of reality later."

They moved. They ran. Limbs and limestone conspired to trip Afrit. People were still picking themselves up off the ground. They started running too.

Behind them an army gave chase. And whatever city it was that they had arrived in, whatever one it was that the Hallows had just violated in the worst possible way—its bad day had only just begun.

The going got tougher as they reached the lip of the crater. The ground sloped up. There were overhangs. Dirt and sand and pebbles gave way beneath Afrit's clawing hands. She gasped. Someone gave her a leg up, and she was genuinely shocked that someone would help her. Then they were up and over and still running. Someone had her by the hand. Cois of all people. There were others here. More bodies. And people blinking out from masks of dirt and dust. Bewildered stares and shouts. Crying children. Crying everywhere. And Afrit wanted to stop, to help, to apologize. But there was no time, because if any of her senses could still be trusted, there was an army at her back.

And then, as she ran through it, it finally struck her. This was *Avarra*. Not just some tragically violated plane of reality. Not just a place where they had arrived. This was *home*. Her home. She had been striving to get back here. And she might not have agreed with Will's methods, or even with his ultimate goals, but she had wanted to come back. Her desires had lain parallel with his. Because this was home.

And then they were no longer fleeing from Gratt's army. Gratt's army was on them.

It was like a mouth closing on the city. All about her was heat and sound and blood. Blood ran through the streets as fast as any feet. Someone grabbed her. Lette threw a punch at Afrit's assailant, sent him sprawling. Out of nowhere Cois put in a kick. And Balur was roaring, and his fists were in—actually *in*—someone's chest. Lette was picking up chunks of rubble and nailing attackers as they charged at them.

And none of it, absolutely none of it, was enough.

The degree to which they were outnumbered was absurd. A tidal wave of the dead was crashing toward them. And she had read myths about this sort of thing. Tales of end times. And maybe, just maybe those particular stories had been right.

And then...then...

Afrit knew she had grown up a sheltered child. She had been born after much of the chaos of the Tamathian civil war had already finished racking Tamar. Her hometown was far to the east of those troubles anyway, close to the tranquil port of Tammsod. Her parents had enjoyed a certain degree of affluence. They had doted upon their only daughter. They had placed her in exclusive schools. They had assured fine references sent her to the finest university, and they had made sure that Tamar was a calm and stable city once more before doing so.

In short, she had grown up without truly seeing any violence.

Lette and Balur had changed much of that for her. And while she would not consider herself particularly well educated on the subject of dismembering one's fellow man, Afrit knew that she knew enough to tell that the mercenaries were uncommonly skilled. Most people, she had come to realize, actually possessed little more than a rudimentary understanding of their weapons.

In most fights it was speed, heft, and ferocity that determined the outcome, rather than finesse. Finesse could beat all three, but like many worthwhile things, it was difficult to attain.

Willett Fallows did not possess finesse. He didn't possess much of the other three either. Ferocity came to him in occasional bursts, Afrit knew, and perhaps that had helped him stay alive so far. Honestly, though, most days she really wasn't entirely sure how Will was alive.

And then... then...

Ten men. No, fifteen. Perhaps more. It was hard to tell as the mass of them thrust down the street like some extruding finger from Gratt's army, come to pluck out their eyes. Afrit and the others were already fighting off ten or more. This would likely be the end of them.

And then... then Will. He seemed to erupt out of the center of their group. He seemed to flow past her. As if he was no longer entirely human, no longer entirely solid. She blinked, and he was among the oncoming soldiers—big men, burly men, men with wrists as thick as her thighs—and Afrit wasn't even sure he had a blade, but something went snicker-snack.

And then...

One man flew across the street, intersected with a bisected building. His back snapped, and he folded in half, heels hitting the back of his head. Then, before the body slumped to the ground, Will was dancing through three archways of blood spraying up from three men's throats, moving toward two more soldiers, and then there was a blur, and somehow their bodies were tangled together, limbs woven back and forth in defiance of their joints, their bones.

And then...

Five left. Then four. Then two. Limbs and pieces of limbs skittering and whirling. The last two men turning to run. But Will was on them. He seemed to touch them only lightly, but gods, there was so much blood.

Five more men came down the street. Five more men died.

Will straightened. Purple eyes and white teeth showing through a mask of blood. He looked back at them. They were all looking at him.

"Well." Balur spoke first. "Holy fuck."

"How?" Lette asked. And there was a look on her face... Hunger perhaps.

Will looked down at his hands. Bits of meat clung to them. "I...," he said. "The power. The Deep Ones..."

And that shook Afrit out of it. That relit the fuse of anger in her. "You said it was spent!" She hurled the accusation as hard and deadly as one of Lette's blades. "You said it was gone, and you could not end this!"

"No, no." Will held up his gore-covered hands as she advanced, and there was enough blood on them that it gave her pause. "I didn't say it was *all* spent. Just... too much. I can't do it again, what I did. But there is some left."

"And you waste it on...?" Afrit was so apoplectic that she couldn't get the words out.

"Saving our lives?" Cois finished for her.

And gods piss on her, it was hard to argue with that.

"Help!" A shout from above them put the final nail in Afrit's argument. They all looked up.

The building Will had somehow hurled one of his... victims? assailants?... into was missing most of one wall. Floors and rooms and lives lay exposed. On one of the upper stories, a family clustered near the edge looking down.

"Help us!" It was the father shouting down.

If it weren't so tragic, Afrit might have laughed. Them? Them save anyone? What did that man see when he looked down at them?

Strength, she supposed. And in this apocalyptic moment that was probably enough.

Then the arguments started, about who was to catch them,

and why they had to catch them. And then the argument morphed and it was about who could catch the most. And it was all so predictable and tragic and stupid in this—probably the least predictable moment of her life.

And she wanted to scream and to rage, but she was too busy wiping blood from children's eyes and tying makeshift bandages and uttering words of encouragement that had an utter lack of sincerity to them.

Then they were moving again, trying to judge the balance point between furtive and fast. Sometimes they made mistakes. Sometimes their efforts mattered for naught. The city was rife with people losing their minds and making sure others lost their limbs.

They all played a part in their defense. Even the children picked up stones and hurled them in imitation of Lette. The adults had staves of wood, or just jagged rocks to lend their punches force. Lette and Balur performed their usual murderous duet.

But it was Will who stood out. Will who moved among the oncoming forces of madness like a needle through cloth, weaving complex, deadly patterns, stitching bodies together in lines of ragged red.

More families came out of hiding. More still. They were no longer a furtive band. They were a crowd, almost a stampede. They had momentum. They crashed into other groups and either left them slain or absorbed them. And yet again, against all odds, against expectations, Afrit saw that Willett Fallows was the engine driving them all.

And then, finally, panting, a moment of respite. Balur and Lette stalked forward, scouting a corner. Will was standing at the head of the waiting crowd, bouncing on the balls of his feet. And this was her moment. This was when she would demand answers and finally get them.

But three steps in, someone caught her arm, spun her around. She almost put her fists up before she realized it was Cois.

"Let me go," she snapped. "This has to end. He has to focus on getting the power back. On being able put everything back."

Cois shook hir head. "Aren't you the smart one?" zhe said. "You know this already."

Afrit squinted at the former god. What was zhe talking about? Too much was happening too fast.

"*Worship*," Cois hissed in exasperation. "You had our power once. It all has the same source. It all lives in the blood. It all depends on worship. You know this. Without worship he is nothing. With it..." Zhe trailed off, staring at Will.

Will Fallows. A fool. A blood-soaked, reality-destroying monster. And to the people who were flocking to them now, a hero. Even though he was the one who had put them in this position. Gods...if the world was ever to be set to rights, people had to worship *him*.

"Gods," Afrit muttered. "Avarra is so fucked."

21

The Only One Who
Could Ever Reach Me

Will had someone's throat in his hand. He could feel it, wet and warm and slippery. He could see its former owner staring at it with the same shock Will felt. Though perhaps the former owner edged Will out when it came to horror. Then the throat's owner collapsed, and Will moved on.

He threw the throat into the eyes of the man coming up on his left. He twisted his body slightly to the right, pushed with his left foot, brought his right out and up. He placed his heel hard into the crotch of another man—even as a sword swept through the space where he'd just been—and pushed off into a third attacker, extending his arms as he went. His thumbs found the man's eyes, and he gouged them out even as he used his weight to somersault over the screaming man, bringing his feet down on a fourth man's skull and bringing his eyeless victim crashing down onto the ground with a spine-crunching crack. Will landed an instant later, didn't stop moving, rolled, applied pressure, snapped the eyeless man's neck. He came up onto his knees whipping the rag-doll-limp body out like a club. He heard the next man's knees snap sideways, heard the scream as he collapsed.

He didn't know how he knew to do it. His body was receiving

signals for some new sensory organ. Something with greater situational awareness, something glimpsing a moment into the future, something that knew far better than he did what to do with the information. He was only half in control of his body. He provided the intent, and then this new... this *other* thing ensured that his body did what was necessary.

His muscles too were far stronger than they had ever been. His joints were far more flexible. There was a powerful rubberiness to his body that had never been there before.

And there should, perhaps, be some terror with that, some existential horror at what he had become or was becoming. Except it was so gods-cursedly useful. What he was doing... it was amazing. It was incredible. It was the sort of thing he had fantasized about as a child, back when he first dreamt of fighting dragons.

But he could also feel it fleeing him. Every overpowered punch he threw, each impossible contortion of his body—it cost him something. Something he didn't know how to replace. The well of power within him was being depleted. And neither food nor drink could replenish it. A return to the Deep Ones perhaps, but he had closed that avenue of escape. There was no way back.

Gods, this... all of this... It was his fault. He had been rash and foolish and full of overconfidence. He had... he had...

He had unraveled the Hallows. *An entire plane of existence.* He had unwritten it from reality. And he didn't know how to put it back. He couldn't do it even if he did know how. He wasn't powerful enough anymore. And now, as he drove his fist through some poor unsuspecting psychopath's nose and into crunching layers of cranium, he was growing weaker still.

People were following him. A crowd. As if he were some great leader. And he had been down this path before, and ten thousand people in Kondorra had died.

And somewhere, in among the carnage and the horror and

the shame and the thrill, was a small voice still whispering: *Barph isn't dead yet. Getting here was just the first part of the journey. It's the heavens next.*

He didn't want it to be there. He didn't want to have to listen to that voice. But also, he knew it was part of him. Part of him far more fundamentally than this power he had grafted into his gut. His desire for revenge was unquenched.

Would I sacrifice Avarra too? Do I want to save it or avenge it?

He had meant to sound sarcastic inside the confines of his own skull. To chastise himself. But he honestly didn't know the answer.

Another wave of attackers struck them. Will didn't know if they were the former dead or the inhabitants of this city trying to defend themselves. There wasn't really the time to sit down and talk it all through. There was just time to cock a fist and unleash.

Bones snapped. Skin burst. Blood explored the hazy aesthetic limits of fluid dynamics. More people flocked to Will. More people looking for protection.

Protection from what he'd done.

It was a head fuck he really could have lived without. Instead it was easier to lose himself in the combat, easier to shed his own power than to accept it. To splash it about the walls in monochrome rainbows of scarlet, crimson, and ruby.

As powerful as he was now, he could not be everywhere. The people seeking his protection still died. The crowd was too big for him to fend off every attack. They were herded, pushed, buffeted. And Will didn't know this city at all, had never been here. He didn't know which way was out.

They came to a cathedral in a square. The cathedral seemed to have suffered from some subsidence. The roof sloped down and almost met the floor. The walls sank into the ground. Some part of his mind thought this looked familiar. This was some landmark he should know. But there was no time to think.

People were coming at them from all sides of the square. Will didn't know if everyone was an enemy, but bloodshed was all around him.

He fought. He pushed. He punched. He grew weaker. He was driven back. Too many, from too many sides. He leapt up, found himself on the cathedral's roof. He kicked and scraped and clawed. Bodies flew away from him. He pursued. He ran up the sloping tiles toward the cathedral's vast dome. He was bleeding now, the flesh of his arm in ribbons. The pain felt distant. He felt as if he wasn't bleeding as much as he should be. He felt weaker. Weaker still.

Somehow he was at the crest of the cathedral's dome. People were swarming up on all sides. He was covered in blood. He was a crimson man picked out by the sun. He was kicking, beating, thrashing, pummeling, stabbing, gouging, hurting, ripping, biting. He was a beast. There was only one action sliding into another. One transgression transforming into yet another distinct horror. There was no time for contemplation or regret now. And yes, there was freedom in that.

And then somehow it was over. He was gasping, hanging on to a massive stone depiction of grapes. The sides of the dome were soaked with red. He was soaked with red. The sun was breaking through the clouds, and he could see the whole city spread out around him.

The cathedral was on top of a hill, and most of the city sloped away to their south. He could see the anatomy of it laid bare, as in a textbook. The veins and arteries of its streets. The thick musculature of its docks and workshops. The throbbing heart of its merchant district.

He could see too the vast wound he had inflicted upon it. The crater that had ruptured and scarred it forever. It was off on the southern edge of the city, tearing through the slums, eating into the more respectable housing at its fringes. He could see the smoke and cracks of lightning from the portal at its core.

And he could see figures too. More and more and more of them. There was a flow to them. They rippled out from the portal, flowed around the edge of the crater, and then spilled into the city streets.

More and more and more of them.

It wasn't ending.

This was a beginning.

He had to get out of here. He had to get everybody out of here. He stared around. And of course, of course they had taken the longest possible way through the city. But from this blood-slick vantage, he could see a way out of here.

He couldn't see an easy way down from the dome without falling, and he knew he was weak now, almost completely out of whatever power fueled him, but he gathered the last scraps of it and he jumped the forty feet down to the crowds around him.

He landed with a blast of dust, and an agonizing crack of kneecap against cobbles. But the bone held. He stood up wincing.

People were staring at him. Everyone was staring at him. He blinked stupidly at them.

"That way," he said, pointing, then coughed on the dust he'd kicked up. "The way out is that way."

There was a moment of hesitation, of more staring. And then everyone turned, and everyone went that way. Will stumbled along with them. He was exhausted, utterly spent.

Someone wrapped an arm around him, helped support his weight. He looked over. He was surprised to see it was Lette. She caught his eye, then looked away, shook her head.

"Holy shit," she said.

"What?" was about all he could manage.

"What?" She took her arm away. He wished she hadn't. She stared at him. "Are you seriously asking me what?"

"I'm seriously telling you I think I'm about to collapse." He glanced down at his injured arm. It wasn't as bad as he thought it had been. Just a few narrow scrapes, nothing worse than he'd have suffered from falling into a bramble bush.

Lette wrapped her arm around his ribs once more. He tried to not sag against her too much.

"Are you," she said, "seriously asking me what after you just killed most of a small army single-handedly on top of the Barphetic Cathedral? I mean, I have seen some impressive shit in my time. But that... that..." She shook her head, whistled. "Holy shit, Will Fallows."

A small army? It had seemed like that at the time, but he had assumed it had just *seemed* like that.

And still he felt powerless.

"Did I..." Finding words and breath was difficult. "Did I save anyone, at least?"

"Well..." Lette's hesitation didn't sound genuine. "Probably only everybody that small army was trying to kill."

"Oh." Will nodded. "Well, that's good then." They hobbled on through the city. No one seemed to be attacking them right now. That was nice. After a while he said, "I know I've heard of the Barphetic Cathedral..."

Lette sighed. "Is there any aspect of a basic education that you did receive? The Barphetic Cathedral is probably Barph's most famous holy site outside of Vinland. Massive landmark in Fount, city in southern Batarra. The country where we both used to live together. Nothing? Not ringing any bells?"

Will considered. "It sounds sort of familiar."

"Well, you just soaked it in enough blood to drown a village, so... you know, maybe now you'll remember its existence."

"Possibly."

Lette gave an exasperated sigh. She didn't let him fall on his arse, though.

Night fell, but the refugees managed to push on and put a line of hills between themselves and Fount. Then, by some mutual unspoken agreement, they all collapsed into the rough Batarran grass. The moon shone above them, owls hooted. For a moment there was peace. And then several thousand people collectively realized they had fled so fast, they hadn't thought to bring any supplies with them.

"This could have gone better," Will muttered to Lette, who was still beside him.

"I'm going to have that engraved on my tombstone."

"How are we going to feed everybody?"

"Why's that on us?"

Will pushed himself into a sitting position. "Because we just opened a portal to the Hallows in the middle of their city, and the dead are crawling out of it, and they're batshit insane."

Lette chewed on that. "Couple of points," she said, counting off on her fingers. "Firstly, I personally think it's a little bit on these people for not having a good exit plan. The very first thing you do in any situation, from sitting in the office of a Verran merchant to settling down as his wife, is make sure you have an exit strategy. That's just basic common sense. Secondly, *we* didn't have shit to do with that portal. That's on you, and I will not have you include me in it. And thirdly, and most importantly, shut up, you numbskull. Do you want someone to overhear and kill us both?"

Will's eyes went wide, and he looked around furtively. That last point was a very, very good one.

"Subtle," Lette said, standing, then helping him to his feet. "Come on, it could get cold tonight."

They walked through the crowds that were starting to mill about and congregate like lumps in one of Balur's traditional Analesian sauces. Will looked around, trying to pick the lizard man out of the crowd, but the darkness masked his distinctive bulk.

They settled by one of the larger fires. People were coming up, throwing more and more sticks on it. Someone else appeared with several rabbits. Another woman had had the foresight to bring down a bird earlier in the day and was now steadily plucking it. A parchment parcel of salted meat was passed around. There was a wineskin.

"This is surprisingly civilized," Will said to the man sitting next to him, the owner of the salted meat.

"My mother was killed today," the man said.

Will shut up.

"Then again," the man went on, chewing and staring at the fire, "it was my brother two weeks ago, my wife three, my father a month back. My sister before that. So for life under Barph...I suppose."

When the wineskin reached him, Will passed it straight to the man. Some, it seemed, had a need far greater than he did.

"It's really that bad?" he asked after a while, unable to hold the question inside.

"Where in the Hallows you been the past six months?" the man asked with something dangerously similar to clairvoyance.

Will's smile felt forced. "Sort of all over them," he said.

The man let out a humorless laugh. "Haven't we all? Haven't we all..." He looked at Will and blinked. "Why are you so purple?" he asked.

"Erm..." Will examined his hands. His nails on three fingers had turned black. When had that happened? "Birthmark," he said.

"I just thought—" A woman cut into their conversation. "I just thought...even with everything else. At least I had my home. The whole world around me fell apart. People were torn down in the street. The stalls were looted. We scavenged for water just to stay alive...But my home...At least I had my home. I had somewhere that was still mine. I still had a piece of...of..." She broke down sobbing. The man put his arm around her.

Will felt numb. *I did this,* part of him thought, but it was too big an idea to hold. *I did this because of Barph* was easier. *It's Barph's fault* lacked the ring of truth to it, but was tempting all the same.

He felt a hand on his shoulder and couldn't help but flinch.

"There you are," Afrit hissed. Will turned. The Tamathian stood between himself and Lette, leaning down. Her face was a mask of fury. "Have you heard what has happened?"

"Will took a bludgeon and a rusty spoon to his conscience, and will never sleep well again?" Lette asked.

Which was a little on the gods-hexed nose, if anyone cared to ask Will.

"What?" Afrit took a break from looking furious to look merely confused and annoyed. "Will...? No."

Which, considering Afrit's usual unbending sense of morality, and Will's eminent culpability in the current disaster, rather caught him off guard.

"Barph has...He has..." Afrit seemed to be struggling with her words. And Will suddenly realized that the brightness in her eyes was not fury, but actually tears, trembling on the edge of capitulation to gravity. Fury was what was holding them back.

"A genocide," Afrit managed. "But not of any one race or creed or...or...He's just torn down all the structures of civility and order. Just insisted that people behave like beasts. Just enacted inhuman cruelty on a scale that encompasses all of Avarra. The sick, the elderly...fucking children. He has seen to it that...Gods."

She spat again, and again. "I feel sick," she said.

"We're going to die out here," said the man who had taken the wineskin from Will. He sounded quite matter-of-fact. Beside him the woman started sobbing loudly.

I did this. Barph did this, Will thought. *We did this. I've united us in something.* Will felt a sense of greasy nausea.

"We have to end him," Afrit was muttering. "We have to

mount to the heavens and end him. I don't know how. I don't think it's possible. But we have to."

"Fuck Barph," someone said from the other side of the fire, plucking the thought—it felt—directly out of Will's mind. He made out a silhouette as it stood and shook an angry fist at the sky. "Fuck you!" the figure screamed, shaking an angry fist at the sky.

"What had we done to deserve this?" someone else said, a few yards off to Will's left. "We'd done what he said. We followed his stupid gods-hexed edicts. Everything, and now..." Whoever was speaking let out an inarticulate sound, something made of anger and grief.

I did this. Barph did this, Will thought. *But people don't know about me. And they know about Barph. And they blame Barph for what I did here today.* A thought was taking root in Will's mind, sinking its tendrils into him, and he didn't think he liked it, but he wasn't sure if that mattered.

"We have to flay his pissing corpse," Afrit was muttering. "Drag him down from the heavens..."

Worship, Will thought. Barph had taught him that. A god's power depended on worship. And of course everyone worshipped Barph. He was all knowing, all seeing, all powerful. You had to worship him or risk his wrath.

Except...

What if you didn't care about his wrath anymore? What if you were standing in a field at night, shaking your fist angrily at the sky, and screaming at him to go fuck himself? What then?

Anger could outweigh fear, Will knew. He knew it well.

"Barph," he said. Not loud enough yet. Just loud enough to get Lette to look up at him, a question in her eyes.

"Barph," he said again, getting a feel for the word. For the thoughts behind it.

"What's that?" said the man with the salted meat and the

murdered family. The woman beside him was still sobbing uncontrollably.

"Barph!" Will was brought to his feet by the force of the word. He bellowed it, howled it across the night. "Barph!" he screamed.

People were looking at him. Even the sobbing woman.

"Barph did this to us!" he yelled.

He could feel the bitterness of the lie in his mouth. He could feel the weight of it in his gut. And this was compounding his crime—this lie, this blasphemy. But he believed in it too. He believed in the value of this lie, of what it could do for them.

The people gathered round the fire started to rumble. Not quite questions, and not quite denials. A susurration of uncertainty.

"Oh gods," he heard Lette mutter.

He had been sitting on a boulder; he stood on it now, put himself head and shoulders above the others.

"Barph did this to us!" he shouted again. "He sits in the heavens, and he calls himself a god, and he demands our worship, but what do we get in return? What does he do that rewards our worship? He does not give us great bounty. He does not protect our homes. He does not bring good health to our children. He does not defend us from our enemies. He does none of these things. He is no god. No savior."

The murmur had died away this close to the fire; it was rippling out, people coming to look and to stare.

"We worship him for one reason," Will said. "Simple and clear. We worship him because we fear him. Because what will the consequences be if we don't? What death and destruction will he wreak upon our lives? Will he..." Will cast about as if searching for inspiration, a rough pantomime at best. "Will he open a portal to the fucking Hallows in our city?"

A grunt, a groan from the crowd. It was too close a blow, too soon for a rueful smile. It made them angry. And that was good, Will thought. He needed them angry.

"We worshipped him!" he shouted. "We got down on our knees and offered up our prayers. We poured our libations. We followed his directives. And what happened? What happened today? What did he do?

"Barph betrayed us today!" he shouted. "He said that we and our worship mean nothing to him. And so I say that he is not the god of revelry, nor of joy, nor even of anarchy. He is the god of meaninglessness. He is an empty and hollow god! He is the god of nothing!"

It was not a handful of people around a fire now. He had the attention of the masses. And not all of them could hear him, he knew, but he also knew his words were being relayed, whispered back, a rustling echo weaving in among all the gasps and murmurs of agreement.

And he felt sick. And he felt giddy. And he felt powerful. And he felt that maybe, just maybe he could make a difference. One that mattered.

Maybe if a lie ended genocide, it was worth it. Even if it masked his own crime.

"Today," he shouted, "I stood upon the summit of the Barphetic Cathedral, at the peak of his highest temple in this land, and I was beset on all sides by madness and horror. I was drenched in blood. And I looked out and I saw this world he had created—this world that he had uncreated."

More gasps from the crowd. Someone...the man with salted meat and no family, stepped forward slightly. "Who are you?" he asked. And there was something like wonder in his eyes.

"I am a man," Will said. "I'm a farmer. I am Willett Fallows. I am the prophet of Kondorra who threw down the dragons from those skies. And I am here, and I have returned, and I have come to tell you one simple thing: Barph is no god of mine! I am nothing to him, and so he is nothing to me! You are nothing to him! He should be nothing to you! From this day forth, from this travesty onward, I say this: BARPH IS NOT OUR GOD!"

Silence. Absolute. Every last murmur laid to rest. Eyes everywhere were on him.

And then he felt it. Before they even said a word, he felt it, and he knew.

Power rushed into him like a drug. He could feel it shuddering through him in waves. He felt light-headed from it. The *other*—the part of the Deep Ones he had taken into himself, that had lain desiccated and spent inside him—suddenly filled, swelled inside him, buoyed him up.

And then the noise hit him. The cheer, the cry, the affirmation, the defiance. And he knew: He had spoken, and they believed.

22

Stuck in the Middle with You

Lette stared at Will as he stumbled down from the boulder he'd been standing on. She held out an arm, and he caught hold of it, leaning more weight on it than she'd expected. He was unsteady, blinking, and still she just stared at him.

How did he do it? How did the stupid bastard manage it? How did he know? How could this idiotic, foolheaded numbskull of a man reach into the ether and find the words that undid her? How did he make her care?

Because she did. She stood here and now, surrounded by men and women who meant nothing to her, by absolute strangers, and yet when Will spoke, she wanted to save them. She wanted to unite with them. She wanted to wield her middle finger at the night sky and shout, *I am here, and I am human, and I reject you, for you care nothing for us. For us. Us.*

Us.

That word. That sense of community. Creating that was a magic far greater than any Lette had ever seen Quirk manage.

Will was trying to pull away from her, from the crowds and the light. People pushed toward him, but he kept pulling away, and then she was propelling him out of the circle, off into the shadows.

We're getting away, she thought. *We are. We have one purpose. We do. Us.*

He sagged to the ground in a small hollow, and she sat beside him.

"What did I just say to those people?" he asked her. "What shit did I just fill their heads with? I can't believe..." He buried his head in his hands. "I'm the one responsible. I—"

"Oh, shut up," she said. And for a wonder, he did. He stared at her, and he looked utterly lost. But she...she felt as if she'd come home.

And suddenly, just like that, the words were so easy to say.

"I love you, you idiot."

He opened his mouth. And so she kissed it. And after a moment he kissed her back. And they kept on that way while all around them, the fires died.

23

When Life Gives You Apocalyptic Disasters

Gratt smiled. It was not, he knew, an attractive look on him. He was not good at smiling. His maker had not gifted him with a mouth designed for smiling. It was a mouth made for biting and rending. And yet still he smiled. Because Gratt quite honestly didn't give a shit what anyone else thought.

Gratt was looking at his city. His Avarran city.

He did not know its name. It lay half in ruins, and the other half was soaked in blood. He had lost tens of thousands of men in claiming it, and yet he smiled. This was a good day.

He heard scurrying behind him. He turned, ready to wet his claws in some misguided attacker's blood. To his disappointment it was just one of his messengers, one of the once-dead, scrambling toward him on all fours.

The messenger bobbed his head one-two-three times in deference. "A message from the portal general," he said in a voice as twisted as his body had been by Lawl's punishments in the Hallows. "General Earrah is dead."

And Gratt's smile forced itself wider.

The portal was still vomiting up souls from the deepest caverns of the Hallows. They came through bewildered, weakened, and confused, which was why Gratt had placed a circle of troops around it with simple instructions. Anyone under seven feet tall was to be forcefully recruited. Anyone over seven feet was to be forcefully murdered on sight.

Gratt had taken this city and murdered every single one of his rival generals from the Hallows all in one day. He had folded their armies into his own, and he stood unopposed.

It was a good day.

The thought of escaping the Hallows had been beyond the limits of his ambition—a dream that had never entered his skull. And yet here he was. Here he stood. In a world ripe for plucking.

And all because of Will Fallows.

Even he could not have predicted how wise an investment that man had proven to be. He was certainly not the first to come to Gratt begging for the route to the Deep Ones. But Will Fallows was the first one either insane or desperate enough to go through with everything and take part of the Deep Ones into himself.

Gods...the things that would happen to...Was Will even a man anymore? He was certainly less of one. Would become even less than that. Would become...

Gratt suppressed a shudder.

Still, there would be a process of becoming, a time when someone as efficacious as Will Fallows could be useful to Gratt. And a time after that when it would be good to know where he was so he could be put down easily.

He turned back to the messenger. "Has any word come of Will Fallows?"

The messenger bobbed his head seven or eight times, which meant Gratt knew the answer before the man even opened his mouth. So Gratt punted him ten yards before he delivered it.

He turned to another minion standing nearby. "We establish order. We establish a hierarchy. Bring my lieutenants to me; I will have them impose order, structure. This rabble becomes an army tonight. Bring me locals. Make me maps. We will plan our campaign. We will chart the cities through which we will march and pillage."

He smiled once more. "And then," he said, "send more men to bring me what's left of Will Fallows."

24

Because We Haven't Heard from Her in Nine Chapters

Quirk knew that riding at the head of an army of dragons was the sort of thing that bards would get very worked up over. There would be refrains and choruses and more synonyms than any good sentence could handle. However, she also found that doing it with a concussion rather took the romance out of it. Yes, there were sweeping vistas, but there was also the pounding headache, and the roiling sense of nausea that the whirling landscape did nothing to still.

The dragons made slow progress. They were, in the end, the elderly, the sick, and the runts. The crossing from Natan to the Avarran coastline had been harrowing as they sank closer and closer to the chop of the waves, as their wingbeats had seemed more and more labored. Eventually they had sagged to the coastline, terrorized a herd of cattle, and then collapsed for the night.

Now they rumbled cross-country, making as direct a line for Batarra as Quirk could manage. That country, she felt, was still the heart of the resistance. She would rekindle the flames she had once stoked there. Begin again.

She tried to herd the dragons away from the major cities, to stick to the farmlands and forests. She knew what the sight of her new companions would do to people. Trying to introduce a hundred or more dragons as a group of saviors had to be done gently, and by degrees. She had to demonstrate their intent, make the people come to her.

She could not hide her army completely, though. She saw shepherds in the Rosalian hills beneath her pointing up and screaming. She saw farmers gibbering on their knees. She saw some road-weary travelers drop to the ground and pray. She could not blame them. There was something apocalyptic about this force she headed. It excited her as much as it caused her fear. This was the end of something.

In the afternoon of the third day, her headache had eased to a dull throb, and the Batarran border was in sight. The sun was low on the horizon as they cleared the trees of the elven Vale and swept up into the rolling lowlands and increasingly scrubby trees.

There was a time when Quirk might have expected a sense of peace, of returning home. Now all she had was grim satisfaction. This part of her journey was done. The next part was about to begin. The great burning of the world.

But it seemed as if someone else had already gotten a head start on that.

The city of Fount crested the horizon, slouched toward them...and yet...not all of Fount. Someone had done some very bad things to the Batarran city.

A huge portion of the southern city was gone, just a desolate wasteland. Buildings lay shattered. Streets were zigzags of ruin, running nowhere. And at its core...a permanent storm. A pit. A portal that crackled with lightning, that heaved with bodies.

"What was done here?" Yorrax looked back over her shoulder.

"Something very wrong."

It was as if a god had pressed his finger into Fount, harder and harder, until the skin of the world broke and reality bled out.

"Barph's work?" Yorrax asked.

And Quirk knew of only one god, so she said, "It has to be."

"Then it changes nothing."

Gods, she had only been away a week, and it had been too long.

They circled the city, trying to make things out. Quirk didn't dare get too close. Around the portal—and she was sure that must be what it was, she had read enough books—the thermals became strange and difficult to navigate, pushing and pulling, and she feared crashing into the crackling maw of the portal more than she had feared anything in a long time.

Yorrax was the first to arch away from Fount. The other dragons followed her. The young dragon had enjoyed a change in status since the decision to come to Avarra. It seemed Yorrax's elevation was a sacrifice worth making for those dragons who wanted to come and establish their dominance over Avarra.

As they progressed toward the periphery of the city. Quirk saw signs of organization among the populace. There were groups all running in step. People parading in military lockstep. Archers mounting to roofs and tracking their progress. Martial law, it seemed, ruled the parts of Fount that had survived. Barph would dislike that. The law, the order, and the discipline. The thought that whatever he had wrought here had backfired made her smile.

The day's light was dying, though, so the dragons broke off from their aerial perusal of the city and went sweeping on, Quirk angling them toward her old encampment near Tarramon. But they had only cleared the first line of hills when Quirk saw the campfires spread out beneath them.

People. Refugees, obviously. Several thousand of them escaped from Fount. She could hear shouts rising up as the dragons passed overhead. And she wasn't sure if their silhouettes would be clear against the night sky, but the sound of their wings would be enough to bring fear.

Refugees. People whose lives had just been ruined by Barph. People who might hate. Who might have the courage to tear Barph's world down. The sort of people she was searching for.

And she was not mentally ready for convincing several thousand people that the dragons were there to help, but opportunities were rarely this golden.

"Turn back," she shouted over the wind, as she and Yorrax flew past the crowd. "Take us in to land."

Yorrax turned her neck, gave her a wicked smile. "We shall eat well tonight."

"No!" Quirk let heat fill her palms. Not enough to hurt, but enough to be felt through Yorrax's thick scales. She turned and looked at the rest of the dragons, shouted as loud as she could over the wind, "We will make allies tonight!"

Yorrax barked a sound that could have been a laugh or a grunt of disapproval, though Quirk was still not entirely sure she could apply human motivations to the various utterances she heard from her new draconic companions.

Then her stomach was lurching, and her head was throbbing, and the ground was rushing up toward her.

They landed with a clatter of limbs, a furious clapping of wings, and the sound of turf tearing beneath Yorrax's talons. All around her, heavy bodies thumped to the ground, scaled limbs crashing and thundering.

And then the screaming began.

At first she thought a dragon had broken ranks, had started to sate its hunger, and in the darkness she couldn't tell who. So she sent a huge fireball up into the night to cast the scene in flickering yellow-orange light.

That made it so much worse.

"Dragons!" people howled, and "Flee!" and "Oh fuck!"

"Peace!" she yelled at them. "We are your friends!" But she was just one voice, and she'd already hurled a fireball into the night, so it turned out she didn't have much authority, or at least not enough of the right sort.

But someone did. "Hold!" their voice boomed. "Hold!" It was a massive rolling sound. And Quirk wondered if somehow these people had a dragon of their own. Or perhaps a clan of hill giants had joined them.

The crowds stumbled in their panic and looked around, not sure if they were willing to comply with this new command.

"We are here as friends!" Quirk shouted again. Hardly anyone heard her. And Yorrax's cynical laughter didn't help at all. The other dragons were stamping and snorting, and Quirk had to admit she was losing faith in her own message. It suddenly felt as if having Barph as a common enemy might not be enough to smooth over all past enmities after all.

She gathered herself, stood precariously on Yorrax's back, waved her arms, desperate to make herself visible. Other dragons loomed over her.

"They do not seem a mighty ally," said one of the dragons.

"Well, if you look at their city, I'm sure it's been a bad day," Quirk said, but she wasn't sure the dragons were listening to her any more than the refugees were.

"I said hold!" the booming voice snapped. "I have killed dragons before, and I can do it again."

Killed dragons before? Who could it be? Some veteran of Kondorra?

"We come as friends!" she shouted for the third time. "We come to aid you in your fight against Barph!"

"We do not join their fight," grumbled a dragon. "They join us in ours. Their fight is puny and stupid. Ours is glorious."

Quirk wasn't sure now was the time to haggle over linguistic nuances.

"Dragons exist to dominate," accused the booming voice. "They exist to impinge their will on others. They are not friends or allies. They are bullies and killers."

Quirk put a hand to her eyes, squinted into the firelight, tried to make out where the speaker was in the crowd of backlit silhouettes. She could see nothing. His volume made his location uncertain.

"We share a common enemy," Quirk shouted back. "A common persecutor. We have a shared goal of revenge." *Gods, let the Batarrans have found their courage since I left. Let there be fertile ground for these words.*

"Yes," boomed the unseen leader, "but you're a bunch of dragon arseholes."

"Dinner it is then," said Yorrax.

"No!" Quirk yelled. *And fuck this.* She filled the night with fire. She demanded attention from dragons and Batarrans alike. "Listen to me!" she screamed. "I have traveled to the ends of the world and beyond to come back here with an army capable of making a difference. And I will not have some petty despot fuck that up for me. So hold. Make nice. And get ready to kick some arse, before I have to get down there and do it myself!"

Gods, she was tired of making speeches.

But it might not have been quite so bad if whomever she was talking to hadn't started laughing. She balled her fists.

"Beyond the edge of the world?" said the voice. "Well, on that issue, I might just have you beat."

And then someone grabbed a torch from a fire and started walking toward her. And then Quirk's jaw dropped as out of the shadows—out of the grave itself—walked Willett Fallows.

25

Death by Bear Hug

Afrit watched dragons descend from the sky. Massive, brutal beasts. Each one the size of a sea galleon, with outstretched wings darker than the night itself. And she knew that this was death. That was it, at its simplest. The dragons had come and they would end everything. There was no time for a plan, no time for trickery. This was a surprise too great for them, and not even Will with his stolen divinity could fix things.

She heard him trying, yelling at the crowd to hold with an artificially magnified voice. The people listened to him—though the gods alone knew why—but it would do them no good. Killed together or separately, they would be dead all the same.

She started to fight through the paralyzed crowd, searching for a way out that didn't exist. For some shadow that could only ever fail to hide her.

There would be no escaping the Hallows this time either, she thought. There were no Hallows left to escape from. Only the Void beckoned now.

Something massive crashed into her, and she screamed, because she knew a dragon had looped around behind them, was poised to devour her whole. But then a more familiar reptilian face gazed into her own.

"Have you been seeing her?" Balur said.

Balur. Fighting the other way through the crowd, heading

toward the dragons. His mothlike impulse to immolate himself against the largest monster available had taken over. And quite frankly, if it bought Afrit another few seconds to run and hide, she was fine with that.

"Honestly?" she said, pushing past him. "I can't imagine Lette is looking to be part of this fight."

Then her forward progress ceased utterly as Balur gripped her upper arm. His fist was large enough to cover her entire bicep. The power of his fingers was painful.

"Not Lette," he hissed, and she could see something that... No, surely it couldn't be panic. "I have been losing Cois."

Not her. Hir.

And he wasn't looking for a fight. He was looking for his love.

"We were getting separated in Fount." His bass rumble was heading for higher registers. He flicked his head back and forth, licked the air again and again. "I am thinking I can taste hir. Zhe is being here."

Afrit flicked her head around. They were surrounded by thousands of people. It was dark. Panic was rampant. There was still a horde of dragons landing before them. Literally a hundred dragons or more. And there was something epochal about this. Part of her felt that this was significant, that she should be mentally recording it. And yet still all she wanted was to get away.

Then Balur was propelling her through the crowd, back the way she had come. "Cois!" he shouted as they barreled through stunned, milling crowds. "Cois!"

She tried to pull away, but Balur wasn't even paying attention, just dragging her along like some stuffed animal seized for moral support.

She could hear Will desperately trying to negotiate with the dragons, though his specific words escaped her. It sounded as if he was talking to a woman.

A woman with the dragons? No... that doesn't make sense...

"Cois!"

They were getting dangerously close to the front of the crowds, back where she had been.

"Cois!"

An explosion of movement in the crowd. Afrit flinched. Some pincer movement was happening. The dragons had been buying time—

No. No, it was a flurry of fabric and flesh, a shriek, and then Cois was on Balur like a rabid kobold, saying his name over and over, and he was rumbling happiness and recriminations, and Afrit was stumbling and discarded.

The pair of them stood in the churning chaos of the evening utterly separate from events, lost in each other.

And suddenly, despite it all, the only thing Afrit could think of was Quirk. Quirk up here somewhere in Avarra, still lost to her. And now Afrit was going to be killed by dragons before she had a chance to find her.

She had to get away.

She turned her back on the dragons, started to worm her way back through the crowd.

And then something made her stop. At first she didn't know what. But then she caught it again. An inflection of voice. A tone she knew. And her heart shivered in her chest. But no. No. It couldn't be.

And still she turned and hunted for it. Where had she heard that voice?

She could hear Will talking again. Saying something that sounded positively stupid in the face of these horrific reptiles, but that, more irritatingly, meant she couldn't hear anything else.

And then it came again. That familiar voice. That voice that couldn't be. And it came in response to Will.

No. No. It couldn't...

She stumbled again. The world felt only loosely held together, as if the moorings of reality had begun to fray. Her body was

numb, a distant thing propelling her tiny lost sense of consciousness forward through the crowd. She was floating, breathless.

And then... then...

She saw her. She saw her step down from the back of a small
blue-and-white dragon. Saw her run across an expanse of grass
and seize Will by the shoulders and embrace him. She saw her.
Her. *Her.*

Afrit stepped toward them, and she tried to say *her* name,
but she couldn't. She couldn't make any sounds. Her throat was
clogged. She could hardly breathe. She thought her legs might
give way. Because it was her. Her. *Her.*

She was smiling, animated, gesticulating wildly. And words
were pouring out of her. Wonderful, beautiful words. And Afrit
couldn't understand a single one. Because her ears were full of
just one word. *Her* name. And still Afrit couldn't say it, couldn't
even raise an arm to attract her attention. Her. *Her.*

And then *she* turned. And then *she* saw.

And then the whole world contracted, became a single pin-
point of reality focused entirely on them. The crowds went
away, and Will went away, and the dragons went away. And
it was just them. And Afrit found she could breathe again, she
could control her body again.

And then Afrit was running. And *she* was running. And they
were in each others' arms in a way they had never been before,
but which Afrit had always dreamt of. And their lips were on
each other in a way they had never been before, but which Afrit
had always dreamt of. And everything was a dream, and nothing could be real, except it was. And *she* was real. And *she* was
here. Her. *Her.*

And finally, finally, Afrit could say her name, could whisper it
into her soft ear, over and over and over.

Quirk.

26

Because Burning Everyone and Everything Is Totally a Plan

Love. Beauty. Peace. They were ideas Will had given up on. They were thoughts from a previous life.

And yet...there was Quirk in Afrit's arms. There was the memory of Lette's lips on his. Even in this world, it seemed, there was respite.

And then a dragon growled, and Will remembered that respites did not last forever.

"I think," the dragon spat at Will, "that you are an agent of Barph come here to disrupt our vengeance. I think that you are to be killed."

Its teeth glinted. Its eyes gleamed. Its breath was oven hot. It had a head the size of farmer's wagon, a body the size of a warship. It was not the largest of the dragons assembled there.

"And I think you are as dangerous to these people as Barph himself," Will snarled back. "I think you are an untamed beast that must either be broken or destroyed. I think both sound appealing to me."

He knew Quirk must have had her reasons for bringing the dragons here, but he wasn't sure he would like them.

More than one dragon roared at his words. Sound and heat washed over him. He felt the crowd behind him quail, felt his strength trembling. He walked a precarious line, he realized. His strength was not infallible.

But these people could fuel him if he gave them faith.

"I am not cowed by you," he shouted into the dragon's face, into all their faces. "I have killed your kind before. I shall do it again."

And he could feel some of the crowd coming with him on this journey of defiance. Their excitement fed his strength.

The dragon reared back on its length. It opened its jaws. And now . . . now he would see how strong he was.

Fire arched over Will's head. It smashed into the dragon's face. The vast lizard scrabbled back like an offended feline.

"No!" Quirk's voice was a whip crack. "No!" She stormed toward them, palm raised and full of fire. She turned to Will. "Gods, you couldn't let me be happy to see you for longer than a minute, could you? You had to jump right back into the same old bullshit?"

"They're dragons!" Will pointed out, not, he thought, unreasonably.

"We are fighting dragons now?" And suddenly Balur was there with an eager smile. Cois was still on his arm.

"Is that . . ." Quirk was momentarily sidetracked. "Is that Cois?"

"Who is this?" bellowed a dragon.

"Burn him!" shouted another.

"Burn them all," came another cry.

The blue-white dragon, the one Quirk had been riding, turned and hissed at its larger companions, but they ignored it.

"If anyone is getting burned alive," shouted Quirk, "I'm the one doing it." She took a breath. "This is Willett Fallows. He is . . ." She looked at Will. He shrugged. He didn't know how to sum his life up any more than she did.

"He is the epicenter of all bullshit," Quirk shouted to the dragons. "He is a farmer. A nobody. He is the prophet of Kondorra from time to time. And somehow he is a catalyst for epochal change in Avarra. And I don't know how, or why. But he is important over and over again. And apparently he is important again here, though I doubt he deserves to be."

"That's actually pretty fair." Lette had joined them. She placed a hand against Will's lower back. "Hello, Quirk." She grinned.

"Also," Quirk said to Will, lowering her voice, "aren't you usually less purple?"

Will shrugged. He wasn't even sure how to get into that.

The dragons hadn't finished growling. There was a moan of fear rising from the crowd behind him. Not all of them, but enough.

"He angers me," stated one dragon.

"He angers everybody," Quirk snapped back. "It's sort of his thing."

And Will wasn't entirely sure how he felt about that. He'd always rather hoped that improbably successful plans were his thing.

"But," Quirk went on, "if he is here—and believe me, it pains me to say this—then he is probably our best ally against Barph. Especially if he has a few thousand people at his back."

And suddenly a lot of things that had been said started to add up in Will's head. "Wait," he said. "Your ally? You're here to fight Barph?" He pointed to the assembled dragons. *"They're* here to fight Barph?"

"Barph didn't just screw you over personally, Will," Quirk said with a sigh. He thought the sigh was a touch unnecessary.

"You expect us to ally with him?" one dragon scoffed.

Will rolled his eyes. "She expects me to ally with you."

"I expect," Quirk snapped, "you to be united by a common goal. Barph is the enemy. Or, of course, we could all fight each other and leave Barph alone to rule over our corpses. The longer this conversation goes on, the less I care."

Lette whistled. "Holy shit, Quirk," she said. "You brought a dragon army to Avarra to wreak war on the heavens?"

Balur grunted. "I am going to have to be reassessing how badass academics are being."

Afrit just stood behind Quirk and virtually vibrated with pride.

And, it had to be conceded, that was a pretty astounding feat. And as much as Will would have liked to rally the refugees and lead them in battle with these dragons, as much as he would have liked to paint the ground with their blood, he could also see their value as allies.

He looked up at the vast reptilian, alien faces staring down at him. "So," he said. "A truce? An alliance?"

The dragons looked to Quirk, and somehow, Will realized, she really had impressed them.

"I swear an alliance with him will actually be less of a pain in the arse than trying to go against him," Quirk said. "And it might even be helpful."

The lead dragon—a massive black beast, not the small blue-white dragon Quirk had ridden—snorted. That seemed to be as much of a concession as the dragons were willing to make.

"All right then." Lette clapped Will on the back. "Seems like it's about time for you to come up with a really stupid plan."

They separated themselves from the main bulk of the dragons and refugees. The world's most absurd war council. Will, Lette, Balur, Afrit, and Quirk, and three of the dragons: Netarrax, Pettrax, and Rothinamax. They were large, belligerent, elderly creatures of a singular distemper. Exactly, Will supposed, the sort of leaders you would expect from a society that favored bullying over diplomacy.

Quirk's blue-white mount tried to accompany them, but the largest of the older dragons kicked her away. The smaller dragon sent pitiful looks after Quirk, and Will saw the former academic swallow something that looked a lot like guilt.

They stopped a hundred yards away from the crowds. It was absurd, really. The dragons were so large they'd done little more than simply turn around. Still, their enormous bodies formed something of a barrier that allowed for privacy.

The three dragons lowered their heads until they were close to Quirk's and the others'.

"Discussion is stupid and human," Netarrax started immediately. "The only true speech is action, and the only thing we have to say is the sound Barph's heart will make as we rip it from his body."

"Oh good," Will said. "You're incredibly stupid."

It was not, he knew, the most constructive thing to say, but in his defense it was hard to let an entire childhood of oppression go just like that.

"I shall demonstrate what we have to say to Barph on you," said Pettrax, exposing his claws.

"I swear," Quirk said, turning to Afrit, "the only reason I'm going to try and stop them from killing each other is because I want to make a good impression on you."

"Oh good," said Lette. "Two people can be condescending at once now."

"Look," said Quirk, loud enough that the dragons would pay attention, "we are not here to play power games. We are here to ensure Barph dies. A singular purpose. Remember?"

"And the way to do that is to rip his heart from his body," said Netarrax.

"Point us at him," said Rothinamax, "and we shall end him."

Will didn't know what line of bullshit Quirk had been feeding these dragons, but the time had come for some reality. "He's a god, you ill-begotten spawn of iguana jism," he snapped. "*The* god. He killed forty or more of your kind back in Vinland without breaking a sweat."

"They were not us." Netarrax, the massive black dragon, was, it seemed, as stubborn as he was stupid.

"You're right." Quirk surprised Will by cutting back into the conversation. "They were younger, stronger, and more powerful."

The dragons stared. That they had apparently not expected.

It was time for some harsh truths. "A direct assault on Barph will lead to death, and probably some condescending laughter on his part," Will said.

Quirk's nodding was particularly aggressive on this point.

"Barph is strong because of belief," Will said, while the dragons worked out exactly how offended they wanted to be. "Because people have faith in him. We need to take that away."

"Exactly." Quirk picked up the argument's thread, carried it deeper into the dragons' hesitation. "We need to take exactly what Barph told you all to do to defeat the old gods, and use it to defeat him," Quirk said. "It's honestly the only viable way to take down a god."

"Wait..." Will held up a finger. "Barph did what?"

"Backstory," said Quirk. "I'll fill you in later."

"I say we try ripping his heart out first," said Netarrax, pulling Will back to the here and now, "and then if that doesn't work, we try the humans' way afterward."

"And I'm saying that if you do that," Will said, "then there won't be an afterward because you'll all be dead."

"Listen to us," Quirk said. And Will expected to hear a pleading note in her voice, but there was only command. "You will still get to rip out Barph's heart. You just need to...to..." She looked to Will.

And what exactly were the specifics of destroying faith in Barph?

"We need to tour all of Avarra," Will said. "We need to convince people to not worship the arsehole god who's destroying their lives. And once we've done that, then you should sharpen your claws."

"All of Avarra?" Afrit's question was, Will thought, a little poorly timed.

The dragons exchanged looks. Will got ready to knock heads.

Balur took a half step forward. "There will be being violence along the way, right?" he asked.

"Finally," said Netarrax. "Someone who speaks sense."

"Yes," said Will, and he heard a coldness even he hadn't expected in his own voice. "Don't worry. I am certain there will be a lot of violence along the way."

27

The Man without the Plan

Barph couldn't resist actually licking the Barphetic Cathedral's walls. Power crackled in the back of his mouth. He felt his left leg trembling slightly.

He very much doubted that Will had meant the murder of a small army as a blood sacrifice, but he had done it on the grounds of Barph's own cathedral, grounds consecrated in his own divine name. Plus Barph wasn't picky.

Barph shook his head. Will had really outdone himself. The Hallows in tatters, a city destroyed, a cathedral bathed in blood. Honestly, Barph was a little jealous—he wasn't sure he could have done better himself.

The god walked into his cathedral, stretching his senses out as he did so, feeling the pulse of the city, of the lands around it.

Gratt—Lawl's creature if ever there was one—was assembling an army nearby, conscripting the once-dead into a massive fighting force. He had set up his troops to attack any rival generals who crawled out of the portal. He was forcing order and control upon this city.

And there, out on the outskirts, was Will. Will actually fraternizing with dragons. Forming an alliance with them. Another little pocket of order, of rule; another flaw in his perfect empire of disorder.

People, Barph realized, were screaming. They were running toward him, waving their little arms in the air. They flung themselves at his feet. His priests. They called his name. They prayed. Their hands scrabbled at his ankles.

Saving them, that was the gist of it. Gratt's army prowled their streets. Dragons were in the skies above their heads. They wanted him to undo it all. To put the dead and the Hallows back together. To rebuild what they knew. To set his plans to rights.

He felt them, these forces massing against his vision. He felt the threat they posed to him. He felt the hatred the actors behind these events felt for him.

"Save us," his priests wailed. "Save everything you have achieved."

He looked at them, at their wide imploring eyes. "We love you," a priest screamed.

Barph trod on the priest. He felt the man's bones crack beneath his heel.

The priests stopped praying.

Barph stared at them in contempt. Did they truly not understand ... still?

He had created perfect anarchy. Perfect disorder. He had undone Lawl's rule utterly. And it had been ... so, so boring. So utterly dull.

But this. This kicking over of all his plans. This destruction of all he had done. *This* was anarchy. *This* was what he had needed. He required an adversary. Because when did one revel? When did one truly laugh, and carouse, and be thankful to be alive?

In victory.

And Barph knew now that Will and Gratt would be the perfect vehicles for his victory.

28

As Unstoppable as a Runaway Steamroller Heading Toward a Kindergarten

Two weeks later, and a hundred leagues farther south, Will stood and stared down the slope of a Batarran hill at a small village. The fields around it had been largely turned to mud, and one home was a smoking ruin, but compared to many settlements he'd seen since his return to Avarra, this one seemed remarkably whole. It was also notable for being built at about 50 percent of the size of all the others.

He turned to Quirk, who was standing beside him. "You're seriously telling me," he said, "that you've never been to a dwarf enclave."

"I study *mega*thaumatofauna," Quirk replied. "And *mega* is almost as problematic a term to use when it comes to dwarves as *fauna*."

Will sighed. Well then...

He signaled back to Lette to hold their forces while he and Quirk descended. There was no obvious resistance to the appearance of several thousand refugees yet, and he didn't want to spook anyone, no matter how much it made Lette purse her lips.

He and Quirk were still a hundred yards out when the dwarves started to appear, filing out of low doors, peering up at them. Will felt a sense of unreality staring at them all. He'd heard all the remaining dwarves in Avarra had retreated to the Verran hills. He'd never expected to see any here.

The dwarves had formed a rough, shuffling mass by the time he and Quirk reached the village's edge. As they got within ten paces, a burly figure was ejected. He was just over four feet tall, which met with Will's expectations closely enough, but in defiance of stereotypes, he was clean-shaven. Will would have guessed he was in his mid-forties perhaps.

"We ain't got much," the dwarf said without preamble. "We ain't got gold. We ain't got jewels. We ain't that sort of dwarf."

It was not the beginning Will had expected.

It also made him want to ask a lot of questions, but he knew that what he really had to do was establish that they came in peace. "We—" he started.

The dwarf, however, seemed to have a different shape for this conversation in his mind. "We don't dig," he spat. "We don't delve. We ain't got mining carts. We don't sing baritone working chants in unison. We ain't that sort of dwarf."

Will and Quirk took the time to exchange a look.

"We didn't—" Quirk started.

"It's racist," the dwarf said. "That sort of attitude. Bringing those sorts of assumptions. We don't all spend our time prettifying dungeons. Some of us are artists, not just artisans. Some of us paint. Some of us sculpt. Some of us work with nature. Julia"—he turned and pointed—"creates bowers that no elf could even pretend to aspire to. Bet you didn't think she could do that, did you?"

"I . . . ," Will said, then looked at Quirk again. "I guess I hadn't thought that about her. No."

"Pissing round-ears." The dwarf hawked a gob of phlegm on the ground. Which struck Will as a bit absurd, as the tips of dwarven ears, if not quite as round as humans', were far from resembling the sharp points of elvish ears.

"Honestly, I hadn't really thought about her at all," Will tried. "I hadn't really thought about what any of you do. But, I guess..." He looked about her. "Well, I hadn't seen any evidence of a mine, so I thought maybe you were farmers." He shrugged.

"I'm a farmer!" said one of the dwarves in the crowd, jumping up and down with his hand raised.

"He is," said the lead dwarf. "And he creates the most beautiful fruit baskets you could possibly imagine." Still, he seemed slightly mollified.

"Thanks, Davitt!" called the farmer from the crowd.

"Davitt?" Will smiled at the lead dwarf. "My name is Will. This is Quirk."

"Round-ears," was all Davitt said.

"Yes," Will said, with an edge to his voice, but Quirk shot a look at him that made him hesitate before pointing out that for a dwarf so concerned with racism, he seemed happy to throw around racial slurs himself. "But all we truly came to say is that we mean you no harm. Neither physically, nor with any foolish assumptions."

Davitt's eyes narrowed. "You making fun of me? Because I'm short?"

"I swear he's not," Quirk jumped in. "Will is often foolish, but he is also painfully sincere."

Davitt grumped. "Well," he said after a while. "You seem all right for round-ears. But I swear, you ask me to forge you a mithril blade and you're going to be shitting blood for a week."

"Thank you," Quirk said, keeping her smile polite.

"But you want something, right?" said Davitt. "Otherwise you would have rode on past, and I wouldn't be stuck out here trying to pretend we're not all shitting in our britches."

Will smiled at that. And Davitt seemed to catch that it was genuine smile, because he returned it.

"Well," Will said, "let me ask you this: Are you having any trouble with Barphists?"

Will watched from an upper-story window as Barph's priests walked into the dwarven enclave. He was crouched low, down on all fours—not just to keep out of sight, but also because the roof of the dwarven building was only five feet above his head. His sword was drawn.

There was no organization to the Barphists as they sauntered in. Will supposed that was by divine writ. There could be no leader. There could be no formation.

Will had, in the later part of his life, considered himself something of a rebellious sort. If you had asked him prior to his personal acquaintance with the gods which of them he found the most sympathetic, he would have answered, "Barph" without a second thought. Barph was the god who flailed against the rules, who fought for his right to kick back and drink and carouse and leave all his responsibilities for another day.

That, though, Will was beginning to realize, required that there be something to flail against. Order and chaos had to fight each other to find balance. When order was killed and chaos allowed to run rampant...

One of the Barphists stopped, turned, and studied the front of a dwarven house. It was small and neat, with potted plants lined up outside and shutters on each window, each painted with a surprisingly lifelike lily. The Barphist nodded, then set about the shutters with her club. By the time the house's occupant was outside, hands in her hair, most of the shutters lay in ruins.

Ignoring the screaming woman, the Barphist also took the time to smash a couple of windows. She stepped back to admire the effect.

Much more chaotic, Will was sure.

The house's owner didn't seem to appreciate the new aesthetic.

The Barphist decided to give her a more nuanced understanding by rearranging her face to the same parameters.

The club went up, the club went down. So did the dwarf. Blood sprayed from her mouth.

Will knew that he should hold. He knew that the Barphists were not, as Lette had described it, "in the snare." They needed them farther down the street. He knew that they had told the dwarves to act as if nothing were different. He knew that he had just preached moderation and patience to the dragons, who were all over a low rise, straining at the leash Will had sent Quirk to put on them.

But he didn't care. All the other Barphian priests were engaged in acts similar to this bully with her club: knocking down doors, knocking down anything that was lined up too neatly, and knocking down anyone who tried to stop them. One priest had a produced an oil flask and was fussing with a tinderbox.

Will had seen too many villages that had received this treatment. They weren't razed to the ground. Not beaten into ruin. But they were villages tortured to the edge of survival. They were villages left crippled and clinging to subsistence: a few houses burned, not quite half the windows smashed, the well water soiled, but still on the edge of drinkable. He had seen villagers' spirits broken and their wounds left to fester.

This village had held out longer than most. It was not easy to stumble over. The dwarves had fended off one pack of zealots. But Davitt had told him that a Barphian temple in Vinter had been sending scouts over the border on longer and longer raids. Forty or more priests had been spotted in the area the previous day.

The ambush had been hastily arranged, but Will was certain they had the numbers to win. He had close to two hundred of his followers hidden around this village. All of them waiting for his signal. All of them waiting for the Barphist to enter "the snare." They were leaner and harder now than when he'd found them. Food had been scarce on the trip down, mostly scavenged and stolen, and often coming with losses. Barphists had ambushed them. Gratt's once-dead had harried them. Their weak had been winnowed from the pack.

And so Will was done with waiting.

He flew out the window as the club went up a second time. He landed awkwardly, struggled up. He yelled. And he could feel the surprise rippling around him. He could actually feel it, the part of the Deep One within him stretching out, probing and touching with unfingers. He knew through it that some of his followers felt shock, and some of them felt disappointment, and some of them felt red-hot rage that he feared might sear his mind, but he knew most of them felt excitement and pride in him, and that each and every one was ready to charge.

And as he broke into a run, he felt their belief.

The first Barphist aimed her club at Will. Will felt his body move at a speed that had nothing to do with his muscles. He felt reality part for him to proceed through it to where he wanted to be. The Barphist's club struck air. Will's elbow struck her jaw, spun her head around with enough force that there was a violent snap and the priest collapsed still on the ground.

Will let out a yell. This might not be stealing belief from Barph, but it certainly would rob him of some believers.

When it was done, Will stood before the gathered victors and licked the dried blood from his lips. There was, he thought, a chance that he should have washed the gore off before he gave this speech.

"What does Barph promise you?" he shouted at them all. "Love? Safety? To hold you tender in the safety of his bosom? No. He promises you none of that. All he has ever promised you is the threat of force."

The dwarves looked vaguely shell-shocked by this idea. He

suspected it had been quite the day for them. A lot of blood had been spilled in their streets. Likely, more of it was their own than they'd expected. The Barphists had fought with zealous fury.

But the Barphists had lost, and Will had talked to Quirk and gotten the dragons up in the air above them, screaming and roaring, and excited to eat the corpses Will and his followers had provided. And all in all the victory felt impressive.

"But what if you kowtow to Barph's threats?" he shouted to the crowd. Most of them were his followers, and had heard this speech or some variant of it many times before. They didn't seem to tire of it, though.

"Are you saved?" he called. "Spared indignity and harm?" His derisive laugh was practiced.

"What if, instead, you defied his threats?" he asked for the umpteenth time. "How exactly would life be worse?"

He carried on with his message. He added a few new ideas here and there, but he didn't truly tell the dwarves anything they didn't already know. All he did was show them a crowd they could hide in.

But that, he knew now, was enough. He could feel the rising energy in them. The hope. The mounting joy. The fierce rediscovery of pride.

How many, though, would be dead after they found the next Barphian temple? And after the next once-dead attack? And after the food ran short again?

But he didn't ask them those questions. Because all the hope his words were giving them was being fed back to him, making him more powerful, making his chances of being one day able to take on Barph just a little better.

And so, despite the coming death toll, he stood there, and he pontificated, and he shouted, and he insulted, and he joked and japed, and he brought them over. He convinced them to leave behind their lives and their homes and, above all, their worship of Barph.

When he was done, he stumbled away, feeling spent, feeling overfull of other people's energy. Foreign voices and emotions chattered in his head. He waited for them to settle, for his own voice to reestablish itself.

Lette found him sagged over a barrel of water, trying to wash the gore and horror away.

"Good speech," she said, putting a hand on his shoulder.

"What am I condemning these people to?"

"A life lived free of the yoke." Her hand massaged tense muscles. "That's not a bad thing."

Will chewed his lip. "Seventy-three dead, Lette."

She sighed. Then grabbed his chin forcefully and made him look her in the eye. "Are you seriously telling me," she snapped, "that you want to stand up in front of this crowd and tell them that you've changed your mind, that it's time to pack it in? Because I'm not mopping up that mess."

"No," he said. Then he hesitated. Because... "I'm just...I don't know."

Lette sighed. "Look, I know I told you I loved you, but that doesn't mean that my tolerance for self-indulgent whining has abruptly increased."

Will smiled. She was right. If he was honest, he didn't want her advice, he wanted to assuage his guilt, and she was far from being the right person for that. That was why he loved her, after all.

And if she could condone his becoming something harder-edged, someone who didn't feel bad about making the hard sacrifices, why shouldn't he? Why shouldn't he just take the power and run with it? He had a cause, he had something bigger than himself to commit it to.

He nodded. "You're right."

Lette stepped in. "Now that's romantic talk." She stroked his brow.

Will reached out to touch her cheek just in time to feel her body go completely rigid.

"What?" he asked.

Without saying a word she slowly pushed back a lock of hair. The look that crossed her face wasn't one that one typically wanted to see on one's lover's.

"What?" he asked again, at greater volume.

"Will…" Lette's voice was barely above a whisper. "You know how you were fairly convinced the purple stuff was okay?"

"Are you trying to make sure I don't anymore?" He was not handling this well, but she wasn't either, and he hoped that gave him an excuse.

"Well—" She hesitated, looked away. "Will, I think you're growing an extra eye."

29

The Pillage People

Bellenet. It had been described to Gratt in so many ways. Batarra's capital. Batarra's pride. Its heart. Its soul. The jewel placed upon its crown.

Gratt was going to have to slap someone's jaw off.

Bellenet was, as far as he could tell from this distance, a stinking midden heap surrounded by fields that lay either fallow or overgrown, providing feasts for rodents and insects alone.

Then again, given what he'd seen of Batarra so far, perhaps this truly was what most of the citizens held as a treasure. For two weeks he'd marched his army through its collapsing countryside. For two weeks he'd kicked over collapsing farmsteads and burned tinder-dry towns. For two weeks the few who had survived these encounters had scrambled over the dead to pay obeisance at his feet. The Batarrans were a craven people, he had decided. A pathetic people. Perhaps it made sense that their capital was pathetic.

It just also happened to make them a truly disappointing people to conquer.

Still, Bellenet had walls. He could make out the people perched upon them, so it had defenders. This could perhaps provide an amusing distraction, if nothing else.

He formed up his troops, bellowing at and bullying his lieutenants, who in turn bellowed at and bullied their sergeants, who in turn bellowed at and bullied and beat bloody the

Batarrans until they stood in rough squares, gripping swords and pikes and knives bound to branches and bits of planking with nails jutting from them and pretty much anything else they had managed to seize.

"Some of you think of this as your home," Gratt growled as he stood at his army's head. "Some of you think you have family in this city. Some of you think your loyalty should lie here." He licked his tusks. "You are wrong.

"Some of you think Barph is your god now. You are wrong.

"Some of you think that death is the worst thing that could happen to you. You are wrong."

He stared them all down. A whole army. His whole army. And some of them, some who had been with him since the start, down in the Hallows when the opportunity to seize control had first come, some of them were grinning along with him, and he almost felt affection for those troops. He suspected many of them would die today, but he felt no sadness at that. Everyone and everything here was a tool, and now all he had to do was hone it.

"I am your god now!" he yelled at them. "I am your home and your heart and your mother and father and your family. I am everything you have. I am your will, and your hope. I am your home. When you breathe, it is because I will it. When you die, it is because I will it. And the only thing you need to fear, the thing worse than all other fates, is disappointing me."

His breath steamed in the air.

"I want Bellenet!" he roared at them. "Give it to me."

His lieutenants roared. Their sergeants roared. His army moaned and shouted and screamed, and they moved, and all he cared about was that last. And they streamed across the battle-field toward his prize.

The heart of Batarra. Its pride. Its soul. Its capital. And it would be his, and so would this land. The first country to fall, but far from the last.

He watched as his troops tore across the fields toward Bellenet's main gates. He waited to watch the arrows fall like rain. He waited for the sweet music of screams.

And he was disappointed.

As he watched, no arrows came. No pitch was poured from the walls. No calls of defiance were screamed. As he watched, he saw the gates of Bellenet open.

He saw his army stumble to a confused halt.

Gratt spat. If you wanted something done right...

He strode across what should have been a battlefield, kicking his troops aside, toward the small delegation that wavered and waved at him from Bellenet's gates.

"Welcome!" a man was calling. He was short, and wearing a wig almost half his own diminutive height. It was made of curls, and mice ran in and out of them as Gratt watched.

"Welcome, brave conqueror!" he called again. "Welcome to Bellenet!"

Gratt stood before him. Towered over him. "What," he said to one of his lieutenants, "is the meaning of this?"

"They..." The lieutenant paused. He knew this tone well enough. He worked his jaw. "They have surrendered, General."

The bewigged man from the Batarran delegation took a few halting steps forward. "We cannot say how happy we are to see you, brave conqueror. We cannot say how difficult the past six months beneath the heel of Barph have been. Everything has gone..." The man's voice broke. "They're eating people in there. They're fucking..." He tried to regain his composure. "We welcome you. Our city is yours. Everything. Our coffers. Our women. Our men. Whatever you want. Just...protect us. Please. Please protect us." He was weeping openly.

Gratt ignored the crying man. He fixed all the power of his stare upon his lieutenant.

"You accepted his surrender?" he growled.

"I...," the lieutenant stuttered. "I...what?"

"What?" echoed the weeping Batarran.

"I said," Gratt growled loud enough for half his army to hear, "that I want this city. Let me be clear." He raised his voice. He roared. "I want this city's bloody corpse! I want its beating heart in my hand! I want its gore upon my tongue. I do not want its limp fucking prick." He turned and buried his claws in the chest of the weeping man. He hoisted his gurgling corpse aloft while the rest of the Batarran delegation cowered and screamed. While his army gasped. He flexed his fingers and the corpse came apart, wet and ragged.

"Give me this city!" he screamed.

After a moment his army poured in.

Gratt stood in fire and rubble. Corpses stretched out all around him. He licked the blood from his claws. All in all, Bellenet had been less of a disappointment than he'd feared. Its citizens, once properly motivated, had provided a passable whetstone on which to hone his troops.

"What does it feel like?" he asked.

He'd had Lawl dragged here, to the heart of Bellenet, to the buildings that had once served as its halls of governance. The roof had gone from this room, the sky occluded only by smoke, not by delicate painted plaster.

They'd found a cage down in the jails, and he'd had it dragged up here, installed his former master in it, away from the other gods. He turned and stalked toward the chained deity. "What does it feel like to be the lowest thing in this world? You created this place, and now it is simply rubble. How pathetic does that make you?"

It was, Gratt suspected, shallow of him to derive so much pleasure from this. To make Lawl wallow in his misery. And yet...so what if he was shallow? Who would dare accuse him of being so? Whom would he let live if they said so?

"Slightly less pathetic," Lawl said, "than the man who claimed to be a god at the open gates of a broken city." He turned a thin smile on Gratt. "Hypothetically speaking, of course."

Gratt growled softly. Lawl was a proud one. But, he supposed, therein lay the pleasure in breaking him.

"And yet you are chained by such a man," Gratt pointed out. He reached down, snapped the leg off a corpse, started chewing on it.

"And yet I know that as proud as you are now," Lawl said, picking himself up off the floor of the cage, "as strong as you think you are, as powerful as you think you are, you are nothing before the bastard child of my loins. Your blood will never fill the font at the heart of the Summer Palace. The worst of us will crush you without even thinking twice about it. You are nothing to him."

Gratt ground his teeth. "And what about you, old man? What are you to him?"

Lawl hesitated. The blow, Gratt saw, had landed. "He shall not kill me," Lawl said stiffly. "I shall endure long after you are gone. Barph's madness will end. He will see my rightful place."

Gratt just laughed at that. It was pathetic.

But Lawl wasn't quite broken. Not quite yet. "Your only chance to stand against him," Lawl said, "has already slipped between your fingers. I gave you your only hope. Remember that. Remember that for millennia you were too afraid to seize the Deep Ones' power. Willett Fallows, a mere mortal, exceeded you, and then he walked away. All you are doing now is marking time until Barph feels crushing you would be amusing."

Gratt suddenly was no longer having fun. He waved, and his men returned to haul Lawl back to the other gods.

"Enjoy remembering what power was," he called after the god. "Enjoy remembering mattering."

And still, as around Gratt Bellenet burned, all he could taste was ash.

30

The Passion of the Quirk

Quirk was quite pleased that Will's troops managed to avoid a battle for a full three days after the dwarven enclave. That was a pretty good stretch for them.

They were skirting the southern border of Batarra, avoiding plummeting into Vinland and risking the wrath of a nation that had been zealously devoted to Barph's worship even before his ascendancy to omnipotence. There were no recruits for Will's cause to be found there. Instead they were angling toward the Vale and the elves, who were always a rebellious sort and more likely to be open to the message of kicking a god in the nuts.

The land here was less populated than the rest of Batarra, and the tangled wilderness of bramble and scrub made a nice change from the desolation of wasted villages and farmsteads. It was more overgrown than the last time she'd been in this part of the world, but it wasn't actively causing people to starve, or serving as a graveyard, so that was nice.

And then, on the third day, as they were making their way through the tangle of a wood, Yorrax landed beside her and said curtly, "A small army ahead," and then started to flap her wings.

Quirk was walking with Afrit. They were holding hands, which was a thing Afrit liked to do, and a thing Quirk was acclimating herself to. Physical contact was still difficult for her, but she was working on it.

She had seen Yorrax a few hours before—she was still nominally in charge of Will's dragon contingent, and still seemed to command some respect there, but Quirk and Yorrax barely exchanged more than pleasantries anymore. Yorrax had been effectively cut out of the dragon leadership, and was used by her brethren as little more than a messenger. Quirk felt bad about the whole situation, but the alliance with the dragons was fragile enough that she didn't want to mess with it further.

Still, she felt oddly embarrassed to be caught here, hand in hand with Afrit. Her time with Yorrax had been oddly intimate. They had shared a strength of commitment she had not shared with many others.

She let go of Afrit's hand.

"Is that all?" she asked.

Yorrax snorted and took off back into the air.

Quirk sighed, then left Afrit to go and find Will.

Planning followed, and arguing, and Balur's insistence that he be allowed to go "blade deep in the rectum of anyone who is putting himself in front of me," and Lette explaining why that was a turn of phrase most people avoided outside of a particular sort of bordello, and Balur's insistence that this was the fault of "stupid human language," and then suddenly the dragons were all in the air, and fire was raining down, and as usual it was all rather academic and far too late.

"To the front line!" Will grabbed Quirk and shoved her forward, in the direction of the screaming. "Get out there! Save people!"

And Quirk ran. This was what she did now, after all. Academia was behind her. Saving the world was before her. This was what it took.

And yet, as the two forces smashed together, mixed, mingled, and swirled about in a wild, bloody embrace, Quirk found that, as was increasingly the case these days, she was only truly interested in saving one person.

Quirk pushed, and shoved, and burned her way through the chaotic tangle of bodies until she found Afrit.

Afrit was standing on a fallen tree, gripping a short sword Quirk had scavenged for her from a Barphian temple. She was holding it in both hands, pointing it at anyone who came near. It was not a particularly threatening sight, but for reasons that would forever be beyond Quirk, it filled her heart with pride.

And she was alive.

Oh gods. Oh gods. Oh gods. Afrit was alive.

Afrit had died to save Quirk's life, and with that act had unlocked some hidden chamber of Quirk's heart, a piece of her soul she had assumed was simply not there. And yet the chamber had remained empty, because its occupant was no longer here, was down in the Hallows, lost forever.

And so Quirk had filled that chamber with hate and rage and war.

But now she had cast that all out. Because the chamber's occupant was—impossibly—returned to her.

She was still in free fall. She was still on the course of that previous life. She could not get her footing, could not even think what she would do if she could.

"Quirk!" Afrit called to her, called her back to the here and now. "Thank the gods, you're okay."

"To be honest," said a voice at Quirk's shoulder, "I don't think any of us had anything to do with it."

It was Cois, who had gotten a crossbow from somewhere only zhe knew and was busy reloading it. Quirk was surprised Balur had left hir alone in a fight. The pair seemed inseparable these days.

Still, she couldn't focus on that. Afrit was still perched on her fallen tree trunk, and Quirk could see a group of three enemy soldiers—surprisingly unscathed—approaching her. And they seemed to know what to do with the swords they were holding.

Quirk sprinted to Afrit's side, pulled on the fire in her heart, set it loose, and sent it spinning toward the three soldiers. Two went down, one dived free. Then a crossbow bolt punched through the steel of his helmet, and he stopped moving.

Quirk glanced over at Cois, who was bent over the crossbow's loading mechanism. Zhe glanced up and flashed Quirk a smile.

Afrit relinquished her two-handed grip on her sword long enough to push sweaty strands of hair out of her face. "You shouldn't be here with me," she said. She seemed to be trying to avoid clenching her teeth, and her knuckles on the sword were white. She spoke between small pants of breath. "You should be out on the front. They need you there."

"I'm not going anywhere you're not," Quirk told her.

"Then I'm going to the front," Afrit said.

"No!" Quirk called, but she was too slow. Afrit was leaping off the tree trunk with an inelegant downward slash of the sword that one of the Barphists dodged easily. Quirk roasted the man with a blast of flame to the face before he could skewer Afrit through her neck.

"No!" she said again, more forcefully this time, running and catching up with Afrit, grabbing her by the shoulder and pulling her back so that another Barphist's sword swipe went wide of its mark. She turned the man into a living pyre who went reeling back into his compatriots.

"I love you," she said to Afrit, "but you are not good at this. You have to stay back. You have to be safe."

"And you," Afrit spat, seeming oblivious to the fact that Quirk had just saved her life twice, "need to be at the front. Every time you save me, you let five others die, and I will not have that on my conscience."

And what could Quirk say to that? That she would let a hundred die if it meant Afrit lived? A thousand? It was true, but how could she say it? And how could she fight for this cause if it was true?

But now was not the time to figure out an answer. Their

argument was abruptly a moot one: The front of the fight had come to them. A desperate push by fifty or so enemy soldiers, clustered in a tight knot of blades, barreling forward, tearing through the lighter arms of her and Will's troops.

Dragons circled overhead, but the two forces were tangled together so tightly now that any more bombardments would kill as many of the dragons' allies as of their opponents. Not that Quirk was completely sure that the dragons cared, but at least they held their fire for now.

Quirk held out an arm, used it to force Afrit away from the oncoming slaughter.

"You should—" Afrit started again, but Quirk shook her head violently. She wasn't going to let loose a burst of her own flame and give away Afrit's position. She wasn't sure she could take down all fifty attackers before Afrit was seriously injured.

Then it was right in front of them: the price Will was still willing to pay for revenge. The price, it turned out, Quirk was willing to pay for Afrit's safety. The unprotected people of Avarra being hacked down as they fought for freedom from oppressors.

Blood was everywhere. Gashes opened up in flesh. Great ragged wounds. People screaming, collapsing. The smell of it almost overwhelming.

Quirk forced Afrit away from it, shoving bodily.

And then suddenly, something changed; there was a violent shift of momentum in the fighting. With her back to it, Quirk wasn't sure what it was at first, but then she glanced back and made it out. Lette. Lette tearing and stabbing, pirouetting in a ballet of violence through the men and women, flinging knives, dancing around blades. It was a beautiful sort of suicide. A deranged attack that seemed to work only because of the sheer shock it caused.

"She's going to get herself killed." Afrit was still breathless. "We should help her."

But they didn't. They both stood, and they watched as

somehow, impossibly, Lette reversed the current of this fight. The knot of attacking soldiers broke apart, spilled away from her. Their own forces fell on the stragglers without mercy.

And then it was over. All of it. They had emerged victorious once more. Everyone was cheering. Lette stood over the fallen bodies of her foes, two bloody swords raised, their blades crossed in a victorious symbol of defiance. People gathered around her, cheering, lifting her onto their shoulders.

Lette, who had risked her life and saved so many.

Afrit shook her head. "That should be you."

Quirk looked at Afrit. Because it certainly wasn't jealousy she felt. And it wasn't guilt either. She was separate from this now. She had become peripheral to the fight that had consumed six months of her life.

"I don't want it to be me," she said.

Afrit's expression wasn't exactly accusatory, and it wasn't exactly sad. Frustrated perhaps. "Maybe not. But they need it to be you."

"They don't—" Quirk started.

"Don't lie to me." The snap of Afrit's words caught Quirk off guard. "Lie to yourself perhaps, but not to me."

"I was protecting you." Defensive wasn't the tone Quirk wanted to hit, but she found herself unexpectedly backed into that corner.

"I don't need your protection."

That was almost a laughable thing to say, but Quirk was self-aware enough to know laughter would be very much the wrong move.

"If I hadn't—" she started again.

"Then I would have died," Afrit finished for her. "But I would have died for a cause. For something that matters. I am here to fight, Quirk. I am here because this fight matters to me, and to this world. This fight is for all Avarra. Neither of us is bigger than that."

"You are to me." It was all Quirk had. It was everything in her heart.

And finally Afrit's anger broke, and she said, "Oh, Quirk," and she almost took Quirk in a hug, but remembered just in time and just held both her hands. "I love you," she said. "I do. And I love that you love me. But..." She shook her head. "How many people died today because we love each other?"

And the answer was *I don't care,* but Quirk couldn't say that. She knew she couldn't. So she nodded, and said, "You're right," and tried to smile as she lied to the woman she loved.

31

The Things We Do for Love

By the time Balur found her, Lette was very drunk indeed. For his part, Balur felt worryingly sober. It was an odd, deeply uncomfortable role reversal.

He stood over Lette as she sat with a group of hard-looking men and women. When she looked up at him she was slightly cross-eyed. There was an open cask of ale to her side and a pair of dice in her hand.

"What is it you are doing?" he asked her, even though it was startlingly obvious.

"Damaging my decision-making process until I lose a substantial amount of..." She looked at the dice in her hand, then the others sitting with her. "What are we betting again?"

"The right to stab Barph in his hairy balls," said another of the women.

"Until I lose a substantial amount of privilege to stab Barph in his hairy balls," Lette said to Balur. "Apparently." She blinked. "I could have sworn it was—"

"Can we be having a word?" Balur cut in.

"It's my throw." She sounded petulant.

"Look," Balur said. "I am going to be the one who is stabbing Barph in his hairy balls, so this whole game is being moot. Be coming with me. We are needing to talk."

Lette sighed, then tossed the dice carelessly into the air. "Doesn't count," shouted one of Lette's fellow players, while she spent several seconds figuring out how to uncross her legs. Once she was done, Balur led her away to a relatively quiet spot where he could embarrass himself undisturbed.

"We are being tribe, right?" he began. Lette nodded with a degree of emphasis that could only be achieved after a certain amount of alcohol had removed a certain degree of gross motor control. With that settled, Balur went on. "And what is being my role in that tribe?" he asked.

"To make really terrible decisions about battle strategy," said Lette.

Balur nodded as sagely as his outlook on life would permit him to. "Yes," he said, which he thought caught Lette rather flat-footed. He generally tried to avoid this level of self-awareness and honesty. It tended to damage his bubbly optimism.

"So," he went on, "I am therefore wondering," and now he came to the crux of it, "what the fuck was that?"

Lette stared at him with at least one of her eyes. "Was what?" she asked.

Balur sighed. She was going to make this difficult. "Let me be giving you a hypothetical," he said.

Lette rolled her eyes, and most of her head went with them. "Just because Cois finally taught you what a hypothetical is doesn't mean you have to use them in every conversation."

"Say there is being a group of fifty soldiers attacking us," Balur plowed on without stopping. "Which one of us is wading arse deep into combat with them?"

Lette shot a finger at him. "That isn't a hypothetical, you jack-ass. That's you using a very specific example to make a pointed criticism."

Which was exactly how Cois had taught him to use hypotheticals, so he said, "Yes."

"Look," said Lette, and waved her hand at nothing in particular. "They're dead. I'm fine. It's all good. You are being a ninny."

Again, Balur couldn't directly refute her claims. "Yes," he

said. "I am. Which I am hoping is emphasizing how stupid what you did was being. I am not being the ninny in this tribe. You are not being the one who wanders into improbable fights. We are having what some people are calling a dynamic. You are messing with that balance. I am here doing the speech you should be giving me. Neither of us is being comfortable. Both of us are wishing it could be over."

Lette blinked at him slowly. She leaned back, failed to stop as she reached her tipping point, rocked back dangerously, managed to right herself with a minimum of grace, and blinked at him again.

"Jealous," she said.

"What?" he said.

"You're just jealous," she said, and flicked hair out of her eyes. "I got the glory. I got the kills. I've got just as much love as you do now. I'm blood-drenched and happy, and you've got a girl-friend who's a boyfriend, and whose tits are, quite frankly, a bit saggy, and you're jealous of me. And I'm glorious like a butter-fly. And you're not."

Balur decided, on the grounds that he had known Lette a long time, and that she was very drunk, and that he had probably said worse things to her, but mostly because no one else was looking, that he would not break her nose.

Instead he cuffed her around the back of the head and left her to regain consciousness. Then he went and made very vigorous love to Cois, and at the end he was satisfied that every aspect of hir physicality was spectacular, and not saggy in the slightest.

Afterward he lay beside hir, and hir thin, gentle arms draped across the solid breadth of his chest. He watched the soft down on them move with his breath.

He realized he was still sober. Cois had a wineskin not far from hir bedroll. He considered getting up and taking it. Per-haps things would have gone better with Lette if he'd been drunk. Life generally seemed more fun when he was drunk.

But he didn't get up. He lay there and watched the soft white hairs move back and forth.

"You're not thinking about me," said Cois, wriggling voluptuously beside him.

"Lette is going to get herself killed," he said. He couldn't see any point in evasive subterfuge. He never had before, he wasn't going to start now.

"Why?" Cois's finger traced convoluted designs across his chest.

"I do not know."

"Does she?"

Balur licked the air, tasted the scent of their bodies heavy on the air.

"I do not think so."

"Would it make you feel better if she did? Or you did? Or both of you?"

Balur licked the air again. He liked its taste. It soothed him the way that caving in a man's skull normally did.

"It would make me feel better if she stopped. If she was Lette."

Cois smiled into his side. He ran a finger up and down the ridges of hir spine, careful to not tear the skin with his claws.

"Put some trousers on and come with me," zhe said.

"I am always having less fun with you when my trousers are being on," he groused, but he did as zhe asked anyway.

Zhe led him out of their makeshift tent and back out into the crowds that were encamped near the site of the would-be ambush. A line of men were still digging shallow graves for the dead. A few dragons still swooped back and forth above the trees. But for the most part, people seemed to be gathering for another of Will's speeches.

"I have been hearing many of these," Balur said. "He is becoming very repetitive."

"I brought the wineskin."

"Fine then."

They found a spot on the ground near the back of the crowd. Cois rested hir head against him.

These days, Will had a makeshift stage of wooden crates that he strode back and forth upon, delivering his speech, railing against all the—incredibly obvious—things that Barph had done wrong in this world. Balur was never quite sure why humans liked having these things enumerated for them, as if they could not do it themselves. Still, the crowd around him seemed happy, and Will puffed himself up like a sparrow in winter as he condemned it all. And there was a sense of energy and excitement to the event that Balur had to confess he quite enjoyed.

"I like to come to these," Cois whispered into his ear, hir breath tickling slightly. "I like to see these people this way."

Balur looked around at the crowd. "Unprepared and defenseless?" he asked.

"They're at their best listening to him," zhe said. "That's what he brings out in them."

"Not their best for battle."

"Look up at the edge of the stage." Cois pointed with hir chin. Balur narrowed his eyes.

Lette was there, standing in what would be the wings if Will had a respectable stage. She paced back and forth, just as Will paced. She didn't look at the crowd but at him as he talked.

"Why do you think she's there?" asked Cois.

"Because she is having terrible taste in men." That was simple enough.

"And why are you here in this crowd?"

"Because you were asking me to be here," he said. "You are knowing that."

Cois pulled away from him, swept an arm at the gathered crowd. "Why are all these people here?" zhe asked. "Why are you here in a forest with them? Why did you end up in the Hallows?" Zhe smiled at him, at his confusion and his irritation, and leaned back against his heavy chest. "I promise, love, if you figure that out, then you'll figure you and her out too."

"This is being like the hypothetical thing, isn't it?" he asked.

"You mean something that you will have to figure out for yourself?" Cois asked, imitating sweetness.

He snarled, but stroked hir hair at the same time.

"Let me put it to you this way," zhe said. "You are here for a reason. Lette has a reason for being on the front lines of every fight. These people all have a reason for being in this crowd tonight." Zhe rose up and kissed him. "It is the same reason for all of you. Although not all of you realize it yet. Apparently."

For all his faults—and Lette had always ensured Balur knew they were many—he was not stupid.

"You are talking about Will," he growled. And he had thought Cois thought better of him than that.

"No," zhe said. "I am not. Or...not exactly. Look at the crowd, Balur. Look at them." There was something beyond hir usual teasing in hir voice, he realized. Something surprisingly urgent.

He looked at them. The poor. The destitute. The desperate. All the fools who always seemed to be clinging to Will's words. Why was he never on the side of the intelligent, well-armed people anymore?

And why wasn't he ever on those sides anymore?

Was that what Cois was getting at?

Because...because...Well, Lette was never on those sides anymore. She had hitched herself to Will and his foolish schemes. And he had...Wait. Was he as weak-willed as all that? Was he following Lette like some lamb waiting for his mistress to take him to the slaughterhouse?

No. He was here because he chose to be here.

He had his reasons for being here.

"Oh gods," he rumbled as realization struck him. "I am having a cause, aren't I?"

Zhe smiled at him. "I'm afraid so, love."

He groaned. "When was this happening? Causes are being for priests and paladins and zealots. Causes are being like giant signs asking for one's arse to be being kicked from one end of Avarra to the other. To be being kicked by me. So I can be making sure the idiots are not talking about their stupid causes." He worked his hands, but there was nothing nearby to crush in them. "Fuck!" he spat.

"They worm their way in, love." Cois stroked his arm.

He looked at hir. "It's not you, is it?" he asked suspiciously.

"You say the sweetest things."

He just stared.

"No, love. As much as I enjoy flattering myself, I am not your cause."

"Good," he growled. However, this still did not tell him what his cause was. He cast about for the offending item.

He could see nothing but Will pontificating, and the crowd. The crowd...

Oh gods. Zhe had wanted him to look at the crowd.

"Oh," he said.

"I'm afraid so, love."

"Them?" When in the Hallows had that happened?

"Yes, them." Cois planted another kiss on his cheek.

Balur looked at them. The poor. The destitute. The desperate. His cause.

"Fuck," he said again.

32

Fired Up

Yorrax was ready to spit fire. She was ready to burn these humans to ash.

Quirk had lied to her.

Or...Quirk had tricked Yorrax into lying to herself *about* Quirk. Yorrax had thought she had finally found a human with the heart of a dragon. But instead Quirk had turned out to be a human with the heart of a craven worm. Just as all the dragons of Avarra had the hearts of worms. Because all the true dragons of Avarra were dead.

All except Yorrax.

She had almost forgiven Quirk for her betrayals on Natan, for her derisive words and her demeaning attitude. Quirk was only human. Quirk could be weak and stupid from time to time. Yorrax could understand that. She had been angry, but then... then they had ridden at the head of an army. Yorrax had finally assumed her rightful place...

But then...

But then Willett gods-hexed Fallows. Might all the heavens pour piss upon him. Might she lick his liver from his fresh corpse.

Quirk had kowtowed to Will Fallows. Quirk had nodded and bowed and scraped, and...Gods, it galled Yorrax. Quirk had *submitted* to him.

Perhaps Yorrax could have forgiven Quirk, if Quirk had not embarrassed her on Natan. If Quirk hadn't made such a show of beating her. If she had held a civil tongue in her head in the presence of others. If, after all of that, Yorrax had not been so kind and magnanimous as to allow Quirk to ride her back...

Yorrax snarled, fire escaping in a rush, and the body of the Barphist she was consuming turned to ash. Fuck.

Yorrax had allowed Quirk to ride upon her back. And then Quirk had *submitted* to Will Fallows's wishes.

Will gods-hexed Fallows. Might he burn in eternal fires. Might she suck the marrow from his bones.

There was no reeducating Will Fallows. There was no reasoning with him. More and more he became the petty despot. More and more he saw the dragons not as his rightful masters but as simple tools.

She was going to kill Will Fallows. She was going to show the other dragons that she bent to no human's will. That she was no tool.

Unfortunately, she was not the only one to have spotted Will's growing arrogance.

"If we were to burn him," Netarrax said, his head high above Yorrax's, slurping at a leg that was stuck between two sharp teeth, "then we would lose the other humans."

"We do not need the humans," Pettrax said.

"He says that we do," said Netarrax. "For belief. We have to make humans believe in something that isn't Barph to win."

"We can win without humans. Without belief," said Netarrax.

This, Yorrax thought, stretched belief. Pettrax was old and rheumy eyed and blunt toothed. And he should be reminded of that fact before he took Yorrax's opportunity from her.

"You," said Yorrax from between the larger pair, "couldn't beat the human who wipes Will Fallows's arse."

Netarrax did not take this well.

A massive, taloned foot pinned Yorrax to the ground. She felt her skull grind against the dirty Vinter ground.

"Do not mistake your place, runt," Netarrax growled.

"I ride at the head of the army," Yorrax spat back at him.

"Yes," Netarrax growled. "That way when something strikes you from the air, the rest of us will all be able to laugh together."

Yorrax felt bile and hatred rising in her. That this old man should use something as pitiable as his own bulk to defy her destiny.

"Will Fallows will strike you down," Yorrax bit back at him. Yorrax knew their fears. Even if poking them wasn't particularly wise. "And then," she pressed, "I shall strike him down, and shit on both your corpses." She bared her fangs, refusing to be cowed.

Netarrax's face darkened. He growled, something low and primal, and despite herself Yorrax blanched. And then Netarrax's growl grew louder, and brighter, and suddenly it was laughter, bold and hawked into her face.

"Will Fallows shall help us kill Barph," Netarrax sneered, "and then he shall die." He looked away from Yorrax and into Pettrax's eyes, though he didn't relieve the pressure on Yorrax's head for a moment. "The lion's share of the work, though, shall be ours, and the people shall know it. They shall not worship him. They shall worship us. And that is when Fallows shall die. And then we shall ascend, and we shall be dominant. We shall not be his tools, he shall be ours. And in his pride, and his hubris, he shall never see it." He nodded his massive head, and then slowly brought it down to hover an inch before Yorrax's own.

"But long before all of that, runt," he said, "you shall be dead."

Finally he released his foot. Yorrax gasped and flapped away, spitting sparks. Netarrax ignored her.

But in that moment Yorrax knew she had spoken the truth.

It would be she, not they, who killed Will Fallows. It would be she, not they, who ascended to godhood. It would be she, not they, who was worshipped. And it would not be Netarrax and Pettrax, because when that happened, all they would be was corpses covered in her shit. This she swore.

And so she began to scheme.

33

That Moment When
Two Is a Crowd

Afrit was the first one to spot the ambush.

It had been a while since they'd seen Gratt's forces. They'd heard rumors of what he'd been up to in Batarra, and about the sacking of Bellenet, but it was hard to know exactly what was true now. Under Barph's rule, sources of authority were as hard to come by as honest politicians.

She was walking with Quirk. Because she could. Because for six months she had lived with the conviction that the woman she loved was lost to her forever. Because even if Quirk had made it to the Hallows, the Hallows were near infinite, and the ways to travel to the Void almost as numerous. Reunification had been an impossible dream.

But it had come true all the same. In an age when she knew precisely how powerless every god was, except the one that was set on killing her, a miracle had happened. She had Quirk back.

And in such a way too. Quirk had arrived at the head of a dragon army. She had arrived on a dragon's back. Their great enemy tamed and turned to their cause. The cause that had reunited them.

And it was the cause that was responsible. Afrit was certain of that. There was a weight and momentum to it. And beyond that there was... Well, *righteousness* felt like a pretentious word, but she hadn't gotten to be a professor at the Tamathian University by being afraid of a little pretentiousness. What they were doing was righteous. It held the interests of every sentient species on Avarra at its heart.

So she walked with Quirk.

And then she saw the once-dead ambush.

It honestly wasn't that hard to spot, but Quirk had her eye on the skies and on the dragons that were looping above them. The beasts had a tendency to raid farms for livestock if they went too long without a major battle and corpses to feed upon. Quirk had needed to drive them away from more than one herd of cattle. Farmers had, in her opinion, a hard enough time now that Barphian priests punished herding as forcing unwanted order onto the inherent chaos of animals.

She and Quirk were at the head of Will's followers, trying to keep a semblance of pace with the dragons. It was harder than usual since they had entered the fringes of the Vale—the elves' traditional home. Flora in general seemed to have benefited from Barph's rules, growing rampant and uncontained. Many of the trails and pathways of the Vale's forests had been lost, casualties to this unconstrained growth.

Some Batarrans, it seemed, had seen a potential advantage in this new tangle and taken refuge in the forest. They had, however, apparently forgotten to ask the elves' permission. She and Quirk were approaching a clearing where arrow-dotted tents were testaments to centuries of race enmity and to a lack of diplomacy on both sides.

Near the clearing's edge, Quirk had put a hand on Afrit's shoulder, made her stop while she "scoped things out," which was ironic, as Quirk still had her eyes on the dragons. And for just a moment—though now it was far from the first moment—Afrit felt more than a little frustrated. Because as incredible as it was to have a girlfriend who had ridden at the head of an army of dragons in the name of the cause that had reunited you, it would be nice to have one who would take you seriously in that fight.

Gods, it would be nice to have the one who had ridden at the head of a dragon army once in a while. That woman would be far less of a mother hen surely...

Afrit had pushed that thought aside. They were reunited. That was enough. Right? Then she had stared disconsolately at the sad little punctured tents.

Which is when she had seen the fabric move, and the man with a bandanna striped in the colors of Gratt's army poke his head and his crossbow out from behind one flap.

"Oh piss," she said quietly. And then she said far more loudly, "Ambush!"

Which, Afrit realized almost immediately, was not the best thing to say when the bulk of your friends were still two or three hundred yards behind you in hard scrub and there was an unfriendly man with a crossbow twenty yards away across a clearing.

Fortunately, the man took longer to realize this than Afrit, which gave Afrit a chance to dive for cover. The crossbow bolt slammed into a fallen tree trunk she had dived behind. It was termite-ridden and incapable of providing exactly the cover Afrit was after, but it at least deflected the bolt so that it glanced away over her hip.

Then Quirk started yelling, and the fire began.

The man and his tent and the surrounding ten feet of space disappeared in a ball of flame.

This, Afrit realized, was probably an even worse idea than yelling, "Ambush!"

The Vale was not a dead or dying wood, and there had been rain, but even live wood would burn if given enough encouragement, and there were more than a few dry leaves lying on the ground.

And so Afrit found herself tackling her girlfriend to the

ground while other panicked once-dead soldiers shot crossbow bolts at both of them.

Quirk stared at Afrit in confusion. "What are you—?"

"Saving us from a forest fire!" Afrit snapped.

Quirk considered. "Oh," was the best defense she seemed able to summon.

The once-dead man had friends, it seemed. They too had successfully identified that the best way to prevent forest fires was to prevent Quirk from starting them. They however, were more predisposed to use pointy metal to express their opinions. More crossbow bolts flew. Quirk rolled, forcing Afrit beneath her. It was, Afrit's racing mind registered, a maneuver she had been rather hoping to enact in a more intimate setting, but this was the first time Quirk's deep-set distaste for physical intimacy had allowed them to achieve it.

"Let me up!" Afrit was still snapping.

"They'll shoot you."

"They'll shoot both of us unless I get back to the body of the troops and let them know what's going on."

"You shouted, 'Ambush!'" Quirk pointed out.

"The trees muffle things."

"I'll go," Quirk said.

"Then you'll get shot."

"So you admit it!"

A crossbow bolt whirled past their heads.

Afrit drew a breath. "The dragons listen to you. You are a mage. You are more important to this cause than I am. If I can draw their fire or get help so you survive, that is the most important thing."

Quirk's face could have been made of steel. "I will not let you sacrifice yourself for me."

"It's not for you. It's for the cause."

It was out of Afrit before she really considered it. But from the expression on Quirk's face, perhaps she should have. But she meant it. And wasn't honesty part of love?

Quirk opened her mouth. No words came.

"Please, love," Afrit said. "Let me go."

Quirk didn't answer.

And then there was a roar, and the sounds of branches ripping and men screaming, and the hammer-blow flaps of massive wings, and both Afrit and Quirk were buffeted with billowing wind and leaves. They shielded their eyes and stared. Yorrax was there, having torn a ragged hole in the trees. She had two once-dead soldiers in her claws, another one hanging from her jaws. She spat the corpse out.

"Puny humans," she said before opening her wings once more and flying away.

34

Dead Man Talking

Two weeks later, deep in the Vale, Will couldn't sleep. He hadn't been able to sleep for three days. He was still figuring out how to close the new eyes.

There were clusters of them on each of his temples. Small, black glistening things, none bigger than a blueberry. He was sweeping locks of hair down over them. And it wasn't exactly as if he saw with them. His visual field was the same. But there was...awareness. A new sense of what was happening in the peripheries that was hard to define. A heightened awareness of the smallest movements.

Lette had been good about them, he knew. She lay with him now in their makeshift cot, her head upon his chest, slowly rising and falling with each breath. It would have been easier for her to scream and run. But she hadn't. She had stayed. He was a lucky man.

He could hear others moving about outside, attempting to be quiet and failing. Despite the moonless night, he could pick out individual leaves in the tree canopy above when he peered through the holes in the tent's roof.

The strange power that the crowd gave him never left him now. Whenever he spent it, there always seemed to be more left over. He didn't really think about it as "spending" power anymore. It was just something he could do. Something that he was. That he had become.

Afrit had asked him about using the power to put the Hallows back. Now that he had recaptured his power it had been nice to be able to say—truthfully—that he had already tried. He wasn't proud of everything he had done since his return to Avarra, but that at least felt clean. Still, it had not been possible. Not even remotely. The initial rush of power that had come with the Deep Ones' first invasion of his body was utterly spent. He honestly believed he would be able to overthrow Barph before he could fix the Hallows. And that...that did not feel quite so clean.

Slowly he extricated himself from beneath Lette and slipped out of the tent, out into the night. Part of him could tell that it was cold, could see his breath on the air, but he willed himself warm. That was new too.

They had only recruited a handful of elves to their cause since coming to the Vale. It was not that the elves were truly faithful to Barph, just that they were distrustful of "round-ears." But, despite this, some still came. Because...because he was *powerful*, he realized. That was the word for it. *I am powerful.* He turned the phrase over in his head. Tried to figure out how it fit into his idea of himself.

It didn't.

"Master Willett." The voice caught him off guard. One of the men posted as a night guard shuffled out of the shadows and then—of all things—took a knee before Will and touched his forehead with one thumb. Two other men looked over, came, and assumed the same position. When had that started?

"Hello," he said. He felt awkward but didn't want to reveal it. "You can...get up."

"Thanks to you, Master Willett," the three men said in unison. They stood, but they stayed there looking at him. There was something vaguely creepy about the whole thing.

Will looked for escape routes. But simply fleeing from them felt rude.

"How is it tonight?" He hoped that he didn't sound as if he was desperately reaching for the nearest topic at hand.

The men looked at each other. It seemed they were as unprepared for this interaction as he was. Then one broke the silence. "Cold, Master Willett," he said, clapping his hands. "But quiet. And that's how we like it. Keep your people safe."

"Put the fear of a god in those Barphist bastards, so you have," said another.

The third just nodded wordlessly.

"It's a good night to have you out with us," said the first, seeming to gain some confidence.

"Aye. Thank you," said the second.

And the third just nodded.

"Well...," said Will, and then stopped himself. Telling these men that he was out here to avoid company was probably not what they wanted to hear.

I am powerful. I am powerful because of men like these.

That he was out here to avoid company was not what *he needed them* to hear.

"Well, I'm glad," he said, trying to cover the hesitation. He nodded. Best to get out of here before he screwed everything up. "Keep up the good work."

They seemed to glow with pride. And there was a time, maybe just a week ago, when he would have felt that. Would have taken in their high regard for him. But now...now it was drops in the ocean. And honestly, right now their attention was too much.

He could hear them whispering excitedly among themselves as he walked away. They would tell others, he knew. More people would "stumble" into his path. There would be no peace.

There was a voice in his head that whispered he was being a selfish ass, that told him he was taking the sacrifices of men and women for granted, as if he—of all people—actually deserved worship, as if this were somehow his birthright and not the result of his taking the Deep Ones into himself.

He ignored it, though. It wasn't even that hard. Instead he used the scrap of illusion that remained to him to step behind a tree and not emerge.

35

She Has Her Reasons, Dammit

Lette wasn't even sure whom they were fighting this time. They were near the end of the ugly, angry tangle that the Vale had become, so really it could be anyone. Barphists? Gratt's once-dead army? Some confused and overly aggressive peasants? In the dark of the day's end and the shadows of the canopy nothing was clear.

Lette knew their opponents' identity ought to matter, of course. It was just that it didn't. Whoever these people were, they stood in their way. They opposed Will. So she fought. They all fought, hurling themselves at their enemy with scavenged weapons and homegrown ferocity.

It was a more vicious attack than normal. It was difficult to position themselves in among the tightly knit tree trunks. It took a little longer than usual to get the momentum of their inevitable victory going. But by this point Will's followers were getting pretty good at the whole fighting business. There was plenty of on-the-job training. Plus they had dragons.

And Will.

She worried about him, of course. Just not in battle. Not anymore. Now he was something else. Now he was graceful and beautiful in battle. He was like a champion stepped out of a bard's story in all his improbability. Now she watched him as he appeared to flow between their enemies. Fighters came apart in his hands like fresh-baked pastries, spilling stuffing and heat. And at the end he emerged unscathed, barely out of breath.

But she did worry. She worried, because it wasn't like Will to be that sort of man. That sort of killer. And she worried because it wasn't truly human to be that sort of warrior, and Will had taken something inhuman into him. And she worried because…because of the coldness that she felt in him sometimes. Not toward her. But toward everything else.

One of the things she had always loved about Will, no matter whether they were tumbling in the sheets or spitting curses at each other, was that when you tore down everything else, there was a core of iron in him that was utterly unbreakable. There was a part of Will Fallows that simply refused to bend. But now…it was as if that core had grown, was pushing away all the softness that made it palatable. And, yes, she did worry over that.

But then she slit a man's throat and the fight was over, and all she could really do was wipe her blades clean and take in the adulation of the crowd.

Will stood a short distance away, ringed by the dead, roaring dragons above his head, the crowd cheering all about him. He looked dazed, eyes not focused on the here and now. She went over, gripped his forearm, trying to make it look congratulatory and not concerned. After a second his hand gripped her back.

"Are you okay?"

He blinked, then nodded. "Of course."

She caught his gaze, made him look her in the eye. He didn't blink or look away. And praise the gods, his hair was covering those other little eyes. Right now he was…just Will. A little tired. A little harried. More than a little blood spattered. But Will. Her Will.

"I'll need to give a speech," he said. He did not sound overly excited.

"That has rather become your thing." She leaned up, planted a kiss on his bloody cheek. "Give them time to recover, though. People have lost family today." Will had a tendency to want to rush through the aftermath of things these days.

"Right," he said, and nodded. He blinked again. A thought seemed to occur to him. "Are you all right?" He reached out, touched her cheek.

Lette assessed. A blade must have nicked her right flank. And to be honest, her ribs felt more than a little bruised. And her knees ached. And someone had stamped on her left foot. And her arms were aching so furiously she wasn't sure she would be able to make a fist for another hour at least.

"I'm fine," she told him.

Will looked around. "I think I need..." He trailed off, looked up to the heavens. And for a moment she thought maybe he would tell her. Not some superficial thing. But what he actually needed. What it was that kept him up long after she had gone to sleep. But then he looked at her and said, "I think I need some time alone anyway. Before talking to them."

He gave her a quick grin. And it was tentative and shy, and so very Will that she couldn't help but kiss him again.

"You deserve it," she said.

"Thank you," he said, and stepped into the adoring crowd, and then was gone. Actually literally gone. Invisible. He was using his tricks of illusion more and more these days, she'd noticed. Another potential worry.

She would find Balur, she decided. She and the lizard man hadn't spoken much since their disagreement over her new-found enthusiasm for battle a few weeks ago. She had been so drunk she wasn't entirely sure what she'd said. But Balur seemed to have taken it badly. He hadn't sought her out often since then, and if that was how he was going to be, then she wasn't going to be the one to go begging to him. Perhaps now, though, enough time and fighting had passed that they could just share a drink and bypass the whole stupid apologizing business.

She wandered through the crowds slowly working through the aftermath of the fight. Some folk were celebrating already, drinking scavenged wine and elven moonshine. Others were industriously cleaning the weapons they'd scavenged from the fight. Others were shoveling shallow graves. Quirk was directing people to gather up their enemy's dead in preparation for the dragons' feeding. Children came out of hiding places and slashed at each other with sticks and fallen branches, shouting crude battle cries. Some wept at the news of who'd been lost this day.

But for all the people she saw, she did not see Balur. No eight-foot-tall lizard man loomed over the crowd. She had glimpsed him back in the thick of the fighting, she knew. But she'd lost track of him before the end of the fight.

She went back to the dead, her heart tap dancing in her chest, but no, he wasn't there, thanks be to the gods.

That left the chirurgeons' tents, though, which was not much better than the pile of bodies waiting to be buried. Half or more of those who wound up in the tents screamed their way to the grave anyway.

Yet when she arrived at that grim boneyard, those with gashes in their arms and chests and skulls still grinned at her and clapped her on the arm and slapped her on her bruised back. They said, "Thankee" and "Much obliged" and doffed caps and helmets when able.

It still struck her as strange, that gratitude. To be congratulated for the chaos she caused? To be celebrated? That hadn't happened even back in her mercenary days. Not beyond a grateful nod and slightly heavier sack of coins, anyway.

"Balur?" she said to the smiling, blood-flecked faces. "Have you seen Balur?" And they nodded, and they pointed, and her heart grew heavy.

When she finally found the lizard man, though, the only blood on him belonged to other people. He was outside a tent, pacing a groove in the dirt. And truly, this was where she had to stop and wonder what Will had done to the world, because Balur was surrounded by a small crowd. A small crowd patting his arms and shoulders and telling him that everything would be all right. That the best that could be done was being done. A consoling crowd. A comforting crowd. And there was no roaring. No flailing of limbs. No rage. Just concern. The crowd for Balur. And Balur for...

"Oh shit," she said. "Cois."

Balur didn't even look up from his pacing, just nodded.

She elbowed her way through the crowd, fell in beside him. "How bad is it?"

"Arrow to the shoulder," he said.

Lette hesitated, fell out of step with him. "Wait. That's not... It's just an arrow to a shoulder." Which was perhaps not sympathetic, and which the crowd around them didn't seem to take particularly kindly, but in the end it was just meat and bone there. There were none of the more vital organs to worry about.

"Zhe is a civilian, Lette." Balur had rounded his turn and was bearing back down on her. "Civilians do not injure like we do. They suffer. Cois is suffering."

"Cois," Lette started, then lowered her voice and fell back in step. "Cois used to be a god. Zhe is not going to die from some poxy arrow in hir shoulder."

Balur ground his many, many teeth.

"Could be worse," Lette said. "Could have been her knee."

"Shut up," said Balur, but there was the slightest of grins on his face.

"Your companion is right," said one man.

"If you tell me about the time you took an arrow to your knee, so help me..." Lette had a knife in her hand. The man backed up.

"I meant no offense. Only to help assuage Master Balur's fears. His lady—"

And there Lette tried not to scoff.

"—is being cared for by the finest chirurgeon in Master Will's host."

His host. Gods. These people were busy deifying Will. That was something else to worry about.

And then she was distracted from that thought by Balur going and putting his meaty paw on the shoulder of the man who had promised a fine chirurgeon and saying, "I am thanking you kindly." Which prompted her to say, "The fuck, Balur?"

He turned and looked her.

"What?"

"Did you just thank someone kindly?"

Balur nodded and pointed. "This man."

"Like a total pussy?" Which was of course fighting talk, but if Balur didn't punch her now then she would know something was seriously wrong.

Of course if he did punch her, then something would be seriously wrong, but with her sternum, and not with her lifelong friend's mental well-being.

He didn't punch her.

"Gods," she said. "Screw the arrow to Cois's shoulder, what about the one that removed your balls?"

Then he did hit her, but only gently, so she just sat down hard two yards away but didn't break anything.

"I spoke to you," said Balur from many feet above her spinning head. "I was telling you that you were messing with the order of things. That you were playing with a successful dynamic, but you were not listening. And so I was having to talk to Cois. That is on you."

"Zhe did this to you?"

Balur's tongue tasted the air. "You are trying to goad me," he said matter-of-factly.

She stood up. "Yes! I am trying to goad you into being yourself." Lette rubbed her head. "I think I was less worried when I thought you were dead."

Balur looked at her with as beneficent a look as his pointed snout could summon. "Why are you throwing yourself into battle like you are being a berserker?" he asked. "Why are these people here?"

"Why are you talking like you took a blow to the head?"

Balur sighed. He looked at the tent.

"Zhe'll be fine," said someone from the crowd. He put a hand on Balur's forearm. It was a familiar gesture.

Balur sighed. "Will is going to be talking soon," he said to Lette. "Be coming with me. We will be watching him. You will see."

She narrowed her eyes. "I watch Will talk all the time. It's always the same crap." And that did get a gasp from the crowd. It felt somewhat satisfying to shock these cattle. There was a chance it would get them to think critically. Not that she wanted them to stop following Will...but...

Gods, she didn't know what she wanted.

She wanted to be steely, but not too steely. She wanted Balur to be happy with his love, but not different. She wanted the crowd to worship Will, but not give in to blind faith.

She wanted to stop worrying. But she didn't know how. And perhaps that meant Balur was not the only one who had changed.

So she went with the lizard man. Because what else—in the names of the gods—was she going to do?

Some people had set up Will's makeshift stage, well away from the chaos of the earlier fighting. He was pacing around at its edge while the crowd gathered. Again, he hadn't washed himself clean. He looked lean, hungry, powerful—a wolf waiting for his chance to lead his pack in baying at the moon. And her heart beat just a little faster looking at him. And everything made a little more sense. She had a purpose here.

"Cois brought you here?" she asked Balur, who was sitting quite peaceably on the ground beside her. He was nodding and smiling to those gathering around her.

"We have been coming often," he said. "For the past two weeks. After the night we were having our disagreement. Zhe was trying to explain things to me."

"What things?"

"Wait," was all he said. Like an irritating prick.

The crowd gathered around them. There was a warm, friendly air to proceedings. People passed wineskins around. Cheese and flatbreads too. People greeted Balur by name, and he smiled back at them. Old blankets and sheets were spread out. You would never have known these people had been fighting for their lives only a handful of hours ago.

Then Will took the stage, and the crowd roared, and again she felt that sense of reassurance. That no matter her confusion, she was on the right path. That purpose was pointing her feet in the right direction. She even got to her feet to clap along with the others, just so she could watch him pace and snap and snarl.

"They came again today," Will said, his voice ringing out, sharp and clear. "They tried to stop us again. Barph tried to resist the tide of change that we represent. And he failed again. So how powerful can he truly be? Compared to us, how powerful is he truly? How scared do we have him running?"

We. Us. Against him. Against Barph. Slowly he wove them together. And Lette watched him do it. And she smiled.

Balur tapped her on the shoulder. She ignored him. There was something meditative to this. She didn't want to be disturbed.

Balur shoved her shoulder. She turned round, glared at him.

"Do not be looking at him," Balur said. "Be looking at them."

Lette furrowed her brow. Whom was he talking about? But then she saw that he was looking not at the stage but all around them, at the people sitting to their left and right. And despite her still-furrowed brow, Lette followed his gaze.

All about her, people of all ages, races, creeds, and colors sat. All about her were elves, Batarrans, Vinlanders, a few rogue Verrans, and Kondorrans. A family of Salerans she had done her best to ignore. The injured. The whole. Children and grandparents. A broad swath of Avarran life. And here and now they all wore a singular expression. Rapt attention. They stared at Will. They watched his every move. They smiled. And it was exactly the same expression she had worn just a moment before. Just before Balur tapped her.

At certain moments Will allowed the crowd to breathe. And it was not a sophisticated speech, Lette knew. It was jingoism and platitudes. But in those gaps the crowd looked at each other and caught each other's eyes, and they smiled. And they caught her eye, and they smiled at her. And she couldn't help but smile back. Because here they were. Here they stood. Together. United.

"We are having a cause, Lette," Balur said softly. "We were doing our best for a long time, and we were having a good run. But we are having a cause now."

And of course she knew they had a cause. Will bound them all together with a cause. His cause had given her a way to be herself—to kill—without losing her humanity. His cause, her cause, their cause was the death of Barph. It was the struggle toward the ultimate end point. It was what he was standing up there shouting about.

Except now she realized that it wasn't.

Her cause was people. Her purpose was people. These people. And she was their purpose and their cause. And Will was too. And they were his. They were knit together by bonds of desire and delight. And she saw all of it now, all of those connections, stretching out. And for once in her life, instead of feeling trapped or confined . . . she felt as if she'd come home.

36

Power Relations

Barph knew he should be watching Will. Will had a plan, after all. He had a track record of landing surprisingly devastating strikes on opponents who outmatched and outclassed him. He had chosen a course of action that had a chance of success—albeit a chance so thin that you could stick a dress on it and pass it off as a Fanlornian princess. Barph should be keeping an eye on Will.

And yet here he sat, feet dangling over the edge of the heavens, Avarra spread out below him, and he could not take his eyes off Gratt.

He waved a hand, caused another goblet of wine to spin itself out of gold, took a sip.

Gratt had them chained right there. Lawl, Betra, Toil, and Knole. Poor Klink was lost to the Void. And Cois was with Will, of course. He should keep an eye on Will…

Lawl was on his knees. He was talking to Gratt as they rolled over the border of Batarra and into Salera. Gratt was pretending to ignore Lawl. Gratt thought he had disdain for Lawl, Barph knew. Gratt thought he harbored ill will toward Lawl for the years of servitude that had been forced upon him. He thought he had been injured by Lawl.

Gratt, Barph knew, was a petty and pathetic creature who did not begin to understand the depths of pain that Lawl could inflict, nor the depravities of betrayal that he enjoyed. Gratt was not nearly as tricky or chaotic an upheaval in Barph's plans as he had hoped for. He was an unimaginative conqueror marching across Avarra with nothing but a hard-on for subjugation in his hand.

He should really be keeping an eye on Will…

Barph adjusted the focus of his attention. Impossible miles above Lawl, he heard every word as clear as a bell.

"Salera is the key," Lawl was saying. "The cities that believe in Barph heart and soul. You need to go there. You need to undo their belief in him. Only then will he take you seriously. Only then will your challenge be serious."

Gratt snorted. "Do you know why you still breathe, Lawl?" he asked.

"Because my advice will keep you breathing," Lawl barked. "And only—"

"Because you amuse me," said Gratt, cutting him off but still affecting a lazy drawl. "Because it makes me laugh that you think you still have power. That you still have influence. That your opinion matters."

"You think this is victory, don't you?" said Lawl. He was on the verge of tearing his beard out. "You think your accomplishments matter."

This was so delicious, Barph would lick it up if he could.

"Your voice," Gratt said, "is like the chirping of a swallow as the cat creeps up on him."

"I have stood where he stands!" Lawl howled. "My blood has filled the font at the heart of the Summer Palace. I have seen what he sees now. I watched a thousand petty conquerors cross this land, and none of them were anything to me. You don't matter. Nothing you have done threatens him at all."

And the undertones of anguish, of despair in those words. Each one was a lazy finger down Barph's spine, stroking him to the edge of ecstasy.

"Nothing you say matters," Gratt replied. "Nothing at all."

He didn't mean it, Barph knew. Gratt stayed up late at night worrying over this. But that just made it all the better.

"You fucking...mortal!" Lawl raged.

Gratt shook his head. "Ah. No," he said. "No, you cannot accuse me of that anymore. Not given your own state. Or should I remind you of Klink?"

Lawl spat. "Murderous scum."

Gratt laughed. "How many lives are on your conscience, old man?"

But Barph has stopped paying attention. *Why had Lawl said murderous?*

Klink was lost to the Void, but that had happened in the destruction of the Hallows, had it not? So many had been. An amusing twist of fate that Klink was denied his fair due. But that was all, wasn't it?

Lawl was weeping now. Why was Lawl weeping?

Barph landed in Gratt's camp without truly thinking about it. His impact threw Gratt thirty feet through the air. Lawl's cage didn't survive, spars of wood and steel spearing through the air and nearby tents. Screams rose.

Barph ignored it all. He strode toward Gratt. "Where is Klink?" he asked. "Where is my uncle?"

Gratt stood shakily, stared at him. "To arms!" the misshapen arsehole shouted. "The enemy is here! To arms!"

Barph could not say he appreciated this. "WHERE," he thundered, "IS MY UNCLE?"

Gratt bared his massive teeth. He towered above Barph now. He seemed to think that mattered.

"He is a memory," Gratt snarled. "He is dust at my feet. He is lost and gone into the Void at my hand."

At my hand.

Barph tried to contain that phrase. Tried to hold it still and peaceful in his head. But it raged through him. It tore through his insides.

"You?" he asked. "*My* uncle? *You?*"

"And now you," Gratt said. His men were running now, holding hastily recovered swords and spears.

Barph had always intended to rebuff Gratt's ambition. He had always meant to knock him back on his arse. He had always had it in mind that this game of anarchy had its limits. He would win. He was god, after all. The only god. But this... this...

It wasn't that Klink was dead. Klink was, after all, a meaningless god. He was a god of an ambition that served no purpose but to sort humanity into the subjugated and the subjugators through the arbitrary medium of shiny pieces of metal. He was, as Barph had pointed out to him numerous times, the god of greed, no matter what he called it. And when Barph had believed him to be a casualty of circumstance there was a sort of hilarity to it all.

But this... That Gratt had dared...

It was the fucking impudence of it all.

Gratt's men charged. Barph swept a hand through the air. Each and every charging man fell to the earth in two pieces, neatly bisected at the waist. They gasped and flailed and bled and died.

Arrows came and hurled spears. Javelins and throwing axes tumbling end over end. Barph brushed them aside, sent them back to their owners with enough force that the impacts could be heard like a drumroll of wet explosions.

Gratt growled, charged. Barph caught him around the throat. He was a little larger than Gratt now, his body shifting in size so fluidly and quickly that he doubted Gratt was even capable of seeing the transformation. He hoisted Gratt off the ground easily. Size was irrelevant to that, of course. It wasn't really muscles that Barph was using to hold Gratt aloft. It was belief. But size seemed likely to make an impact on Gratt's thinking.

"Lawl," he said into Gratt's frothing face, "was right." He threw the general into the dust. "You think yourself a king. You

are a fucking beggar at the table of power. You are a craven crippled child, and I bestow upon you nothing but my piss."

Gratt growled, and Barph was on the verge of kicking the
general squarely in the head and ending this distraction once
and for all when a voice interrupted events.

"You fucking peasant! You call him a beggar? Better a beggar
than you! Better a worm than you!"

Barph paused, turned. Lawl had recovered from his sprawling pratfall, was standing there, apoplectic with rage. His beard,
once so well groomed, was a tattered ruin. "Ah," Barph said.
"Father. Grandfather. So good to see you."

"You are the beggar!" Lawl frothed with obscenity, seemed
unable to contain himself.

Gratt took the moment to pick himself up, hurl himself at
Barph. Barph caught him by the face, squeezed until the nose
was broken, flung him away.

"Oh, Father," Barph said. "If that were true, then why are you
here? Why are you caged and locked and bound and so very,
very, very, very powerless?"

He reached out and stroked his spitting father's cheek. Lawl
clawed ineffectually at Barph's skin. He might as well claw at
steel.

"Do you know what power is, Father?" Barph asked Lawl.

"I know you're why people preach against inbreeding," Lawl
spat.

"All your years shouting how you were in charge," Barph
said, "and I don't think you ever learned at all." Barph smiled.
"Power is letting you live. It's knowing that I could end you at
any moment, and letting you live with that knowledge. That's
power, Father. Now you know. Goodbye. See you soon."

And with that he left them all there. The screaming, the
dying, the belittled, and the enraged.

It was good to be god.

37

Enhanced Interrogations

In all honesty, Will had expected the Barphists in Tamar to be better organized.

Of course he knew organization was anathema to them, but it was so much a part of the stereotype. Afrit and Quirk with their tight-lipped disapproval of everything were so Tamarian sometimes it was laughable. Tamar was... It was a prissy nation. There was no getting around the fact. So surely even Barphists in Tamar would approach things with a sense of urgency.

And yet it was almost two weeks after they emerged from the Vale until the horizon darkened with a line of the nation's famous horsemen. Dark-skinned warriors astride white-flanked horses—a scene from Will's mother's tales, told by firelight to a wide-eyed child.

There should have been a sense of wonder to it, Will thought. There was a time when there would have been.

That time was past.

The numbers were pretty even for once. Several thousand Barphists all lined up. And they had horses. A tremor ran through Will's forces as the line of men started to pour down the hillside toward them.

Will had dragons, though.

The famous horsemen of Tamar came pelting down the hill in a swirling mass of sweating horse flanks and flashing bridles and whirling manes. Scimitars were hoisted to the skies, whirled like flags on a saint's day. Ululating cries were launched like spears.

And then it all disappeared into flame.

The dragons came in waves, the largest and heaviest plummeting out of the skies first, wings tucked tight, necks outstretched. And then, when it seemed far too late, the wings flared and the long sinuous necks flexed. They pulled out of the dive, skimmed barely seven or eight feet above the surface of the earth. Downdrafts hurled dust and grass into the air. They raced ahead, vertical velocity transmuted into forward momentum. Their massive jaws unhinged. Scales glinted in the stark Tamarian sun. Fire bloomed.

And then the next wave, and the next, and the next. One after another. Five at a time sowing death like rain.

Will had seen some of it before. Back in Batarra he had learned exactly how devastating his new allies could be, and it had turned his stomach slightly. But this was the first time they had faced a massed enemy. This was the first time in a long time that the dragons had been able to attack without worrying about the tree cover of the Vale.

So now, as Will watched his forces realize that they would not be needed, that this attack was aborted before it had begun, all that sickness that had possessed him back in Batarra was nowhere to be seen. Now there was grim satisfaction, even the slim edge of pride. He watched Barph's worshipers fall. He watched the faith of his own people renewed. He swelled.

Five minutes, and it was over. Only the screams of men and horses were left to oppose him. Only the smell of roasting meat drifting over the battlefield.

There was silence. It took him a while to pick up on the feelings of the crowd. Awe touched with horror. And it didn't feel like that at all to him. And he could understand what they felt only because... How did he understand it? It was knowledge that appeared out of nowhere.

"We move on!" he shouted. There was little else to do, to be honest. The dragons would eat these dead, then they would catch up. Some were already landing among the dead, bones crunching and blackened meat spilling juices across scale-covered lips.

"We move on!" he called again. This time they got it, began the slow trudge past the bodies.

He got perhaps five hundred yards before he heard the shrill cry. "Will! Will, come quickly!"

He almost used an illusion to duck away. It was almost instinctive now. But there was something about the tone, and the voice made him think he knew this woman running at him, shouting.

"Will! Come quickly!"

Afrit. How in the gods' names had he forgotten her name?

"Why?" he asked, trying to cover his confusion.

"She can't stop them," was all the answer he got.

He sighed, considered ignoring her, but she was giving him an excuse to get away from the crowds. And running didn't really make him tired anymore. Nothing made him tired anymore. And yet somehow he was always tired.

He caught up with her, not even truly jogging, just allowing his footsteps to devour a little more space than they should have. A subtle folding of reality. Soon Afrit was trying to keep up with him. But he already knew where she was trying to lead him, her intent reflecting in the landscape clear as a beacon. He left her behind.

Quirk stood at the edge of the battlefield, hands on hips, railing at three dragons. They were big brutes. The travel and hard living of the past month or so had left them lean and muscular. They were not easily cowed anymore. One of them stood, its body between Quirk and the others, its head turned away for all that Quirk's hands were full of fire.

"Stop!" Quirk screamed, and Will could hear a raw edge in

her voice. The dragons wouldn't respect that, he knew. He could read their contempt in their postures.

"What is this?" Will made his voice just loud enough to cut through. Heads flicked around.

"They're…they're…" Quirk's face was pale to the point of sickness. Spots of color stood out against her naturally dark complexion.

Then Will was past her, and he saw.

The dragons had someone on the ground between them. A man. No…what was left of a man. Someone just on the edge of death. Someone who wouldn't be there much longer.

As Will walked forward, one of the massive dragons put a claw into a wound already gored in the man's side. The man convulsed.

"Where?" A voice came sharply.

Will realized there was another dragon he couldn't see, one obscured by the bulk of the others. He pushed around the bulk of the dragon who had his back to Quirk.

Yorrax leaned over the tortured man. And *tortured* was indeed the word.

The man gabbled and spat words. Yorrax leaned close.

The dragon torturing the man twisted its claw. The man screamed.

"When?" Yorrax asked.

"Stop it!" Quirk yelled. Will hadn't realized she was following him. She pounded his shoulder. "Stop them!"

"No," rumbled one of the dragons, looking up from what was left of the man. Will recognized it now as Netarrax, the massive black beast who styled himself head of the dragon forces.

"We grow impatient of this pathetic war of attrition," Netarrax growled. "We are dragons. We fight tooth and claw. This man will give us the information we need to find Barph, to tear him from the heavens."

"This is inhuman," said Quirk.

"Well, they aren't human," Will commented. Though he supposed that wasn't helping.

The man on the ground made dying noises.

"Why aren't you stopping this?" Quirk was staring at him, eyes wide.

Will wondered about that. He looked at the man. So much meat and bone. Barely any wants and fears left in him now. No belief at all. It reminded him of being a farmer on the days they'd needed to slaughter cattle. Gods, that had been a long time ago.

He shook his head, tried to clear it. "What's he told you?" he asked Yorrax.

"That's not fucking relevant!" Quirk screamed.

"A Barphian temple," said Yorrax. There was red on her teeth. "It's important. It's just two days from here."

"Why is it important?" Will asked.

"You are fucking endorsing this, you heartless shit!" Quirk yelled.

Will nodded. "Take your claw out of its guts," he said to the offending dragon.

For a moment their eyes met. His purple. Its yellow. Slitted pupils narrowed. Then with a slick noise the claw slipped out. The man gasped, then the life slipped out of him too.

No more hopes or fears for him now. Just the peace of the Void.

Will looked back to Yorrax. "Why is it important?"

Yorrax shook his head. "He won't tell us now."

"Fuck's sake." Quirk was blanching.

"We should destroy it," said Netarrax.

"We should destroy you, you murderous shit," Quirk muttered. Netarrax growled.

"Yes," Will said. Both Quirk and Netarrax turned their murderous gazes on him. "The temple," he clarified. "Obviously."

"This is tainted information." Afrit, it turned out, had decided to join the group. She was pointedly not looking at the corpse. "We can't use it."

Netarrax looked to Yorrax. "You are knowing humans, runt," he rumbled. "What are they jabbering about?"

"Weakness," said Yorrax. And she looked at Quirk with a sneer.

So, Will thought, *that's gone south.*

And he did understand where Quirk and Afrit were coming from. Or…he thought he did. Or…he remembered what it was like to feel what they were feeling. But in the end the goal was Barph's death. Or…the freeing of Avarra. Or…revenge. It was one of those. All of those. Maybe they were all the same thing.

"We have the information now," he said shortly. He didn't argue with people anymore. He was done with that. "We're going to use it."

The dragons smirked. Quirk and Afrit both opened their mouths. And Will twisted illusions and disappeared before they got a gods-hexed word out.

As promised, it took two days to make it to the temple. The skies remained a pale blue above them, the sun rode high. Dragons circled on thermals.

"Is being an odd place for a temple."

Will started. For a moment he almost slipped into invisibility. But then he recognized Balur's voice and tortured semantics, and turned to see the lizard man.

Cois was with him. Of all the gods, zhe seemed to have taken the loss of power the best. Will wondered why. Perhaps it was to do with Balur. With hir relationship. Will thought of Lette and of what she gave him. Yes, he could see that.

"A temple," Balur said again. "I am not thinking it belongs here."

Will finally took in the content of Balur's speech. He looked around the low Tamarian hills. "Why not?" he asked.

"A temple is being like a basket," Balur said.

Will gave Cois a look. "Metaphors now? Really?"

Zhe grinned.

"A basket in the center of a community," Balur plowed on. "The people are bringing their prayers and their coins there. The temple is collecting them." Balur looked around exaggeratedly. "There are being no people here. No villages. This is being farmland and plains. There is being nothing for the temple to collect."

Will shrugged. "We don't know why it's important. Maybe it does something different."

"That," said Balur, with more of a sarcastic lean than Will was used to these days, "is sort of being my point."

"So," Will double-checked, "your point is that you don't know anything? Well, that's helpful." He increased his pace.

"Perhaps," Cois said to his back, with deliberate slowness, "we are not here to serve your great cause. Perhaps we have our own cause."

Will stopped, looked back at them. He forced his displeasure into the air. Made it something tangible. He watched Balur grimace. "There is only one goal," he said. "There can only be one until Barph is gone."

Balur furrowed his brow and spoke despite the force of Will's irritation tainting the air. "Be being careful with these people," he said. "Do not be spending them as if they are meaningless."

Will squinted at Balur. Because...Well, first, *Balur* had just said that to him?

But pointing that out probably wouldn't help anything. So he dealt with the second absurdity. "I don't think they're meaningless." Of course he didn't. It was a ridiculous accusation.

"Then being careful with their lives will be easy," said Cois. And zhe was looking at him in a way Will didn't fully understand. Something knowing in hir look.

He shook it off. "Of course." He tried to sound irritated, not chastened. He wasn't sure if Cois bought it.

They walked together for a while. The dragons still circling in the air. A few scouted ahead. Then suddenly Yorrax swooped down, landed heavily beside them.

"There is something ahead," the dragon said without preamble.

"The temple?" asked Will.

"No," said Yorrax. There was no apology in the dragon's voice. "Something else where the temple should be."

"What thing?" Will was tempted to beat the word *something* out of the dragon's vocabulary.

Yorrax didn't blink or look away. "Perhaps a vineyard."

"Perhaps?" Will balled his fists.

"Perhaps you wish to fly and look for yourself."

"Perhaps you no longer deserve to fly."

Yorrax started to growl.

"Every life," he heard Cois whisper. At a volume only he and zhe could hear.

And perhaps tearing the limbs off a creature for a lack of specificity in its messages might not set the right tone.

"Thank you," he managed between gritted teeth.

Another foothill, and they saw the structure perched in a shallow valley. And there were indeed neat rows of vines covering the sun-soaked slope. A villa accompanied them, and several barns.

"That is not being a temple," said Balur.

"We should raze it to the ground." Netarrax landed this time. The massive black dragon made the ground quake as he walked alongside them.

"We don't know why it's important," Cois said. "Or why a tortured man was jabbering about it."

"We do not need to know," Netarrax growled. "We raze it. It ceases to be. It ceases to be an asset to our enemy. We weaken him."

Will considered this, and there was some temptation to the thought. The razing of his enemy.

He looked back at the host trailing after him. They had traveled most of the day. They were tired and slow. And despite himself, he wanted to prove to Cois that he cared, that he could be magnanimous.

"A small force," he said. "Twenty of us. To investigate. No dragons."

Netarrax growled.

"Do you wish to dispute this with me?"

For a moment their eyes locked. Then Netarrax looked away. "As you say."

"As I say."

Will resisted the urge to hold Lette's hands as they walked up the dusty road to the vineyard. There were those here who did not know their history, who might interpret it as weakness.

They'd be right, of course.

And still, as they got closer, as the warmth of the sun grew, as the sound of the grape leaves rustling reached them... there was something of this place that reminded him of his long-abandoned home in Kondorra, and of the farmstead he and Lette had briefly owned together in Batarra. How much of this would have been avoided if she had stayed with him there? Would they be happy? Would their lives be simple and sweet?

But Lette had hated farming. His dream had been her nightmare. And now he was here, with power in his fists and an army at his back.

Two dark-skinned men hurried out of one of the barns. They wore linen aprons stained purple. One had salt-and-pepper hair and a beard streaked with gray. The other was younger and had no beard but bore the same nose and eyes. Father and son, Will would guess.

"Can we be helping you?" It was the father who spoke. He

had a broad, helpful smile and open hands, but his voice shook slightly at the end.

"What is this place?" Will flexed a little magical might to increase the volume of his voice, to deepen its tone.

"Show-off," Lette muttered, but he could tell she was smiling.

"Just a simple vineyard, sir." The man had opened his hands. "Though we make a good wine, even if I do say so myself. Enough people have told me that I think it's all right to repeat—"

"What is this place?" Will thundered the words now. Made the hills ring with them.

The two men dropped to their knees.

"Please," said the father. "We've done nothing to offend nobody. We're good people here."

"My mother is in there." The son pointed back at the villa. "My sisters. Have some mercy in your heart."

And Will didn't want to destroy this place. He truly didn't. "Then tell me," he said, "what this place is."

"We just make wine," the father pleaded. "That's all."

Will walked toward them, made the weight of his presence lie heavy in the air. "So you worship Barph," he said. And he could not keep the hatred out of his voice.

"No more than the next winemaker, sir." There was desperation in the man's voice. "I mourned the other gods when they went, I swear, sir."

And there was truth in this man. Will could sense it, as if it were a tangible thing, a scent pervading the air. So why was he here?

He looked around, trying to think. The clean white walls of the villa. Its terra-cotta roof tiles. The neat rows of vines.

Neat rows. Ordered.

"This place is untouched," he said to himself. Then he looked to Lette. "This place is clean, tidy. It's ordered." He looked back to the winemaker. "Barph let nothing like this stand," he said. "He forced chaos everywhere. Except here. Here stands clean and clear." He rounded on the two vintners. "Why?" he demanded. "The wine," the son gabbled. "It's the wine."

And still Will sensed truth, but he could find no sense. "What about the wine?" He tried not to shout. He didn't try very hard, though.

"He likes it, sir," said the man. "That's it. That's all. I said to you, I told you, we make good wine. Our grapes grow well. We know our craft. It's *good* wine. And Barph...He...he likes it, sir."

"Barph *likes* it?" Will had been doing his very best not to sound bewildered. It didn't sit well with who he was anymore, but...what in the Hallows was this man talking about?

"Yes, sir." The father nodded. "He leaves us alone. He lets us make it the way we always have. Doesn't want to mess with the process."

Will glanced back at the others. Lette shrugged. Cois looked nonplussed, albeit slightly relieved that no sharp knives had been produced yet. Balur was looking mostly at Cois's arse now that it seemed there would be no bloodshed.

And then Will found it, the incongruity. He turned back to the two men. "And how," he asked, "do you know this? How do two lowly vintners know the mind of a god?"

He set his feet for the fight.

The two men exchanged a look. The father looked back at Will, and his face was as open as a book. "He told me, sir."

"He...?" was all Will could manage.

"He likes our wine, sir," said the son. "He comes for it himself, personal-like. He manifests and takes it back to the heavens with him."

"He...he manifests here?" Will looked about as if expecting to see Barph standing in the wings at this very moment.

And then a voice behind Will said, "Yes. Yes I do."

38

A Break from Your Regularly Scheduled Programming

Long ago, Barph had found there was boredom in omniscience. When, millennia ago, he had first become a god, and humanity was new upon the face of the world, there had been a voyeuristic thrill to peering into someone's life, their thoughts. And yet, over time, everything became a little predictable. The same lives lived out over and over again. The parts merely scrambled into new combinations.

And yet Barph found that he took distinct pleasure in the predictability of Will's expressions. Shock first, as he spun around. Then slowly mounting horror. And...Wait for it...Yes, here it came. The rage.

And then the thought slowly transformed into action.

To be fair, Will's blow came far harder and faster than Barph had expected. But that was pleasant too. A surprise. Wasn't that the very spice of life, in the end: the unexpected, serendipitous, unanticipated stick in the spokes?

He stepped back, and Will's fist swung past his chin, the wind of the blow ruffling his beard. It was closer than he had expected, but his dodge probably just looked more impressive for that.

And then came the follow-up. Will was nothing if not persistent. He didn't even give the surprise a chance to set in. He used his momentum to come round with his foot. And Will had certainly learned some moves since Barph had last seen him.

Barph caught Will's foot. And another surprise was the strength behind the blow. It didn't hurt, but it sent his feet skidding back across the ground.

Barph readjusted the density of his manifested form and heaved Will away, sending him spinning. And now the others were starting to react. Balur charging headfirst at him, Lette's blades arcing through the air. Men and women he didn't know on a first-name basis waving swords and hatchets at him.

All so very predictable.

He batted Lette's blades out of the air, sent them in carving arcs, slicing through arms and legs, dropping some people before they even got their rage appropriately on. Then he put a hand out, placed it in Balur's face, sent him plowing into the dirt.

Then Will was back. The boy had landed on his feet, was whipping through moves that were, quite frankly, alien to Barph. A flurry of feet and fists. And yet Barph anticipated and found no problem following each one, batting it away. *New and unexpected* was not the same as *threatening*.

He started to laugh. And the rage on Will's face just made him laugh harder.

"Oh, little puppy," he said, as Will panted and heaved. "Oh, with your snapping and snarling. You are so fierce. You are so brave." He backhanded Will across the face, sent him reeling—and yet the boy still kept his feet. Then Balur was back up, so Barph kicked him in the crotch so hard he flew across the courtyard and into Lette.

"All of you fighting so very hard, and for what? For my attention? To have some meaning? Some purpose? To prove how important your lives are?" And he laughed harder at the looks on their faces as he picked arrows out of the air. He threw them all back at the archer, made a pincushion of him.

"There is no meaning, little puppies," he said, batting a few more of Will's blows away. "For I am meaning. And I am meaningless. I reject it. And you rail, and you shout, and you clench your tiny fists, and..." He smiled. "You achieve nothing. There is nothing to be achieved."

He slid a solid gut punch under Will's guards, lifted the boy off his feet, sent him flying across the courtyard, watched him crash into the villa wall. Stone chips flew. Barph hoped he hadn't done too much damage. He liked this vineyard.

"All you do," he said. "Everything you achieve." He kicked someone in the head, heard their neck snap. "Is going to add up to nothing. It will simply prove my point."

He knew Will was listening. Lying in the dirt and listening to him. And oh, rubbing Will's face in it—his ridiculous, earnest face—was just so much fun.

And then a very familiar voice said, "You always were a sanctimonious prick, Barph."

He turned through the chaos, brushed aside another attack, and saw, kneeling beside Balur, his mother, his lover, Cois.

Zhe shook hir head at him. "I know you like to pretend to be the rebel, the iconoclast, to talk about ripping Lawl down from his high table. But all you ever really want to do is pontificate yourself. You just could never stand that Lawl's voice was louder than yours."

"Oh," Barph crooned. "Oh, Cois. Oh, Mother sweetest. Who did you fuck to get back to this plane of existence?"

Someone came at him with a sword. He disarmed them. Literally. At the shoulder.

"Your petty jealousies and insecurities." Cois tutted. "Even now you cannot help but be a victim to them."

Barph smiled again. Oh, how he smiled. He had missed this. This backbiting. The snip and spit. And part of him was tempted to take Cois the way he used to do after their arguments and resolve things with the thrust of a blunter sword.

"It was Will, wasn't it, Mother?" he said. "He warms your..."
But then he saw the truth of it. Hir hand on the lizard man's
shoulder. And he had known he should pay more attention to
Will's antics. They contained hidden hilarities that had escaped
him until now. "Balur? Mother!" He knew how zhe hated the
gendered noun. "You always did like a bit of rough trade."

For a moment he thought zhe wasn't going to respond. And
his smile faltered, because for all that he wanted the gods to
know that they lived beneath his bootheel—that they lived at
his mercy, that their plans would always be fruitless wastes of
time—he wasn't sure he wanted them broken. He wanted them
to struggle. He wanted plans to spoil.

How many of Cois's plans had he ruined over the millennia?
How many indiscretions had he ensured hir husband, Toil,
"accidentally" discovered? How many of hir auguries had been
misinterpreted? Because of him. All because of him.

And for all that Will was up on his feet, snarling and tearing at Barph, he was not quite the opponent that Cois was. He
wasn't *family*.

Barph beat Will away, eyes on Cois. Zhe opened hir mouth
and he grinned again, ready to spar with hir.

"You poor broken thing, Barph," zhe said. "You sad little child." Zhe dropped hir eyes, stared at the ground and the
bleeding lizard man at her feet. "I should never have let Lawl
do it to you," zhe said, quietly and just for him. "I should have
stepped in and protected you. I am so sorry."

"You..." He tried to find the words. Because what was this?
Was it...was it fucking sympathy?

"Condescending bitch!" he yelled at hir. Because how dare
zhe? Mother, lover, foil. That was what zhe had been. That was
what they had all been, in one way or another. That was what he
missed. That was what he wanted.

"Whore!" he screamed. But words were not enough. Not even
at a volume that blew hir back across the courtyard and cracked

tiles. He grew and he grew and he grew. He towered over them. His feet crushed grapes. And fuck them. Fuck his need for wine. This was important. This needed to be understood.

"I am your god!" he bellowed. "I am your everything! That is how it is now!"

And somehow Will was still up, was still hurling himself at Barph's ankle like some ferocious hamster. And would he not go down? Would he not fucking listen? Barph kicked him, sent him flying.

"You are nothing!" he howled again. "There is only me. I stand alone now! Alone!"

And he looked down from his great height. And he saw Cois lying sprawled on hir back in dirt and blood intermingled, and zhe looked up, and zhe met his eye, and zhe nodded, and said, "Yes. Yes you are."

39

Thunderstruck

Quirk had dedicated most of her adult life to the study of dragons. There had, of course, been dalliances with other megathaumatofauna. She had spent a semester at university obsessing over the breeding cycles of Chatarran wyverns. She'd spent six months working on a paper about the social structures of Atrian giant tribes. But every time she had come back to dragons. Their legends. Their history. Their influence on human social structures. The contents of their hordes and the hidden ratios within their treasures. And then beyond simply studying dragons—actually fighting them. Interacting with their social structures. Battling their political machinations. And now here she was working alongside them—integrated, in a way, into their social fabric.

But never had any of her reading or research indicated to any reasonable extent exactly how much gods-hexed moaning there was going to be.

"We should have gone to the vineyard," Pettrax grumbled.

"We should have burned it to the ground," Rothinamax whined.

"We wait on a human." Netarrax's voice was full of disdain. "We are no better than we were."

"We are working," Quirk said as loudly as she could, *"together.* Cooperation is not the same as capitulation."

"Cooperation is not being ordered about by creature of weak flesh." Pettrax loomed over her.

It was a challenge, Quirk knew. An attempt to assert dominance. Because it always was. Because every time the dragons talked to her, it was an attempt to find weakness. It was transparent, and ever so slightly pathetic for its repetition.

It was also bowel-looseningly terrifying.

"If you want a say," Quirk growled, imitating aggression in direct defiance of every impulse in her body, "come up with something worth listening to." She let smoke waft out with her words.

Pettrax snorted fire, but it shot over her head. Then the dragon looked away.

"We wait," Quirk shouted to the assembled horde of dragons, "because it is the smart play. We wait because information is valuable. And only after we have retrieved it can you dumb bastards go do the one thing you're good for."

And gods piss on it, that was not a message that would foster the cooperative mind-set she was angling toward. The problem was that when dragons were involved, cooperation seemed to involve one party getting its way and the other party becoming an appetizer. Quirk knew which side of the equation she wanted to be on.

Finally she risked looking away from the dragons, toward the hills that blocked the vineyard from her sight. And at the exact moment she did so, the massive figure of Barph suddenly lurched up into the sky and towered over everything.

Because... because gods piss on it. Because there were no reasons anymore. There was just the mockery of all she strove for. Every gods-hexed time.

"Okay," she said, turning back to the dragons. "*That* you can probably rain death and destruction on."

But they hadn't really waited for her cue. They were boiling up into the air. Downdrafts battered her and forced her to her knees. Dust and dirt were a storm around her. Then the dragons were aloft, screaming, bellowing, roaring, shooting flame, and racing toward their enemy.

Barph was looking down at the ground, and Quirk could glimpse only the edge of his face, so his expression was hard to read, but for a moment she could have sworn it was one of sadness, or perhaps regret, and then it changed and was a look of perhaps the purest hatred she had ever seen. Something that put ice in her heart and made the words, "No! Come back!" form in her mind, but the dragons were already out of earshot. And anyway, as Barph looked round at the collective roars of the dragons, his face wore only a smile.

And thank all the gods that Afrit had stayed back here with her, was not there in the vineyard.

Then there was a shout from behind her. No. *Shout* was too insubstantial a word. Five thousand people shouted as one. Five thousand people charged.

"No!" she screamed. "Don't!" And then, because she felt someone should point it out, "It's fucking moronic!"

They ignored her. Of course. They had seen their cursed enemy, the renounced god, their own personal demon. Of course they charged, roaring up the hill, seizing what weapons they could, shaking fists against the heavens, full of the piss and vinegar that was about to be mashed out of their mangled bodies. They had to charge, no matter how stupid and suicidal it was. They had staked too much of their identities on it not to.

The first dragon was almost on Barph now. Netarrax out in front, no longer the fat, heavy beast Quirk had found on Natan but a lean, sleek beast, scales shining in the sun, wings folded back, body angled like a lance, jaws stretching to encompass infinity. A world eater, a god eater, full of fire and rage, come to fulfill the very purpose for which he had been built. Death and absolute destruction.

Almost lazily, Barph pointed a finger at him.

Out of the clear, blue, cloudless sky a bolt of lightning came. More than a bolt. A cataract of electrical energy. A god's fist of crackling white light. It smashed into Netarrax. It smashed *through* him.

The dragon's charge was utterly negated. All forward momentum obliterated in an inversion of flesh and bone as Netarrax's face caved in. Caved in to his neck, which was sent smashing into his body, half disemboweling the beast in midair and turning his charge into a tumbling, messy pratfall. And then what was left of a once-majestic beast was out of sight behind the crest of the hill, only the dull crash of bone and flesh against soil to mark his fate.

Barph's grin grew wider.

The rest of the dragons shrieked and split apart, spreading out around Barph like a shroud, skimming past him.

Barph closed one eye, narrowed the other, pointed his finger.

Another thunderbolt smashed down through the sky. Another lance of divine rage. Another dragon's head snapped viciously sideways, its body spinning limp and out of control. It plowed to earth out of sight.

Another dragon dived, ducked beneath Barph's outstretched arm, raked its claws across his chest, shredded his white robe, left streaks of red.

Barph didn't even flinch. He aimed again. A thunderbolt struck home.

Quirk could hear the human contingent of Will's army still charging, heedless and idiotic. She looked around. She was the only one left here. Everyone else was gone.

Everyone.

Afrit!

She stared. And no, surely no, because Afrit was hers, and was beautiful and wise and full of intelligence, and she had too much to live for. She had Quirk to live for. She would not have... could not have...

But she had. She had gone with the others. She had gone to immolate herself at the feet of a god.

So now Quirk had to as well.

She started running, pulled up her skirts in a fist and ran and ran. Above her head dragons were screaming. Lighting flared again, again, again. Fire blossomed in great red blooms, yellow petals curling away in wilting beauty. She crested the hill and saw Will's army spread out in front of her. A great unorganized rabble. Dragons crashed to earth in the middle of the heaving mass of them—flesh bombshells kicking up earth and bodies in vast cresting sprays to spear those nearby with roots and bones.

Barph had been slashed again and again. His robes were ribbons, his chest crosshatched with bloody gashes. His beard was on fire. And he was laughing, and murdering. Almost a third of the dragons lay dead on the ground.

And Quirk ran. And she ran. Her breath came ragged and urgent, but she did not slow. A stitch clawed at her. The dead tried to trip her. And she did not slow. She fought through Will's army as half of it broke in the face of such destruction, as half of it redoubled its efforts to murder this god of nothing, this unmaker of their happiness. And she did not slow.

And above them Barph laughed and murdered and cackled. His massive feet came down, and lives ended beneath them. Bodies squashed flat, bones bursting their skin. People clung to his ankles, were shaken free, went sprawling. And still the people were undeterred. Still they rushed forward with knives and spears and swords, slashing uselessly at flesh as hard as iron. Arrows and crossbow bolts stood out like pins against his flesh—even provided handholds for some foolhardy assailants—but barely a trickle of blood flowed from the wounds. And Barph pointed again and again and again, and the lightning came down like rain.

"Afrit!" Quirk's cry came out as a wheeze, a whisper against the roar of the battle and the roar of the dragons overhead. It was inaudible. But she called out again. "Afrit!" Everything was chaos. Everything was madness. It was everything Barph could ever hope for. Utter anarchy. There was no way she could find Afrit in this.

And then she did. Somehow. Impossibly.

Afrit was standing atop a crest of dirt. Torn vines were all around her. And she held a kitchen knife clenched in one raised fist. Around her a crowd of archers were desperately seizing arrows from their quivers. To Quirk it looked as if Afrit were standing still. But that couldn't be. That had to be a trick of adrenaline and fear and hope and the fact that she only glimpsed her for a moment, and then the world turned white.

The thunderbolt crashed to earth, seared a hole in the earth and Quirk's vision.

She screamed. She found her volume then. Because…because… Gods…

But there were no gods left to pray to.

She was falling back, collapsing as the shock wave hit her. She was half-blind, her vision seared.

And then she saw her. Afrit. Still there. Not obliterated. Out of the immediate blast zone of the lightning strike. But close to it all the same. Closer than Quirk. Up in the air now, rag-doll limp, spinning over and over. Flying. Falling. And Quirk would catch her, would cushion her, would protect her, but here she was flat on her back, pain only starting to stretch its fingers through her body and past the barriers of her shock.

Afrit slammed to the earth two yards in front of her, skidded through the dirt, a tumbling, tangling pile of disjointed limbs. She was a blur, barely recognizable as human, whirling just out of reach of Quirk's flopping hand.

Quirk heaved herself over, found she could get to all fours. The world swam about her. She tried to focus. Afrit. Afrit needed her. She had to get up.

She made it to her knees, to one knee. Then a final heave and she was on her feet, stumbling, staggering, but she could see Afrit lying in front of her. Afrit covered in blood. Afrit unmoving. Afrit twisted and broken.

No. No. No. It could not be. It could not be.

But gods, there was so much blood.

The horror, the fear, the shock—it was all too big, too overwhelming. She felt crushed by it, unable to process it fast enough to stop it bearing her to the ground, destroying her utterly.

And then it was gone, subsumed, sublimated. Then all it was was rage.

She turned away from Afrit, unable to bear the sight of that beautiful, broken body. She turned away to see Barph, still towering, still huge, and she understood, she knew perfectly why that crowd was there, why they were hurling themselves futilely against his ankles.

Barph had to die. Anything, no matter how small, she could do to hasten that fate, she had to do it. It was everything. It was all the meaning in the world.

She became fire and fury. She was not a conduit. She was not a gateway. The fire did not flow out of her. She *was* fire, utterly and purely. She was a torrent of endless rage pouring across the battlefield, ripping uncaring through Will's troops and careening madly into Barph. She battered and battered against the seawall of his flesh, grinding and grinding away layers of divine protection.

She could feel fire above her, the sympathetic call of elemental siblings. The dragons were pouring it onto Barph even as their numbers thinned yet further. They were diving through their own bursts of flame, risking scorched wings and burned flanks to claw more and more chunks of flesh from the god who had tricked them, who had slain so many of their brothers and sisters.

And somehow, impossibly, Barph was staggering back, was being taken down by the ferocity of the assault on his body. Somehow he was yelling and flailing. His thunderbolts were going wide of their marks. The ferocity of the dragons' assault seemed only to grow. A thunderhead of flame, claw, and rage tearing into Barph. Will's human followers were at his feet, his ankles, his calves, carving and slashing their way into divine flesh.

And for a moment, even with Afrit lying behind her, she exulted. She gloried. Because this was it. This was revenge. This was victory. This was all she had left to accomplish in the world. And then she could be done. Then she could rest. Then she could join Afrit.

And then, as suddenly as he had appeared, Barph wasn't there. He vanished into thin air. People who had been clinging to his body, climbing the great height of him, were suddenly hurtling to the ground. Ankles and legs snapped. People howled. Quirk howled. She howled in rage and frustration. He had fled. Her enemy had run from the battlefield to lick his wounds and fight another day. And another. And another. On and on, unending. Days empty and hollow of meaning.

From the peaks of exultation, Quirk tumbled toward despair.

And then, out of nowhere, someone caught her.

As she knelt on the scorched earth, smoke still drifting from her shoulders, a heat shimmer above her head, she felt a hand on her shoulder. She looked up. There, bloody, beaten, but still somehow alive, was Afrit looking down at her. And there was, it turned out, still a reason for being alive.

40

He Who Controls the Past

Will stared around. Chaos and destruction. The villa was nothing more than a pile of rubble. A dragon's corpse was draped across it. The vineyards were burning. The earth was churned. Bodies everywhere. The injured and the bereaved screaming. The scents of blood and smoke mixing in the air. All of the beauty and peace of this place were gone.

For the first time, Will wondered if he could blame Barph for this. The god had come here in peace, after all. If Will and his followers hadn't been here...

But what choice had there been? This was why they were here: to defeat Barph, to take back their world. Could they have just sat by?

He probably should have. He had known it even as he flung himself screaming across the villa's courtyard. He had been too weak. He had the support of a few thousand. Barph had the support of a few million. He should have fallen back and bided his time. And still there had been no choice. If he had been seen to quail, to hang back and refuse to fight? It would have been a disaster. It would have undermined him utterly.

But now? Here? In the middle of this death and destruction? In the middle of this unmitigated defeat? He wasn't sure it was any better.

He could *feel* the crowd's loss of faith. He could feel their doubts. Their rising panic. He knew that already some of them were looking to the horizon with a sense of longing. The desire for anonymity and escape growing, taking them from him, stealing his power, undoing all the work he had done.

He could feel the thing that was of the Deep Ones lying within him starting to panic too. He could feel its knowledge that its sustenance would be lost. And he tried to tell himself that all that fear and dread was alien to him, was being layered onto his thoughts by something that worked for him and that was within his control. And yet...

His breath was starting to come hard. His skin felt fragile. He had to turn this around. Yet there was no way to turn this disaster around. There was...

Unless...

He looked again, tried to look closer. Almost half of the dragons lying dead. Several hundred humans. Some of them crushed by the dragons meant to be protecting them.

Unless...

He walked forward, walked toward the remains of one of the fallen villas, toward white rubble and black dirt. He stepped up on unsteady mounds of rubble, stood precarious before them all.

They weren't looking at him. He was the least of their concerns.

"People," he said. And they didn't hear him. "People," he said again, and he put power into the word. The power they gave him. The power he needed. Needed so much more of, if he was ever to finish this. And this time, for the first time in a long time, he felt the cost of its use. He felt the loss of power that this volume required. But they looked. They looked and they stared.

"People!" he said. And he tried to force cheer into his voice, excitement. And gods, he was a farmer—or had once been a farmer—not an actor, but he did his best. "People!" for a fourth time. He raised his arms into the air. "See how Barph flees from us!"

This was met by a rather incredulous silence. People continued to stare at him, but they did little else. There were no cheers here. No raised fists. There was…confusion. Confusion starting to coalesce into something harder and uglier. He had brought them to this.

Will could feel his reserves dwindling even as he spoke, but it was either gamble everything or watch it trickle away. He had no appetite for the latter. Not anymore.

"We fought a god today!" he roared. "We the people of Avarra! Not heroes out of legend. Not undying warriors bestowed with divine gifts. But you and I! Your neighbors. Your friends. Your brothers. Your sisters. We, the downtrodden, the dirty, the unkempt. We, the everyday citizens of this world. We took on a god!"

And he knew that he was no longer any of the things he described. That he was somehow, now, special. That he had assistance that was more than a little divine. And that almost all the damage done to Barph had been done by the dragons. But truth wasn't what mattered now. Hope mattered. Belief mattered. Belief in this fight. In him.

"Did he hurt us?" Will asked them. "Did many of us die today?" He knew he could not appear too far out of touch with reality. "Yes." Will nodded. "He did. And my heart bleeds with every victim out there. I mourn with everyone bereaved. I feel every loss."

And that was true, though perhaps not as they took it.

"But what did we achieve?" Will asked them. "What did we do today? Who ran from this field of battle? Who stands proud at its end?"

And, to be honest, he didn't think many of them were sure of the answer to that question. Or why it was a question. But he could take that uncertainty. He could use it.

"We stand here!" he bellowed. He felt the ground tremble at the force of his words. He felt his insides hollow out as the power rushed out of him with them. And he prayed desperately for it to come back. "We still hold this field! A god flees before us! A god tucks his tail and runs! From us! From the people of Avarra. We are here, and he is gone. For we have proven him what we know him to be: NOTHING!"

And this was it. The last of it. The final scraps of his power. The final desperate lies. It felt as if something was thrashing in his mind. "Barph is nothing compared to us!" he yelled through the pain. "His power is nothing compared to ours! His might is nothing compared to ours! And in the end, his reign of a few months will be nothing to the reign of peace and prosperity we establish for this world! His future is nothing! Ours"—he swept his eyes over the broken and bedraggled crowd—"ours is everything."

And that was it. He was spent. He tried to stay standing there at least, to keep his chest puffed out and defiance in his eyes. He tried to not visibly give in to the rising agony.

The moment hung in the air.

Come on. Come on, you little fuckers. Do something. React. Believe me. Give me what I need, you shits.

He stared at them. Streaked with blood and dirt and tears. Sweating and panting. Their clothes ragged and torn after months on the road. Their hopes lying smashed into bloody pieces around them.

Oh gods...what was happening to him? What sort of insane death march was he trying to force these people into? People had died here today. People were in mourning. And he was... *Gods.*

He could feel the hunger inside him. The desperation for adoration. And what had he brought into himself in that space below the Hallows? What had his desperation driven him to do?

He opened his mouth to take it all back. To tell them that this was a foolish, desperate fight. That he was a liar and a fool. That he was spelling out a death sentence for them. That they had to flee from this place.

Then it hit him like a tidal wave. Their cheer. Their roaring, upraised voices. Their clenched fists hurled skyward.

It flooded him. Parts of his brain felt as if they were detonating. Wave after wave of ecstasy breaking over him. Because, yes, yes, yes, they believed Will. They had fought a god today. And the price? Well, the price had been worth it.

Will shook and shuddered, tried to contain all the power as it filled him. Each gasp of air he managed to suck down was a white-hot lance into his lungs. His eyes felt as if they were straining against the limits of their sockets.

And still they cheered. And still they roared. And still they believed.

41

Quitting Time

"I'm okay," Afrit said.

She was not okay.

She repeated it anyway. When that didn't help, she tried, "Please let go, Quirk. You're hurting me."

And that did work, at least in the short term, because Quirk finally let go, and she stopped crushing the ribs that Afrit suspected might well be broken, or at least badly bruised. However, looking at the worry—the naked fear—in Quirk's eyes, Afrit was not truly convinced it would help in the long run.

"Why?" The word seemed to emerge from Quirk against the woman's will. She looked as if she were examining the air between them for it so she could swat it away like some intruding insect.

For her part, Afrit was too beaten up and exhausted to be offended. So she asked, "Why what?"

"Why," Quirk said, the words emerging slowly, "did you attack Barph? Why did you run toward him?"

It was Afrit's turn to hesitate. "You think I should have run away?"

Quirk shrugged helplessly. "We can't beat him."

Afrit drew a long breath. It hurt. She suspected everything was going to hurt for a week or two. "I charged because..." She tried to track back to the moment. A lot of recent history was fuzzy around the edges. "Okay," she said, "I don't think these are going to sound like good reasons, now that we know how everything turned out.

"I fought because of everything we've seen. Because of all the hatred and heartache Barph's poured into the world. Because of how offended I am by everything that he stands for, and by everything he's done. I fought because of how very fucking angry I am. Because of how horrified I am. Because I'm scared for this world, and because I'm tired of being scared. Because being defiant was being better than being cowed. Because I hoped. And it was stupid hope. But gods... everyone else in that moment hoped. We all hoped together. And it was huge, and it was bigger than me, and I was part of it. I thought... maybe. Just maybe."

She sighed. Her chest and throat hurt now. Too many words. "It turns out that it was a pretty stupid idea."

"No," Quirk said, and put a hand on Afrit's shoulder. Afrit tried not to wince. A lot of the skin was missing from that shoulder. "It doesn't sound stupid."

"Can you let go of me again?" Afrit was forced to ask. It wasn't often that the requests went that way round.

"Sorry." Quirk winced. She licked her lips. They were chapped, Afrit saw. Quirk's eyes were red, her skin raw. Her attack on Barph had, it seemed, not been without its cost. Afrit had never seen Quirk lose control with that degree of ferocity before. It scared her a little.

"Are you okay?" she asked.

Quirk shook her head. "No. I thought you were dead, Afrit. I thought you were dead again. I thought there was no way back this time. I thought everything was over." She bit her lip. "It..." She paused, looked around. "It hurt so much. And last time... last time... that's what it took for me to realize how I felt, what you are to me. It took you dying for me to realize I can actually feel love. But now I do. Now I love you. And last time, that realization, it hurt, but there was something beautiful in it too. That revelation that I wasn't totally broken, that you had healed that part of me, or found a way to dig it out. But this time..." She shook her head, seemed to fold in on herself, as if something were collapsing, or...as if she were being punched in slow motion. "This time it was just over. It was just pain." She took a long, ragged breath. There were tears in her eyes. "Last time I could hate. That was how I could cope. I could tear the whole world down. But this time...this time Barph was right there. And I could fling myself at him. But all I was really trying to do was die. Because it wasn't worth it. Life wasn't worth it. Because nothing I did stopped it from hurting. And I can't...I can't lose you again. I can't take that hurt again. I can't. I can't." She sat there, shaking her head. "I can't."

And there were tears in Afrit's eyes too now, and not just because of the pressure Quirk was putting on her raw palms. Because the beauty she had always seen in Quirk was so close to the surface now. The tender, fragile part of her that she kept so guarded from the world.

And because she knew that she would almost certainly hurt her just this way again.

She pulled her hands free of Quirk's grasp, took her love's head in her hands, and kissed her forehead over and over.

"I will always fight to stay with you," she said. "Everything I can do, I'll do it. For you."

Quirk looked away from her. "Will you?" she asked. "Because..." And then she trailed off.

And Afrit knew where this was going, had known since before they entered Tamar that this moment was coming, had known it since perhaps before Quirk had. But still she wished they hadn't arrived here.

"Because perhaps we should quit?" she asked.

And gods, she wished she could pretend she hadn't seen the hope flare in Quirk's eyes.

"I—" Afrit started. But before she was done, Quirk held up a hand.

She licked her lips. "This world," she said, "has so much wrong with it. And everything you are about to say about what Barph has done to it is true. He's destroyed so much that I loved." She finally looked Afrit in the eye again. "But it has you in it. And for me, if it is a world with you in it, then it is still a world with beauty in it. I cannot hate a world that has you in it. And I would rather live in this world with you than lose you in a fight for a better one."

She smiled at Afrit, even though she was still crying. "I choose you over everything, Afrit. Over my old dreams. Over my old values. I choose you. And if you say no, then I'll choose that with you too. I just . . ." She choked off, unable to finish.

"No," Afrit said.

Quirk was very quiet for a very long time.

"I can't," Afrit said, because she had to in the end. She had to explain. This was, in the end, love. "I can't be someone who sacrifices the world for themselves. I can't. That will not be me."

Quirk still didn't look up. Still stayed staring at the ground.

"Quirk," Afrit said. "You're holding my hands."

Quirk didn't look up.

"Quirk," Afrit said, "my skin is starting to smoke."

And finally Quirk looked up, and still it was a moment before she let go of Afrit's hand.

"I understand," Quirk said, and her voice was very small.

"This is who I am," Afrit said, though she wasn't entirely sure why she was defending herself. She was being the bigger person here. "If you love me, you love this piece of me too."

"I love you," Quirk said, but her voice was still in retreat along with the rest of her emotions. And then she turned, and she almost fled. And Afrit knew that the wound she had just inflicted was as deep any other done that day, and would take just as long to heal.

42

Compromising Situations

He had done it again, Lette thought.

Will had taken the broken pieces of his army and he had fused them back together. The people around her, on the edge of breaking, of running—they were cheering now. Somehow he had turned this into a victory.

She recognized the artifice in it all. She had heard the little lies Will wove to create the large one, but she admired him all the more for it. The end, here, justified the means. If lies were what it took to prop up these people's hope, then they were what it took.

She went to him as he stepped down off his improvised podium of rubble, put an arm around his waist. He seemed slightly shell-shocked, blinking in the face of all the adoration being hurled at him. People clapped them both on their shoulders as they made their way through the crowd. She clasped hands with people for him, smiled into their beaming faces.

And seeing those faces, those gleaming eyes, she thought perhaps there had been an element of true victory in this fight. The force that stood before her now was diminished in numbers, yes, but it had also been forged into something stronger, harder, more savagely edged. And, yes, dragons lay dead, but their blood served to temper this army's steel.

She raised a fist to the heavens, and around her a hundred fists lifted to the sky, and cheers echoed off the fallen walls.

*   *   *

Later they managed to find some peace. Makeshift tents were thrown up, the celebrating died down, and the hard work of burying the dead began. The dragons showed no compunctions about eating their former fellows, so that lightened some of the load at least.

Lette and Will climbed into as much privacy as a thin sheet of canvas could afford them. Will seemed to have come back to himself a little. Or as far back as he ever did these days. There was still a distracted look in his eyes—his human ones at least—as if he was seeing something beyond the rest of them. As if the here and now could never quite fully capture his attention.

She knew he didn't sleep anymore. She hoped he would stay the night with her, though. Sometimes he did, and she would wake in the darkness and curl against his body. She would feel his muscles soften slightly as he relaxed into her warmth, and then she would slip into sleep again.

Other nights, she would wake and there would only be cold, empty space beside her.

In the confines of the tent, she turned to him, pushed her hands through his hair, kissed him. He hesitated, then kissed her back. Hungry kisses, she thought at first, the sort of passion he'd shown when they first reunited. But as they progressed, she thought perhaps the word *desperate* was more accurate.

They made love with that same frantic urgency. And it was beautiful and wonderful and slightly heartbreaking all at the same time. It was as if Will was clinging to her, fearful he might lose her. And she didn't know why, and she didn't know how to comfort him. So all she could do was hold him as tightly as he held her, meet his passion head-on, and stroke his hair when they were done.

He lay there, panting, his head nestled against her chest, almost feverishly hot as the sweat cooled her skin.

The silence stretched, but she could bear it. She wouldn't be broken by a little thing like that. Still, she felt that he needed her to ask him, so finally she said, "What's wrong?"

"I'm scared, Lette."

She knew he was serious, but she chuckled despite her best efforts. "What could you possibly be scared of? You tried to punch a god today."

He fell silent again, and she regretted her words. It was a strange thing to love someone, she thought. To have your happiness tangle with theirs.

"Tell me," she said.

Still he was silent, but she would wait now. He would be ready eventually.

"I mean...," he said finally. "Just fucking look at me."

And he would have to push harder than that if he wanted her to break. She had just screwed his brains out. If his looks were a barrier she would have fled screaming already.

"You're a little purple," she conceded.

"I have fucking bug eyes on my forehead, Lette!" There was something shrill in his voice. "Look at this!" he held out his arm to her. The skin near the inside of the elbow was so pale it was almost translucent, marbled with veins and purple stains. "That's new," he said. "It's still happening. It's not stopping."

And he really was scared. She cupped his face. "The bards talk about this sort of thing being skin-deep," she said. It was a line that had been tried on her before, and she hadn't bought it at the time, but Will was a romantic sort.

And the hysterical breathing did stop at least. But everything seemed to stop. He went very still.

"I lied to everyone earlier," he said eventually. "I lied to them all."

"To be fair," she said, picking her words as if she were picking her footsteps across a Thassalayan Whisper Floor, "that is not the first time we've lied to the masses."

"I know," he said, "I know. But..." He shook his head, as if trying to free himself of something. "No, it wasn't different. I was different."

Oh, Will. If only he could just be at peace with himself. With his own efficacy in the world.

"It's okay," she said. "It's okay to be in charge. To be what these people need. To be good at being that person. It's okay."

"No." The shake of his head was less violent this time, but his words were just as urgent. "This cause...It's important to people because they're being oppressed. Because they need to be freed—"

"And you're doing that for them."

"I'm being worshipped by them."

"Because of what you do." Why couldn't he see that? "You have fought this fight harder than everyone else. When we were in the Hallows, I lost my way. I lost my hope. And you pulled me out of that. Out of the fucking Hallows, Will. You have done so many impossible things. You deserve to be worshipped."

"No," he said again, his voice rising. "Don't say that."

She pulled away, looked him square in the face. "You, Willett Fallows, deserve to be worshipped."

He put his face in his hands. He dug his fingers into his skin with an urgency that frightened her. "No," he said again. "That's the problem. I'm not telling them to fight for the cause because I want them to be free, or because I want to end oppression. I'm telling them that because it means they worship me, Lette."

He looked at her, anguished. "I'm losing my way. I'm losing my cause. The worship is becoming the thing." He clawed at his face again, white-knuckled. "I looked out at them today and I didn't see people. I saw fuel. And yes, I've lied to people before, but I've also known it was wrong before. Part of me has always regretted things needed to be that way. Gods, part of me has even hoped they'll see through my bullshit. A stupid part of me perhaps, but...I can't find that part anymore, Lette. I can't find so many parts of myself. I'm becoming someone who looks at people and doesn't recognize himself in them anymore."

He pulled his hands away from his face, and there were ten little crescent cuts in his face where his nails had scored his flesh. But even as she watched, the skin knit back together, the blood was sucked back into the disappearing wounds.

"I'm becoming something that isn't human, Lette." There was absolute terror in his voice. "And it's more than skin-hexedly deep."

And Will. Oh, Will. Why did he always have to give voice to the secrets she hid from herself? Why couldn't he ever let her live with the peace of self-deception?

She knew all this. Of course she knew. She saw him. She had always seen him. And she had always seen through him. And now she saw what lay beneath all the physical changes.

Will was a good man. That was his steel. That was the part of him that wouldn't bend. He would not, could not, be anything but a good man. He could be furious, but he was righteously furious. He could lie, but always in the service of a greater good. He could kill, but he would do it for a reason and with an awareness of the cost. Dragons had oppressed him from birth. Riches had offered the temptation of corruption. And still he had not bent. Still he had been exactly who he always was.

But now . . . now there was corruption within. The Deep Ones' power ate at him, rotted away at that core. And she saw it. And it was slow, barely noticeable. But it was constant. The erosion of the ocean upon rock. And eventually there would be none of Will left.

And the question—the question she avoided, the question he was truly asking even if he didn't realize it—was when it would be too much. When would there not be enough left of the man she loved for her to stay?

"I need you," he said to her. "I need you to help me. To keep me here. In myself."

And she knew that too. And she knew more. She knew how the crowd saw them. She knew how she was wrapped up in the mysticism and the worship of Will. She was a part of the legend. She knew that there was loyalty to her, that she was seen as a protector of the people. That if she left now, if she abandoned Will, it would be nothing short of a schism.

More than that too, she knew that there would come a time when she wanted to leave, but when if she did she would leave the people unprotected and without a voice. Because part of Will's magic—part of why she loved him—was that for the first time in her life she truly cared about the crowd. She fought not just for herself, but for them.

Will and them and her. Love, loyalty, and desire all tangled up. Will binding them tighter and tighter together, but fraying as he did so, threatening even as he cared. And here he was looking at her, imploring her for help.

So what else could she say but, "I know. It's okay. I'm here. I'm fighting for you. With you. I'll hold you together. I promise"?

And she didn't know if she could keep the promise, but here in the darkness, with Will curling into her body in the dark, she knew that for a while the fact that she had made the promise would be good enough.

All she had to do was figure out a way to help him kill Barph before she broke it.

43

Halfway There

Yorrax stared. So many dead. More dead than she could have imagined. Dragons laid out limp and lifeless one after the other. Their once-bright eyes gone dull. Their flames gone out. Half of all the remaining dragons in Avarra dead in one single swoop. A genocide.

It was brilliant.

Half of the petty, pathetic, iguana-fucking dragons who abused and derided her were gone. Half of those who stood in her way removed as obstacles.

Yorrax took a large bite out of Netarrax's neck. In death, as in life, he was salty and bitter.

Heavy footfalls approached from behind. She ducked her head, and tried to sneak a look at who was coming. Pettrax walked with Rothinamax, the large brown dragon wearing an expression of anger.

"You are not in charge," Rothinamax snapped at Pettrax.

"I will be if you lack foresight," Pettrax bit back. "Look around you. Barph was defeated on the backs of our bodies. The humans did nothing but nip at his ankles. We were the ones who drove him away."

Pettrax looked down at Netarrax's body, toeing at a limp wing. He seemed to notice Yorrax for the first time, and promptly kicked her out of the way.

Yorrax snarled, but Pettrax's attention was already back on

Rothinamax. "We were victorious, but whom do the humans celebrate? Who claims the glory?"

Pettrax leaned in close to Rothinamax. "It is as we always suspected. The humans can think of us only as tools. Will Fallows will betray all his promises to us. So we must betray him first. It is now only a question of when, and how to make it count the most."

"He is already too powerful—" Rothinamax started.

"You have the balls of a gecko." Pettrax cut him off. "The only reason you have survived today is you lacked the bravery to truly engage in the fight."

Rothinamax bared teeth. Pettrax didn't waste a second. Flame engulfed Rothinamax's face. There was a flurry of wings and talons, and then Rothinamax's head was slammed to the ground, his neck pinned by Pettrax's claw.

"I yield," the old dragon coughed. "I yield."

Pettrax sneered. "Of course you do."

But Yorrax was barely paying attention. She was no fool; she knew these power games were taking place far above her head. But perhaps now she had a path to the top that was more reliable than waiting for Barph to kill all her opponents.

When, where, and how to betray Will Fallows. That was the key to it all. That was what would make the dragons dominant over all Avarra. And the dragon who provided the information on how to do that…

Yorrax knew she was small. Knew she lacked the blunt power of many of her kin. But that was not the only path to supremacy.

I swore, she thought, looking at Netarrax's corpse, *to kill Will Fallows while standing on your corpse and Pettrax's.* She stepped up onto Netarrax's dead body and surveyed the land. *Well, now I am halfway there, old beast.*

44

I Would Do Anything
for Power, but I Won't Be
Allowed to Do That

Gratt roared. Gratt raged. Gratt swept his claws through the wall of a ramshackle barn. Rotten wood cracked and split. Gratt dropped his shoulder, burst through the ruined wall. Cattle were screaming and thrashing. He hoisted a cow aloft and hurled it into the crowd. More animal screams. Human ones too. He waded in. He waded out red with gore.

He emerged from the barn and saw the rest of the farmstead in flame. A few people were running across the fields. His troops were in pursuit.

His troops...

Gratt roared. Gratt raged. But there was no one left to kill.

He had held all of Batarra. He had seized a city and crushed its heart as if it were nothing. He had ripped the life from a country and taken it for himself.

And then Barph. Barph casually stepping out of a tear in reality to rail at him about Klink. Barph screaming and frothing. Barph decimating his army. His troops.

Half of his army had been killed in mere minutes. And almost as if Barph weren't truly paying attention to it. A mere sweep of the hand and a third had died. A single volley of arrows that was turned back, each shaft burying itself in life after life. Half of them dead like that. As if it were nothing.

And then the desertions. The despair. And all his acts of rage and discipline did was speed things up. His troops scattering into the night. Even his lieutenants, who had come out of the Hallows with him. His power sputtering away with each act of cowardice he couldn't control.

He still held a few hundred men and women to his cause. There were still those too loyal or too cowed to flee. But a few hundred troops could not take a country. They could not unseam Batarra and spill its wealth into his hands. The rest of Avarra was a joke.

And so here he was, razing this farmstead to the ground. Here he was, seizing cattle and chickens and a handful of horses, all so... so what? So he could annex another farmstead somewhere else.

It was pathetic. It was rage inducing. And here he was with no one left to kill.

He picked up one of the panicking cows and killed it instead. It was about as satisfying as annexing a farmstead.

"I keep telling you: It's about faith."

Gratt honestly wasn't sure why he still kept Lawl alive. They were long past the point where the gods' subjugation was amusing. Toil still wept each morning, and there was something in that, but it had lost most of its edge through repetition. Knole was essentially catatonic these days, lost so thoroughly in her head that she was impervious to taunts. Betra was occasionally pliable, but her attempts to win favor through seduction were so painful that they had become more sad than anything else these days.

And Lawl. Still offering advice. Still so convinced of his worth.

"These people believe in you. These people are a start," Lawl went on, sitting cross-legged in his cage. "Make it about faith.

About belief. You can become the god you want to be through them."

The worst of it was the nagging doubt that perhaps Lawl was right. Perhaps that was what he should have done, and perhaps now things wouldn't be so desperate. But to take his advice now. To go crawling to Lawl for advice. Just the thought of Lawl's smug smile.

Gods. Why hadn't he killed Lawl yet?

Why hadn't he?

Perhaps there was someone left to kill today, some violence that could still put a smile on his face.

"Will Fallows could still be bent to your will." Lawl was prattling on. "He has the right idea. He has a cult. Make him your creature, and the crowds are your creature. Do it now, before he tries to put his own blood in the Summer Palace's font."

Gratt crossed to where Lawl's cage sat on the edge of what he was charitably thinking of as the battlefield. He tore the door off it.

"I'm glad to see—" Lawl started. Then Gratt's fist was around his throat, yanking him out of the cage.

"I have had enough," Gratt spat, "of your advice, old man. You have not learned to curb your tongue, and so I must remove it from you. I think it starts somewhere around your neck." He flung Lawl to the dirt, yanked out his sword, and yes, he was smiling again. This was a piece of bliss that could warm his heart.

Lawl twitched and flailed and shrieked in the dirt. Gratt raised the sword, lined up his blow.

And then he brought the blade down.

And then the blade stopped.

Lawl screamed again.

The blade was three inches above his neck.

The blade was resting in a man's hand.

A god's hand.

Barph was there. Barph holding the edge of Gratt's blade. Saving Lawl's life. Thwarting Gratt's desire.

"Tell me," Barph said. "Tell me you weren't just about to do that. We had words about this. I explained very carefully. You don't get to kill these people. That's a pleasure reserved for me. So tell me, very nicely, that you weren't about to fuck that up again, Gratt."

Gratt decided to explain by screaming, "Die!" very, very loudly and ripping out Barph's throat.

It didn't go as well as he had hoped.

When he could sit up again, he did so. Barph and Lawl appeared to be yelling at each other.

"—don't need your help!" Lawl was yelling.

"—so fucking proud!" Barph was yelling at the same time. "So petty and absurd. This is why you wallow, Lawl. This is why—"

"There is no love for you in this land! You give people wine and still—"

"—you are nothing to me. Why I let you twitch and twitch. Your inability to learn is my constant amusement."

"—they hate you! You are an empty impotent god unworthy of the name."

Barph backhanded Lawl across the face. The god flew like an arrow from a marksman's bow. "I am twice the god you ever were!" Barph screamed. "I am seven times the god!"

Barph was, Gratt noticed as his head cleared, not arrayed with his usual majesty. His beard appeared to have been burned off. He was missing an eyebrow. His clothes were ragged and slashed. Had Lawl done that? Lawl couldn't have done that.

"I am the god!" Barph was yelling. "I am your god!"

Gratt picked himself up. Barph had his back to him, was facing Lawl, utterly absorbed. Gratt licked his claws, stalked forward.

"You shall worship me," Barph howled at Lawl. "You shall

bend your head and your knee, and you shall beg me for forgiveness!"

"I would rather worship my own piss."

"You—" Barph started.

Gratt leapt, claws outstretched, teeth bared, silent and deadly.

Barph caught him in midair. Gratt wasn't even sure the god had turned around. He had just simply been facing one way, and then he faced another. The intervening motion seemed to have been snipped out of reality.

"I am having," Barph growled, "a private conversation."

There was a pause after that. Barph seemed to notice for the first time that the few hundred troops Gratt still controlled had stopped in their wanton pillaging and were all staring at this exchange.

"Fine," Barph muttered. He swept a hand at the troops.

And again. Again. How could it happen again?

Half of them dead. Half of his men dead. Just dropped lifeless to the ground, their veins black and bulging. Gratt howled.

Barph shook his head. "There," he said, almost to himself. "Perhaps you'll learn now."

He looked at Lawl, still lying on the ground, dirty and bloody, and with a face full of hate. He shook his head again. "I don't…," he started. "You don't… You mean nothing to me."

And then he was gone.

Gratt fell to the ground. He was still screaming. Half his men were screaming. Screaming at the dead half on the ground next to them.

"You must…," Lawl said, grabbing at Gratt, hauling on him.

Gratt turned murderous eyes on him.

"Will Fallows," Lawl spat. "You have to turn him to your will."

And gods. Gods. It was all the fucking gods' fault. Gratt wanted to tear this fallen creature's throat out. He wanted to scatter his limbs across the world. But he could not. Because of another god.

He couldn't bear the sight of Lawl anymore. Not of any of them.

"Get out!" he screamed at Lawl. Lawl stared at him. Gratt stalked toward the cage with the other gods, with Betra and Toil and Knole. "Get the fuck out!" he yelled. He couldn't stand the sight of them. "You're a fucking hex!" he bellowed.

And it was true, he thought. It had to be true. It had to be someone else's fault. Lawl's fault. The former gods' fault. The current god's fault. Barph's fault.

He tore the roof off the cage holding the other gods, tumbled them out onto the dirt. They were all staring at him.

"Go!" he roared. "Go! No more will I have you bring death to these people." He had to make his troops see it as the former gods' fault. That's how low he was. He was pandering to these plebs.

Slowly Lawl got up, started to stagger away. Then the stagger broke into a run. And the other gods stared for a moment and then finally got up and broke into their own running jogs, half falling over the landscape, mounting a rise and then disappearing over it as he watched.

Gone. They were gone.

He felt oddly relieved, oddly bereft. The two emotions wouldn't reconcile, just swirled together inside him.

He looked back to his troops. What was left of his troops. Just one lieutenant left to stare at all his dead compatriots. Gratt beckoned the man forward. He lowered his voice. Hopefully nobody else had really listened to his conversations with Lawl.

"Okay," he said. "We have a new objective. Every resource we have left now goes into finding and capturing Willett Fallows."

45

Back to Our Regularly Scheduled Programming

"No," Balur said.

Everyone stared at him. He didn't particularly care. Unless one of them had spent the entirety of their acquaintance hiding the fact that they were a basilisk in an extraordinarily convincing disguise, staring at him wasn't going to do any damage.

"But—" Afrit said.

"No," Balur repeated. He was thinking that he had been pretty clear the first time, but apparently it bore repetition.

"But the Analesians are your own kind," Afrit said, which Balur was forced to assume must be indicative of some sort of learning disability.

Fortunately he had fists.

Will, though, apparently wanted to be punched more than Afrit did. "It doesn't matter what Balur thinks," he cut into the conversation. "This isn't a democracy. I have said we'll go into the desert to try to recruit some Analesians, and now we're going to do it."

"Is this not the point," Balur asked, looking at Afrit, "where you are pointing out that he is being an asshole dictator, and that the geopolitical contours of Analesian society are not being conducive to recruitment?"

"Geopolitical contours?" Afrit looked at Balur with an insulting amount of surprise.

"Why don't you want to go back to Analesia?" asked Cois, still with hir hand on his arm.

"Which jackass brought up Analesia?" Lette walked into the impromptu discussion. They were all sitting around a table in a burned-out farmstead. The owners were long gone, but somehow a dining table had survived the worst of the blaze, and that had been enough to recommend the site as a camp for the evening.

"The Analesians will make excellent shock troops, and supplement our numbers after the loss of our dragons," Will said. Balur had the distinct impression he was talking at the air instead of to any of the individuals actually standing in front of him.

"Oh, shit." Lette's eyes went straight to Balur. "Are you okay?"

Balur shrugged and tried to pretend that he was.

"Why should he not be okay?" It was sweet of Cois to worry, and also definitely not helping the situation.

Will stood before Balur had to worry about an excuse. "I'm tired," he said to Lette. "Let's go to bed."

Lette sent another worried glance at Balur. He shook his head as fractionally as possible. He didn't want Cois fretting over him. And Lette had enough on her plate with whatever Will was becoming without needing to worry about him.

Lette hesitated, but then she and Will linked arms and headed back toward the door Lette had just appeared through.

"We are all knowing you don't sleep," Balur called after Will. "We all know you're just running away."

Then he waited until everyone else had left, just to make sure no one had a chance to accuse him of the same thing.

Three days later, Cois walked with hir delicate hand in his clumsy one as they traipsed toward the Analesian Desert.

"Are you going to do the strong brooding thing the entire way?" zhe asked.

Balur thought about it. He supposed he hadn't said much since Will had set them on this course. But he knew exactly what zhe wanted to talk about.

"I am supposing so," he told hir.

"Hmm." Zhe grimaced. "Well, then I suppose you're lucky that it's extraordinarily sexy on you."

Zhe grabbed his ass. He found it did raise his spirits a little.

Since leaving the Analesian Desert, Balur had discovered that humans had a lot of poetic names for different parts of the world. Salera was the world's gateway to the Amaranth Ocean. Atria was the Lost Island. Kondorra was, to a certain subset of tavern-goers, Avarra's Cock.

No one had a poetic name for the desert. There was nothing poetic about it. It did not have drifts of golden sand. It did not have sun-tarnished slopes. It was not Avarra's heart, because if it were then Avarra would have a septic, necrotic heart that was rotting the rest of the world from the inside out.

The Analesian Desert had only one purpose: to kill you and everyone else stupid enough to wander into it. It was a swirling wilderness of jagged rock, biting sands, razor-edged winds, and creatures either too stupid or too stubborn to go anywhere else.

Balur didn't know which category the Analesians fell into. Probably both.

Most of Will's followers, in Balur's estimation, fell into both camps as well. However, there were degrees of stubbornness and stupidity. After just four hours in the desert's heat, Balur could sense that Will was losing some of his support.

"You were raised here?" Cois's voice was muffled by the makeshift scarf zhe'd pulled up over hir face to block the flying sand.

"The brood mothers raised me," he said. "Yes."

"Brood..." Cois shook hir head. "You know, I never paid much attention to the Analesians when I was divine. Your race was never truly interested in romance. Lawl was the one who cared for you. Lots of fighting and discipline, as I recall." Zhe squinted at him, and not just because of the sand. "You don't seem big on discipline."

"Once the birth mother's eggs are hatching," Balur told hir, choosing the focus of his reply carefully, "the young are being taken to the brood mothers. The brood mothers are being the females who are too old to be birth mothers. It is being them who are teaching the young Analesians what they are needing to know, how to be surviving in the desert. You are listening to them or you are dying. Many are dying. Those who are not dying are strong enough to be Analesians."

It was more than he'd ever told Quirk about Analesian society, he supposed.

Cois weighed the information. "Living in the Analesian Desert is stupid," zhe said.

He nodded. "Yes. But it is making you strong."

Cois squeezed his bicep. "Yes indeed." Zhe wiggled hir ass as zhe walked beside him.

But Balur was thinking that he hadn't lived in the desert for a long, long time.

They came in the night, as Balur had known they would.

Will's followers had wasted an hour trying to set up their tents, trying to cook supper. In the end they had wrapped themselves in blankets and eaten what food they could manage raw. Conversation was muted. Will had walked among his faithful, seemingly unaffected by the biting sand and suddenly plunging temperatures. He had settled the few rumbles of resentment Balur had overheard. Still, no one was happy to be here.

There were sentries now, walking their routes, blinking against the flying sand, calling out to the shadow shapes of those looking for a quick place to piss in peace.

He'd known the sentries wouldn't do much good. Still it was better to have them. It would give the Analesians something to focus on.

It was dark as pitch when the screams started. Balur cursed, scrambled up, started running. It took a while, but he had wanted Cois as close to the center of the camp as he could manage. It would take the Analesians longer to get to hir there. It would give Will longer to pull a miracle out of his ass.

In Balur's mind the best-case scenario would have been to run headlong into a scene of bloody chaos. Unfortunately, what he arrived at was a scene of carefully coordinated slaughter. The Analesians were systematically moving through the rows of guards that were forming up, killing them one by one with very little apparent effort.

Balur grimaced. As much as he loved a good fight, this was going to be no fun whatsoever.

He roared. He charged. He sank his claws and teeth into scales. He bit. He tore. He clawed.

And his opponent did it right back to him.

Someone hit him on the side of the head with a fist like a war hammer. He reeled away, lashed out with his tail, felt it collide with hard muscle. Strong arms gripped it, wrenched it painfully. He stepped into the maneuver, buried his knee in his target's guts. They doubled over, opening their jaws to savage his underbelly. He drove his elbows into their spine. They flicked their tail up to smash into his skull.

Again. Again. Again. They threw claw and tooth, fist and tail against each other. An unending deluge of crushing blows, with only one purpose: to see who was stronger, who would be left standing.

And if he survived this, all Balur could do was throw himself against the next Analesian in line.

But the desert made Analesians strong, and Balur had not lived in the desert for a long time.

A blow snuck through his guard, collided with the side of his temple, spun him around, landed him facedown in the sand. His snout twisted with an agonizing wrench. A foot landed in his spine, applied pressure. His vertebrae screamed.

Someone shouted his name, which was nice, he supposed. It was nice to be mourned. And it was good to go out fighting.

Then the weight was gone, and he was sucking in air, even through the pain in his snout. He heaved himself to all fours. Still he didn't die. He got to his knees. Still he didn't die. Then he was on his feet.

Everything was curiously silent. He turned around. And... oh gods...he was never going to live this one down. No matter that Will was semidivine these days. No matter that he possessed speed, strength, and skill that no human should possess. No matter that he was half-purple. There was simply being no way that Balur could ever be living this down.

Will had saved him. Will stood with the throat of an Analesian warrior in his hand. Will stood facing down a tribe.

And...Well, when the gods pissed it poured. Of all the tribes in all the deserts...

"Balur," growled one of the Analesians. "Exile."

Balur nodded to the speaker. "Ralk," he said. Ralk was bigger than he remembered him. A full foot taller than the last time they'd set blazing eyes upon each other. Broader in the shoulder and chest too. He looked down on Balur now, yellow eyes in a coal-black face, scales a series of sharp triangles like a skin of teeth.

"You are not being worthy to speak his name," another Analesian spat at Balur.

He picked the face out of the crowd. "You were always being a lickspittle, Alack."

Alack balled his fists, curled his legs.

"I will kill you where you stand." Will sounded almost bored.

Alack hesitated. And Balur wasn't entirely sure how Will had killed the lizard man who had been crushing his spine, but it must have been mighty fucking impressive.

There were about twenty Analesians standing before them, hulking shadows looming out of the black night. A full war party. Balur recognized perhaps half of them—their sloping foreheads, their flickering tongues, their craggy hides. The rest were younger members of the brood. Perhaps he had known them once. Perhaps they had looked up to him. Once.

His old tribe. His tribe before Lette. Before Cois. His first tribe. His people.

What a bunch of dickholes they were being.

"Be stepping aside, Will," he said. "I am having things to kill."

Ralk laughed, long and loud. It was an obviously false laugh, but Ralk clearly didn't care if anyone knew that.

"You?" he said. "Exile? Be killing us? When this human was having to save you from young Bolloxt? The runt was having you on the ground. You were being the runt's plaything. And you are thinking you can be taking us?" His tongue licked the air, long and lasciviously. "You are being weak, exile. You have always been being weak. You will always be being weak. The soft lands of the humans will be killing you before long." His tongue flickered up in amusement.

More people were coming now. People with torches and drawn swords. They were wild-eyed and confused. The sand smelled of blood.

"Hold!" Will called, holding out his hand toward them. "Hold!"

"No, little human," said Ralk, stalking forward. "This is being the way of the desert. Tooth for tooth. Claw for claw. This is being a place of strength. This is being a place for shedding weakness. Be letting them come. Be letting them find their strength. Or be letting them see if we are finding them wanting." He opened his mouth, showed jagged teeth.

Oral hygiene. That was another thing humans had brought to Balur's life that he had a hard time being sad about.

"We are not here to fight you," Will tried.

"Then you are being here to be being killed by us. To be letting us drink your blood and be feasting upon your flesh." Ralk had always been a monotonous bastard.

"Shut up," said Balur, stalking past Will, coming face-to-face with Ralk. "You are posturing like a broodling still trying to figure what he should be using his prick for. He is here to be recruiting you to his great fight against Barph. You will be refusing."

He looked over his shoulder to Will. "See, that part is being taken care of. Now we are fighting. And we shall win. And those who are left will be stronger for it. Then we shall either be repeating this process or be leaving. Because I was telling you this was being a stupid idea."

He turned back to Ralk. "Now," he said. "Be ready."

But Ralk did not spread his arms and straighten his tail. He did not prepare for combat. Instead he straightened up and turned his back on Balur. "No," he said.

Balur couldn't actually believe it. He'd known Ralk was a prick, but... "Coward!" he roared at Ralk.

And then Ralk turned and Balur brought back his fist, but before he could strike, Ralk had him by his injured muzzle and was twisting and heaving, sending Balur to his knees.

"No!" Ralk roared. "You are not daring! You are not daring say that to me! Not you, exile. Never you. He who was not being strong enough to accept his tribe's weakness. He who was betraying the codes of battle. He who was betraying his new kin. He who was slaying those with their guards down. Simpering lickspittle of the brood mother's teats. Will-less child. Exile. Never you. I am not deigning to fight you. You are not being worthy of me. Killing you is showing no strength on my part. I would rather be fighting a human than you."

Balur struck and struck at Ralk's arm, at the hand that ground against his wound. But Ralk's arm did not move.

And here, in front of all of them. In front of all the gathered crowds...his weakness revealed. Gods...

"Stop it! Stop it!" Someone was shouting. And gods...But of course a god was here, and that was the problem.

"Stop it!" screamed Cois.

Cois trying to defend him. Fuck.

"Oh, look!" Ralk crowed, still not releasing Balur. "She who would be sullying herself with the exile has come to beg for his life. To be pleading for us to spare his weakness."

Balur tried to growl at Cois to stay back. But Ralk's thumb kept his jaw firmly closed. He hissed and spat into the bigger Analesian's palm.

"Oh, tall, dark, and scaly," Cois said, "I think I have a little more than you can handle."

Ralk laughed. And even as Cois made things worse, Balur loved hir.

"I am thinking," said Ralk, "that once I am being done killing your boyfriend, then I shall be showing you what a real Analesian is being."

"I am thinking," said Will, "that I'm going to kill you and see if there's someone smarter I can talk to."

Ralk grinned. "Now that is being a challenge," he said, "that I would be willing to be accepting."

Will cracked his knuckles. Ralk dropped Balur to the ground. Balur tried to pick himself up quickly, but his limbs betrayed him with their shaking.

"No," someone said for what had to be the hundredth time since this whole pissing conversation began. Apparently Lette had decided to join the chorus.

Ralk's question came out more as a bass growl.

"No," Lette said again. She had a torch, Balur saw, and was striding toward the center of this whole shit show. "We do not deign to fight with you. You who betrayed the codes of battle. You who attacked brood mothers after the fight was won. You who murdered babes. You who abused his victory. You who lied to his brothers and exiled a good warrior to hide his shame."

Ralk, it seemed, wasn't done growling.

Lette turned to the gathered crowd. "They accused Balur of being dishonorable. They exiled him for this accusation. But what is dishonorable to the Analesians? What do the codes dictate they do when the warriors of two tribes clash? When a defeat has been acknowledged?" She turned to Ralk. "Do the two tribes not then come together in peace? Do they not evict the weak and join their strength together? Does not the slaughter stop?"

Now she turned to Balur, finally picking himself up off the ground. And he wished Lette would be quiet. None of this would change anything. This was history. This was all still stupid.

"They say Balur did not stop. That is the crime they lay at his feet. To continue fighting for his clan once his defeat was acknowledged."

"They say the truth," Balur rumbled before Ralk could do it himself. He would own this. It was true.

Lette nodded. "They do. They do. But Ralk would like us to forget why you fought. He would like to hide his own crimes. Because you were not the only one who continued to kill once the fight was over, were you?"

She looked over at Balur. He grimaced at her. He saw no point in this. The Analesians would not suddenly throw up their arms in horror and abandon Ralk. Whatever else he had done, he had delivered victories, and that was all Analesians cared about.

Lette rolled her eyes at him. "Come on, big guy. Play for the crowd." Then she wheeled on Ralk again. "And Ralk here—big, strong Ralk—didn't fight warriors, did he?"

Ralk's growl ended, and he leapt. His massive talons aimed

straight for Lette's throat. And gods hex him, he was fast for a big lizard.

Balur was moving, but gods, he was too slow.

Will wasn't.

Somehow he slipped past Balur. Past Lette. Somehow he traversed space that should have been impossible to traverse that fast. And then his fist was connecting with the tip of Ralk's snout, and the big lizard man's momentum was reversing, his body only catching on slowly, performing a cartwheel in the air and landing him on his arse.

Surreptitiously, Will nursed his knuckles.

Ralk stared up at Will, dazed.

"Ralk—" Lette said, and Balur finally noticed that she wasn't talking to the other Analesians here, all of whom were staring at Will and Ralk in amazement. Lette was talking to the gathered human crowd, telling them a bedtime story. "—with victory declared, with the fight over, went to the defeated tribe's brood pits. Went to their young. And he proceeded to slaughter the brood mothers. The caretakers of the young. Then he killed their young. The innocents. After peace was declared, he murdered babes. And so Balur attacked Ralk. He defended the defenseless. His people. His tribe. He defied the laws and the rules to do what was right. He stepped the fuck up. Because that is who he is. That is why he fights with us. It is why we fight with him."

And now, finally, she turned to the Analesians. "And if you want him," she said, "then you'll have to come through us."

The crowd roared. Even with their dead at their feet and the scent of shredded organs in their nostrils, they cheered. And for just a moment, Balur felt just a touch of pride. These people.

This new tribe of his.

At Will's feet, Ralk growled again, started to pick himself up.

"Fuck it," Balur heard Will mutter.

Then Will kicked Ralk in the temple. Ralk's head flew around, and there was an audible crack from his neck. Then the lizard man fell limp to the ground.

His new tribe.

Balur roared. He fucking roared. And he saw that lickspittle Alack, his brood brother, he who had been first to condemn him. And he saw the lizard man's eyes go wide. Because while the desert made Analesians hard, some had flaws that betrayed that strength.

Balur waded into the crowd of Analesians. And yes, he had lost this fight once, and yes he was injured, and yes he hurt, but gods piss on it, he was back in the desert, and the desert made you strong or it killed you. And he would not die today.

Alack dropped his weight, lunged. He was lean and lithe, strong and fast.

But he did not have a sword.

And then he did. Lodged in his throat.

It was cheating, perhaps, Balur reflected, as Alack gurgled at him. It was not the Analesian way. Their way was red of tooth and claw. But Balur had been gone from the desert a long time. And in the end, a reach advantage was a reach advantage.

"Who is being next?" he roared.

There weren't any volunteers.

"That is what I am fucking thinking." Balur spat blood at his feet. Gods, his snout was messed up.

Finally one of the Analesians dropped to his knee. "We acknowledge your strength," he said to Will. "We bow to your tribe's superiority. We beg to be joined with you."

Balur spat again. "No," he said, not giving a shit what Will had been about to say behind his back. "We reject your request. We do not want you. You are not strong. You are not our tribe." He turned to look at the people gathered around him. Petty and weak and stupid, but also good and hopeful and—above all—bound together by common dreams and aspirations.

"This," he said. "This is my tribe."

It was, Balur was fairly sure, a glorious moment. It might even be a bardic moment. There was some gods-hexed poetry in it.

And then Will went and rather undercut everything by putting his hand on Balur's shoulder and saying, "Remember how I said this thing wasn't a democracy..."

46

Can't We Have an Upbeat Chapter?

Gratt's once-dead forces caught up with them again the day after they left the desert, and entered Verra.

It was not a large force, but the ambush was well prepared, and there was a sense of desperation to the fighters in spite of the numbers they faced.

Will's followers had bedded down at another farmstead, this one inhabited and very grateful to receive an alternative to Barphian dogma, even if the large pack of Analesians that now traveled with Will did give them some pause.

Lette woke early, the morning light still a barely realized dream. Will was gone, off on his nocturnal wanderings, and her bedroll was cold. She lay there for a moment, waiting for a cockerel to curse, but the crowing didn't come. That was not what had wakened her.

She went to the window, and then she heard what it was that had roused her from her slumber.

The clink of chain mail.

Most of Will's followers were enthusiastic amateurs in the fighting game. They had learned a lot in their months sojourning around Avarra, but still most of them were distinctly lacking in armor, and of those who possessed it, few were in the habit of donning it first thing in the morning.

She listened. Fifty bodies perhaps. Making their stealthy way through the camp.

Lette made judgment calls one by one in her head. If she called out, a lot of people sleeping in makeshift tents would die. Will's followers would win eventually. The algebra of battle was wildly in their favor. But a lot of them would die. If she set about them by herself... fifty was a lot of people. Five she might have felt confident about, but fifty... She didn't know where Balur was. He'd been sulking ever since Will had overridden him in Analesia and recruited the lizard men to his cause.

The lizard men would be prepared for battle almost instantly, but their tents were pitched at the outskirts of the camp, far enough away that they wouldn't scare the animals...

The animals...

Verran farms, it turned out, had some very interesting animals...

As quietly as she could—and far more quietly than the men creeping through the camp looking to assassinate Will—Lette slipped out of the room.

Ten minutes later, Lette made considerably more noise.

The beast beneath her bucked and squealed and gnashed vast tusks, and then it just fucking charged.

Verran war pigs. Holy shit.

She had heard of them, of course, but she'd never had a chance to see them up close before. Most of her mercenary wanderings had taken her to the east, not the west. And she appreciated that the east had been a profitable place, that it had allowed her to face down dragons twice, and that it had led her to the man she loved. But at the same time, she was beginning to think she had made a mistake in missing out on war pigs until now.

They were vast slavering beasts the size of oxen, covered in sharp bristles and thick drool. Their mouths were nightmare slashes of broad yellow teeth, and they had the eyes of true psychotics. Lette would never have gotten on the back of one if she hadn't had the farmhands with her. She had roused them as she made an exit from the farmhouse. There was no need for the once-dead to find them sleeping there.

A quick run to the sties and the strapping of a saddle onto a belligerent monster. And now here she was, charging the fifty confused-looking once-dead recruits emerging from the farmhouse.

The tusks of her mount took the first of the once-dead in the gut. He was hoisted aloft in a spray of gore, sent flipping feet over arse, sprawling through the air.

Verran war pigs were, in Lette's opinion, fucking brilliant.

The rest of the pigs came now, the farmhands on their backs armed with pitchforks and shovels, wielding them with wild abandon, screaming and shouting at the top of their lungs.

The rest of the camp started to wake to the danger.

But the once-dead in the camp weren't alone.

One of the once-dead lifted a horn to his lips that seemed to be largely made of human tibias. He blew short panicked notes. Calls answered. And suddenly two hundred or so more troops were charging into the slowly rousing camp.

It might have been worse if it hadn't been for the Analesians. They boiled out of their beds and directly into the face of the once-dead charge. It was as if Barph himself lowered a divinely sized hand drill into their enemies. Blood and gore seemed to fly away into the air, like discarded chaff.

It was short and bloody and vastly exhilarating. Lette's beast galloped wildly through the camp, one enemy combatant caught on its tusk, the body flopping obscenely. By the time she got to the Analesians, it was a rout.

Lette threw a victorious fist into the air and shouted Will's name to the heavens. People gathered around her and the Analesians as she dismounted, clapped them on the back, shouted with excitement and praise. The Analesians, after a moment of confusion, settled on looking supremely smug.

Balur was still nowhere to be seen.

The pigs tried to get a start on consuming the dead before the dragons did. The dragons, though, when they arrived, were in no mood to share. In all honesty, they had been in a vile mood since the encounter with Barph and their failure to do much but die at his feet. That the Analesian sands had grounded them and that they had slept through most of this fight did nothing to improve matters.

Lette found one riderless pig who seemed to be questioning whether the vast size difference between it and the dragon in front of it really mattered. It was the sort of idiocy she found charming in Balur. She did her best to push the huge animal back toward its farm.

"Thank you!" A farmer was running up from the newly liberated farmstead holding a brace of bridles. Five or six more men were coming up in his wake.

"Here, Alice!" the farmer called to the pig Lette was heaving against, and the slab of muscle abruptly moved, almost spilling her on her arse. "Thank you," he said again to Lette.

"That's our paladin," said someone else. One of Will's soldiers. Charliss, his name was. One of their better fighters, and a good-hearted man to boot. She liked him. He clapped her on the shoulder as he walked past, a broad smile on his face.

She'd been hearing the term *paladin* more of more of late. She wasn't sure where it had come from. She certainly hadn't started it. In her experience, people who called themselves paladins were the sort of people who liked to commit mass murder and then make excuses involving the gods. She took great pains to keep the divine out of her excuses.

Still, she couldn't stop a smile from creeping up at the corners of her mouth when Charliss raised a fist to the sky and shouted, "Our paladin!"

"Our paladin!" cheered back those who had been fighting with her—bloody, sore, and victorious.

"Idiots," she said, but she couldn't put much feeling into the word.

"Not many who can inspire folk like that," said the farmer, sharing her smile.

"Me?" Lette huffed a laugh. "Gods, I'm just the tip of the iceberg."

Later she found Will down in the farmstead. He was leaning against the fence around one of the vast pigpens.

"So," she said, running a hand up his spine, "did you come here for the fine aroma, or the stimulating conversation?"

He didn't look over at her. "You know," he said, "in my head all this...all this with the dragons, and you and me, and everything...It all began the day I tried to kill my pig. She was called Bessie. And, gods, she was nothing like these pigs. Just a regular sow. Old and tough and heading to the great trough below soon enough. And I needed to kill her and sell her parts. But I didn't want to. My heart wasn't in it. Not at all. So I failed. And she lived. And that night soldiers burned my farm to the ground. So I ran into the woods, took shelter in a cave—"

"And met me," she finished the story.

"And met you," he said.

She wrapped her arm around his shoulders. "A lot of miles traveled since then."

"Yes."

"How are you?" She didn't like asking the question. She hated the answers more. But she knew it was important. She had to help keep Will grounded, keep him in the here and the now. With the people. She had to be their champion here more than on any battlefield.

Their paladin...

Will stayed staring at the pigs for a long time. Her heart prepared for the drop.

But then he leaned over and put his head on her shoulder and said, "Good. Today I'm actually doing good."

And thanks be to all the gods. Even Barph, if that was what it took.

"That's great, Will," she said. She turned and kissed the top of his head.

He put his arm around her and squeezed. "I think I just like pigs," he said.

"If that is in any way a comment on my eating habits, these people are going to be worshipping a man without genitals."

"It's weird, right?" he said. "The whole worshipping thing."

"Deeply."

The pigs shuffled around, grubbing in the ground for roots with their curiously mobile snouts.

"But," he said, "eventually it'll stop, won't it? I mean...if we do everything right, if we kill Barph. If we succeed. Then...then it's over. Then there's peace."

She thought about that. And to be honest it was a good thought. But...

"We didn't do so well together last time there was peace," he said so she didn't have to.

Six months. Six months of living together on a farmstead like this, and she'd been going out of her mind. And rather than confront Will about it, she'd just fled. It wasn't a high point in her life.

"I like pigs," Will said again. "And you don't."

The pigs kept on shuffling around in their slow circles, grunting to each other.

"I do like riding them, though," said Lette, finding a way back to happier thoughts. "I could do that again. That would be pretty gods-hexed brilliant. A whole cavalry charge of pigs.

Nobody would know what to do." She laughed to herself, and she felt Will laughing too. And it was nice to hear his slow chuckle once more.

"I bet," she went on, "that a line of pig cavalry could take on an equal number of Analesians, just on the strength of absurdity alone. They wouldn't know what to make of it."

"You're right," Will managed between chuckles. "I am fully behind this plan."

She squeezed him tight, felt the warmth of him, the humanity. But...

"You probably wouldn't like riding war pigs into battle, would you?" she said.

"I think it might push the absurdity a little too far."

She nodded. Still, it was nice to think of an afterward.

"But," Will said, "a band of mercenaries riding war pigs would need someone to look after the pigs. They'd need somewhere to get new pigs if something happened to the old ones. I imagine there's a lot of maintenance involved in war pigs."

She pulled back a little, turned and looked at him.

"Are you," she said with a soft smile climbing up the corners of her mouth and toward her eyes, "coming up with a plan, Willett Fallows?"

He grinned at her. And gods, when the light hit him right, he was a pretty man, even now, even through all the changes wrought upon him. "I might be," he said.

She kissed his forehead. "Tell it to me."

Will smiled. A really genuine smile. The sun was on his face, and it seemed as if he was staring straight into it as he spoke. "Imagine," he said, "riding off to war, your war pig between your thighs—"

"If you mention your cock next..."

"Let me finish." He was still grinning. "You ride off, astride your pig, with your war band at your back. And you do whatever it is you do for money. Probably murderize people, but

I'm going to pretend it's for good reason. And maybe it takes a week, or two, or maybe even a month. But then you ride back. You come home. You saddle up your porcine steed and you ride back. To a farm in the hills. To a place where there are droves of pigs in their sties. Where grunts ring in the air, and the stink of shit is as thick as stew."

"You're losing me."

"And me," he said. "And me, waiting for you to return. Waiting with open arms. Waiting to share all the future with you."

And his open arms folded around her, folded her into that future. And for a moment it felt real and possible, almost a certainty. For a moment she believed in it.

And for just a little while, that was enough.

47

With Friends Like These . . .

Back when he had had priests, Lawl had always been very clear with them that the whole "Pride is a sin" thing was bullshit.

Pride was what had gotten Lawl out of bed in the morning. It was what had helped him tolerate all the petty grievances of divinity. It was what had kept him from wiping away all of reality and starting everything over again. Pride had been air to him. He had been proud of what he had done, of what he had accomplished. He had been proud that he could look down every day and see a world that only he had created, that only he controlled. He had been proud of his physique, his position, his prowess.

Lawl was not proud anymore.

Lawl was footsore, body-sore, and gods-hexedly heartsore. He was bedraggled and hungry and exhausted. He was also thoroughly sick of what was left of his family.

"I can't go on," Betra bleated, which was what she said every five minutes despite the fact that she always seemed to eat twice as much as any of them and still maintained what could generously be called a svelte figure beneath her filthy robe.

"It takes forty days for the average mortal to starve," Knole replied, as if that were somehow relevant.

"It will take a minute for me to murder you and gain meat enough for a week," Toil snapped back, sounding as if that was distinctly within the realm of possibility.

Lawl debated for a moment and then backhanded his son across the face. Toil mewled and cringed.

"Shut up, all of you," Lawl said. "We will not go to Will Fallows as beggars. I refuse."

And yet, Lawl knew, that was exactly how they came. Cast out by Gratt, unable to support themselves in this new world, they were falling back on their protector from the Hallows. On the only viable challenge to Barph's authority in Avarra. On Will Fallows.

And Lawl was not proud of that at all.

They finally caught up with Will deep in the Barrons of Verra. The hills rose and fell around them, steep and low, as if a storm-tossed ocean had come to a sudden halt and grass had crept up on it over time. Herds of the goats and sheep Verra was famous for dotted the slopes.

Lawl almost turned back when he first saw the crowd. If he had been on his own he would have. How could he face Will now? How, with a crowd that size? How, when he came with nothing?

How had Will even amassed that many followers? So paltry compared to what Lawl had once had, and yet so many more than he had now.

But with Betra and Toil and Knole clinging to him like the clap, how could he ever live down walking away?

He tried to hold himself erect as he entered the swarm of bodies. He ran his fingers self-consciously through the tangle of his beard. He tried to walk as if the broken figure of Toil weren't really associated with him.

No one truly spared them a glance. They were just another group of weary travelers come to take refuge under Will Fallows's protective wing.

And if he had been a less proud man, maybe Lawl could have lived with that. Maybe he could have just slipped into the crowd and clung to the little bit of peace that came with belonging.

But he was Lawl, and he had been king of all the gods, and he had made this world, and so he could not.

Lawl let his little entourage through the thickening crowd to the edge of a makeshift stage on which Will Fallows was pacing back and forth.

For a moment Lawl didn't recognize the man. He had seen the purple blotching on the skin down in the Hallows, he had expected that, but the rest of it...Things had progressed.

Will was thinner than Lawl had ever seen him before. It was as if all the softness had been carved from him. Something of hard angles and lean muscle was left behind. He was taller too, maybe. Or was that an illusion due to the loss of weight? The time when Lawl would have known was lost to him.

The purple staining of the skin was more pronounced, and was offset by other, paler skin. It looked almost translucent in places, scaly in others. And for all that Will played with his hair and wore it long in the front, Lawl still saw something that looked like eyes bulging from his temples.

And, of course, there was the power. Lawl might no longer have access to it, but he had been around magic long enough to feel it coming off the man in waves. Will had an almost feverish heat emanating from him.

Lettera Therren was still with him as well, proving she had a stronger stomach than Lawl would have guessed.

Will didn't look up at their approach. Lawl cleared his throat. "Fallows," he said when that didn't work.

It took Will a long time to react. And when he finally did, it took even longer for Lawl to realize that Will simply was not going to recognize him.

"We are returned," he said, playing desperately for time. "Escaped from Gratt's clutches."

"Well...," Toil began, but fortunately Betra was there to elbow their son in the ribs for him.

And then, finally, thankfully, Will figured it out. "Lawl!"

he said. "Betra! Toil! Knole! You…" He looked at Lette. "You know," he said, "I have to say I'd rather forgotten about you."

Lawl ground his teeth together. "Well," he managed, "we have not forgotten about you or the plight of the Avarran people, and we are here, and committed to this cause."

He had fallen from grace for now, but grace could be reclaimed. If he positioned himself close to Will for now, he could grow to eclipse the little upstart once more. This would not necessarily be defeat.

Pieces of emotion seemed to flicker over Will's face. Nothing quite readable or truly whole. He looked at Lette again, seemed to gather himself. "I have to speak to the crowd."

Lette chewed her lip, looked at the gods. "They expect him," she said. And she at least had the decency to sound apologetic. She knew her place.

"Perhaps I can assist you," Lawl said. There was no time to work on his resurgence to power like the present.

Something that might have once been related to a smile appeared on Will's face. "Yes," he said. "Yes, why don't we do that?"

Lawl smiled.

"All of you," Will said, and there was the snap of command to his voice now, "on the stage."

It was not how Lawl wanted it, but Will's back was already to them. Lette opened her mouth several times but said nothing. Then she slipped away.

The sun was fading as they mounted the creaking boards. Oil lamps had been lit around it, casting flickering illumination up at Will as he paced back and forth. It was harder to see the discoloration of his skin in this light.

"To throw down a god," he boomed. His voice was amplified beyond the capacity of his lungs. "That's why we're here, isn't it? To reach up into the heavens and hurl him to the earth." He paused, looked around. And it was a beautiful imitation of human emotion, Lawl thought. Pitch-perfect. He even puffed out his cheeks. "That seems like a lot, doesn't it?" he said, almost conversationally. "A god. Us. Mere mortals. How can it be done?"

It was a good imitation of nerves, just enough to rile the crowd, safe enough because they knew Will would give them an answer.

"But of course," Will said, "it's been done before."

He turned, and now he smiled at Lawl and all the other gods. The first genuine emotion Lawl thought he'd seen. Something wolfish and hungry.

"We have guests!" Will boomed. "Newcomers to our family! Visitors from distant times come to jog our memories." He beckoned to the former gods with fake enthusiasm. "Come, come!" he called.

And if he could have walked away now, Lawl would have, but he had his pride. So with the others stumbling in his wake, Lawl stepped fully into the light.

"May I introduce Lawl!" Will cried. "Betra! Toil! Knole! Once gods of this world. Once our gods."

A gasp, a silence, a moment of wonder. And could it be, Lawl knew they all wondered, could these figures truly be their former gods?

Well, all he could do was seize the moment. He flung his arms wide. "We are returned to you!" he called, his voice sounding small and empty in the wake of Will's cries.

A flurry of activity in the front row, someone emerging, squealing with...Gods, was he about to be attacked? But then there was Cois leaping up onto the stage, seizing him and staring at him, smiling.

"You are an ugly, stupid old man," zhe whispered to him, "but you are family." And then zhe kissed him. Zhe kissed all of them. And Lawl found he might even be glad to see hir.

"Cois too!" Will yelled. "Truly a reunion to be remembered!"

Lawl stared out into the crowd, and he could see Balur there,

standing in the front row, eyes narrowed. And it was a look of . . .
Was it fear on the big lizard man's face?

Lawl did not feel this was going to go well.

"Look at them!" Will cried. "Look at all of them here. Our
gods!" The moment hung. The crowd just on the edge of uncertainty.

"Once," Will said. And all noise seemed to drop away at the
word.

"Once," he said again. "Before. Previously. Our *former* gods.
No longer."

And there was a bite to Will's words now.

"They were cast down, these gods. They were deposed. They
were replaced. And who did that? Who threw them down, as
we would Barph?"

Lawl needed to gain control of this situation quickly. "Your
enemy!" he called. "Barph—"

"You did!" Will rode over him with a voice like cannon fire.
"You took your faith in these failed figures away. And they
fell. They tumbled. That is your power. You toppled gods. All
of you. You have trod this path before! You tread it again! Your
refusal to be oppressed! Your refusal to bow to tyrants!"

And Lawl felt it now. The worship. The adoration. The fervor.
As the crowd chanted and howled and yelled, he felt it all rushing past him, flowing through his fingers and pouring into Will.

"You refuse again!" Will was still shouting. "You stand proud
again! You lift me up! You place me upon your shoulders! You
give me the power to throw down Barph! You! You make me
your champion! Your power in me!"

He strode the boards now, like some carnival barker. Lawl
and the others were forgotten, discarded props, straw men
already burned down.

"There will be no more tyrants. There will be no more petty
power-mongers. No more gods of nothing. Now there is me!
Now you have chosen me!"

And now Lawl saw Will's face truly in the light. He saw the wolfish smile again. Saw the way the skin was draped over the leering muscles and the bared teeth. He saw the hunger in Will, and he knew what this was.

And proud as he was, Lawl fled the stage.

48

The Voyeur

Barph watched the world slip by beneath him. He watched as his priests kicked and beat at those who defied his orders, at those who struggled so futilely against the chaos he had decreed be sown. He watched as those very people stuck spears into his priests' guts. He watched his priests die, their eyes cast imploringly up at him. He watched their hope die with them.

He stood in a heavenly garden, leaning on a wall. The bricks, once so neatly pointed, now crumbled beneath his arms. Someone had tried painting some of them. They smelled faintly of piss and stale wine.

He began to walk through the tangle of overgrown weeds and brambles. Toil had used to care for these gardens. He had cared so very much for them. He had killed mortals who had dared to compare their gardens to his. The memory made Barph smile. Then it did not. He stopped, chewed his lip pensively. He pulled a rose from the nearest tangle of branches and rolled it back and forth between his fingertips, feeling the thorns prick at his skin.

He had expected his and Will's confrontation back in Vinter to be the end of Will's little venture. The conflict had come earlier than he had been hoping for, but he had known the fun couldn't last forever. Will could not ever actually win. He could just twist futilely, fighting with just enough vigor to make life interesting, but eventually even Will would realize exactly how pathetic his efforts were.

And so, face-to-face with Will, Barph had decided to end things then and there. And he had done it with joy. It was best to go out on a high note, after all. And so Barph had defeated Will and mocked him. He had killed Will's dragon allies. And he had annihilated the spirit of Will's men.

Perhaps, looking back, the price had been a little higher than he had expected. Perhaps he had left the field of engagement a little earlier than he had anticipated, but…he had won. He had crushed Will and his rebels.

A thorn on the rose pierced Barph's skin. He winced, dropped the rose, ground it beneath his heel.

Will Fallows had not gone away. He had not faded into amusing insignificance. He had not even taken to drowning his sorrows in a bottle.

Will Fallows had had the audacity to thrive.

He could feel Will's power now, like a slight pressure against the side of his head. A sense of depression.

He could still end things if he wanted. Of course he could. Their last meeting…He had been caught off guard. Will's power was still nothing that could truly affect Barph's dominance. But it was still there. Still nagging. Still refusing to go away.

And what if Will's power continued to grow? What if they met and Barph was caught off guard again?

He summoned a thunderbolt to replace the discarded rose. He held it crackling in his hand. It was almost weightless. The electricity tickled his skin.

He looked down, saw Will Fallows. He was back in Verra after his little trip into the Analesian Desert. It had been amusing to push Balur's old tribe into their path. Certainly the slaughter had not quite lived up to Barph's expectations, but watching Balur squirm had been fun all the same.

Now Will paced back and forth among the sleeping forms of

his followers. Occasionally he looked blankly up at the heavens. His eye failed to see Barph looking back down at him, though. He was little more than blind.

Barph hefted the lightning bolt. He could throw it with enough force that Will would be nothing but a smear across the pages of history.

And yet… and yet…

He had always mocked Lawl for throwing thunderbolts. Had always told his father that he used them because he was too stupid to come up with a better solution.

Barph hesitated for a moment, enjoying the memory. The look of outrage on Lawl's face. Betra's eyes wide. Cois failing to hide hir smile. The sizzle across his arse cheeks as Lawl had flung the bolt at him.

He smiled. Old days.

Dead days. And it was the other gods who had killed them.

Barph let the thunderbolt fizzle. There were other—more amusing—ways to deal with Will Fallows.

49

Breaking Faith

Another guard tugged his forelock as Will walked past. Will only just remembered to acknowledge the gesture.

He had owned sheep before. He remembered it clearly. It was as if he had seen a play about the whole thing. Quite recently. He remembered the players, the names. He remembered the emotions that had played across their faces. He remembered how it had felt to own sheep. Counting heads. Fretting when one went absent. Caring for their needs. Feeding them. Helping them thrive. And then, when it was time, holding their heads back so he could slit their throats.

My flock, he thought. *That's how I think of them. Like they're sheep.*

He knew that was wrong. He knew he shouldn't feel that way. But he did.

He should talk to Lette. Talking to Lette helped.

Lette was asleep. He should let her sleep.

She still felt human to him, at least. And Quirk and Afrit. Balur too, which made him smile, given that Balur wasn't human at all. Cois, if he concentrated hard enough, could feel meaningful. But the rest of them? Not even Lawl felt as if he mattered much. Not even the dragons.

What if Lette stopped feeling that way to him? What if he stopped caring whether she got the rest she needed or not?

What if she stopped caring for him?

What if she worshipped him?

He rubbed his head, trying to excise the thoughts. Trying to find some sort of peace. He wanted to sleep. He wanted to curl up beside Lette and find oblivion.

He kept walking, away from the camp, away from the sleeping bodies, and away from the throbbing pulse of their adoration. Maybe if he walked far enough away he could get some rest.

He headed out into the hills. And he could have walked faster. He could have folded space and fled. He had that in him now. But he did not. He knew he wasn't really running away. A shepherd didn't leave his flock.

One of the hills of the Barrons was taller than the others, rising up to a sharp peak overlooking the resting horde. An old ruin was perched at its summit—an old temple to Toil or Cois perhaps. Maybe even to Barph. He headed there, clambering hand over hand when necessary, waiting for the soothing strain of aching muscles, but it never came.

When he reached the summit, whatever power had once resided in the place was long gone, drained away into the centuries. Now it was just broken stone columns, shadows, and ivy.

But...wait. Seriously? Was there really an actual shepherd out here?

An old man was jerking upright from where he had been lying against the ruined stump of an old fountain. Will could see a bedroll and the dying remains of a fire. He held a crook and was wrapped in a thick traveling cloak, the hood pulled up to obscure his features.

"What?" the shepherd said, blinking into the darkness. "Is someone there?"

Will almost laughed. Almost.

"You are a poor actor, Barph," he said. His initial surprise was over. The time when such illusions could have fooled him was long past now. But still he threw up his own. He clothed himself in an image of himself, something he could fling one way while he dived another. And that time was coming. Beneath the illusion of easy indifference, he tensed his muscles.

The shepherd straightened, pushed back his hood. Barph grinned out at him, teeth as white as stars in the night.

"Hello, Will."

This would be the end of it. Just the way Barph said the words, Will was sure of it. And would he be strong enough? Fast enough?

He knew he was not. He knew there were still so many miles to go. And if he fought here, he would never get to travel them.

But surely Barph knew that too.

And Barph was not attacking him. Could there be an opening here? A moment when he could seize an advantage?

"Why are you here?" Will managed to growl.

Barph shrugged. A movement too careless to actually be careless. "Just to talk. I have no one to talk to anymore, Will."

A strange play for sympathy. So misplaced. So unbelievable. Could it be a sleight of hand somehow? Still Will started to close the distance.

"You lie," he said. "All you do is lie."

Barph shrugged. "Honestly, my trade is more in half-truths than straight lies. It's far more entertaining that way."

"Anything you're here to tell me," Will said, "I can't trust." He could feel his anger like a beast inside him, raising its shaggy head. But he had to bide his time.

"You haven't asked what I want to talk about," said Barph. "Quite frankly, that feels a little impolite."

And he turned his back on Will.

Will's anger almost got the best of him, almost sent him skittering forward in a suicidal charge. He heaved back on its leash. He had to play this smarter.

Instead, he sent his illusory self stepping forward, gathered shadows around himself, stood where he was. And when Barph turned back, where would he look?

"I have no interest in hearing it," he had his illusion say. "It will be a lie."

"A half-truth," said Barph. "We went over this."

Will again resisted the urge to rush Barph while his back was still turned. He had to be stealthy. He slipped off to the side, slipped a knife from his belt.

"I remember a time before I took the Deep Ones' blood into me," Barph said, looking off over the Verran landscape. "A time before I was divine. I remember what it was like to change. We all do. All of us gods."

Of all the things he could say, Will had not expected that.

"Hard," Barph said. "Isn't it?"

And what was this? Why was Barph here? This had to be an attack. But was it more subtle than that? Was it an attack on his confidence? On what the power was doing to him? Will knew he was different now. But this was what it took. He kept stalking.

"There is no truth here," he had his illusion say again. It was as much for him to hear as Barph.

"I know how you feel about me, Will," Barph said. He still hadn't turned around. "I know so many things now. It's..." There was a slight hitch in his voice. A pantomime, Will was sure. "...different now. With all of this inside me. With all that I am now." Will kept moving. "And it strikes me that of all the people in the world, there are not so many people who could understand that."

Will almost laughed before he could throw the sound to his illusion. "You're appealing to my sympathy? I thought you were meant to be the trickster god. Don't you have a reputation to maintain?"

"No, Will." Barph's voice was distant. "Not sympathy. I'm

just...nostalgic. Simpler days. When I was Firkin. When we sat and talked."

For twenty-five years Barph had pretended to be someone he was not: a mentor, a friend, almost a father figure for more of those years than Will cared to think upon.

And gods, whichever way this went, Will would be glad for an opportunity to fight this god. "Well," his illusion said through gritted teeth, "you should have thought about that before you cut my throat."

Barph cocked his head to one side. And then, so very, very slowly, he began to turn.

Will held his breath. Because this would be the moment that everything hinged upon. This could be the decisive moment in Avarran history: Was Barph talking to him or to the illusory simulacrum of him?

He had penetrated Barph's own illusions easily, of course. It was likely Barph could do the same to his. Except...Will knew that not every flavor of divinity was exactly the same, and his illusory powers had not come directly from the Deep Ones. Rather they were secondhand, transferred to him from Cois. Who knew what the cocktail of divine sources would allow him to do?

"You'll lose her," Barph said, still turning, still bringing his eyes around, yet to find their resting place.

And Will couldn't even answer.

"We all lost people," Barph said. "It's inevitable." He shrugged. "Or maybe that's a half-truth. A lie you can ignore. Perhaps you won't leave her."

And he said it to the illusion.

Will actually couldn't believe it. This was the moment to strike. It couldn't be clearer if his own followers suddenly burst out of nowhere and sang a jaunty tune about how this was the moment to strike.

Forty yards left to close. Still moving slowly, still keeping shadows and silence clustered about him, Will kept on closing the distance. But he needed to buy time.

"You came here," his illusion asked, "to give me relationship advice?"

"No." Barph shook his head and Will braced. But Barph just stood where he was, looking oddly contemplative. "I didn't come here for any of this. But now...now I suppose what I really want to do is talk about old times. About the world when it was young. About who we used to be. Me and Cois and Lawl and all the rest. About when Lawl first united us. When we had just risen up and stolen power for ourselves. A time before I hated all of them."

Will was thirty yards away now, creeping, body held low, praying that he wouldn't kick a stone or be sent sprawling by a stray root.

"There was a time when Lawl wasn't a dick?" he had his illusion say. It bought time.

Barph smiled. And it was a genuine smile.

"Does he grate on you, Will?" he asked. "And no, he was always a prick. But he used to carry it better. One can be a prick when one is full of revolutionary fervor. Once one is in control, though, it rapidly loses its appeal. But he liberated us all. It was his plan that set us free. And so we tolerated him." The smile became a sneer. "Does any of that sound familiar, Will?"

Both Will and his illusion grimaced.

"I'm not the one in control," he said. "I'm not the sole god reigning over the world. I didn't connive for that position."

It was Barph's turn to grimace. "No," he said. "You are not." He turned. Will froze. Barph's eyes were about to sweep straight over him.

And they did. And they kept moving. Barph made no indication of having seen anything.

Twenty-five yards.

"Regrets?" Will's illusion said. There was the hint of a weak point here.

"No," said Barph, almost flinching. "They deserved it. I deserved it. This is justice. This is right. This is…this is what the world needs. I'm what the world needs. I've set it free. I've liberated it from the strictures Lawl put on it."

"Liberated?" Will's illusion was as outraged as he was. "You've visited death and destruction on the world! You've ruined lives! You've killed thousands, hundreds of thousands. Perhaps millions. That's not liberty. That's genocide."

"So *humans* are worse off." Barph shrugged. "What about the birds in the sky? What about the squirrels in the trees? What about the giants hunted and oppressed? What about the Analesians trapped in the desert? Why are your human concerns so important, Will? Am I not god of all things? Wheat grows free now. Hedgerows can sprawl as they were intended to do. Why are their concerns less important to me?"

"You're insane."

It really hit Will. Barph was out of his fucking gourd. He had always thought it was something vindictive or petty or cruel, but Barph was just utterly nuts.

"I simply have a broader perspective."

"That's why the other gods punished you. That's why they condemned you to eight hundred years of solitude. Because you're unhinged."

Barph leaned forward, civility slipping away, teeth bared. "They did that because they're fucking animals, Will. They're beasts, and they deserved to be treated as such. They had been beautiful and wonderful. And I had strived to make the world beautiful and wonderful just for them. I kept their lives interesting, exciting. I *entertained* them. I made the millennia pass. Do you have any idea how fucking boring eternity is, Will? Are you hoping to discover it with that petty scrap of divinity in you? I made the years tick by. I brought them highs and lows. I brought them unpredictability. I brought them chaos. I brought them wine, for fuck's sake, Will. And what did they do to me?"

"They stopped you," Will's illusion said. "Because you had to be stopped."

Ten yards now.

Barph stared at him, wild-eyed, for a moment. And then, abruptly, all the tension went out of his body, and he threw his head back and laughed. He roared at the heavens.

Eight yards.

"Oh, Will." Barph wiped at his eyes. "I have so missed having someone to talk to." He nodded. "You're not quite the sparring partner Cois is, but... Well, zhe's satisfied with lizard dick, so perhaps I overestimated hir for all those years." He shook his head. "It's a terrible thing, Will, to discover your lover has left you for a penis with scales."

Seven yards. Moving at a crawl. Desperate to do nothing that would give himself away, barely enough concentration to maintain the illusion, the conversation.

"Well," he managed, "you did kill hir."

Barph waved a hand. "Details." He sat down suddenly, folding his legs, leaning forward, looking up at Will's illusion. "You should have seen hir in hir prime, Will. Zhe was amazing. Zhe would walk into a room and people would collapse on the spot. Zhe was pure chaos. Love, Will. Love. That's the real madness, isn't it? And I loved hir. I loved all of them, Will. If anything has driven me mad, and maybe you're right, maybe it has... but if it has, it was that. I loved them."

Three yards. Two more paces.

Barph straightened up, stood. Will froze, holding his breath. Barph stretched, looking up at the heavens, rolling his head from side to side. "I really meant to kill you as soon as I came down here," he said. "But I'm glad we had this chat. It's been good for me, I think. Perspective and all that."

Will was almost directly behind Barph now, so he couldn't

see the smug self-satisfied grin on Barph's face. But he could imagine it.

"Still," Barph said, "to business."

Will lunged.

Time seemed to slow. Will was an observer of his own body as it carried out his commands. A yard away now, the knife held low at his waist, the cutting blade facing down, the wicked, curving point held parallel to the floor. His arm jabbing forward, a slight upward movement, the beginning of a curve designed to carry the blade into Barph's kidneys and up into his lungs.

Barph was bringing back his own fist, preparing some brutal blow aimed at Will's throat, something to tear the life from him and to scatter his blood around this old, dead place. His head was rearing back.

Will's illusion was flickering, his concentration fleeing him, everything focused on the power of the blow.

Barph's head turning, twisting, the movement of his arm hesitating, losing momentum.

Will was gritting his teeth, was starting to scream, to put everything he had into the blade. All the pent-up power of ten thousand believers driving the knife forward. The blade beginning to glow. And this would matter. This would count. This would achieve something.

And then suddenly Barph was flowing like quicksilver through the molasses flow of dilated time. Was twisting impossibly fast, was defying Will's movement, and Will tried to change the direction of his thrust, but it wasn't enough. Could never be enough.

The blow caught him like a kick from a dragon. It slammed into his cheek, lifted him off the floor. Will pinwheeled through the air, smashed into a column, shattered stone. He collapsed to the floor, sense and breath knocked from him.

His vision cleared. Barph was in the air, leaping high, fist cocked.

Will rolled. Barph slammed into the ground. Barph's fist made the earth shake. Flagstones exploded, flew. Shrapnel peppered Will.

Will scrambled to his feet, sent an illusion running left as he went right. And he still had the dagger. He still...

Oh shit. Oh shit. Oh fuck.

Barph picked up a broken flagstone, threw it at Will with the force of a cannon. "You think you can trick me?" the god screamed. "You dare?"

The flagstone passed harmlessly through the illusion's back. Barph roared. Will struck.

Again that moment of exhilaration, of hope. Again the slippery sideways motion of Barph at the last moment, sliding around the blade, his will enough to bend reality, to negate Will's own.

A fist like a sledgehammer into the side of Will's ribs. All the air rushed out of him. He skittered across flagstones, slammed into the wall, collapsed in shadows. His head rang like temple bells.

In shadows. Shadows.

He faded. Disappeared into darkness. Gods, he could barely think. He tried to get to all fours. That was far beyond him.

A chunk of flagstone, hurled like a ballista bolt, struck him in the midriff.

"Just because I can't see you now," Barph said, "doesn't mean I didn't see where you went." He paused, then added, "You fucking idiot."

Will had to move. He had to get away. This was a trap as obvious as Barph had made it appear. And his faithful weren't far away, but they were far enough. They couldn't rally behind him. They couldn't propel him with fresh reserves of belief.

He was alone. And he was fucked.

He rolled. It was all he had. His ribs screamed at each rotation. A flagstone flew over his head. Barph was advancing. Will lay panting, trying to silence his breath. But Barph was about to trip over him.

He gathered the strength left to him. Sent another illusion skittering away. Just a noise this time. Running feet skittering and stumbling. Barph whirled.

"Idiot," Barph muttered. He took steps away from Will. A thunderbolt appeared in his hand.

Will made it to his feet as the far end of the temple ruins exploded in a wave of heat and sound that mashed against the back of Will's skull. He tried to ride the wave, use it for extra propulsion.

His bellow of pain was enough to attract Barph's attention even through the rumble of collapsing masonry. The god spun around, hurled a curse in Will's general direction. Will knew in his bones that a thunderbolt was about to follow.

He held on to his invisibility. He sent illusions scattering left and right, weaving in between columns and tangles of leaves. He headed for the open pasture beyond, zigzagging wildly.

Another bellowed curse from Barph. And then a roaring wave of destruction pulsing out, Barph at its epicenter. Fear and disaster chasing Will, nipping at his heels, and for a moment he thought he was finished. And then he was flinging himself into soft grass, and the shock wave was pulsing over him, crushing him against the earth. But he was still whole. His heart still beat within his ribs.

He rolled over, lay on his back.

The ruins were gone. The hilltop was gone. There was just a smoking crater that ended a few scant yards from his aching heels.

Barph was gone.

He lay on his back, stared at the night sky. He held on to his illusion of invisibility like a cloak.

And slowly, slowly he started to chuckle. Because he was

alive. Because he knew more now than he had before. Because perhaps he knew a way out of all this.

As powerful as he was, Barph could not penetrate Will's illusions.

Barph could be tricked.

50

Reptile Dysfunction

"Because," Balur said with more than a little heat, "it has been becoming nothing more than self-aggrandizing bullshit."

He did not like arguing with Cois. In fact, he would rank it as one of his least favorite things in life, as long as one discounted all the things that involved his organs being punctured.

Cois laid a patient hand on his arm. "Going to the speeches has nothing to do with Will," zhe said. "It's about being with the people. Being part of their cause." Hir patient tone wasn't helping as much as zhe thought it was.

They were out of Verra now. One night, Will had woken up, refused to talk about the smoking crater where a ruined temple had been the night before, and started a forced march toward Salera. They were blazing through the craggy landscape of Chatarra now, not stopping, even for recruitment, unless they had to. Winds whipped down the sharp valleys, and herdsmen regarded them from high ledges, eyes peering from the depths of thick-wrapped furs.

There were warriors here, Balur knew. Chatarra was famous for its longships and its berserkers. And Will had been so interested in shock troops when they had been going to Analesia. He had been so happy to recruit a bunch of savage idiots in the desert. But where was his desire now?

It was bullshit. And the epicenter of all that bullshit was Will Fallows.

"My *cause*," Balur said, and he still said the word with distaste, "is being the people who would overthrow Barph. My cause is being their willingness to fight without quarter. To not be giving ground when a god stands against them. That is being a fight I am wishing to be part of. Those are being people I am wishing to die next to. My cause is not being a crowd of sycophants all fawning to tell Will Fallows how mighty and great he is."

He spat onto the cold Chatarran stone.

"They still fight, love," Cois said. "Will is just their hope. And their hope is growing. Their taste for the fight is growing."

Balur ground his teeth.

"Were you not being there?" he asked. "Were you not standing on that stage when he had them laugh at you? When he held you up as a defeated enemy?" And gods, it had taken everything he had at that moment not to get up on the stage and rip out Will Fallows's throat. Because nothing about that had felt as if it was to do with defeating Barph. It had all felt like Will standing astride the world and shouting that he was god now and touching himself.

"Have you not been being with me," he went on, "when we walk among these people? Have you not been seeing the looks they are giving you? Have you not been hearing their words?"

Because Will had given them all license to spit on the old gods. And that was fine when it was preening Lawl, or pathetic Toil. But it was not okay when it was Cois. That was asking to see the color of your own liver.

"Our cause is bigger than me." Cois stepped in closer to Balur now. There was an urgency in hir voice. "These people are more important than I am."

"No," Balur said, and his voice was deeper than usual, catching in his throat. "That is not true."

"Come," zhe said, pulling at his arm. "Please."

He would have had more of a chance standing against a horde of Cyclopes.

The crowd was gathered on top of a steppe, the wind whistling among them. In the cold, Balur felt sluggish and irritable. Cois pulled a cloak tight about hirself and pulled him to a stop. Most ignored them. A few threw dark glances, and Balur growled back at them. This had been a place he had come for comfort once. Now he itched to do violence.

Cois had a distinct destination in mind, it seemed. Balur supposed he should have known. The other old gods were all clustered together at one edge of the steppe. They were in an even sorrier state than the one they'd arrived in. They huddled together in rags, no one apparently willing to lend them a blanket or bedroll for warmth.

"No," he said as they got closer. "This is just making things worse."

"They're family."

They sat, and Lawl offered them a mirthless smile. He was shivering, and snot was matted in his tangled mustaches. Neither Betra, Toil, nor Knole even turned around.

Around them the looks darkened, and so did Balur's mood as they waited for Will to mount his stage and talk about what a good idea it was to worship the ground he walked upon.

Then a raucous noise, shouting and bluster. A few cries of alarm, a few roars of laughter. The other Analesians had arrived. They were plowing through the crowd as if this were a battleground, storming and stomping through clusters of people, pushing and shouting. A few men and women drifted toward them, as helpless before their obvious displays of power as iron was before a magnet.

Their destination was already obvious to Balur. Toil too, it seemed, as he groaned and sank deeper into himself.

"Traitor!" boomed out one of the lizard men—Kallor, Balur

thought. "God lover!" There was laughter around him. It was coarse, rough laughter. It was the sort of laughter Balur loved. Except when it was directed at him.

"Weakling," Balur snapped back. He was on his feet without truly thinking about it. Cois reached out, placed a hand on his leg. "Don't," zhe said. And there was an edge of pleading in hir voice. An edge of weakness. And it was these fuckers who had put it there.

"I am being weak?" Kallor looked around at the small crowd of Analesians and humans that traveled with him. "I am being the one who clings to old beliefs and old ways? I am being the one who is needing a god to feel strong? I am being the one who cannot imagine throwing down a god if I do not have another one at my back? In my bed?"

There was more laughter at this last piece. Balur's growl deepened.

"You are being weak," he managed among the flexing of his claws, "because you will be eating the dirt at my feet eight seconds from now."

"Don't," Cois said while Kallor laughed, but there was a sense of resignation.

In Balur's defense, he didn't hit Kallor with the blade of the sword. But he did bring the hilt down on Kallor's snout with enough force to break bone.

There wasn't much else to be said about Balur's defense as eight other Analesians knocked him to the dirt and kicked him while Kallor lay mewling on the rock. They finally let him up once at least one of his ribs had been broken in retaliation. He lay there panting. One of the lizards spat on him.

A circle of women and men were watching now. There was an almost eager look on their faces. What else was going to happen here?

"You are worshipping old gods," said one of the Analesians.

"You are worshipping a man," Balur spat back.

It was said in haste, and anger. But he lost the crowd with that one.

Someone booed. Then more did.

"Be fucking off." Balur sat up spitting blood.

Another of the Analesians was looking around, enjoying the reaction he was getting.

"So," he said, "you are not worshipping Will Fallows? You are rejecting him?"

Balur was wise to answering that question directly now, though. "And you?" he asked. "You are being a proud Analesian and you are licking this man's boots?"

But the crowd wasn't having that either. More boos followed. An angry shout was hurled.

"I told you not to." Cois was staring at the ground. The other gods sat even more huddled now.

"Will Fallows is being a great warrior," said the thick-skulled Analesian. "He is being the champion of those who stand opposed to Barph. He is being our champion. But is he being yours?"

It was hurled like a challenge. And there was a smart time for knowing when you were outmatched and it was time to go home.

Balur had never been known for making smart decisions in fights.

"I am worshipping no man," he said. "And I am worshipping no god. I—" He had a lot more to say, but it was drowned out by the shouting.

And gods, he wanted to shout at them now. He wanted to tell them to be better than this, to be who they had promised to be at the beginning of this. But Cois's hand was on his arm, and zhe was pulling him away, and he could watch his own bones be broken if it was in the name of his honor, but he couldn't watch hirs.

"Run, traitor!" the Analesian shouted as Balur pushed away into the crowd, using his arms to shield Cois from the hurled hatred. "Run away. We stay here. The true Analesians. The true warriors of Will Fallows."

And Balur wanted so much to turn and tear the smug smile from the lizard's face, but Balur fought for a cause now, and in this moment it felt as if that cause was already lost.

51

The Protestant

Days on the road turned into weeks. Chatarra turned into Salera. And if anyone wanted Balur's opinion, Will did not look well. In fact, Will looked like eight sacks of cow shit shoveled into five sacks of human skin.

No one asked Balur about his opinion.

They finally came to a halt on the hills overlooking the Saleran capital, Essoa. More than a few Salerans had joined them on the last leg of their journey, and Balur suspected that their numbers must exceed ten thousand by now. It was not a great army, nothing that would define an age, and no more than they had ended up leading through Kondorra when he had first faced off against the dragons. But still, it was not an insignificant number. And they were all worshipping... Well, this thing that looked as Balur imagined the Will of old would look if he'd had a particularly harrowing encounter with a disease-ridden banshee prostitute.

Here, before Essoa, Will had called for a war council of sorts. Balur had resisted coming; his ribs and pride both hurt, and Will's tendency to talk about what a boon to humankind he was had done nothing but grow. Cois pushed him here, though.

"Who else will beat his swollen head back to size?" zhe had asked, and Balur had no answer.

Now the body of Pettrax—the surviving dragon leader— formed a wall against the rest of the camp. His breath had lit a campfire. Will stood beside it, and the rest of them sat with their backs to Pettrax's enveloping bulk—Lette, Quirk, and Afrit joining Balur and Cois. The lights of Essoa flickered below.

"You grew up down there, didn't you?" said Cois, leaning over to Lette.

Lette shrugged. "It feels like that was more years ago than it actually was."

Above them Pettrax snorted with a sound like thunder. "Are we here to talk of war or not?" he asked.

Will was staring into the flames. He looked up. "Essoa," he said. "A Barphian stronghold." He didn't seem to be looking at any of them directly. There was a strange light in his eyes. It was the wrong color for reflected firelight, Balur was sure. "A source of power for our enemy." Will chewed his lip.

Balur looked over at Lette. This could not be comfortable for her. The city of her childhood enslaved to a tyrannical god. Her lover raving like an alcoholic.

"People to be liberated." Cois smiled at Will and then Balur. "Freed from the tyrannical yoke of my former lover by my new one."

Balur smiled thinly. Zhe was trying to pull him back into this. And had it only been a month ago that he stood in the Analesian Desert shouting that this was his tribe?

"Liberation," Will said contemplatively. "Perhaps." He shook his head. "Of a sort."

And then...wait. Balur blinked, shook his head. Because while Will stood by the fire, Will also came walking up the hill. And there were two Wills. And they both looked like sacks of purple shit. Both of them stretched their mouths in humorless smiles. Then the Will that had been standing by the fire flickered out of existence.

"Barph can't see through my illusions," the new Will said. "He can't penetrate them." The Will that had been by the fire came back, and the Will that had walked up the hill faded from sight. "This is a demonstration," Will said, because apparently stating the obvious was a thing he did now.

"Pissing illusions," Balur groused.

"Wait." Cois leaned forward. "Which one is the real you?"

"Neither," said Will. Except it was a third Will, standing way off to the left. The Will beside the fire flickered away.

This was the sort of shit that made Balur's head hurt. He wanted to hit something. Preferably Will.

"Quick question," Lette asked. "Have I ever fucked an illusion of you? Because . . . Well, I may have to kill the real you, and I'd like to know."

Will smiled again, and there was something genuine to it, finally. He seemed to come back from wherever he had been and focus. "I am always real with you," Will told Lette. "Always."

Cois shook hir head. "And people say Balur and I are gross."

"What have any of these parlor tricks got to do with smiting our enemy and rending his heart?" asked Pettrax. Balur didn't like much about Pettrax, but he did like the idea of making this discussion as short as possible.

"This," said Will.

And Pettrax disappeared.

"No!" Quirk shouted, and Afrit said, "Gods, Will," in horror because Will had just annihilated a dragon in front of them. He had just—

"What?" said Pettrax's voice from the middle of nowhere. And gods piss on Will and his stupid trickery.

"You're invisible," said Will.

"I am?"

"I can't see you," Cois added helpfully.

"Are your eyes closed?" Pettrax checked.

Lette started shaking her head.

"You're invisible." There was a little more volume to Will's voice than seemed natural to Balur.

"Well, that's great," Pettrax said. "Is my enemy dead too?"

Another advantage of being larger than your average barn, Balur thought, *is that it is making it very hard for you to sound petty.*

"In our last encounter with Barph," Will went on—the real one, Balur thought, as long as he had been following this game of three-Will monte correctly—"you dragons almost took Barph down."

Pettrax became visible just in time for everyone to see the dragon's smug expression.

"If Barph had had less warning of your attack," Will went on, "you could have done significantly more damage." He turned away from Pettrax, looked down at Essoa. "I propose to hide you. To let you get close. To let you unleash your full potential for violence."

"You can do that?" The shock in Cois's voice made Balur look at hir.

Will didn't appear to notice. "Yes."

Balur caught Cois's eye. "What?" zhe said. "That's a lot of dragons to hide. That's a lot of power."

"Yes," Will said again.

"Can you put the Hallows back?" Afrit asked.

"No," Will said.

Afrit didn't seem to like that answer, but didn't push it.

"But what," Quirk asked, "does any of that have to do with Essoa?"

Balur was surprised that Quirk didn't get that. They'd done this a lot now. "We are going to be liberating them, and having them as allies in our fight," he said. "And then Will is going to convince them that his prick is being bigger than Barph's so they should be worshipping him instead. And his head is getting bigger, and he is getting creepier."

"So this is more of the same," Pettrax growled. "More slow attrition. More wasting time."

"But if it's what you've done before," Quirk persisted, "then what does that have to do with hiding you from Barph? He's only ever shown up once before."

"Essoa is bait," Will said.

He did not say it loudly. It was little more than a whisper really. But they all heard it very clearly.

Balur felt his muscles go tight.

"What?" Lette asked. She looked at Will, then looked down at her home.

"A Barphian stronghold," Will said. "A source of power for our enemy. One he will have to protect. It is too much for him to lose."

"Lose?" Quirk's voice rose.

"He will come to defend it," Will said.

"From what?" Balur asked. Though it galled him, Balur knew he couldn't quite reach the bass depths of Pettrax's growl, but he thought he did well enough.

Pettrax leaned down, and his face split in a vast, jagged smile. "From me."

"Then it is time for me to be killing another dragon," Balur said. Because this...No, this would not stand.

"No," said Will, and the sheer physical force of his word held both would-be combatants in place. "The dragons must be hidden. The dragons must not be seen, so they can hurt Barph when he comes."

"So what is attacking Essoa, Will?" Lette asked.

"We are." The bastard didn't even blink. He didn't even look away in shame. "We attack. We kill. Barph comes. The dragons attack. They kill Barph."

"Wait—" said Quirk, who finally sounded as if she was on the same page as Balur.

"We are attacking Essoa?" Balur checked, still feeling the rage burning in the back of his throat.

"Yes," Will said. He looked around at them. "Is this hard for you to understand? Am I being too complicated?"

He appeared to be genuinely concerned, and that just stoked

the fuel in Barph's gut higher. That Will should worry about *that*, and not about the thousands of lives he was willing to so casually snuff out...

"We are killing the people who are living there?" he managed to get out.

"Balur..." Lette could see the warning signs.

"Until Barph shows up, yes," said Will. "Would it help if I drew pictures?"

"I am going to be tearing off your balls and beating you to death with them now," Balur said. "I am imagining they are very small, so it may be taking a while, but I am feeling patient."

Will blinked. "What?" he said, as Balur approached. "It's killing people, Balur. You like killing people."

"These are being the weak," Balur said. "These are being the unprotected. The innocent. Ending these lives is not proving strength. It is not offering a life red of tooth and claw. These deaths are pointless, ugly. These are the acts of a coward, afraid to test his strength."

Will blinked. He didn't seem to be overly concerned that Balur had him by the throat and had lifted him off the ground. He dangled unconcerned. He wasn't even red in the face. "You once burned convents to the ground to distract a force following you through Vinter. Why are you concerned about these people? What are they to you?"

And there was a long and complicated answer to that, but in the end Balur was more concerned with another question. "Why aren't they something to you, Will?"

"My neck is more powerful than your hand, Balur," said Will. "Please put me down."

And he had such a reasonable unconcerned fucking tone. Balur slammed his spare fist into Will's face.

"Fuck!" he roared, because it was like punching a mountain, and he thought perhaps he had broken his hand. He dropped Will, nursed it between his thighs.

"They are meaningful," Will said, landing lightly on his feet. "They are the means by which I shall save all the rest of Avarra, Balur. They are the sheep that must be slaughtered so their meat can buy grain for the other animals. Some blood must spill."

"And we shall kill Barph," Pettrax said. He sounded very satisfied. "The dragons shall be doing the deed."

"That's the plan," said Will.

"I like this plan," Pettrax told everyone as if that settled things.

Balur turned to look at Lette, still wringing his sore hand. "That is being your home," he said to her. Because of all of them she could still get through to Will. "You are being fine with him beating on it like iron in the forge?"

And Lette clearly was not. Her face was twisted up as she stared back and forth between Will and Balur.

"I'm sorry, Lette." And Will genuinely did look sorry. "It's Barph's greatest stronghold in the north. It's the only place that makes sense."

"It is not making sense," Balur bellowed. "Fighting Barph is making sense. Because he is being a prick of the greatest magnitude. But now in this fight, you have been becoming a prick of the same girth. And so now I am needing to fight you."

Will spread his arms. "You're welcome to," he said. Like a prick.

"Balur." Cois was trying to get between them. "Please. Don't do this."

"You are being fine with this?" Because zhe was the one who had done this to him, had made him realize he cared about these things.

"Of course I'm not," zhe said. "It's a monstrous plan. But he can beat you. I'm sorry, but he can."

"Of course he can be beating me," Balur said. "I am not being a prick. I can be telling when I am outclassed. I am not going to be fighting him with fists. I am going to be fighting him where it is mattering to him. With his precious followers. I am going to be pointing out to them that that they are worshipping a limp cock of a man who is incapable of achieving anything meaningful."

Will laughed. Not loud, and not long. But enough. Enough to mean Balur would end him utterly if he could.

"And Lette will be doing so too," he said. "Their paladin will tell them the truth, if she is being worthy of the name."

And still Lette's face was twisted up. "I . . . ," she said. "I never said I was worthy of that name."

Lette too? Lette who knew exactly what they would be destroying?

"You will be letting him do this?" he asked her. And he tried to stop his voice from sounding broken, but he wasn't sure he achieved it.

"I'm not letting him do anything." Lette managed to reach for some of her normal bite. "No one here is a child. No one here is asking for permission. He's going to do it." She thumbed at Will. "I'm just . . . I'm saying I see why. I'm saying I can see the logic of it."

"Just like that?" Balur pressed.

"What? Are you asking if it hurts? Of course it fucking hurts, Balur. That's my home. Or it was. Or it was the home of someone I was once. But it hurts that they've embraced Barph too. It hurts that I've been beaten around the head and neck all the way through Avarra by Barphian idiots. A lot of things hurt. But you keep on living. You survive. And that's why we're here. To make sure Avarra will survive. I want that. And if it takes Saleran blood, if it takes Essoa, then that's what it takes."

"I'm sorry, Lette." Will looked distracted again, chewing at his lip. "I didn't . . . I forgot . . ."

She shook her head. "I'm a big fucking girl. A lot like Balur, apparently."

Balur clenched his fists. He wanted to throttle Will some more, but his hand still hurt. "I will stop this," he said instead.

"I will stop you." And the gods knew he was no orator, but even a child could see how heinous this plan was.

Cois took his hand. "We will stop you."

Will spread his hands. "You're welcome to try."

People were already gathering for the nightly sermon. The Analesians had set up a loud raucous group in the center of things. Some women were dancing in the center of a ring of them. Men were handing out bottles of liquor to them.

The dragons were at the back of proceedings too, or in the air above, sending sheets of flame back and forth. Balur wasn't sure if Will had asked them to do it for effect, but he wouldn't put it past the prick.

He wasn't sure where Will was. Or whether, if he saw Will, it really would be him or just some illusion the idiot had summoned. He didn't care. Real or not, Will had a stupid plan. And he would stop it.

Not everyone had arrived, but, looking out at the sea of faces, Balur figured it was enough.

He stepped up onto the boards.

"Balur!"

He turned and looked, and...Gods, he found a chance to smile. Lette was there.

"You are seeing sense finally," he said.

But apparently she wasn't. "Don't do this," she said.

He tried to take a moment. He tasted the air. The anticipation of the crowd did nothing to calm him.

"Be going away, Lette," he told her, "before I am doing something I am regretting later."

"He will destroy you."

Balur sneered. "He is welcome to be trying. I have been killing bigger things than him."

"Not...not like that, you big idiot. He will turn them against you. I swear it. You're already on thin ice. You know how they feel about Cois and the other gods."

"And you are being okay with that?"

"Of course I'm not. I'm not okay with so many things. I'm not okay with you doing this. I'm not okay with what you'll do when this crowd gets ugly."

"They will see sense."

She shook her head. "It's too far gone, Balur."

And that sounded a lot like defeat. Balur looked at her. "I have not given up. I am getting up there. What will you do?"

She hesitated. "I'll protect the crowd."

"From Will?"

She clenched and unclenched her fists. He didn't think he was the one she wanted to punch, though. "Will wants to save Avarra. The crowd lives in Avarra. Everything is subjugated to that now. That's the sort of fight we're in."

"What about the innocent in Essoa? What about the brood mothers who live there?"

"There are no pissing brood mothers in Essoa, Balur. This isn't the desert."

"No," he agreed. "The desert makes you strong."

And with that he turned his back on her and mounted the stage.

The crowd stared at him. The weight of their eyes fell on his shoulders. Thousands of them. It was a different sort of weight to the kind he normally bore. But piss on it, if Will could do this, then so could he.

"You are knowing me," he shouted to them. "I am Balur. I am an Analesian. I am tribe with you." He could see people straining to hear his voice. And of course he had no magic to amplify it. And where was Quirk when you needed her? He had been sure her self-righteous bullshit would cause her to align with him on this.

"God lover!" someone shouted. There was laughter from the circle of Analesians.

"I am being tribe with you," Balur shouted again. "Tribe. That is being an important word to Analesians. To me. Tribe is fighting for each other. Tribe is dying for each other. Tribe is living for each other. Tribes are not being individual people. People are dissolving into each other in tribe. Your kill is becoming my kill. My kill is becoming yours. Your defeat is becoming my defeat. My defeat is becoming yours."

Even the people who could hear him were looking confused now.

"Tribe," he said, "is not killing each other. Tribe is not wasting each other's lives. To be doing that is to be killing yourself. And that is being stupid, is it not?"

Will liked to ask questions that had obvious answers. People seemed to like that. And some people were shrugging in agreement, so that was something.

"You're no tribe of mine!" shouted another heckler.

Balur licked the air, tasted his own uncertainty.

"But where is our tribe ending?" he asked, plowing on regardless. "Who is being our tribe in this fight? Who are we fighting for? Who are we killing, and who are we dying for?"

Not even shrugs this time.

"We are killing Barphists," he said, and that, finally, a few people seemed able to get behind. "We are killing Gratt's once-dead pricks." There was a cheer. "We are killing them because they are threatening our tribe. They are threatening the world we are trying to save."

Even the people who couldn't hear him seemed to be getting into the cheering. Balur felt a little more certain in his righteous bellowing.

"What about Essoa?" he asked. "What about the women and children who are living in that city? They are not traveling with us. Some of them are worshipping Barph. They are not fighting with us. They are not dying with us." He looked about. "Are they tribe?"

The crowd lost their momentum.

"Get off!" A clearly Analesian voice this time. "Go love a god!" Laughter again.

"If they are not tribe," Balur continued doggedly, "can we just be killing them? If they are not being with us, are they being against us? Is it okay to be killing women and children who have been forced to be living in fear? Is it okay to be killing those who are not knowing there is an alternative to their lives as they are being now?"

Silence. Absolute silence.

"Well," he said, "that is depending on what sort of tribe we are being. Are we being here to fight for the weak? Are we being here to protect those who cannot be protecting themselves? Are we being here to save Avarra? Or are we being here for the self-aggrandizement of a man who has become a complete and utter prick?"

He saw a field of puzzled looks. Gods hex them all. He took another breath.

"What a lot of cryptic questions, Balur."

And there Will was striding out, his voice booming across the stage, smiling broadly. There was something savage in his eyes.

"What," Will went on, "could you be talking about?"

He turned to the audience, cocked his head to one side. Balur could see the smiles rippling out.

Balur opened his mouth. Savaging Will in front of these people might actually be fun.

"Maybe I can add some light to the matter." Will cut him off and drowned him out with his booming voice. "I think you all know where we are. In Salera. Looking down on Essoa. The stronghold of our enemy."

Booing from the crowd. And gods, they molded themselves into the palm of his hand so quickly.

"I say we go down there. I say we pick a fight. I say we draw Barph out. I say we make our confrontation here. I say we take back Avarra now. I say this is our time."

Cheers. Insane cheers. The crowd losing its goddamned mind. Just like that. Every single question Balur had put in their heads obliterated by the fire of Will's speech.

Lette had been right. She'd been completely right. Will would destroy him up here.

Finally the cheering died down. Will looked at Balur, cocked an eyebrow.

"At what cost?" Balur shouted at him.

"At what cost?" Will turned the question over. He mused on it quietly, and everyone heard. And it was the right question to ask. It was the question that mattered. It was the question that could undo Will, but Balur just did not have the strength to throw a killing blow in this arena.

This was not life red of tooth and claw, but it was every bit as savage, and Will was the apex predator.

"Balur cares for the people of Essoa," Will said. "He thinks their lives too precious. He thinks my plan a step too far. He asks at what cost. He wants you to see the blood my plan will spill and hate me for it. As he hates me for it."

Silence. Just as absolute as before. And yet for Will, it did not seem so unkind. They were awaiting their cue. And Balur wanted to give it to them, but he did not have the words.

"It is a great cost," Will said. And gods, he sounded so reasonable now. He sounded so connected to these people when he talked *at* them. If only they could talk *with* him and see what a mess he was. But of course, he would never allow that.

"It's a terrible cost," Will went on. "Hundreds of lives. Innocent lives perhaps. Perhaps more than hundreds. Barph is an uncaring god, and maybe he will be slow to defend his faithful. That is the cost." Will nodded.

"You ask these people to be murderers," Balur said. It was the best he could think of. And he did see some faces wavering. He did see a current of concern. If only he could somehow make it a tidal wave.

"Yes," Will said. "Yes I do. And I do because of the very question you ask. At what cost? At what cost does our inaction come? At what cost do we ignore Essoa? At what cost do we allow Barph to rule? To thrive? At what cost, Balur? What cost would you have us pay? Would you have the world pay? What sort of man... or almost-man, I suppose, looks at this world and says it is okay to let it continue on its current path? Looks at it and says, a little longer under Barph won't hurt? What sort of not-quite-man feels sympathy for Barph's faithful servants here? For the people who have slashed into our ranks? Who have cut the throats of our loved ones? Who cherishes their lives? Who, Balur? What sort of faith does that man hold?"

The crowd was on its feet. The sound was immense. Will's magically amplified voice barely audible. And this was the tidal wave. This was the power in the room. This was everything Balur had tried to capture. But he had failed. And now it was turned on him.

Lette had tried to warn him. *He will destroy you.* And he had thought she meant just defeat. But no, that was not it. *He will destroy you* meant "He will tear down what you stand for. He will turn you inside out in the minds of these people. He will make them hate you. He will make you the enemy." That was what she had meant.

He should not have picked this fight. Not this way.

He looked off the stage. Cois was there. And there was fear in hir eyes.

The crowd was pressing in on the stage. They were pressing toward her. And Will's smile was so wide it seemed to encompass the world.

Balur growled, set his feet. And perhaps there was something good in this. A clean death. A death where he tested his strength against the strongest thing he could find.

What a fucked-up world it was, where that was Will Fallows.

But then there was a hand on his arm. Cois's hand. "Balur!" There was so much fear in hir voice. And this was not the death zhe wanted. His death could not save hir. And he did want to save hir.

"Balur!" His name again. Lette at the back of the stage, beckoning to him. "Move, you big arsehole!"

He hesitated. His claws itched for blood. People were clambering up on the stage.

"A tactical withdrawal!" Lette was almost screaming. Cois was hauling on his arm, dragging him toward Lette.

Will cocked his head to one side, a question Balur longed to answer.

But then Cois screamed. And he turned, and he ran.

They found shelter in the shadows of the slope leading down to Essoa. They crouched behind bushes. Cois was still trying to catch hir breath. Lette looked around.

"You can find refuge in the city," she said. "For tonight at least. No one will look there."

"No!" he said. Fury was still in him, still making him shout despite the packs of people looking to take out their anger on him. "Will has been taking these people, and their anger, something fucking pure, and he has been making something awful of it. Something perverted and wrong. And you are helping him."

"I am helping you!" Lette's voice was raised too.

"But you are not helping your people."

"Avarra, Balur!" Lette was in his face. "Avarra is not just these people. These are ten thousand. There are millions to free. Millions. There are nations. It is a question of scale."

"It is being a question of this whole plan having lost its way and having clambered up Will Fallows's arsehole!"

And suddenly all the fight seemed to sag out of Lette in a great rush.

"He needs me, Balur. He needs me to hold on to his humanity."

Balur laughed. It was loud and barking, and ill-advised enough to make Cois clutch at him again. But he couldn't help it. "This is being him holding on?"

"Imagine how much worse it would be if I wasn't here."

"He has been going rabid, Lette." He tried words one last time. "He is needing to be put down."

Cois seemed to think this wasn't enough. "Your boyfriend," zhe said, "has become a fucking psychopath."

Lette looked back up the hill. And there was so much pain in her expression Balur just could not hold on to the urge to damage her into seeing sense. "He's still our best hope against Barph," she said.

"Then there is being no hope." That was all Balur could see now. The only place left to go was Essoa, and tomorrow an army would fall upon it.

Lette stepped away. "Good luck, Balur. Go quickly."

"Be coming with us." He knew it was weakness to ask, but she was tribe, and he couldn't help himself. "Be finding another way."

"These people need me."

"These people are lost," he said.

"Well, me leaving isn't going to help them find their way."

And that hurt.

"This isn't a zero-sum game," Cois said, picking up what Balur could not. "It isn't just Will or Barph. We can find another way."

Lette shook her head. "Getting you into Essoa is the best way I know how to help you. I'm sorry. Please, go. People are coming."

Balur shook his head. It felt heavy and clouded and full of

ugly thoughts. He took Cois's hand. It was solid, and definite at least, for all that it trembled. Zhe pressed against him.

And then Balur turned his back on Lette, and Will, and the people who followed them. He turned his back on his cause, and he walked away.

52

Causality's Casualty

There was chaos in the camp. Quirk felt storm tossed in it. People were everywhere, running and shouting and hunting for Balur—the lizard man who had somehow proven himself their champion, the one who was trying to save them from Will's apocalyptic plan to pitch them all into a battle they couldn't win. *That* was whose blood they were baying for.

A pack of men ran past her brandishing swords, screaming, "Death to the god lovers!" Someone crashed into her from behind, carried on without pausing to see if she was all right. Torches were lit. Quirk wondered if somewhere a cache of pitchforks was being broken out.

It was absurd. All of it. A farmer dreaming of deification. That farmer's plan that they defeat a god with the aid of parlor tricks and sleight of hand. The willingness of the crowd to buy any line he tried to sell them, no matter the price. It was all falling apart. Whatever this dream had been, it was becoming a nightmare.

She needed to find Afrit. They had become separated in the chaos. She needed to talk to her about what to do about this. About what could be recovered.

She fought through the throng. She paused in pockets of still bodies and empty ground. She shouted Afrit's name pointlessly—her voice drowned out by a thousand other shouts, some angry, some as lost as hers.

She plunged back into the stream of bodies who had some-how still not lost their enthusiasm for the search. They jostled and knocked at her. She was thrown to the ground more than once, almost trodden upon. Fire licked at the back of her mind, but that was the last thing this chaos needed. The dragons were already in the air, baying back and forth, spraying sheets of flame into the night sky, sending sheets of yellow illumination flickering through the crowds below.

It seemed as if hours had passed. Quirk felt exhausted. She was about to give up, about to head back to her tent, where in all likelihood Afrit had been weathering the storm, when she half tripped over a form in the dark.

"Gods!" she spat in misplaced anger, and then recovered herself a little. She had just kicked someone. Someone on the ground. She knelt.

"Are you...," she started. Then the words died on her lips.

Afrit was lying on the ground.

"Afrit!" she shrieked. She shook the woman. Because she couldn't be...she couldn't...

She wasn't.

Afrit groaned, raised a hand to her forehead. There was an ugly-looking tear in the skin above one eye. Blood coated one of her temples. "Think I took a tumble," she said weakly.

"Gods." Quirk lifted Afrit in both arms, carried her through the fields. She summoned fire now, heedless of what damage it might do, used it like a wedge to break up crowds and to fight her way back to their tent. When she got there, she lay Afrit down on the bedroll. She soaked a cloth in water from their skin and washed the worst of the blood away. Afrit smiled softly at her.

"What would I do without you?"

"Rest," Quirk said. "I'll pack."

Afrit closed her eyes. Then she opened them again. "Pack what?"

"We're leaving." Quirk was surprised Afrit even had to ask.

"What?"

Quirk looked at her. Was she truly going to try to argue this point? She counted off the points on her fingers. "Will has gone power mad. The crowd has become a mob at his beck and call. He's chased Balur and Cois out of this camp. He's picking an unwinnable fight with Barph tomorrow. You just took a blow to the head." She'd run out of fingers. "We have to leave."

Afrit shook her head, then groaned and put a hand to it. "I'm not leaving," she said.

"We're leaving," Quirk repeated. Afrit wasn't even in a fit state to argue, in her opinion. "Just lie there. Rest. We're going to have to travel soon, and get far away from this place. There's no telling how much destruction tomorrow will bring."

Afrit struggled to a sitting position, grunting as she did so. "Didn't you hear what Will said?" she asked. "We're facing down Barph tomorrow."

Quirk stopped stuffing old clothes into their traveling packs. She fixed Afrit with as steely an eye as she could manage. "Did *you* not hear what Will said?" she asked. "Will is about to pick an unwinnable fight with a god and get us all killed."

Afrit grimaced, trying to settle herself. "Why are you so convinced it's unwinnable?"

"He's a god, Afrit!" The vehemence of Quirk's cry caught even her off guard, but she couldn't stop. "Barph killed us all once already, and now he is infinitely more powerful. This is a seat of his power. We will die here. All of us."

"All of us?" Afrit took the hand away from her cut. Blood was trickling down her forehead again. She blinked it away from her eye as she looked at Quirk. "I told you, this is bigger than me. This is bigger than us. This is all of Avarra."

Quirk felt something rising inside her. Something like fire. And she did not want that here. Not with Afrit. *Be the calm lake*, she told herself. *Be the absence of wind. Be the still trees.*

"You mean more to me," she said as calmly as possible, "than all of them. I can't help that. I can't change that."

"I don't want to mean that." Lette shook her head grimly. "You can't hang that much on my shoulders."

"It's not on you," Quirk argued. Why was she so thickheaded about this? "This is me. This is how I have to live. We have to leave."

"And what if everyone feels that way?" Afrit pressed. "What if everyone who is scared or afraid or in love—what if they flee now? What if they think their needs are bigger than the crowd's? You say this fight is unwinnable. It will be if we run. If everyone thinks only of themselves. This is humanity's chance. If we stick together. If we consider the needs of the whole. We can do amazing things."

And they were all the right words. Of course they were. Afrit always had the right words. But just because they were the things one ought to say didn't make them ring true in Quirk's heart. And that dissonance just seemed to amplify all her frustrations.

"Why are you so set on dying here?" Her shield of calm was melting under the heat of her anger.

"Why are you set on abandoning everyone else to die?"

"Because I love you!"

And it was such a strange thing to shout those words in anger.

Lette paused, bit her lip. "And I love you," she said. "But I won't leave."

"If you loved me, you'd leave." It was out before she could stop it. And it wasn't the right thing to say, but it was the honest thing. It was finally what she felt.

"If you loved me, you would never have said that."

And now the floodgates of honesty were open, Quirk couldn't stop herself. "That is such sanctimonious bullshit!" She stared around. "Who do you think you're performing for? Who is judging you? Not every opinion has to be the correct one. Not everything you feel has to align with an agenda. It is okay to be selfish about the people you love."

Afrit was shaking her head, blood dripping from the cut as she did so. "I don't lie, Quirk. Never. And I would never lie to you. If you think you're hearing some performance, then you're just projecting your own insecurities onto me."

"I am trying to save your life!"

"You're trying to save yourself from hurt." Afrit was unremitting. She gave no quarter. "Do you think you are the only one who has felt hurt? Do you think I spent my time in the Hallows rejoicing over our separation? Emotion isn't a badge people wear. It isn't an award. It is life. You have to accept it. The good and the bad. And I fear your dying, I truly do. But I will bear that pain and that hurt if it means Avarra survives."

"Even if we don't."

"Even if we don't survive this conversation."

And there it was. A gods-hexed gauntlet. Right there. Stay here and watch Afrit die again, or leave Afrit behind right now.

The breath caught in Quirk's throat. All the flames gone now. And there were tears stinging her eyes.

"Either way," she said, "I end up without you."

"You don't know that's true. Nothing is written in stone. Not Barph's victory. Not our fate." And finally Afrit's stony façade started to crumble. "Don't leave me here, Quirk."

And now the tears fell freely. "I can't watch you die. Not again. I can't."

"You don't have to."

But that was only if Afrit came now. And Afrit was refusing. Afrit was here committing suicide. And Quirk's words and her love could not reach her.

Quirk reached out. She held Afrit's face in her hands. An

intimate touch, and one she avoided most times, but one she needed now. The smooth warmth of her skin beneath her palm. One last memory to hold in the nights to come.

And then Quirk grabbed her pack, and slipped out of the tent, and left Afrit behind.

53

All the Usual Hazards
of Playing with Fire

Quirk stumbled away, blinded by the night and her tears. But she would hear Afrit's running footsteps soon, wouldn't she? She would feel Afrit's hand slipping into her own. Afrit's fingers finding their typical grooves. Wouldn't she?

And still she stumbled on. And still the darkness pressed down on her. And still Afrit did not come.

She felt cold. She felt her body shivering. She tried to summon fire to warm herself and light the way, but she could not.

She went on. She wanted to collapse and sleep. She wanted to scream. But she could not.

She went on. Over the rise and fall of the Avarran landscape. She clambered over broken-down fences and pressed through sprawling hedgerows. She went on and away. That was all she had left. All she could do. She had to flee from this place. She had to leave Afrit's death as far behind as possible. She couldn't face it. She wouldn't. It would be something distant. Soon all this would be distant. Soon this wouldn't hurt.

Wouldn't it?

The darkness began to lift from the landscape without her truly noticing it. She was lost in herself and in the landscape. Everything was unfamiliar to her.

And then the sun lifted its head above the horizon, and Quirk realized its significance. Day was here. The day Afrit would die.

She fell to her knees and retched violently.

When she was done, she tried to get to her feet again. She had to get away. She had to.

She could not.

She stayed there on her knees, paralyzed by all the decisions she'd made and failed to make.

Voices finally freed her from the prison of her own skull. Voices out in the hills rarely heralded good intent for a lone woman. And while Quirk was not exactly afraid of any lonely shepherds who fancied their chances, she was not in the mood for such petty encounters. She wanted to be alone.

The voices, though, she began to realize, were pitched lower than she had anticipated. And there were more of them. And as the voices rose, she realized they were not human at all.

The dragons, she knew, often roosted a mile or more away from the human encampment. She had encouraged it herself. The dragons were not at their best when first awoken, or when hungry. A little distance, she had reasoned, could save a lot of lives.

This morning, though, the dragons seemed to have awoken angrier than usual. And they were farther from the camp than she would have anticipated. She must have traveled more than a mile, surely. So, what were they doing out here? Why were they shouting at each other?

She should have no interest in such answers, of course. She was leaving this place. She was leaving everything behind. She was in mourning for a life she had imagined by Afrit's side. She was in mourning for Afrit herself.

And yet...what if she heard something that would let her know more about what would happen to Afrit today? What if she heard something she could use to change Afrit's mind?

And so she approached slowly, hunched over, until she reached the crest of a low rise and looked down on the gathered assembly of dragons below. It was still a sight that could take her breath away: the low morning sun glinting off scales and wings, the size of the beasts stomping and grunting and bellowing below her, the sinuous grace of muscles as large as houses, the twisting mass of bodies.

Pettrax was in the center of it all, twisting back and forth, jaws open. Rothinamax was rearing back, front claws flashing. And in the thick of the scrum, in defiance of logic, Yorrax was there too.

"We hold to the plan," Pettrax was shouting. "We slay the god. Barph falls at our feet. We will be the ones responsible. All will see who it is who is truly victorious over the god. We shall ascend to our rightful place."

"You mewling idiot," Rothinamax snarled. "You have us do as the human Fallows tells us, and the next thing he shall do is turn around and slaughter us."

"You were born a coward," Pettrax called, "and you have lived all your life as one. You are an insult to all dragon kind." He shot fire into the sky. "If Will Fallows wants to try his hand at striking me down, then I shall enjoy feasting on his heart."

"I am the coward?" Rothinamax roared. "You are the one who crawls and grovels at the human's feet! You are the one who does his bidding without question!"

"I am the one that sees beyond the limit of the human's plans. I am—"

"You are both fools!" Yorrax's screech brought everything to a crashing, crawling halt. Quirk watched as both the larger dragons brought their massive ire to bear on the small blue beast.

Yorrax was unbowed. She turned to Rothinamax. "We need Will Fallows to kill Barph. If you believe anything else you are a fool. Barph is divine. The Fallows man has tapped into divine power himself. Without it we stand no chance."

And Pettrax couldn't help but preen slightly at this damning of his enemy.

"And you"—Yorrax wheeled on Pettrax—"are a fool if you think that the Fallows man will suffer us to exist a moment beyond the defeat of Barph. He thrives on worship. If anyone threatens to steal the crowd's adoration, then he will end them." She stared at them both as if daring them to strike her. The whole crowd of dragons seemed to be waiting for violence. Perched above it all, Quirk waited for it. Waited to see if she still had the capacity to care if Yorrax lived or died.

And yet Pettrax and Rothinamax seemed to be struggling to fault Yorrax's logic. She spread her wings and launched herself into the air, flying around their heads, like a starling buzzing around a pair of eagles. She stretched her jaws and screeched fire.

"Listen to me," she cried. "The Fallows man would use us as tools. We must make him ours. We must use him to defeat Barph, but then we must defeat him. His power comes from the people, from the crowds. Once Barph lies dead beneath our claws, we must not stop. We must keep up the slaughter. We must remove Will Fallows's source of power. We must kill his worshipers. Every last one."

Quirk had thought she had lost her capacity to feel. She had thought last night had eviscerated what was left of her emotions and left her hollow and heartbroken. And yet this found a chink in the shell of numbness she had built up around herself. This she felt: a sluicing blast of shock.

Because...Kill all of Will's followers?

And yet this was the dragon who had wanted to burn the world with her. Perhaps she should not be surprised. Perhaps the only true surprise was how long it had taken her to realize that this was the obvious conclusion to everything.

And apparently this plan was the obvious outcome to all the gathered dragons too, even as Pettrax and Rothinamax tried to reestablish control. The gathered dragon kin launched themselves up into the air, roaring and howling and filling the air with fire. And atop this roiling inferno, borne aloft by scale and claw, wings spread, was Yorrax. Yorrax arching and diving and reveling in this newfound moment of leadership. And as the streaming trail of dragons stretched out toward the horizon and Will's camp, all that was left for Rothinamax and Pettrax was to take to the air and chase after their fleeing roles at the head of this army.

Quirk was left on the hilltop, staring up at the retreating army she had brought here to Avarra. The one she had committed to Will's troops. The one now hell-bent on betraying them all.

Except...hadn't she already written this battle off as a loss? Wasn't that why she was here? Because there was no hope for this fight? Because every man, woman, and child with Will was bound to die? Weren't all the dragons' contingency plans for naught, because the fight would never get that far?

Wasn't there no reason to go back? Hadn't she left her only reason behind?

Quirk hesitated. She had felt hollowed out before. Now she felt cored. She had nothing left.

And perhaps Afrit was right after all. Perhaps it wasn't just about saving Afrit. Maybe it was about saving herself from hurt. And could she really live with the pain of knowing she could have done something, that she could have perhaps prevented the inevitable?

Oh gods. Afrit.

Quirk picked herself up and started running after the dragons, back toward Will and the army and her abandoned love.

54

The Ants Go Marching
Two by Two

Lette watched the sun rise like a blight on the day. She watched it vomit light onto the twisting mass of streets, alleys, homes, shops, stalls, temples, cathedrals, theaters, museums, livestock, and people that made up Essoa. She watched the way it reflected off windowpanes, pooled in the thoroughfares, and rendered the rooftops as a chiaroscuro of black and white lines across the city.

It had changed, Essoa, since she had last been there. So many years ago. When she was someone very different from who she was today. Were her parents still down there? Her sisters and brothers? Aunts and cousins? What did they look like now? Who were they? How many were dead?

She hoped Balur might seek them out. That he might ask for them, try to protect them from what was to come. She hadn't wanted to ask it of him. Pride and embarrassment and good old-fashioned stupidity getting in her way.

Still, among all the changes, there were familiar contours to the city as well. Rooftops that continued to conform to recognizable patterns. Routes she had scampered through as a child, her pockets full of stolen pastries and an uncle in pursuit.

Nostalgia and dread. There was an emotional mix she didn't get every day.

She heard footsteps approaching, knew it had to be Will. She didn't turn to face him. She couldn't quite. Not today.

"I really am sorry," he said.

"I know."

"I wish I could see another way."

"I know."

And he did mean the words. Here. Now. When he was with her, when she was on his mind. But it was too often now that he slipped away, not just from her, but from thinking of anyone else as being truly real. When their thoughts and concerns no longer mattered. Would he be sorry five minutes from now? She didn't think so.

But she didn't see another way either.

"The dragons are hidden?" she asked him. The practicalities of the day were almost easier to deal with.

"Yes. They arrived a few minutes ago. They're eager for this fight."

"You'll be with them?"

"Yes."

She nodded. "You should go then." And she did glance at him then. She couldn't quite help herself. And she could still see, in that moment—with the wind tousling his hair, and concern and love writ large in his eyes—the farm boy she had met cowering in a cave in Kondorra. And even through all the changes that time had wrought, he still looked beautiful to her.

Nostalgia and dread, and just a little bit of heartbreak too.

"Go," she told him. And he did.

She raised her arm into the sky. "Defenders of Avarra!" she bellowed. "Are you ready?"

The army gathered at her back bellowed.

She stood at their head. The defenders of Essoa were gathered at base of the long slope below them. She drew her long sword, raised it to the heavens. Light gleamed off the polished blade.

"Charge!"

She was not up for speeches today. She was up for getting this over and done with, come what may.

The army didn't need speeches anyway. Will had filled them up with speeches. His words had made them into so many powder kegs ready to blow. So that a single shout from her was enough to light the fuses.

They charged. A great flowing mass of humanity pouring down the grassy slope. Legs pumping, carrying bodies at full tilt. Weaponry and homemade banners waving in the air. Shouts emptying their lungs.

"For Avarra! For Will! For all of us! Death to Barph! Death to Essoa!" On and on, an outpouring of love and hate, carrying Lette along, buffeting her at their head. Carrying her forward to wreak destruction on the city of her birth. Because she was their paladin.

Essoa's defenders were not organized. They were not allowed to be. Their god opposed such things. They did not, she thought, in the odd calm of the charge, even have captains or corporals. There were no sergeants to beat the soldiers into line.

The defenders of Essoa, she thought, were going to fall.

And then she was on them, hurdling one soldier's clumsy pike thrust, planting her foot in his chest, knocking him to the ground. She stabbed down into his young face, ducked a sword blow from another, drove her blade up under her attacker's chin. He spat his life out onto her chest in a bloody gout.

Next to her, someone was dying on the end of a spear. Someone was bringing a shield down over and over into another man's face. Someone else was hacking at arms with an axe. Another had found a morning star somewhere and was in the process of bringing the thing crashing into his own midriff. When he fell, he crushed a woman's foot, sent her howling and flailing. Someone else with a short sword ended her screams.

It was chaos and madness. No one had uniforms. No one could tell who was fighting for whom. She just kept cutting and thrusting, letting her momentum dictate her allies. Were they heading with her, toward the city? Then she would defend them. If they were not, she would kill them.

She ran out of throwing knives, save for the two she kept for emergencies. She drew her short sword to pair with the long sword in her right hand. She carved through soldiers like a butcher on a feast day.

The grass turned red beneath her feet, and the city of Essoa grew closer. And the defenders of Essoa fell.

So many dead. And where was Barph? Where was he to defend his city? Was Will right? Did he care? Did he have to defend this place to stay dominant?

And then there was laughter. And it came from all around her. It crashed into her, massive and oppressive. Her charge faltered. Everywhere the fighting faltered. Everywhere people turned, looked up, stared.

Barph stood among them. Barph as she had never quite seen him before. Barph massive. Barph monumental. Barph truly the god that ruled all Avarra.

He dwarfed cathedrals. He dwarfed dragons. His head must have been level with the top of the slope she had just charged down. He was as tall as the hills. A literal mountain of a man. His feet were the length of houses.

He stood between her and Essoa. He beamed down broadly at them. He laughed.

And now all she had to do was help kill him.

55

The Greatest Trick the
Devil Ever Pulled...

Will could actually feel the strain of it—the effort of will required to hide fifty dragons behind a curtain of illusion. This was not magic that was natural to him. It did not come straight from the Deep Ones that he had taken inside himself. This was magic come secondhand, via Cois, from before his death. His new almost-divine powers supplemented this magic, made it stronger, but the interaction of the two was not perfect. And he felt it.

He felt so little these days. There had been something back when he'd been with Lette. Something nagging and sad, but also sweet for all the bitterness of it. He wasn't sure he could capture it now. Now there was just this sense of strain, this dull ache at the back of his mind.

And then Barph appeared, massive beyond imagining. His shadow blotting out a full third of the city. His face like a sun in the sky, full of teeth and curving lips.

And Will felt hatred. Will felt rage. Will felt savage.

He felt the dragons at his back. Their joy that this fight had come to them, that they were finally about to slip the leash he had put on them. He felt the wind of their wings spreading, the downdrafts as they beat at the air.

All around him the dragons ran at the crest of the slope leading down to Essoa, leading to Barph, to the fight for Avarra, to glory, and to death.

The dragons—hidden, invisible, deadly—took to the air, and Will felt himself smile.

56

All the News That's Fit to Shout Semiarticulately

Quirk felt as if she'd been running for days. Her lungs burned. Her legs ached. The final uphill slope almost defeated her. But she struggled and heaved and cursed at her aching legs until they moved.

But as she penetrated the first layers of the camp, she realized that it was empty, just a shell village of tents and bedrolls. Abandoned wagons and livestock surrounded her. Food left half-eaten.

No. No. Let me not be too late. Please let me not be too late.

"Afrit!" she screamed. There was no answer.

Then she heard the sound of fighting, and she knew she was too late.

"No. No." The word was a power unto itself, self-generating. Unstoppable.

She was still moving, still stumbling forward. "Afrit!" she called again. But there was no reply. And gods. Oh gods. Afrit was over that hill. She was in that thunderclap of violence.

And still…she didn't hear the roar of dragons. Not yet. So maybe there was some time left to her. Maybe if she could find Will, she could still warn him.

She staggered past the places where people had slept, the grass still flattened where they had lain. She passed their still-smoking campfires. She could smell their cooking. The density of their bodies. The sense of life just gone was heavy in the place.

And then she saw—at the crest of the hill—a lone figure. A man standing, looking down on the scene beyond.

"Will!" she called out, trying to convince her legs to break out into a run again. "Will!"

He didn't turn around. But it had to be him. She knew him too well to be mistaken.

"Will!" She was a step behind him, reached out, put a hand on his shoulder. And then she was on the crest of the hill, seeing what he saw, and all her words died on her lips.

A great slope of grass stretched out below her, acres and acres of meadowland sweeping down to a bustling cosmopolitan metropolis. And on that field, two armies clashed. One small and ferocious. Another large and bewildered. The former was on the attack. Will's army, she realized now. Her army too, she supposed.

And...

And also...

How had Barph gotten so large? How was that possible? Had any of the other divinities ever manifested at that size? Gods, his head was almost level with her, and he stood at the base of the valley.

Barph's foot came down. Fifty lives ended. He was laughing.

"He's going to kill everyone," she said.

"That's his aim, yes," said Will. And, finally, it was Will's utter lack of concern that snapped her out of her horrified trance.

"Afrit's down there!" She was almost screaming. "We have to save them!" And gods. Gods...that was why she was here. And then the absurdity of her saving an army from...from...from the thing Barph was hit her. "*You* have to save them," she said. It was all she could think of.

"That," Will said, "would take a miracle." And could it be that there was a hint of a smile playing around his lips? It suddenly felt to Quirk that something was very wrong with Will.

"We...we..." She grasped at straws. Everything was a tumult in her mind. She had to go down there. She had to save Afrit. There was no way to save Afrit. No one could save anyone from this. From Barph. Not even the dragons.

The dragons!

"The dragons," she said, trying to crack Will's shell of indifference with her urgency. "Where are they?"

"Close," Will said.

"Well, if you're relying on them to save those people," she snapped, "then they're about to betray you."

"I know."

For a moment Quirk couldn't even process this answer. It was too far from the realm of possibility for her. And Afrit...Afrit...

Except...

"You...," she managed. "You...you what?"

"I know," he said. He turned fully to her. His face was simple and open. It was almost a child's face. "I know so much these days, Quirk. I see so many things that were hidden to me before. It's all clear. It's all under control. So I have obscured the dragons behind an illusion. They have told me they're going to kill Barph and save my people. But I know that truly they're planning on killing both Barph *and* my people. And then, when I'm powerless, they're going to kill me."

Quirk felt her mouth open and shut of its own accord. She had burned with this knowledge. Afrit was down there dying. And he knew? He fucking knew? And he didn't care?

Will still had that small smile toying around his lips.

"The thing is," he said, "I'm not going to give them the time to do it."

"What?" she managed.

Will's grin grew fractionally wider. "You see, Quirk," he said, "I'm going to betray the dragons first."

All she could do was stare.

Will closed his eyes. And she saw pain then. And impossible strain. An effort that she didn't think it was within her grasp to understand.

And then suddenly, flapping urgently toward Barph, the dragons of Avarra appeared in the air. They were not there, and then they were. Exposed and startled, staring about, wings fluttering as Barph's wicked eye fell upon them. As his grin grew wider.

But then, in that same moment of unexpected revelation, something else. The army at his feet... Will's army, in midpanic and midrout—before Quirk's very eyes, they vanished. They were gone. No longer there to be crushed by Barph.

Gone.

Saved.

And Quirk stared down at a miracle.

57

Seeing Is Believing

Balur looked up from Essoa's shadowed streets. He saw the battle laid out like a theater performance. An epic, bloody tableau that transfixed every man, woman, and child in the city. Just the way Will had planned it.

A prick he may be, Balur thought, *but Will does have a surprisingly sophisticated sense of drama.*

Balur had spent the morning trying to make his way through this tangled death trap of a city, trying to set himself and Cois on a path for the city's harbor and a boat bound for as far away as they could get. Some island in the Spatters perhaps. Somewhere they could be ignored for a long, long time.

He was being thwarted, though, by every idiot jackass in this idiot jackass city standing in his way. And now he had taken a wrong turn, and he was in a market square, and pretty much the only way out was going to be by treading on people and feeling their rib cages explode beneath his weight.

Normally he wouldn't hesitate. This crowd was on edge, and a good rib stomping in a crowded square was just the sort of thing that would set it off. And then it would be rioting and chaos and a bloodbath, which he would normally really enjoy. But today he had Cois. And Cois's small slender fingers were tight on his arm. And zhe...Well, zhe would enjoy some riots, he was being sure, but today was not a good day for hir and riots.

And so he paused, and he looked back, and he saw, and, well…Well, it was quite a show.

Barph towered over them all, as tall as the hills, and—as insensitive to human emotion as he was—even Balur could feel the mixture of fear and awe and adoration that ran through the crowd. And even he, as much as he had spent the night rinsing his hands of concern for Lette, felt a shiver run down his spine as he thought of the madness on the battlefield right now. Even he felt his fists tightening as he watch Barph's feet come up, the soles stained red with the blood of the masses.

And seeing the slaughter written in Barph's red footprints, Balur knew that Lette and Will had bet wrong. Barph would win this fight. He would win it easily. This was the slaughter of hope. This was the death of dreams.

Victory would take a miracle.

And then…

Balur understood. At a certain level, he was aware of exactly what Will had done. He knew about his former friend's powers of illusion.

But…

An army vanished. A second one revealed. All the dragons of Avarra flocking toward Barph. Red of tooth and claw. Lungs full of fire.

And he saw the momentary confusion and disarray in the dragons' line before they resumed their flight toward Barph. And he knew that this had not been discussed. That something was amiss.

But…

A sophisticated sense of pissing drama.

"He saved them!" someone shouted. "All those people. Willett Fallows saved them!"

That is being, Balur thought, *an odd use of Will's full name.*

"A miracle!" someone else shouted. "Will Fallows performed a miracle!"

And the crowd hesitated. As their god stared around, his bewilderment written massively above them. Barph's confusion was utterly apparent. It was not, even Balur was forced to admit, being very divine.

"A miracle!" came the cry again. And Balur turned to see the person shouting.

And...

Gods. It was deception and trickery and absolute bullshit that took his breath away.

He *recognized* the woman shouting about miracles in the crowd. He had broken bread with her. He had diced with her. She was Will's woman. She was one of his followers.

"A miracle!" the woman shouted again. "Will Fallows saved them all with a miracle!"

Essoa worshipped Barph. Its people believed in him. They were a vast source of power for him. And Will...Will—who protested so hard that he was a simple farmer—would always be a thief at heart. No matter how divine he became, he would always be a con man.

Essoa wasn't the sacrifice. The dragons were. This city's inhabitants weren't meant to be slaughtered cattle. They were meant to be converts. A fake miracle, with fake men and women to proselytize in the crowd.

Will was going to steal Essoa from Barph.

58

Tricked Out

Barph felt it. He felt the faith of a city flicker. He felt doubt, like poison, enter its heart. He felt himself grow weaker.

And the worst of it was that he, just like them, was left staring. Was left wondering what had just happened. There had been an army at his feet. He had been merrily mashing them like a barrelful of grapes. He had been laughing and happy.

And then Will...Will had *tricked* him. Somehow. And he wasn't sure how. He still couldn't see it. And now his city doubted him. A piece of Avarra had slipped between his fingers and lay in Will's grasping hands.

And then, before he could work out how to seize it back, the dragons attacked. Because he had hesitated. He had reeled. He had been given a chance to prepare himself for this, and he had missed it.

Flame raked over him. Claws slashed at him. And he felt the two competing realities. The one where his skin was as thick and impenetrable as iron. The other where he was scalded and lacerated, where his blood burst forth in fountains.

He wrestled for control. He wrestled to be master of reality instead of mastered by it. He reached out. He called down lightning in a storm. He cared nothing for accuracy. He cared nothing for collateral damage. He cared nothing for the lightning striking and scouring his own skin. He needed to establish who he was, what he could do.

He needed these dragons to die.

He saw dragons rupture and burst before him, lightning crackling through their bodies—more than they could contain, pieces of them raining down on the ground below. He caught another of the lizards in one of his massive hands. He squeezed and felt blood and bone ooze between his fingers. He raked his hand through the air, swatted beasts to the ground like so many insects, felt the sprays of earth their broken bodies kicked up.

But he also felt their fire, their claws, their teeth. He felt himself cut and ruptured and despoiled in a thousand places. For every dragon he killed, ten more seemed to wound him. He howled in rage and pain. And as he did so he could feel himself growing weaker. The people caring for him less and less.

This was that fucking vineyard all over again. This was worse than that vineyard. That had been a private embarrassment and a private pain. This struggle was writ large and displayed for all the world to see.

He felt talons scrape across his face, felt the blood running down into his eyes. He felt fire crackle over the skin of his chest, felt his beard burning.

He felt afraid.

He lashed out again, again, again. This had to end. This had to stop. He was a fucking deity. *The* deity. He had beaten Lawl. He had beaten all the gods. He had tricked all the world. It was his now. He would re-create it. He would set it free. He would be liberation, and glory, and he would be loved in a way that Lawl never had been. Never could be.

He was god, and this could not be.

And yet it was. And with every passing second he felt his grip on the world grow looser.

Another dragon died on the end of his fist. Another one exploded under the force of the thunderbolt he flung at it. Another dragon was crushed beneath his foot. Another died. Another.

But he was reeling. He was staggering. He was doubling over in pain. He was weeping and screaming.

Death to these things. Death to them all. He forced his will out. A black spreading cloud of choking, harrowing death. Acidic air that burned the dragons' lungs, that seared the flame from their throats.

And finally, tattered, choking, on all fours, he was left alone. There was silence. He was on fire. Blood fell from him like rain. He felt hollowed out, violated by doubt.

But the dragons... He wiped blood from his eyes. Two, three perhaps. Falling back. Running for the hills.

Now Will would come. He knew it. Now his enemy would try his hand. With the city at his back vacillating over where its loyalties lay. With him at his weakest.

And fucking Will Fallows actually stood a chance. He would hide. He would use his little magics to slip unseen like a knife between Barph's ribs.

He howled his rage. He roared his hatred. Somewhere on this fucking blood-soaked plain, Will Fallows was there. Mocking him. Thinking he had outsmarted him. Thinking he could kill a god.

"Nothing!" he roared. "You're nothing! Not you! Not Lawl! Not any of your companions! You are nothing to me!"

And he called the storm of lightning bolts down once more. With the last of his strength. He would burn this whole fucking plain. He would burn Will Fallows. He would scorch him from the earth.

There would be no victories here. No simple narratives to be spun before eager-eyed children. There would be only his legacy. Only chaos.

59

The Eternal Fate of
Smug Bastards

Quirk had watched as Will's face changed and as Barph had stared around in confusion. She had watched as the dragons recovered from their initial surprise and swept toward him. She had watched as fire and blood filled the sky.

Will had been smiling. His face had looked fit to burst from the strain of it.

"Essoa," he had said, almost grunting the words, "they're starting to believe."

"Believe what?" She hadn't been entirely certain she'd wanted to know the answer.

"That their god will fall." Beads of sweat stood out on Will's forehead. "That I'll win."

And that had been good. Quirk had known that was good. But at that moment it hadn't felt quite as good as it should have.

A dragon had plunged out of the sky, crashed into the plain. The slope Will's army had just occupied.

"Where are they?" she had asked. "Your followers?" But really she had meant, "Where's Afrit?"

"Still there," he'd said. His eyes had looked on the verge of bursting from their sockets. "I've just hidden them. I can't move that many people."

Still there...

"So where that dragon just fell...," she'd said. "There were people...?"

Will had shaken his head. "I have enough."

"Enough...," she repeated. The word hung there between them.

"To win," Will had clarified. "I have Essoa now."

And gods. All those people. All those who had followed him since he emerged from the Hallows into Avarra. Who had followed him on the strength of the lie that it was Barph who had ravaged Avarra. All of them nothing more than grist in the mill of Will's revenge.

"You...you..." The enormity of her outrage had stuck in her craw for a moment. "Afrit is down there! You...fucking...arse-hole! You—"

But then the lightning storm had begun and cut her off. Bolt after bolt raining down among the dragons. The earth scorched black. Lizard bodies crashing down like battering rams. The earth rising in bomb-blast sprays. A fog of acrid black smoke exuding from Barph's body that seemed to choke the life from everything it touched. Then the hillside running red with blood.

They were still there. All those people. All those lives. Afrit's life. In the middle of the madness and the slaughter. They were there and—unseen—they were dying.

"We have to do something." She was desperate. She reached out, seized Will's arm. She jerked back. His skin seemed to sting her, crackling with energy that left a taste like bile in the back of her throat.

"Soon," Will whispered.

There were seven dragons left in the sky. Then six. Barph fell to his knees, to all fours. Blood seemed to be dripping from every part of his body. His beard was on fire, smoke rising above his head. It began to rain.

"Yes," Will breathed. "Now."

The last three dragons were flapping away. Three. Gods. She

remembered Natan. She remembered the teeming skies. She remembered racing across the ocean back to Avarra at the head of an army.

Three. All that was left of the dragons of Avarra. The creatures she had dedicated her life to studying—for all that that life was left behind in the ashes of a broken world. And even with the mountain of grief already heaped upon her shoulders, she couldn't help but mourn them. She couldn't help but feel horror at her own culpability. She had brought them here. She had embroiled them in this extinction.

Will cracked his knuckles. Barph was looking up, and Quirk was struck by the pathos in his ragged, stained features, by the horror and the loss. She was struck by how vindictive Will looked in this moment.

This moment. Gods. This was everything and nothing they had fought for.

But maybe...maybe Afrit was still alive. Not everyone had been lost. She was sure of it. Will had saved some of them. Perhaps even most. Perhaps the odds were not so stacked against her. Maybe...

And then Barph stretched out a ragged and bloody hand, palm outstretched, fingers spread, as if to ward off Will's coming. And then the whole hillside seemed to quake. The very earth vibrated beneath Quirk's feet.

Lightning. Lighting as dense as rain. A storm like a roiling beast, like a crawling, scribbling finger of death swiping over the plain.

And the dragons were dead. And Barph was on his knees. But the slaughter had not ended.

Quirk didn't know what Barph was trying to do. What he thought he was achieving. But...

Afrit. Afrit and all those people. All of Will's army. All of his faithful. All the people he had only hidden, not moved. And Afrit.

They were still there.

The ground boiled. Lightning was everywhere. They must be dying by the hundreds.

Quirk turned to scream at Will. To assault him somehow with her horror and rage. And she would break through somehow. She would make him feel this.

She saw Will's face change once more. She saw the grin of overpowering joy become a rictus, become stricken, become gaunt. She saw the sweat on his forehead stand out more and more even as his cheeks began to sink in.

"No," he said. "No!"

And he did feel this. There was something left in him, perhaps. Some sort of compassion. Or perhaps it was just the selfish grab for power.

"No!" he shouted again, and started a step forward, but then stopped.

"He's killing them!" Quirk grabbed him again, heedless of the sting of his skin. "He's killing Afrit! You have to save them!"

"But—" Will looked down at his hands. "I...I need them to save them..."

"You fucking... You have Essoa! You said you have Essoa!"

"I..." Will looked utterly devastated. "They... Barph's not... They don't..."

Oh gods, she wanted to... to tear into him somehow. To tear out his heart and expose it to all the pain he had caused. But she didn't have words. And she didn't have time. Down on that hill, Afrit didn't have time. She didn't know what she could do, but she had to do something.

She left Will standing there with his horror-filled eyes. She left him standing motionless. She left him and took off, tearing down the hill, heading pell-mell forward, desperate to save the people there, somehow, any way she could.

Her footsteps faltered. She couldn't even see the woman she was trying to save.

And then, with a feeling like a soap bubble bursting over her whole body, she seemed to step through the edge of the illusion, and she saw.

Oh gods. Oh gods. She saw.

Terror. Terror writ large. Terror no longer a word or an idea. Terror come alive. Terror grown limbs and eyes, and mouths with which to scream. Terror become a crowd. A crowd become a wound.

The dead were everywhere. She could see them scattered below her by the thousands. She saw their faces lit by the lightning bolts that added to their numbers. She saw people dying and dying and dying, their bodies bloody and raw, laid out exposed.

She saw two women holding hands, scrambling up the hillside. Lightning reached down, evaporated one, sent the other flying through the air like a catapult stone, fire jetting from her mouth, her eyes. She saw men clawing over each other. She saw a mass of bodies transform from something scrambling and urgently alive into something quivering and dead in a single white flash.

And what could she do? What could she do?

"Afrit!" she screamed. She couldn't even hear her own words. "Afrit!" It was an exercise beyond the pointless.

Someone stumbled into her. A woman. For a moment Quirk's heart leapt. But no. No, she didn't know this woman. She was just one of many, almost collapsing from exhaustion. Blood and tears streamed down her face. "Please," she begged Quirk. "Please help me."

And Afrit was in there somewhere. In the maelstrom of death.

But this woman was here. Her desperation was here. And Quirk was not yet someone who could ignore that.

"Come on," she said. She grabbed the woman, hauled her up toward the crest of the slope, pitched her over its edge, toward the possibility of safety.

Someone else was there, scrabbling and slipping. "Come on!" she took a step forward, grabbed him by the arm, propelled him upward. "You can make it! You're almost there."

She waded into the crowd, into the storm, armed only with platitudes and the last scraps of her energy. And perhaps, perhaps it was enough. Perhaps she would find Afrit this way. Perhaps she would haul her to safety and this nightmare would be over.

And yet she also knew it was nothing but a drop in the ocean. For everyone whose hand she held, two were blown apart. Two were turned inside out. Another was set on fire and sent screaming to pinwheel into a friend, a father, a mother.

Above them all, Barph was become something else. Not just a god of chaos. Not just a god of drunken revelry. Barph was become death itself. A conduit to the Void. Because there were no Hallows left for these people to be condemned to. No. This was an undoing complete and utter. And who had seen to that? Who stood paralyzed by his own culpability on a hill behind her?

Barph and Will. Neither was any better than the other, she thought. Petty, powerful men, sacrificing thousands of others to satisfy nothing but their own egos.

Lightning smashed into the ground beside her. She felt the heat of it slap at her, couldn't hold back her cry of fear. Flying mud stung her face. She scraped it away, staggered on. She grabbed someone's outstretched arm, heaved, trying to pull them to their feet. Was it Afrit? No. She didn't recognize this face. Then, under her efforts, the woman's torso slithered free, while her legs stayed lying on the ground. Quirk gagged.

Something touched her arm. She flinched away.

"Quirk! Quirk!" It took her a moment to recognize her own name. Someone was shaking her arm and shouting her name over the fury of the storm.

Could it...? She spun ready to embrace Afrit. But no. No. It was not her.

Still she did recognize this woman.

"Lette?" The mercenary's presence caught Quirk utterly off guard.

"Having fun yet?" The mockery of a smile on Lette's lips was a horror to behold.

"We have to . . . we have to save these people!" Quirk screamed. And it was an absurd thing to say. Nothing could save these people. But they had to.

"I know!" Lette shook her head. "That's all I know! I don't know how. I don't . . . I don't . . ."

Quirk stared about. The sky seemed to have closed over them. A solid fist of clouds wearing lightning as knuckle-dusters pounding the ground over and over, grinding the people upon it into nothing. Nothing at all.

"We have to do something!" Quirk felt the emptiness of her words.

"Come on then!" Lette heaved Quirk toward an injured woman with a wound in her chest leaking blood into the mud of the hillside. Lette grabbed one of the woman's arms, looked at Quirk. Quirk stared down at the woman. She was barely alive.

"Come on!" There was steel in Lette's voice.

Lightning slammed into the ground to their left. Quirk flinched. Someone else screamed. Afrit was in here somewhere. Afrit alone. Perhaps dying. Perhaps in need of help.

But so was everyone else.

"What would Afrit want you to do?"

And of all the questions. Of all the times to be asked it. She grabbed the woman's arm anyway. It was as good as anything.

They heaved. They struggled. Their feet slipped in mud and rain and blood. Lightning struck the ground again, again, again. People died all around them.

They were almost at the crest of the hill when the woman they were heaving on started to spasm wildly. She bucked, and

Quirk lost her grip, slipped and fell. When she picked herself up, the woman was dead.

Lette was panting, wiping her brow. She looked at Quirk. Her jaw was set. "Another one then."

It wasn't a question.

They went back into the heart of it. Into thunder so loud Quirk couldn't hear herself think. The air tasted of ozone. Her hair stood on end. They found a young man missing one arm, screaming. They grabbed him by the legs started to pull.

The world in front of them was a solid wall of white. There was no path forward.

Quirk looked back. Barph was a barely distinguishable shadow above them. She screamed at him. She flung fire at him. It disappeared into clouds and rain. She fell to her knees. She screamed again.

"Come on!" Lette's voice was barely audible over the storm.

Quirk stared at her. Because what the fuck was the point? What was the madness driving this woman?

Lette shrugged. "We either die on our knees or on our feet."

And maybe, in the end, that was really all there was to it. Maybe that was what Afrit had been trying to tell her all along.

So Quirk picked herself up. She seized the one-armed man by the leg. And then she walked into the storm.

60

Powerless

Will flung everything he had at the bleeding, tattered body of Barph. But all he had was less and less.

His people were dying. They were dying faster and faster. Barph's desperate, hate-fueled storm scoured them from the earth. It undid lives. It undid faith. It undid Will.

And as the dragons fled, as Will's people died, the citizens of Essoa did not come to his aid. They had doubted Barph, yes, but that momentary flicker of unbelief was gone. Their god had stumbled, yes, he had been injured, yes, but he was still a mountain of a man, he was still vast beyond imagining, he was still breathing. He was still there.

They almost couldn't help but believe in him. And with every moment that Will failed to finish the job, it got worse, and victory slipped further and further away.

And then, suddenly, it was over.

Suddenly the lightning stopped. Suddenly the skies cleared. Suddenly Barph was gone.

Will stood alone on the hillside.

Will stood alone with the dead.

Will wept.

There were so many. So very many. The dead were everywhere. They were fused with the land. Their hands reached up, imploring him. And he had ... he had ...

Nothing.

It was gone. All the power was gone. Everything he had been. He had spent it all. He had wasted it all. All in this gambit. And everyone...everyone was dead. All his followers dead. No one believed in him anymore. Even the handful who had survived had no belief left for him.

He was...human. Nothing but human.

And the enormity of what he had done hit him. The sheer scale of his hubris, his vanity, his recklessness, the totality of his idiocy.

And all the words were too small.

Ten thousand had died in Kondorra. Ten thousand had died fighting against the dragons. But fifty thousand had survived. Fifty thousand had emerged from that fight victorious and free. Ten thousand had died for *something*.

Ten thousand had died here for *him*. And that was just another way of saying that they had died for nothing at all.

He had not freed Avarra. He had not defeated Barph. He had just murdered all these people. And now, without the defense of even his own ego, he could not deny it.

So he wept.

He walked through this garden of the dead, with its reaching black-and-red limbs and its blooms of gut and bone. He walked, putting one foot in front of another, not sure what else he could do. He felt...not numbness, exactly. His horror was simply too monumental, too encompassing. There was no room for the flavor of other emotions that would give it contrast. It was everything he saw and heard and tasted and knew. The whole color of the world had changed.

And then, finally, near the top of the hill, near the edge of the vast field of the dead, he found two bodies he recognized, two bodies whose forms were not bent so far out of true as to spare him this final piece of knowledge. Two bodies. Two women.

Quirk was dead.

And...

He swallowed. He swallowed again. His mouth was dry. His lips were coated with ash. His knees were betraying him. He was falling. He thought perhaps his throat was closing. Maybe he would die as well. Maybe that would be a good thing. The Void this time. An end to him and his hateful anger. His stupid, useless mind finally finding the simple pleasures of oblivion.

Quirk was dead.

Lette was dead.

PART 3: BAD MOFOS

61

Catharsis Through the Medium of Punching Dickheads

Afrit sat up. Her head hurt. She put her hand to it and winced. When she pulled the palm away, flakes of dried blood were there.

It came back to her then. The whole ugly mess of it. Balur on the stage baring his heart and Will convincing the crowd to step on it. The charging chaos afterward, getting knocked down, getting trodden upon. Quirk finding her. The fight...Oh shit, the fight.

She couldn't believe Quirk had walked away. Had she never...? But of course she *had* never been in a fight with a lover before.

But Afrit had been in no mood for being understanding last night, with her wound and her emotions raw. Instead she had been in the mood to collapse and cry and sleep.

And now...

She poked her head out of her tent flap, looked out onto a gray day. The camp was...ghostly. Nothing moved. There was no sound. There was a smell in the air as if a thunderstorm had just passed through.

She clambered out of the tent, careful to hold her head as still as possible. She looked around. Smoke drifted from a few fire pits, but no food bubbled over them. No people gathered around them, laughing or talking.

How hard had she hit her head?

They were marching to war today. Was everyone already gathered to march?

She went blearily up the hill, rubbing sleep from her eyes, her sense of dread growing. Everything was abandoned. As if life had been paused, but now seemed uncertain if it could ever return.

A tent flap twitched open, and she stifled a scream. A head emerged, and after a moment of almost blinding panic, she realized she recognized it.

"Lawl?" she managed.

The former deity looked up at her. He looked old and haggard. "Is it over?" he hissed at her.

She looked around, looked up to where the knot of clouds had been. "Is what over?" she asked. "What happened here?"

But Lawl just grunted and retreated back into his tent. She looked from the rough canvas to the suddenly blue sky, uncertain what to do next. But any answers from Lawl would be hard-won.

She walked faster now. Lawl was proof of life. The pall of death was just an illusion, was just—

She reached the crest of the hill.

Her breath left her. She tried to catch it, but it was racing away, fleeing from the horror before her. She felt the strength go out of her knees.

How could there be so many dead?

She couldn't take in the scope of it. It was too much. All of it. The slope went on for . . . gods, it must be miles. A city at the bottom of it, untouched. But all that space in between . . .

It was covered with the dead, matted with them, their twisted bodies burned and blackened. Already birds were starting to land among them—crows and gulls and vultures. A few feral dogs were slinking among the bodies, their mouths and fur smeared obscenely with black.

She looked back at the abandoned camp.

"All of them...," she whispered. And she had...she had... slept through it? Grief and head trauma had left her unconscious, and she had...

This was her fight. This was the fight she had sacrificed Quirk to be a part of. And she had...she had fucking missed it?

For a moment the image of Quirk down in the twisted mess of all those bodies flashed through her mind, and she thought she was going to throw up. But, no, Quirk had fled all of this. She had left. Quirk was alive.

Surely some of these others had survived. Surely someone down there was still moving. Still needed her help.

Despite her desperate urge to look away, Afrit scanned the crowd for any sign of human life. She felt the tears leaking down her face.

Finally movement caught her eye. She stared. A figure on their knees. Bringing their hands up to their face.

She tried to run, but the bodies were too thick on the ground. She picked her way, ghoulish limbs reaching up toward her.

And still part of her somehow thought she was going to see Quirk there. Somehow. Impossibly. Thoughts of reunion dancing in the back of her head. Hope against a backdrop of defeat.

But it was not Quirk. It was Will.

She barely recognized him. Last time she had seen him he had seemed almost to glow. He had been sickly looking, yes, but he had also seemed taller, broader, radiant...Now his hair was dull, matted to his head by rain. His clothes were mud streaked and tattered. The purple on his cheeks looked like a dull stain. The almost translucent patches just looked pale and washed out. This was the abandoned husk of the man Will had been the day before.

"I didn't know," he said to her. "I wasn't myself. I thought I could...I could..." He didn't make it through the last sentence. His words dissolved into his tears.

"What happened here?" she asked. And she didn't know why she asked, because once she'd said it, she was certain she didn't want to know the answer.

"All I ever wanted to do was protect them."

All the bodies. All the dead stretching away around them. And those were not the words of an innocent man.

"You," she said, her mind grappling with the edges of the concept. "What did you do?" And still she didn't want to know. But she had to know.

"It wasn't me." Will was begging her to believe something she already couldn't. "It was Barph. It was the other thing. The thing inside me."

And then she realized that Will was holding on to something. A body. His hands were covered with ash and smeared fat and blood. He was gripping a blackened, tortured arm. And she stepped to get a better view even as her horror grew, even as a voice inside her head screamed, *No! No! Turn and run!*

And she recognized…

"Oh," she said. "Oh, Will, I'm so…"

"No!" His voice was harsh, and he moved, shifting his weight, almost as if to block her view.

She reached out to him. No matter what the surroundings… she knew what Lette had meant to him. "It's okay." She took a step toward him.

And then she saw the second body. The one Lette's corpse was gripping. Their fused limbs. She seemed unable to focus on anything else for a moment. That one detail was more than she could handle. It obsessed her—the blackened, stunted fingers seeming to almost flow into the ugly raw flesh of the burned arm. The red wounds where the nails might once have been. The fact that she could no longer determine exactly where the knuckles had existed.

Then the whole of it flashed into her mind. The whole of that body and a single word.

Quirk.

No. No. She rejected that. That wasn't what she was seeing. That couldn't be what she was seeing. Quirk wasn't here. Quirk was miles away. Obstinate and stupid, but alive.

Afrit's gaze went back to the arm, traced its way up. The muscles twisted, curling, the shape only just recognizable. So much of the skin gone...

Her beautiful skin.

No. No. That wasn't... That couldn't...

The angle of the shoulder had become something foreign, almost something unnatural. Everything was fused and melted. Afrit's gaze ran along what must have been the shoulder blade. What was left of the neck seemed almost impossibly thin, parts of it carved away by whatever horror had been... had been...

She couldn't get the air into her lungs. Will was saying words that bounced off her consciousness. There was no room in her head to process them.

Because the face... She couldn't look at the face. She couldn't. It was too... It couldn't... She couldn't... It wasn't...

And then she was looking at the face. And even like this, even with the skin peeled back, the muscles contorted, the hair gone... Even like this...

She remembered her laughter. She remembered the way her gaze fell on you, so intense, so unafraid, peeling you open, searching for your secrets. She remembered the feel of her hand twining fingers with her own, palm pressed to palm. She remembered the softness of her lips. She remembered her hair—her trimming it as she stared intently into a mirror, eyes narrowed with self-criticism. She remembered sharing wine, sharing bread. She remembered seeing her again after all the time apart, after escaping the Hallows themselves.

She remembered.

And then memory faded, and she stared at reality once more. She stared at Quirk's crooked, burned corpse before her.

"I didn't," Will was saying. "I didn't."

She didn't know what he was denying. She didn't care.

"You."

Her voice sounded strange to her. It was distant, choking, as if something were throttling her.

"You."

She was pointing her finger at Will. An accusation. An attempt to discover within herself the gift of fire that had always been Quirk's. That had always made her skin run hot and left Afrit sweating on the nights when they shared a bedroll. When she was alive. When she was alive. When…

"I didn't," Will said again. He was backing away from her.

But he had. She heard it in his voice. This was his fault.

She didn't know what she was going to do about it. She just stood there like a revenant, finger outstretched, while Will backed away, arms raised defensively, hands stained gory black with his guilt.

"DIE!"

A single word. A guttural howl. The summoning of all the blackest thoughts in her heart, condensed and hawked up and flung at Will like a crossbow bolt.

But it did not come from her. Someone else was screaming in rage.

She couldn't look away from Will, from Quirk's…from Quirk's…

"Murderer," she whispered the word to herself as Balur tore into her vision. The lizard man was charging, going full force, a sword raised above his low-slung head. The sword came down.

Will flung himself to the side as the sword carved a trench in the earth he had just been cowering upon. Balur tore it free, swiped viciously at Will. Will kept rolling, barely a pace away from the blade's gleaming edge.

"Balur! No!" A not-quite feminine voice. A voice Afrit could almost place. Then Cois chased into Afrit's vision, grabbed hold of Balur's arms. Balur shrugged hir off. He barely seemed to have noticed hir at all.

"DIE!" he bellowed again, hacking at Will. Will skittered back. There was no beauty or finesse to Balur's movements. This was blunt savagery. This was grief transmuted into blinding hatred.

And with that realization, it was as if the lizard man had provided an escape route for Afrit's own grief, her own over-whelming hurt. Rage clenched a fist over her heart.

Will Fallows would die for this.

Balur was chasing after Will, bringing his sword down in massive overhead blows over and over and over again. Will was crab-crawling away, eyes wide and staring as he barely out-paced the blade again and again.

Afrit ran at him, pulled back her foot and kicked one of his arms out from under him. He collapsed back, sprawled. Balur raised his sword, grinned. Will screamed.

The sword came down. Will rolled. The sword bit into the earth less than a quarter inch from Will's body. He was still screaming. Afrit was screaming. She hurdled the sword and kicked and kicked and kicked.

And part of her kept expecting Will to strike back, for him to reach out with some of that massive, divine power he had pulled to himself. Some part of her was waiting to be swatted. And that wouldn't be so bad, because it would be an end at least. It would stop the pain from overwhelming her rage and leaving her curled up and bawling on the ground.

But he didn't. He curled up around her foot and howled, but that was all. And somehow the fact that it was pathetic and cra-ven made it all worse.

Balur abandoned his sword, took Afrit's lead. He kicked Will so hard that the former farmer flew through the air, started roll-ing down the hill, crashing through burned bodies.

Afrit gave chase. Will was on his feet when she got to him,

tottering, clutching his ribs with one hand, trying to fend them off with the other.

"I'm not…," he managed between ragged breaths. "I'm not…"

"You are being responsible!" Balur roared. "Do not be daring to tell me you are not, or that it was being Barph. Do not be daring. Not even once. You were picking this fight. You were calling this a plan. You were the one who caused this. You were the one who killed her."

"I'm not that person anymore," Will said. Tears were still coursing down his face. Whether it was due to pain or sorrow, Afrit couldn't tell. She didn't really care.

There was a lump of steel slag on the ground. Something that had perhaps been a sword once. It was just a twisted mess of metal now. It fit snugly in her fist.

"I was someone else, when I…when I…Oh gods, Balur. I'm so sorry. But you have to believe me."

Afrit threw the lump of slag. It missed his head by inches.

"Gods!"

A god. He had pretended to be a god. When all he had ever been was a self-centered fool. And now she would kill him.

Balur again followed Afrit's lead, found something on the ground, hurled it at Will. It was someone's head. It caught Will full in the midriff, knocked him to the ground.

Then the pursuit was on again. Her hurling objects, Balur trying to get close enough to deliver a killing blow. The lizard man tripped over a corpse, and they came to another impasse. Will stood, breathing hard, hands held out to them, beseeching them.

"I was mad," he said. "I was sick. And I couldn't see it. The power in me…It wouldn't let me see it. If I could…if I could take it all back…"

Words. It was all words with him. All bullshit. They bounced off her. The same way something would off his skull as soon as she found a suitable missile.

"I loved her, Balur! I loved her! I would do anything to save her. I thought that's what I was trying to do. I was just so fucked in the head that I couldn't...I didn't..."

"You are not being properly fucked in the head," Balur said. "Not until I am boring the hole in your skull myself."

"More death is not going to fix this." Afrit had almost forgotten Cois's presence. And hir words meant even less than Will's. She found another lump of...something...She threw it. Will dodged to the side. Balur was circling around that way, weight held low, tail whipping back and forth in the air above his head.

"It was the Deep Ones," he begged. "It was what they put inside of me."

"You put it inside of you!" Balur roared, and charged.

Will flinched back, but not fast enough. Elation and sickness mingled inside Afrit as she watched Balur's claws close on...

Nothing.

An illusion.

Balur howled in rage.

"I'm sorry!" Will was standing five paces away, arms still out, still beseeching. "I'm trying to save my life. I swear this is all I have left. Parlor tricks. All the other power has gone. I can see now. I can see everything I've done."

He started to sob again.

"You cannot be hiding from me." Balur picked himself up off the ground. "I will be hunting you to the ends of the world."

"Is that what Lette would have even wanted?" Cois was trying to get between Will and Balur. "She loved Will."

"He was killing her!" Balur barked at Cois. "That is a betrayal of love. She would be wanting me to be tearing off his head and pissing her revenge into the stump."

"She chose him over you." Cois spoke quietly, but Afrit still winced at the impact of the words.

But finally, it seemed, she had found a way to halt the unstoppable force that was Balur's rage.

"She shouldn't have," Will said almost to himself. "She shouldn't have." He spoke through tears.

They seemed to have forgotten her, Afrit thought. Could she get close enough? Could she make him pay for what he had done?

The sensation of nausea that had passed through her as Balur's talons had closed on Will's neck came again. And no, perhaps she could not.

"What about Quirk?" she said. "What about her?"

Will snapped around, blinked at her. "Oh gods..." He sank to his knees. "All these fucking people. All their families. All their loved ones. He got to his knees. Not a collapse but a slow, deliberate movement. "Do it, Balur," he said. "Just fucking do it."

"Shut up, you arsehole," Cois snapped. "Just because I don't want you dead doesn't mean you're off the hook for this."

Will wasn't really listening to hir. He was still blabbering on, caught somewhere between making excuses and trying to pay penance. "I never meant for any of this to happen. I swear, I never did. I couldn't. I didn't know what I was doing."

"Shut up, Will!" Afrit snapped.

She didn't want to kill him, she thought. She didn't want to listen to him anymore. She wanted to ignore his existence.

"I wouldn't have done it this way," he went on, oblivious to them all. "Not if I was in control. I wouldn't have tried to fight him head-on. That was...Gods...We can't take the heavens by force."

"She was choosing him," Balur said, finally seeming to recover from the body blow Cois had dealt him. He spoke in a low rumble, the worlds hard to pick out. "And so perhaps I cannot be killing him for her. Perhaps she would not be wanting that."

"There's been enough death today." Cois sounded hollowed out.

"But I can still be killing him for me."

Will was shaking his head, but he didn't seem to be listening. "We can't take the heavens by force," he said again.

Afrit just felt tired. Felt defeated. She felt as if all the emotion had been punched out of her heart. She had nothing left for this.

"No, Balur." Cois raised a restraining hand that had no possible way to restrain Balur.

"For me," Balur said.

"We couldn't take the heavens by force," Will said a third time. He sounded as if he was broken. But then he looked up at Balur, and his eyes were bright.

"But," he said, "before you kill me, I think I can tell you how to steal them."

62

Loyalties and Lying

Cois had always believed that Balur killed beautifully. He killed in the way that others created paintings, in the way that others danced and sang. He was an artist of murder. When Balur killed, there was a light to it, something that shone within it.

Zhe was not, zhe thought, bloodthirsty. It was hard to know exactly. When zhe was a god, hir perspective of such things—zhe recognized now—had been skewed. Zhe was certain zhe had never been as bloodthirsty as Lawl, or Toil, or even Barph, who had used murder as a punch line when it suited him. It wasn't that zhe was averse to bloodshed, zhe had just never seen much point to it. Zhe had always preferred the fecundity and savage lust of man. To hir, the creation of life was more interesting than the ending of it.

Balur, though, was different. Balur was a creature of pure purpose. Everything about him was designed to deliver death. All the pleasure he brought hir along the path of his life was almost incidental, almost an accident. And there was something about that that set a fire in hir loins that no physick's ointment could appease. And when he killed . . . He was at his most beautiful when he killed.

And perhaps things would be easier if zhe just let him kill Will. Will was, in the end, responsible for all the deaths spread out around them. And maybe the blame was not totally his, but it was he who had created this situation. It was he who had forced these people and Barph into confrontation. It was his pride. His folly. And yes, there should be punishment. And yes, death was the obvious one.

But... what then? What would come after Will's death?

What would happen to Balur?

Balur had loved Lette. Cois knew that. Zhe knew it in the way that only someone who had competed for that love could know. Zhe knew it in the way his attention wandered. In the questions he asked. In the small unthinking moments that left hir utterly sidelined. Zhe knew.

And now Lette was dead. Lette had been killed. And so Lette was poised to climb onto a pedestal. And if Cois allowed that, then Lette would become the very poison that would kill Balur. That would unman him.

Balur needed continuous motion, continuous purpose. Lette was an ending. Killing Will was an ending. And to stop was to die. It would kill both Balur's spirit and hir happiness in the lizard man's arms.

Balur, zhe saw, needed Will. Will was a cause in human form. He was a cause zhe could never fully believe in. It was a cause to kill hir son, hir former lover. But it was a cause. It was hatred and anger. It was a focus and a destination for Balur beyond the immediacy of Lette's death. It was an engine that could fuel him.

And so, no matter how beautiful it would be, no matter how justified his wrath, no matter how much zhe hated Will for what he had done here—for what he had become, for his pathetic, craven excuses—zhe needed Balur to cease and desist from Will's murder.

The problem was, Balur wasn't listening. His grief was too big. It clogged his ears and his sense. And so hir only hope was that Will fought for his life harder than Balur fought to end it.

And then Will betrayed hir. He knelt and offered his neck to Balur. And zhe could see the rage getting ready to end, the grief getting ready to take over.

And just as Cois gave up hope, Will finally reached into the depths of his metaphorical arse and yanked out a way for hir to save Balur.

I can tell you how to steal the heavens.

Oh, Will pissing Fallows. This was the way he gave hir? Save Balur, but destroy everything else? Of course that was the choice. It always pissing was.

"I am not wanting to hear shit from you." Balur growled at Will, and advanced on him with his sword drawn.

Will seemed to be having second thoughts about his penitent death now that a plan was setting fire to his brain. He scrambled up off his knees and backed away from Balur.

It could still all be over in a second, though. And then Balur would be undone.

"How?" Zhe didn't want to ask it. Zhe didn't want to know. But zhe had to know if Balur was going to survive this.

"The font," Will said. He pointed at Cois, while still backing away from Balur. "You said there was a font of blood in the heavens. You said whoever's blood is in the font—they control the heavens. The Summer Palace attacks everyone else."

And gods, zhe didn't know what zhe'd been hoping for, but it wasn't that. What did zhe say? Where did hir loyalties lie?

Wait. That had been Lawl's watchword when they first arrived in the Hallows. *Wait for as long as it takes. We have long lives and long plans. The humans and all the other mortals are but flickering candles. Wait. Bide our time. Because the moment will come when we can recapture the heavens. If only we are patient. If only we stay loyal to each other and who we truly are.*

Lawl was a prick, to be sure. And Cois liked Balur's prick, to be sure. But mortality…Waking up and feeling aches in hir muscles for the first time in the millennia of existence. Waking up and not having the world fold to hir whims. Waking up and being cold and alone and afraid. Counting those cold, lonely, frightening days one by one in a slow march where the aches would get worse until zhe was so frail zhe couldn't even shit hir own pants right... Mortality was far from being hir favorite thing.

But if Will got the heavens... Well, then, zhe and the other gods would never have a chance to claim them for themselves, zhe was sure. That would be an end to that dream. That would be an embracing of mortality. And regardless of all the questionable people and things Cois had embraced throughout the ages, zhe still did not know if zhe could embrace that.

"Do not be listening to him," Balur said, leveling his sword at Will. "He is a liar, full of lies, and I must cut them out of him from balls to brow."

But mortality did have Balur.

All those divine years as the god(dess) of love and to only now have found it hirself. Ah, the bitter, bitter irony.

"Yes," zhe said to Will. "There is a font, and it functions that way."

"I am wondering"—Balur still pursued Will—"how your bowels will be functioning when my foot is up them."

"The font is the key!" Will almost tripped over a tangle of blackened limbs. Balur closed the space between them as he recovered.

"How?" Afrit asked.

If Cois still had hir powers, zhe would have made the woman's nethers rot on her like fruit left too long on the vine. Zhe did not need any more specificity. The slow grind of striving, that was what Balur needed. The distraction of a purpose. Zhe needed Will's plans purposeful but hopeless.

"The blood in the font," Will said. "That's how Barph actually took the heavens. It wasn't killing the gods. It was putting his own blood in the font. So if we take his blood out of it, and put our own blood in..."

And that was very far from vague. That was very far from hopeless. That could actually work.

Shit.

"At least," Balur said, "when you are dead your tongue will stop flapping."

And would it be easier to let him kill Will after? Would it be easier to let him topple into the abyss of depression and then try to pull him back out?

Will looked at Balur. "Please. I am truly trying to make these deaths meaningful. To make this cause be anything but lost. And I know I have to die. But please, let me give you this plan before I go."

"Your plan killed Lette!" Balur roared. He thrust a finger at Afrit. "It killed Quirk!"

Cois's eyes flicked to the Tamarian. And she seemed to crumple around the words. If Balur was trying to ignite a fire, he was failing. In Afrit the grief was taking over. It was consuming her.

And Balur was so close to being this same useless, racked thing. Cois knew it. With Will dead, this would be him.

If zhe was silent, this would be him.

"Yes," zhe said to Will. "Yes, that could work. The font is the seat of power." Zhe looked at Balur and Afrit. "Not all power is from worship. It's…it's not a system with rules and numbers. It's not even a system. It's about symbolism, and hope, and belief. It changes. But the heavens mean something. They're a seat of power. Possessing them changes hearts and minds. But hearts and minds change it as well. It's fluid."

"We seize the font, we seize the heavens," Will put in, "we can help define what they mean. We can help put Barph in his godshexed place."

"I seize your neck," Balur decided to add, "I squeeze it, and fire your head like a catapult stone into the sky."

"But you wouldn't get to the font," Cois interrupted. Zhe tried not to sound too eager. But perhaps zhe finally had a way to redirect this. "The Summer Palace will attack anyone who enters it, if their blood is not in the font. Lawl built it that way.

The very fabric of the palace rejects people who aren't meant to be there. Not unless Barph gives you permission to be there. And let's face it, you and he are not exchanging feast day gifts at the moment."

"Another failure," Balur said. The words were a curse in his mouth. "That is what this plan is being." He pointed at Will. "That is what his plans are doing. They are failing, and they are killing, and they are murdering. And there must be being a reckoning. A balancing. But now he is to die, he is wishing to embroil us in his schemes. He is trying to perpetuate the death. The ending of things."

"I didn't want Lette to die!" Will roared it. There was something of the old arrogance there. The last flickering embers of power. "If I had anything left to give, I would be pouring it into Lette now. I would chase her into the Void if it could do her any good. I loved her. I loved every part of her. Even at my most fucking lost, I loved her. Truly. Fucking purely, Balur. That was the pure part of my life. The one thing all this shit didn't touch. All the corruption inside of me. It couldn't get to that. And so I would give anything to get her back. Your grief is not larger than mine. It is not better than mine. It is not more earned than mine. You want to kill because she is dead. So do I. I just want it to be Barph. I just want it to fucking matter." He spread his arms. "But if you don't, come do your worst. Come kill me and pretend it's in her memory. Pretend it's what she would have wanted. Pretend she wasn't a better person than either of us. Pretend we had a right to have been...to have..." He could go no further. Tears choked him off.

And whatever else Will Fallows might be—and Cois happened to think he was many, many things—Will always managed to be genuine. And if he ever failed at that, then perhaps he would stop being so compelling. But zhe was not entirely surprised when Balur hesitated.

"But Cois said the heavens will kill us," Afrit said. "So this is all pointless. So…" She looked around. "So why don't we just kill you?" And perhaps the little Tamarian was more bloodthirsty than Cois had given her credit for.

"Lawl built the Summer Palace," Will said, without ratcheting back his intensity even a single notch. "He built the font. Lawl is still alive. He can be our guide. He can minimize the danger."

And piss on him, Will was surprisingly thorough when it came to his plans.

"There are other guardians," Cois said, although zhe knew zhe was grasping at straws at this point. "An army. We are just four—"

"We'll be three," Balur growled, but he made no move toward Will now.

"Gratt," Will said. "Gratt has an army. Gratt hates Barph as much as we do. His war has been as much against Barph as us up here. We bring him in. Bring his army in. We promise them the heavens."

"Aren't we taking the heavens?" Afrit looked confused.

"We lie!" Will snapped. There was a slightly manic edge to him now. "We betray him. When our blood goes in the font, and his doesn't, the Summer Palace rejects him for us."

"More betrayals," Balur said. "More deaths."

And Will stopped. The air seemed to go out of him. He looked around. The whole field of dead around him.

"Yes," he said. "Yes, I suppose you're right."

He looked as if he were collapsing in on himself, the energy and life slowly going with him too.

For a moment Balur looked triumphant, standing over Will, towering massive and brutal. For a moment he shone.

But then… then zhe saw the hurt setting in. The realization that it was over. That this was reality now: loneliness and hurt.

"You would need to get to the heavens too," zhe found herself saying. "And that isn't a place you simply follow a map to. It isn't a place you can just walk to and knock on the door."

"No," Will said. And he seemed to diminish even further. And it was like a disease, an infection spreading through Afrit and Balur.

Zhe hesitated then. Where did hir loyalties lie? What lines would zhe cross?

Who was zhe now?

Zhe licked dry lips.

"But," zhe said into a silence punctuated only by the calls of carrion birds, "I might know a way for us to get there."

63

Prayers Answered

Afrit showed the others where she had last seen Lawl. The tent was shabby and dirty and, Afrit thought, potentially made out of a much-stained bedsheet.

Will cleared his throat. Lawl appeared at the tent flap. His hair, Afrit noticed, was gray and matted. His robes were pock-marked with food and filth. And there was a sharp ammonia-laced smell that accompanied the opening of the tent flap.

"Piss off," the old man spat, then ducked back into the tent.

Will cleared his throat again.

Lawl reappeared. "Did I stutter?"

"Oh, Lawl." It sounded as if there was genuine sorrow in Cois's voice.

"We have a plan," Will said. "You can help."

Lawl started to laugh. "Is it going to go as well as the one you just fooled around with?"

Afrit saw Will's fists ball. "Listen," she said quickly.

Lawl looked up at her. "No," he said.

For a moment she feared there would be violence, but then Will just started talking. In the end, the easiest thing to do was to ignore Lawl's petulance. If he retreated back into his tent, he would still be forced to listen to the plan. Its cloth walls offered no privacy at all.

When Will was done, Lawl's expression was as dark as one of

the thunderheads that used to make him famous. "You fucking traitor," he spat at Cois.

Balur stooped, caught Lawl by the throat, hauled him bodily out of the tent. "You will be speaking nicely to Cois," he informed Lawl, "or you will be shitting your own teeth. Which I am hearing is not the most fun in the world."

"You overgrown—"

Lawl didn't get to finish the insult. Balur threw him onto the ground. Lawl landed flat on his back with a grunt. Balur raised his foot to stomp.

"Don't." Cois spoke quickly, stepping forward. "He's just..." Zhe shook hir head. "I'm not the traitor, Lawl. I'm not even the dreamer. Or the idiot. I'm just the only one who's accepting what's actually happened. I'm mortal, Lawl. You're mortal too. And so are Toil and Betra and Knole. All of us are. And we can't change that. We can only figure out a way to live with it. So that's what I'm doing."

"There is no living with mortality," Lawl sneered from the ground. "That's the whole point of it."

"He's never going to take us back," Cois said.

Afrit tried to follow the change in conversational tack.

"He was never going to come back to power," Lawl snapped. "Never going to kill us all and imprison us in the Hallows. But he did."

"He's losing it," Cois said. And there was information here that Afrit hadn't fully grasped. Cois saw things through different eyes. Barph had been, she remembered, Cois's son, hir lover.

"Look at this place," Cois swung a hand at the world. "Look at what he's done. This carnage. This isn't Barph. Gods, this whole world isn't Barph. He was the god of revelry, Lawl. The god of good times. And yes, he was always callous, and callow, but not vindictive. He was anarchic, yes, but always with a play-ful edge."

Zhe leaned in close. "We broke him, Lawl. We did this. You did. His exile made him unravel, and this power is accelerating the process. Things are only going to get worse."

And something about that seemed to perhaps have penetrated Lawl's thick skull. For a moment his stare seemed to lengthen to encompass the infinite time he had once expected to live. Then he shook his head. "Worse for the mortals," he said.

"Worse for the mortals?" Cois stared at Lawl. "What do you think we are?"

In the end, Lawl's best comeback was just spitting on the ground and ducking back into the tent.

The four looked at each other.

"It is striking me," Balur said, "that Lawl is overly confident about the structural integrity of his tent."

Then Balur started stomping.

A lot of yelling followed, and the snapping of tent poles. Balur had a savage grin on his face as he kicked. Cois stood back next to Afrit.

"We all grieve differently," zhe said.

Finally Lawl emerged from beneath the trampled scrap of cloth. Then others appeared too. Betra was there, and Toil, and even Knole. Afrit found herself wondering if Lawl truly did possess a few remaining scraps of magic. How had they all managed to fit into one tent?

But no. It was not magic. Just squalor. They were all as bedraggled as Lawl. All as dirty and wretched.

"Gods...," Cois breathed. "Once you were gods."

"Him"—Lawl pointed angrily at Will—"and him"—he pointed up at the heavens. "They are why we are reduced to this."

"We need a guide." Will was still focused at least.

Cois shook hir head. "We don't. Lawl knows the tricks of the Summer Palace far better than I do, but I will suffice. I will get us where you need to be."

Afrit watched Will as he looked over the collection of former deities arrayed on the ground before her. His expression of distaste mirrored her own. "Fine," he said.

A noise that had been almost subsonic slowly made its way into the audible range. Everyone looked at Balur. He was growling again.

Cois sighed. "What is it, love?"

"I," he said gruffly, "am not wishing to be one of those overprotective people. Because those people are idiots and deserve to have their heads used for target practice by people perfecting the fine art of shovel throwing—"

"Of course they do, love," Cois said soothingly.

"But it is striking me that if the Summer Palace is going to be attacking us as we go through it, then the situation is going to be one that could loosely be being assessed as a combat situation. And while you, Cois, are having many fine features, not all of which are being physical, although as you are knowing there are being some physical features of which I am being very fond and would be liking to spend considerable time—"

"Today, love," Cois said, slightly less soothingly.

"It is striking me," said Balur, still gruff, "that the chance of dying in the Summer Palace will be being higher than it is normally being. And I am generally being of the opinion that of all the people I know, I am wanting you to die the least. And so I was thinking perhaps—"

Cois stepped up to Balur, wrapped hir arms around his leathery shoulders, and—as he hoisted hir aloft—whispered into his ear.

Lawl made a gagging noise.

And it was all so stupid and petty. And Afrit was still ravaged by grief, and if there was a plan, then gods, she just wanted to get it over with.

She leaned down, looked Lawl in the eye. "What exactly," she said, "do you think will get worse if we get rid of Barph? If you help us with that?"

And Lawl shook his head, but he couldn't meet her eye.

"Please," Afrit said, because honestly, no one had tried that yet.

Lawl hung his head. "Fine," he said, and his voice was that of a broken man. "Fine. I'll do it. If there's one person I hate more than all of you combined, it's Barph. So if you can get me to the Summer Palace, I will take all of you bastards right to its heart, so you can rip it away from him. Because that's one of the few things left in this world that might cause me to smile."

And that, Afrit found, she honestly did believe.

"Sold," said Will. "Now let's keep moving."

64

The Gratt in the Oyster

Very rapidly, Balur came to wish that he were more willing to spend Cois's life like a copper shek. Or, alternatively, that he were allowed to cut Lawl's tongue out. And potentially cut his arms off too, so that he couldn't gesticulate in a sullen, miserable, pain-in-the-arse way. And perhaps put a bag over the former god's head so he couldn't give anyone any of his excessively annoying stares or rolls of the eye.

Neither Will nor Afrit would allow Balur to do this. Not that he was exactly willing to concede that anyone had authority over him, least of all Will, but they both made it clear that they would go on and on about it if he did give in to his baser instincts, and then he'd have to listen to them. So in the end Balur decided it was easier to simply club Lawl around the ears every time he was irritating. And nobody seemed to object to that. Well, nobody who wasn't Lawl, anyway.

Even more galling was the next part of Will's plan: waiting.

Still, they didn't have to wait long. It was evening when Gratt arrived.

Rumors and talk of the once-dead had pursued them throughout their journey around Avarra. Word of travesties performed by a slathering horde of dedicated warriors. And when Balur had matched that image to Will's proposal to storm the heavens...Well, it had been a fine image. It was also an image that did not match the sorry bunch of soldiers that dragged themselves over the Saleran slopes and down onto their little assemblage.

They did not seem much recovered from the beating Will and the others had dealt them in Verra with Lette on the back of a war pig. At the time Balur had assumed that was some extrusion of Gratt's forces, an army grown so large that it could send expeditionary forces out across the world to try to rein Will in. Now he wondered if it had been something more desperate than that. If it had been more of Gratt's army than he had anticipated.

There were perhaps two hundred or so men, road-stained and battle weary. And yet, as hunchbacked as they were, Balur did not think that they were broken, not yet. These last who clung to Gratt had steel in them.

The massive general himself—now striding at the head of his forces—had grown no less ugly since they had last seen him. His skin was still red, pockmarked with calluses and horns. His face was still a half-formed blasphemy. He was still monumental, built from solid slabs of muscle that rippled and stretched as he paced back and forth between his army and Will.

Balur generally didn't trust anyone bigger than he was. Anyone bigger than he was was, in Balur's humble opinion, asking to be cut down to size. The knee was always a good joint to start on for that, although with one particular giant, Balur had needed to start halfway through the midriff.

Lette had given him absurd amounts of grief for that. They'd been supposed to be asking the giant about some kidnapped girls.

They never did find those girls after that.

Gods...Lette.

He should be killing Will. No matter what Cois was saying. Lette should matter more to him than Cois, should she not? Her memory. Her need for vengeance.

Except Barph also needed to die. He was as responsible for Lette's death as Will. More so perhaps. And if Balur was to kill

Barph, he would need Will. And the gods alone knew, if anyone could work out how to bring Lette back from the Void, it would be Will. And while Will could be trusted for little else, Balur was sure that he could trust Will to try to recover Lette.

So he would just have to wait to kill Will until all that was done.

But he would kill Will.

For now, though, he would stand here in the mud and dirt of an abandoned camp, and watch Gratt strut toward them like a pompous motherfucker.

"We surrender!" Will yelled back, hands raised high in the air.

"Well," Gratt said in his gravel-pit voice. "Well, well, well."

Generally, in Balur's experience, saying *well* a lot meant you didn't have a clue what to say. Which meant that despite Gratt's specifically coming here to try to capture them, he still hadn't figured out how to start this conversation. Which meant he hadn't grown much smarter since they'd last seen him either.

Balur found that he had, much to his surprise, some faith in Will.

"You have lived longer than I expected," Gratt told Will.

"I'm lucky that way."

Gratt tsked as best as his malformed lips allowed him. "Still with the mouth." He looked around. "But no longer with your army. No longer with your power base. Now only with..." He looked at the small gathering. Will and Afrit, Balur and Lawl. Cois had led the other gods away down into what was left of Essoa before this confrontation could happen.

"Only with dregs," Gratt said finally. "Word of your disaster is already reaching out across Avarra. Word of it has reached me. And so I know that no matter how fast that jaw works, you have no words left to stop me." And he smiled a savage smile.

"I have bargaining chips."

It was remarkable to Balur that Will could find such unadulterated confidence within himself. It seemed absent so much of the time. So much had to be done to him to drag it out. He could never understand how Lette had been able to put up with it.

Lette...

He should kill Will.

Gratt raised something that might have been supposed to be an eyebrow. He looked around. "Where?"

Will just tapped the side of his head.

Gratt strode forward toward Will and put two massive hands on his shoulders. He bore Will to the ground, and then kept on pushing. The pain stood out bright and bold on Will's face.

"You seem to think you have some kind of value to me as entertainment," Gratt said. "Let me disabuse you of that notion."

"I can get you into the heavens," Will grunted. "I can get you the keys to the Summer Palace. You can own the heavens."

And for just a moment Gratt hesitated. He didn't release his pressure, but he didn't increase it either.

"You know I've delivered before," Will said through gritted teeth.

Gratt licked one of his tusks. He stared over Will's head at the horizon. "I know you are a liar and a deceiver," he said. "I know you model yourself after the trickster god, who seeks to rule Avarra."

For a moment Balur actually thought Will was going to manage to surge to his feet. There was a look of the purest hatred on his face.

"I know," Will grunted, "that you've been nothing but a fucking sideshow compared to me for months. I know that the only reason Barph hasn't scrubbed you from the face of the earth is because you haven't been interesting enough. I've been busy capturing all his attention. But now I'm gone. So I know exactly how fucked you are. But I'm beginning to question if you're smart enough to realize it."

Gratt was clearly not the type to suffer such abuse gladly. The mask of civil words slipped, and he backhanded Will clear off his feet. Blood and teeth flew. Will landed on his back, spitting out molars.

"You will not—" Gratt started.

"You have no plan," Will said, blood dribbling down his chin. "You have no way to defeat Barph. You've been flailing around in a land grab like this is the pissing Hallows!" The color was rising in his cheeks, cords starting to stand out in his neck. "You don't even know what sort of fight you're in! You don't have the imagination to fight a god, and you know it. Well, I do. But I don't have an army anymore. And you do. So either you kill me and keep pissing in the sand until Barph gets around to crushing you, or you do something that actually makes sense, and you help me kill him."

Will stood. And for a moment it was as if he were the one who was twenty feet tall.

Gratt worked his jaw. Savage teeth showed.

"And after that?" he asked, his voice full of false refinement.

"The heavens. They're yours."

"Just like that?"

Will shrugged. "How could I stop you?"

Gratt looked at them all one by one. For a moment he and Balur locked eyes. And then Gratt sneered. Every tooth showed. His long black tongue licked his tusks. "A deal then," he said.

Balur could almost hear Lette telling him she found that smile as trustworthy as a sailor promising to guard a princess's virginity.

Lette...

And before he killed Will, Balur was going to make sure that part of Will's plan involved him murdering the shit out of Gratt.

65

A Better Class of Hitchhiking

Will just about managed to meet Gratt's eye as the general asked, "So, how exactly are we getting to the heavens?"

Gratt's eye was honestly one of the few he could meet now. The enormity of what he'd done—the disaster that he had personally orchestrated—still weighed around his neck like a millstone. More than the destruction of the Hallows, this was an obscenity too far. Indeed, his previous actions only compounded this final error. None of the dead from the field outside Essoa now rested in the Hallows. None found second chances in the plane below the world. It was straight to the Void with them. Straight to their unmaking.

Lette was there. Lette was lost in that black oblivion. Irretrievable. Lost forever.

Was that true? Everything he had ever been told said that was true. The Void was the last resting place. It was beyond the end of things. But he had seen so many impossible things come to pass now ... He had *made* so many impossible things come to pass.

Shouldn't that be where his energies lay? With Lette? With finding some path to rescue her? To defy the laws of reality one more time and bring her back to life?

Except wasn't that what had gotten him here in the first place? That sort of hubris? And didn't he owe something to all the countless dead? Not Lette alone?

There were no answers, of course. He was no longer so deluded as to think there was a single certain path he must walk. Or to think that anyone distracting him from his current path was trying to undermine him. There was only his best hopeless guess. And right now, all he had was this one last best guess at how to take down Barph.

It would kill him, he thought. He hoped, almost. The Void seemed like a blessing now. Oblivion. Free from the weight of the guilt and the grief. He hadn't earned such an ending. But perhaps, if everything went well, he would achieve it.

And so this was the path he walked, narrow as a tightrope, and with the end shrouded in mist.

"The answer," he said, "will come to us, as long as we light a big enough fire."

It had been Cois's idea, whispered to him before zhe left. And it was risky, but it carried a certain amount of poetry to it as well. And so Will led them all to the peak of the tallest hill they could find, and there they lit a vast inferno of a bonfire.

Nothing happened.

Gratt grew impatient, but Will found he still had some stoicism left. Of all the people left in Avarra, he owed Gratt nothing, at least. He owed so much to so many people, but Gratt was as big a murderer as he was. Gratt he could betray happily.

On the evening of the second night, with the fire raging even higher, he saw shadows on the horizon.

"They're coming," Will said.

There were just six of them. But it was more than Will had thought were left. Some must have hidden from the final fight with Barph.

They blotted out the setting sun as they flapped across the sky. The last dragons of Avarra.

They landed on the hilltop, wings held high and imposing, mouths open and fire in their throats.

Will reminded himself that he deserved this.

Yorrax landed at the head of the group of dragons. So she was still alive. That surprised Will at little. And it reminded him of Quirk, so it hurt him as well.

"We are here to kill you," Yorrax told him.

"I know." He nodded.

This seemed to be a little disappointing to Yorrax. She reared slightly, trying to make more of her bulk, despite the fact that she was dwarfed by her five companions.

"We fear you no longer, betrayer," she roared.

Will honestly wasn't sure that was true. The other dragons had a lost, vacant look in their eyes. Gods, they were allowing Yorrax—the runt—to lead them. Barph's devastation had unmoored their certainty in their own dominance. They were as lost as he was.

"And I do not fear death." He spread his arms, a welcoming gesture.

He could feel his own companions' hesitation, their doubt. And it was more than a little tempting to just leave it at that. To let Yorrax recover from her confusion and remember that other species had the word *surrender* in their vocabulary. It was more than a little tempting to give in to the inevitable end of things.

Except he hadn't earned that peace. Not yet.

So instead he said to Yorrax, "We are the same, you and I."

"We are noth—" Yorrax started to snarl.

"We are creatures of violent purpose," he said. And he had no magic left to amplify his voice. He could not shout her down. But she listened all the same. She was wrong-footed and uncertain, and he could keep her that way. Yorrax had never been as strong as she thought she was.

And he was telling the truth anyway.

"We have launched ourselves at Barph's heart twice," he shouted. "Together we have gone to tear him down. And twice we have missed. But now a new path is open. A path straight to Barph's exposed underbelly."

Glory. Dominance. Her own chance to rule the heavens. That was what Yorrax wanted. What they all wanted in the end. He could use that, take advantage of it. And it would be another betrayal, one to add to his betrayal of Gratt and his betrayal of ten thousand others, and his betrayal of Quirk and of Lette, but all his life dragons had been the oppressors, the aggressors. He could find little sympathy for them.

It was the people still left in this place. The people he hadn't killed yet. The Salerans, the Batarrans, the Verrans, and the Vinlanders. The people of the Five Duchies and the Fanlorn Empire. It was all Avarrans. That was whom he owed. And if it took the lives of Gratt and the dragons...

Gods, hadn't he been a farmer once? When had he become this heartless broken thing? He kept blaming the Deep Ones, but had it just been that? Or had it just magnified something that was already within him?

He could still feel it with him, that piece of the Deep Ones. It was a rotten weight in his gut and his mind now. A starving creature, licking its wounds and twitching in pain. But he would not feed it again. And any pain it caused him, he deserved.

Yorrax was staring at him.

"A path...," Yorrax said. The other five dragons were staring at them, dead-eyed. All pretense of fury gone now. They had subjugated their will to Yorrax. She at least still pretended to have purpose, but she was conflicted now.

"A gate straight into the heavens," he said to her. To her violent, narcissistic heart. "A path to the Summer Palace. So we can catch Barph in his very home. So we can tear the heavens from him, just as the dragons were torn from the heavens. So we break his spirit and his will. So we leave him weak, easy prey."

Yorrax lowered her head. And small as she was for her kind, she could still have ended him with a single snap of her teeth, a single exhalation of flame.

"Another betrayal," she said. "Another lie."

"Perhaps," said Will. "I can't prove that it's not. I can only ask you how I could betray you again. I am stripped of my powers. I am weak. I cannot overpower you. What could I do?"

There were no answers. Just doubts, fears, uncertainties, and ambition. And a heartless bastard willing to take advantage of them.

Just him.

"Take us to the heavens," he said to Yorrax. "Fly us into the sky. Let us be pathfinders for you. And once we're there, do as you will. Perhaps we will try to betray you. Perhaps you will try to betray us. Perhaps we will work together and destroy Barph as one. Perhaps we shall fail. But this is our last, best shot. And we can only take it together."

And before she even spoke, Will could see that the last piece of his plan had fallen into place.

66

Castles in the Sky

Yorrax almost abandoned the plan as soon as Willett Fallows climbed upon her back. It would be so easy to reach back, to separate his head from his body, to end the lies spilled by his treacherous tongue. Saliva flooded her mouth at the thought.

But killing Will Fallows had seemed so easy ever since they had tracked him down, she and the five others: Blottax the idiot, Gerrax the frail, Terrax the coward, Chessax the child, and Flerrax the doddery old bastard. All who were left. All who had survived the encounter with Barph either through luck or through fleeing the battlefield and their pride. The dregs of dragon kind.

Her perfect five.

There wasn't a complete backbone between them. They barely had functioning minds. They were utterly lost. They kowtowed to her completely. Her will became theirs.

It was perfect. And in some ways, she supposed, she should thank Will for this. For her moment of dominance.

Yet in every word he uttered, and in every turn of his body, she could sense his rejection of her authority. She could smell his insolence hanging around him like a cloud. He was one who never bent his knee.

This assault on the heavens was another betrayal, of that she was sure. He had as much as said so. Last time, his betrayal of dragon kind had been preemptive, and had undermined their own attempt to betray him. That, though, was under the leadership of Pettrax, and Pettrax was bloated, and weak of mind and loins. She would not make the same mistakes as him.

She did believe in Will's promise of a gate leading to the heavens, though. That was too absurd a promise for it to be false. And she saw Gratt at Will's side. He had bought into this promise too. So, yes, that part, she suspected, was true. The hook supposed to dazzle and blind her to everything else. The betrayal would come afterward.

But she was not blind. All she had to do was bide her time and spot the opening when it came.

So she bore Will Fallows's weight. And she bore the weight of Quirk's mate, Afrit. And she bore the weight of the little lizard man and the angry former god. She spread her wings and took to the sky, careful not to show the strain it took for her to lift all four of them. Her compatriots were laden down with twenty or more of Gratt's soldiers each. Gratt had pushed for more, but he had been barked back into his place. He was large, yes, but he was no dragon, and he did not know where the gates to the heavens were. He could be expended. And once he understood that, he had stopped his hollering and his demanding, and Yorrax had established her position with him.

Now up they went. And up. Avarra dropped away below them, the fields and farms become toy versions of themselves. Animals that she would have feasted upon became specks, then negligible afterthoughts. Cities sketched themselves in rough oblongs and jagged triangles over the landscape. The coastline became visible, a scribbled line of yellow and blue up against the vibrant green of the Saleran plains. The Broken Peaks were visible through a haze to the east. The world was a playground.

Soon it would be hers.

"Up!" Lawl called from her back. "Up still!"

The muscles in her back strained. The air was thin and chill. She could hear the labored breathing of the other flimsy creatures.

"Up!" the former god called again. She wondered if someone else knew the directions and she could eat him.

Her own breathing grew heavy. She fought to keep ahead of large, lumbering, spectacularly stupid Blottax. The big dragon was still beating away at the air, seemingly unaware of both the soldiers on his back and the fact that they were going nowhere. Her lips curled back in a snarl of frustration and effort.

Could this be the ploy? Were Will and his fellows somehow more resistant to these elements than she and the other dragons?

"There!"

She glanced back. Lawl was standing between her wings, pointing toward a single cloud floating in the field of scattered gray above her head. It was a small cloud. Yorrax could barely discern it from all the others, except perhaps there was a slight golden hue to it, as if a forgotten ray of sunlight had somehow picked it out.

But a cloud? It was small and pathetic, and made of water vapor. It did not seem to possess many heavenly attributes.

"It is the portal," Lawl shouted over the wind whipping around them, as if reading her thoughts. "It hides the gates to the heavens."

"'And gold shall be their fabric, and glory shall be their name, and destiny shall be their intent,'" Afrit said. "At least that's what it says in the First Book of the Law."

"To be fair, I might have been a little drunk when I dictated those." Something in Lawl's tone made Yorrax snicker despite the effort.

"There will be defenses, won't there?" Will called over the wind.

"Guards," Lawl shouted back. "Divine warriors. Creatures created without a will of their own, driven to obey the masters of the Summer Palace. Creatures both restless and tireless."

"Gods, you were being a paranoid bastard," said Balur.

"So that's our first hurdle." There was something like eagerness in Will's voice.

Yorrax didn't care. All she wanted was the gates. That was the promise, the deal. She would get him there. Then all agreements were off.

She kept her eyes wide open as she entered the clouds, the gray-golden mist folding over her. She would not show fear. Not even to these idiots.

The mists went on and on. They went on longer than they should have. It had been a small cloud hanging just below the body of the main bank above. And yet she had been beating her wings for a minute or more now. The exertion of each stroke seeming to grow exponentially.

"Hold the course!" Lawl shouted. "Hold the course!"

And then suddenly there was light. Suddenly there was heat and warmth, and updrafts beneath her wings. She almost sagged with relief, caught herself only just before she fell.

"Oh," she heard Lawl say. "Oh no."

And then Yorrax truly took in her surroundings.

The gates lay before her. They were massive things, imposing even to a dragon. Wrought iron curled in ever more intricate curves and spirals. Images of the gods had been rendered in exquisite detail. Eyes seemed to shift and move with the viewer. Muscles seemed to ripple with continued exertion. Gold and jewels were intertwined with everything, shimmering and glittering in the rays of sunlight that backlit the entire creation.

On the flip side, the gates had also had the shit beaten out of them.

They hung askew from their frame. Their carvings were bent and deformed. Deep scratches had been gouged through the faces of many of the figures, obscuring their identities. "Lawl gargles goat balls" had been painted over them in red, along with other, similar claims suggesting the former king of the gods should never be left unattended in a farmyard. Vines and brambles had wound their way through the lower reaches, snarling the gates in a tangle of leaves and thorns.

"What has he done?" Lawl said. There was anger rising in his voice. "What has he done?"

"Cois said Barph was losing it," Afrit said.

Personally, Yorrax didn't see what they were all getting their underwear knotted about. The gates were big, yes, but what did it matter what state they were in? They could enter through them. What else was important? Humans got caught up on the stupidest of details.

"There are supposed to be guards." Lawl sounded pathetically appalled.

"*Supposed to be,*" she couldn't help but growl. "What does that matter when we are here *now*?"

"But...," Lawl said. "He's ruined everything."

The space beyond the gate was a riot of vegetation. Plants grew out of control, sprawling over broken pathways. Yorrax smashed through the twisted gates, landed on cracked flagstones. Weeds and thistles were crumpled by her feet. Will was the first to slip from her back as she looked back and forth taking it all in.

A creature lay on the ground, vaguely humanoid, but built on too big a scale, the limbs with an odd rough-hewn quality. The skin was ochre, and slightly furry. Heavy sheets of armor were strapped to the creature. Its broad red gash of a mouth was open, and it was snoring loudly.

"There," Yorrax said, "are your guards."

Lawl was on the ground now. He knelt beside the figure as the other dragons landed around them.

"Pollark?" Lawl said. "Oh, Pollark, what has he done to you?"

The figure belched and Lawl reeled back, bringing up a hand to cover his mouth.

"I believe he has gotten him horribly drunk," said Gratt without a note of sympathy in his voice for either Lawl or the spread-eagled creature. Then, to reinforce this unsympathetic impression, Gratt pulled out a sword and jammed it through the creature's throat.

Lawl gasped as blood sprayed upward. Then he gagged and spat out the blood he'd just inhaled. "What are you—"

Gratt wheeled on Yorrax. "You," he barked, "beast of burden—"

Yorrax growled.

"No!" Will was shouting into the chaos. "This is not the way. This needs to be controlled and tactical! We need to draw any fighting away from the Summer Palace. We need to keep the attack contained. We need—"

Gratt's troops were swirling around them, already disembarking from their dragon mounts.

"Back down, and get me more men!" Gratt shouted to Yorrax. Blottax even started beating his wings, like the small-minded fool he was.

Gratt turned to his troops. "Take the heavens!" he bellowed. And his troops didn't hesitate before beginning to charge into the mess of foliage.

"No!" Will shouted, but no one was listening to him.

They were listening to Gratt.

To Gratt. And not to Yorrax.

Yorrax roared. The idiot general had stolen her initiative. He was trying to steal her heavens. They were all always trying to take what was hers. And she would have it no longer.

She whipped around, smashing her tail through as many people as she could, battering her wings against the air, lifting up. She exhaled fire.

"The heavens belong to the dragons!" she cried.

Blottax gave her a confused stare.

"They will belong to the dragons!" she corrected. It was helpful to be as literal as possible with Blottax.

"We will take them with fire and claw and tooth!" she called. "No one will stand in our—" She broke off. There was no way that Blottax was going to interpret *stand in our way* correctly. "No one will prevent us!"

Blottax's face cleared. He nodded eagerly.

"Fire and claw and tooth!" she bellowed again.

Blottax happily set fire to several things. Terrax the coward was looking nervously at Will, who was still shouting, "No!" at everyone as if that could make a difference.

His eyes met Yorrax's. The moment held. She smiled at him with many, many teeth.

And then Will ran. And the race to control the heavens began.

67

Home Awful Home

Part of Will knew he should be staggered. He should be amazed. He stood in the very heavens themselves. The home of the gods. He could catch glimpses of the Summer Palace between the trees. Golden spires winked and glittered. Arches leapt and buttresses flew. Jewels sparkled. And for all that half the windows appeared smashed, it was still the very ruling place of the gods. He could see a literal legend.

But he didn't have time for any of that shit. Because every single being in the heavens was an arsehole, and he was in a race with them for the fate of a world.

To be fair, Will did not have any conviction that he and his friends weren't arseholes. It was just that if any brand of arsehole were to be imposed on Avarra... Well, Will had his preferences.

The fighting seemed to spread with the strength and ferocity of a wildfire. Gratt's once-dead soldiers were wrestling with gaggles of bedraggled, confused guards who for all their sluggish, drunken movements were also almost twenty feet tall, built on a scale that equaled Gratt's. When their blows landed, the once-dead folded around their limbs. When their swords connected with flesh it sheared, and limbs and torsos flew free of each other.

The guards, however, were far from invincible. Will passed the same scene repeated over and over again: three or four of Gratt's once-dead bearing a guardian to the ground and turning their yellow fur red, blades rising and falling in the steady rhythm of slaughter.

"Faster!" he managed between bursts of breath.

"I was thinking," Balur grumbled, "that we were agreeing that you would not be giving orders anymore on account of you being a genocidal prick."

That felt a little below the belt to Will, especially when he was trying to psych himself up for an epochal battle to save the world.

As they raced, the physical evidence of Barph's ruinous reign in the heavens surrounded them. Walls and pathways had collapsed into rubble. Weeds, vines, and brambles reclaimed the once-manicured grounds. The vegetation was riotous and uncontained, blocking their path, forming dead ends and obstacles. It snagged their clothes and their feet, swiped at their skulls with gnarled claws. Statues once elegant and elaborate were now defaced and disfigured, scrawled over with chiseled and painted obscenities. Gazebos had collapsed into jagged piles of splintered, splintering wood.

Three of Gratt's soldiers tried to waylay them as they scrambled over the remains of some formerly elaborate trellises. Balur laid into their attackers with obvious glee, claws ripping and rending, teeth snapping obscenely into vital parts. Lawl too seemed to have some aggression issues to work out. He picked up a branch and battered one of the once-dead into bloody submission.

"There's no time," Will tried to explain as he pulled Balur away from committing the coup de grâce. "The palace is the only thing that matters. If we lose the palace, we lose everything."

Balur took a parting kick at one soldier's head, then started running again.

Will had run before. Had run for his life. Had run to try to save lives. Had run toward and away from redemption. But he tried to run now as he had never run before. He tried to put everything he had into it. He had to beat Gratt. He had to beat Yorrax.

He failed on both counts.

The Summer Palace had obviously had its heyday. In the golden sunlight that suffused the heavens, its walls still glowed like something living, like something with the spark of life within. Fragments of the palace's former glory could still be seen in the broken shards of stained glass windows that still clung to their limestone frames.

Vines and brambles had taken their toll here as well, though. The same obscenity-laden hand had brought its chisels and paints to these walls. Some damage was even more recent, however. A dragon had smashed through one of the palace's massive windows and then somehow gotten itself turned around and hung wedged in a gash of masonry, breathing fire down on the gathered guards below, who thrust spears upward, peppering its sinuous neck with jagged wooden adornment even as they died. Another door had been smashed to pieces, but the doorway itself was now ringed with the bodies of the once-dead. The attackers' arms and legs were crushed into obscene parodies of limbs. The exact source of these injuries was nowhere in sight.

"Well," said Will, "that's not completely reassuring."

"Do not be hesitating now!" Balur roared. "Be pretending you still have balls!"

Will would probably never admit it to Balur's face (mostly because he anticipated being dead within the next fifteen minutes or so), but he rather enjoyed it when Balur got in these boisterous moods.

They careened along the wall of the palace until another doorway lurched at them from around a curve in the architecture. This one had the benefit of not being ringed by the dead.

Balur's foot connected with wood. Rusted hinges gave way. The door flew. And then they were in.

They were in a corridor, the opulence of the palace still apparent despite Barph's tenure. The marble tiles on the floor were dirty and stained, but still retained their luster beneath the grime. Dust had collected on the ornate wainscoting, but the craft and care that had gone into its construction was still clear. The vases perched on ornamental tables might have been surrounded by dead blooms and full of stale wine, but the delicacy of the painting beneath their rich glaze still held its power to transfix.

And then a wall tried to hit Will in the face.

He had trouble working out what was going on at first. He was running, panting hard, scanning for danger, and then a wall that hadn't been there a moment before was abruptly six inches before his face. He pulled up hard, turned sharply to take the impact on his shoulder. He stared about dazed. Then one of the ornamental tables lurched across the corridor and poleaxed Lawl and sent him facefirst into the floor. And then suddenly the tiles were slipping beneath Will's feet, sending him stumbling, and a heavy oil painting of Toil wearing far too few clothes was lurching away from the wall, trying to smash its gilt frame into his chin.

"The defenses!" Lawl yelled from the floor. "Those idiots have already triggered the defenses!"

And this was what Cois had described. Their blood was not in the font at the palace's heart. Its very fabric was trying to attack them, to reject them.

"Quickly!" Lawl was scrambling to his feet. "It's only going to get worse!"

And so they ran.

"This way!" Lawl pointed through a set of rooms lined with paintings. Will's lungs burned.

They piled into the room. Its walls started firing their paintings across the room, heavy, hard projectiles spinning with all the grace of an Analesian learning ballet.

"I have done some ridiculous shit with you!" Afrit said, as a rendition of Betra and Klink showing more than familial affection almost decapitated her. "But this..."

Gilt, plaster, and wood showered them as a frame collided with Balur's shoulder and drove him to the floor.

"Be fucking this shit," he yelled.

"Faster!" Lawl and Will said in unison, the former god picking up on the refrain even as they tripped and scrambled. A frame caught Will a glancing blow on the head, turned him around. He stared, dazed, as blood fell into his eyes. Afrit grabbed his arm, steered him toward further dangers.

Velvet curtains tried to smother them. Brass pipes unfurled like snakes. A tumor of ornamental swords barreled down a corridor toward them. Chandeliers fell like catapult stones, and then their fractured crystals whirled up into deadly hurricanes of glinting, spiraling blades. Floors gave way beneath their feet, trying to spill them down onto jagged basement tiles. Doorways grew teeth.

Every step seemed to make it worse. Will walked through a room with his arms clutched over his head as every tile peeled itself off the floor and shattered against his arms. His clothes and skin were shredded. Sheets of blood fell to the floor, only to be blown back against his bruised flesh in stinging flurries. A curtain snagged Lawl around the neck and the former god had turned blue before it was torn free and set alight. Every baluster on a sweeping staircase cracked Balur across the shins hard enough to shatter. The splinters flew in a storm around Afrit, stinging her again and again.

They were gasping, bleeding, and bloody.

"Faster!" Will urged.

"Fuck you," Afrit told him.

"We're almost there," he told her.

"We're halfway there," Lawl replied.

"Fuck you," he told the god.

Curtain cords whipped them. Tables chewed them. Statues swung marble fists.

They passed bodies along the way. Errant gangs of once-dead who had penetrated farther than Will had given them credit for. One room contained a dragon's corpse, the furnishings all burned to ash. The ruined remains of a ceiling beam were lodged deep in the back of the dragon's skull. Everything was curiously quiet, all the room's armaments spent on the former attacker. They crossed cautiously, and Will felt an unexpected sense of gratitude toward the dead beast.

Somewhere along the trek he stopped feeling truly human. Not the way he had before, not when he believed he was a god. This was a new sensation. A new kind of torture. The distinction between whole and broken flesh became fuzzy. The sense of pain was absolute. He was just a collection of wounds. He was just hurt. He just wanted to lie down and let the Summer Palace kill him.

"Faster," he said, only just aware that he was on his hands and knees.

"Faster." He was crawling. Something was beating against his back. He thought he remembered seeing flying books with inch-long fangs.

"Faster." Maybe he said it. Maybe someone else did.

It took him a little while to realize the attacks had stopped. He lay down, his hot, bloody face pressed against cool white tiles. His breath bubbled in the blood and snot and spit leaking from his nose and mouth. He watched as his fingers spastically dragged his hand through his field of vision, still desperate to make some sort of forward progress.

"Be coming on." Balur's voice was ragged. There seemed to be significant dents in his massive frame.

"Is it..." Afrit's voice seemed to come from a long way

away. There was the sound of ragged breathing. "Is it..." She descended into coughs. She tried a third time. "Over?"

"The eye...of...the storm." Lawl was in no better shape than any of them, perhaps worse. The former god seemed to be missing some fingers.

"We're here?" Will found the strength to roll over onto his back. He began the slow, laborious task of sitting up. "We've reached the font?

"Through..." Lawl raised a shaking hand. He'd definitely lost some fingers. "Through those doors."

They were in a large stately room, bare except for its ornate, gilded wall paneling and its statue of Lawl giving everyone the finger. Will couldn't tell if it had been originally carved that way or was a victim of Barph's malevolence. The room's exact purpose escaped Will. For once, though, its purpose wasn't to kill him. That seemed like enough for now. Because he was finally here. All the lives lost. All the damage done. One more door, and he could bring it all to an end.

It was worth it, wasn't it? This made sense. He was saving the world.

Wasn't he?

Will honestly wasn't sure. He'd lost his way somewhere. For all the evil he'd done, there had been a sort of peace in his previous certainty. Things had been simple then. Everything was a question now. Nothing was an answer.

Except...Through those doors. Going through there. Ending this. That would be an answer of sorts, wouldn't it? Perhaps not the one he'd intended. Perhaps not even one that was better than the answer Avarra was living with now. But an answer nonetheless.

He stood. It hurt, and it took an effort that almost staggered him, but he would see this through. If for no other reason than that Lette would have wanted him to. She had stood for this answer, or something like it. She had fought for this. She had seen the world with far clearer eyes than he ever could, and she had maintained this course alongside him. The best he could do was hold it in memory of her.

"Okay," he said.

And then there was a crash. And a roar. And his hope sagged to the floor.

Another set of doors—directly opposite the pair Lawl had pointed to—crashed to the floor. In the broken frame stood Gratt.

"Gods," Afrit said, still on the floor. "We really cannot catch a break today, can we?" She looked up at Will. "I think you're fucking hexed, I really do." She spat a long wad of blood onto the floor.

"You," Gratt growled at Will. "There are no words that will save you now."

Will thought about that. "You know what?" he said. "I think that there is one, actually."

Gratt was a far less complicated being than he'd like to pretend, but even he hesitated for a moment. Just long enough for Will to smile.

"Balur," Will said.

Gratt's eyes narrowed in confusion. Then Balur smashed into him with all the force of siege weaponry.

The once-dead general reeled under the impact, staggered to one knee. Balur was a bleeding, dripping, broken-limbed ball of fury. He rained down blows. He bit. He kicked. His ferocity was an obscene refutation of all his pretenses of civility. This palace had stripped Balur down to his essence, to his purest self. Far more than the Analesian Desert ever could, this palace had made him strong.

"Now!" Will yelled. He was already running.

Lawl was somehow ahead of him, at the doors, heaving them open. Afrit was on her feet, yelling curses, scrambling forward.

Gratt was delivering a two-handed blow to Balur's midriff, driving the lizard man back.

The moment seemed to stretch forever. Will covered half the distance to the door. Half again. Half again. Half always seemed to remain.

And then he was through, and it was the beginning of the end.

68

Well, What Did You Expect?

Afrit dived through the door. She landed hard. Every part of her hurt. She wondered why she had dived. What had she been trying to avoid?

"Well," said a voice, "if I'd known I was going to have guests, I would have tidied up."

Afrit blinked and looked around. Were there meant to be voices in here? She didn't think there were.

Wasn't there meant to be a font?

They were in a hall, long and grandiose. The ceiling seemed very far away, vaulting over massive columns painted blue and red and gold. Tapestries and banners hung beneath them, though the edges were ragged. There were windows high above them, the golden light of the heavens outside falling down in great cataracts. And there was a throne.

And on it there was Barph.

And there was no fucking font.

Afrit picked herself up slowly. Will was transfixed beside her, staring at the god, their tormentor, their enemy. Barph wore an expression like a cat who had just been presented with a very large bowl of cream.

Lawl, though, against all sense, was hurrying toward the front of the hall as fast as his broken body would carry him. His head was bowed. He held his hands clutched together out in front of him.

"I've brought them to you," he said. And his voice was no longer full of anger or pride. His voice was suddenly a broken cracked thing on the edge of a wheedling tone. Lawl unclenched his hands long enough to wave them back at Afrit and Will. "I bring you tribute."

"What?" Will said beside Afrit. "What the actual fuck?"

"Hello, Father," Barph said, full of smug magnanimity. "What a pleasant surprise this is."

A surprise... But... what was happening?

"I thought..." Lawl was almost at the foot of the throne. "Perhaps... I would... You could..."

"What would you do, Father?" Barph asked, and there was something a little less than magnanimous in his voice now. Something with a serrated edge. "Would you insult me again? Would you belittle me? Banish me? Spurn me? Hate me? Castigate me? Destroy my works and my memory? What would you do, *Father*?"

"No." Lawl reached Barph now, actually dropped to his knees. He stared at the floor, utterly craven. "I am a proud creature. I know that. I have always known that. You have always known that. But pride made a of fool me. I was..." Lawl hesitated, seemed to swallow. "I was smug and self-centered and blind. And I didn't recognize... I couldn't see... I'm so sorry." He risked a look up. "Son."

And Barph started to laugh.

Will wasn't laughing, though. He was apoplectic. "You... you..." Words seemed to froth out of him. "You *arsehole*. You absolute, utter, fucking, total shithole." Obscenity burst from his mouth like blood from an artery. He stalked forward, fists balled with impotent rage.

Afrit was paralyzed, because... because... this was the end, wasn't it? She had been beaten, bloodied, and bruised, and now she had been betrayed. And she simply had nothing left to give. The only way she'd ever had to defeat Barph was to believe in

Will, and Will had killed Quirk. He had killed the best thing in her world. And so she couldn't believe in him. So she had nothing. This was the end.

"Son." Barph stopped laughing, rolled Lawl's word around in his mouth.

Barph looked...different from the way Afrit remembered him. The broad strokes were still the same: an old man, a long tangled beard, long white hair swept back from a high forehead, a wiry frame, hands and feet slightly too large for the body that held them. But in between those features, the details had changed. The sour twist of the mouth. The deep lines etched into his face. The unkempt wrinkles in his clothes. The stains beneath his nails that might have been dirt or blood. The glint in his eyes that made Afrit's heart stutter and made her far too afraid to get any closer right now.

"I just...Please..." Lawl was going on, the words pouring out of him. "I made a mistake. I was a fool. And you have shown me the error of my ways. I among all of the gods know what an idiot I was. So please, please, please...just...let me back in."

He seized the hem of Barph's robe. "Just let me be a god again. I won't challenge you. You will be king still. I'll just...I just won't be mortal. I can't be mortal. I can't, Barph. Son. I can't anymore. I can't. I can't." He was sobbing.

"I will fucking end you!" Will was screaming. Whether it was aimed at Barph or Lawl, Afrit couldn't tell.

"I brought him to you." Lawl was almost babbling now as Barph stared into the space above his head. "I brought you Will Fallows. Your challenger. Your tormentor. His companions. I brought you all of them. Tribute. Payment. So please, please...You'll welcome me back, won't you? You've always been such a good boy." He pawed pathetically at Barph's knees, apparently oblivious to the monumentality of the lie contained in that last sentence.

"Son," Barph said again. His teeth were very evident as he bit out the word. "Father."

"Please," Lawl whined.

Barph stood. He was perhaps eight or nine feet tall today, not titanic, but still towering over all of them. Lawl sprawled backward, lay at his feet.

"Forgive me," he begged.

Barph licked his lips. "Forgive you," he said. "Forgive you, *Father*. Welcome you back. Because your suffering is too great to bear..." He stared off into space again.

And would he actually do it? There was, Afrit thought, beneath Barph's false civility and beyond his savagery, some genuine pain in the god's voice. Something tremulous, small, and hurt. A son perhaps, abandoned by his father, and left alone in the cold and the dark.

Lawl made it back to his knees. He was...he was actually crying, Afrit realized. Tears were falling down his cheeks. "It's too much," he sobbed.

And then, whatever prevarication had raged in Barph's heart resolved, and he hardened, and he stiffened. The spark in his eyes flared.

Afrit started to step back. Will was still heading recklessly forward, and she wanted to call out to him, but her nerve failed her.

"Eight hundred years!" Barph howled. The words were propelled out of him with enough force to crack the marble tiles around Lawl. The former king of the gods spasmed at his bastard son's feet. "Eight hundred years as a mortal, Father. And you come to me at eight months? You tell me at eight months that it cannot be borne? That it is too much? Your suffering is but a drop in the ocean of pain you poured upon me. This begging, this pleading. This is mockery, *Father*.

"Father!" Barph made a sound that was almost laughter, but that was too savage, too wild to deserve that moniker. He kicked Lawl viciously in the head. "And you call me Son. Son. A blasphemy. An insult. A fucking obscenity in your mouth, *Father*.

You who call a fraction of the hate and pain you poured on me a step too far."

He stooped, picked Lawl up by the throat, dangled him above the floor.

"And when I was ascendant. When I sat in the heavens. When I said how I would see Avarra governed. What did you do then, *Father*? Did you see the error of your ways? Did you have obeisance in your heart then? Or did you align yourself with my enemies? With those who would drag me down? Tell me, *Father*, where did your paternal instincts guide you?"

He pointed at Will. "You bring him to me as tribute? Or do you come with an invading army? Do you attach yourself like a leech to those would continue to seek my destruction?"

Lawl couldn't answer. Barph's fist was white-knuckled around his throat. Lawl's lips were turning blue. His legs were twitching and spasming.

"You want my forgiveness?" shouted Barph. "Eight thousand years you shall shuffle and grub in the dirt of Avarra! Eight thousand years shall you be powerless! Eight thousand years of pain I shall visit upon you! Eight thousand years of being nothing and no one! Lawl shall be an insult on the lips of the peasants who watch you, old and gnarled and racked by disease! Then—" Barph leaned in close, his spittle flecking Lawl's cheeks. "Then you can ask me for forgiveness. Only then will I hear your prayers. Only then can you come crawling to me, on the foul, stinking stump that will be all that remains of your body. Only then can you grovel and beg. And then, then, Father dearest, once that is done, I shall lean down and I shall whisper in your ear." Cords stood out in Barph's neck. Lawl's eyes stared sightless. "And I shall say no, Father. No. Do you hear me?"

He shook Lawl. Lawl flopped limply. "Do you hear me?" Barph roared. Glass cracked in the ceiling above, shards raining down. Afrit screamed and started running, though where she could run to she had no idea.

"Do you hear me?" Barph screamed. Cracks ran through the walls. Wind howled. Afrit was knocked to her knees.

She glanced back. Barph was staring at Lawl. His eyes bulged. His lips were pulled back in something between rage and horror. And in his hands, Lawl lay dead.

69

Daddy Issues

Barph stared at the body in his hands.

The body.

The corpse.

Lawl's corpse.

Lawl was dead.

No. No, that wasn't right. He was...mistaken?

No. Barph couldn't be mistaken. He was god. The god. The one god. The only god.

So Lawl was dead.

Except he did not want Lawl to be dead. And his will was absolute. Now Avarra would bend itself to obey.

Except Lawl was dead.

So...so...so of course he wanted Lawl dead. Lawl was the worst of them. A hypocrite and a liar and a craven mongrel. Lawl deserved nothing but death. Barph had been merciful in granting a death this peaceful.

He had wanted his father dead?

His father?

Lawl had never been much of a father. The name was as much an insult, a taunt, as anything else. And it had been so easy to bridle Lawl. So easy to worm beneath his skin and watch him itch and twitch. Half the reason Barph had started fucking Cois was to show that he could mount hir as easily as Lawl could. Gods, how he had laughed. How they had all laughed. And

Lawl had laughed too when the joke was pointed at Toil, or Klink, or even Betra. There had been so much laughter.

And then they had stopped laughing, and they had condemned him to a life of pain.

And he had hurt so much. And he was going to hurt them so much.

And he had. He had had his revenge. And he was god. The god. The one god.

And they...

He had been going to forgive them, hadn't he? Eventually. Not now. But in eight hundred years perhaps. Once the joke grew stale. Once the point had been made.

Hadn't he?

But now he couldn't. Because Lawl...Lawl...Because there was a corpse in his hands. A corpse he had made.

He must have wanted to make a corpse.

He hadn't wanted to.

He must have.

A schism in the church of his mind. A breach to be resolved or descended into never to return.

And no matter all the might-have-beens, all the possibilities...He held a corpse in his hand. The Hallows were gone, and Lawl had been sent to the Void, never to be returned. He was condemned to oblivion. By Barph. And by Barph alone. That was the one truth of events. That was the only way things had turned out.

So there was only one thing he could want: Death. Destruction. Terror and damnation.

So that was what he wanted. Even if he didn't want it. That was the world he had made. For that was the will of god. And he was god. The one god. The only god.

And so he rained destruction on the world.

70

This Hurts Me as Much as It Hurts You

Gratt's fist plunged directly into Balur's face. Balur felt his bones break. He felt his skin rupture. He tasted blood. Pain clenched a fist around his snout and ripped at his face.

Balur had been outclassed in fights before. It wasn't even that rare. Hippogriffs, griffins, sphinxes, giants, wyverns, and tree-men all outweighed him. Some trolls did. Some humans who had trained long and hard enough had more skill than he had ever had the patience to muster. Sometimes he was simply out-numbered. He had faced odds of fifty to one and worse. And when it wasn't kobolds or goblins or rioting office clerks, that could count for something.

There were ways to prevail when you were outclassed. Bal-ur's preferred option had always been to fight dirty. He had no qualms about blows placed in very specific spots below the belt. He would happily throw dirt in his opponent's eyes. The aim of a fight, in Balur's opinion, was not to demonstrate what an upstanding member of society one was. It was to get some liver on your teeth.

When even dirty tricks failed, there was one other quality that had kept Balur alive through all the years: tenacity. The simple truth was that he often wanted to win more than his opponents. Every fight was, in a way, a fight for his life. Not in the specific blood-gushing-out-of-wounds way, but in a more metaphysical way that Balur had long ago decided to ignore. Fighting was his being. He fought, therefore he was. So even when wounds that should fell him were inflicted, he fought on. He didn't just eviscerate people literally, he also tore at their will, their hope. And he prevailed.

The problem today was that Gratt was cut from exactly the same cloth. His need to win matched Balur's pound for pound, just as he matched Balur blow for blow. And his muscles ... Well, his muscles were fucking enormous, and Balur just couldn't compete there.

Balur roared as pain racked him. He tried to sink his teeth into Gratt's cheek, but his mouth would no longer open all the way, and he had to satisfy himself with sinking his talons deep into Gratt's chest.

It was a pitiful hold. Gratt seized him by the back of the neck, tore him away, flung him across the room. Balur crashed onto broken tiles. He tried to get up. Gratt was already running across the floor. His foot entered Balur's gut. Something ruptured internally. Balur flew. He hit the floor again.

Be getting up, he told himself.

His limbs didn't appear to be listening.

Gratt bent down, seized Balur by his injured snout. Balur sprayed pain around Gratt's fist.

"Not enough, little lizard," Gratt said, grinning with his ugly gash of a mouth.

And he was right. Balur simply did not have enough. He was outclassed. He was beaten.

Except Balur thought perhaps he wasn't. He was not here to win, after all. He was here to buy time. He was here, taking this beating of a lifetime, so that Will and Afrit could get their blood into a font, seize control of this palace, and have it beat the everliving shit out of Gratt and the dragons and Barph.

How gods-hexed long did it take to get your blood into a font? Open a vein and pour.

Gratt seemed to decide Balur should find this out. The general's muscles bunched, and he flung Balur through the doors into the font room.

Except, lying dazed on his back, Balur noticed that the room he was now in was not the font room. Apparently it was the Barph-pitching-a-shit-fit room. He casually wondered how they'd made such a catastrophically wrong turn.

Barph was ten feet tall and growing. He was holding Lawl in one hand. Things didn't look as if they'd gone very well for Lawl. His tongue and eyes were bulging from his abruptly pale face. He appeared to have crapped himself somewhere along the way. Balur could have been warning Barph that would happen if he throttled someone. He was having experience.

That said, the scale of Barph's tantrum seemed out of proportion to getting a little dead-person shit on his hands. He was smashing at the walls of...

Was it a throne room? How had they been making that mistake?

Barph's fists smashed into masonry. Stones flew free. Above him windows shattered, and glass rained down. The very air around him seemed to vibrate with rage.

There were others here, Balur noticed. Gratt had followed him in. Afrit was there, heading toward the back of the room at considerable speed. And Will too. Will frozen and in great risk of being hit by a chunk of falling ceiling.

Gratt was hesitating. The general was staring up at Barph just as Balur was. It made for a nice break from him pummeling Balur's kidneys.

Afrit marked Balur's violent entrance. She froze, pressed against a wall, looked at him with eyes full of panic.

"Is there a font?" he managed. He wasn't sure Afrit could

hear him. He couldn't make a lot of noise, and Barph was shouting a lot.

"We have to get out of here!" Afrit screamed back. "He's lost his mind!"

"I compel you!" Barph was howling, flailing Lawl's body into the walls. The corpse was little more than a bloody rag in Barph's hand, most of it smeared over the walls. And yet with each blow the very fabric of the castle seemed to crack and moan. The floor was splitting. The wall behind the throne was starting to collapse.

With great and laborious effort, Balur turned over and started to get to his feet. A massive chunk of ceiling smashed to the floor beside him. Stained glass shrapnel peppered his side. Given the state of his wounds, it didn't make much difference.

"Will!" he growled as loudly as he could. "Will, get moving! Will, you have to find the font!"

"This is my decree!" Barph howled. Lightning punched through the walls like ballista bolts.

Will glanced back over his shoulder, saw Balur. He blinked, seeming to shake the paralysis off for a moment.

Gratt stepped between them. Balur tensed. He tried to pretend it wasn't fear he felt. It didn't go so well.

Gratt wasn't looking at Balur, though, and he wasn't looking at Will. The once-dead general's eyes were fixed on Barph, now towering thirty feet above their heads.

"Child!" Gratt roared. "Infant god. Puerile one. Player of petty games! You have pretended to your grandfather's throne for too long. You have played at being king, and all you do, all you have done is play with your own shit." Gratt puffed out his not inconsiderable chest. "Your time is done, child. It is time for a true warrior to take over."

Barph took a break from screaming madly to stare at Gratt. Confusion and anger mixed on his face. "No," he said. "Shut up. I do not want to listen to you. That is my decree. That is what I command. And I am god. The one god. The only god. I compel you. Only me. Me alone."

"Child—" Gratt sneered.

"I COMPEL YOU!" Barph's words were a wall of sound. They tore through the room, ripping tapestries from the walls, shattering cracked columns, ripping sconces from their settings in the wall. Stones and rubble blasted past Balur, sent him skittering down the room.

For a moment Gratt weathered the storm, and then Barph stretched out a hand.

Lightning struck.

Where Gratt had stood was a fine red mist. A violent crimson smudge haloed where his feet had touched the floor. Of the rest of the general, there was no sign.

Barph threw back his head and laughed, a shrill, high-pitched sound.

"Fuck," Afrit said from beside Balur.

The roof of the palace was in full collapse now. Masonry bombarded the room, the sky above peering down as clouds began to clot and the golden light grew dim.

And Balur stared at the stain on the floor that had been Gratt. That had been the creature who had beaten each and every shade of shit imaginable out of him. Dismissed. With a wave of a hand. Become nothing more than meat mist.

His heart was beating fast in his chest.

"What was that?" Barph yelled at the stain that once was Gratt. "I can't hear you." He laughed again.

"We have to get the fuck out of here."

Balur wasn't really listening to Afrit. The curse was the only reason he really caught the words. It was strange to hear it coming from the academic's lips. Something inside her seemed to have been damaged by events.

"Will!" Afrit shouted. "Will! Come on!" She was hauling on Balur's arm now, trying to get him back on his feet.

Will half turned. He didn't seem to be able to look away from the space that Gratt had occupied either.

The room was continuing to collapse. The walls were caving in. Barph was still growing, his head sticking out through the rent ceiling, exposed, into the heavens. Rain was falling.

Slowly Balur got to his feet.

"Come on!" Afrit shouted again. "This is not the fight we came here for! We can't win this!"

Will took somnambulistic footsteps toward them. Rubble crashed to the earth around them. The floor shook.

Barph turned his attention, fixed it on the three of them, the intruders in his throne room.

Balur shook off Afrit's arm.

"I am the god here!" Barph told them. "Not you. Never you. Only me."

"The font, Will!" Afrit was almost screaming.

Will seemed to wake from the dream. "Oh shit," he managed. He started to run.

"You think you matter to me?" Barph asked them. "You think you matter more than my own father? You think I won't kill you?"

Balur looked into Afrit's panic-stricken face. And through the pain he found he still had a smile left in him. "Be holding my beer," he told her. "I am having this."

"Your beer?" Afrit blinked at him.

He walked away from her. He walked past Will.

"Balur! No!" Afrit yelled.

He walked toward Barph.

Life. It made you strong or it made you weak. And if you were weak, it would kill you. And the only way to know if you were weak or strong was to test yourself again and again. To find the greatest challenge you could and fling yourself against it, discover if you were strong enough to survive.

There would always come an enemy who was your better.

There would always come the thing that you could not defeat. The only question was whether it would be mighty or feeble. Whether your death would be glorious or laughable.

Balur had tested himself before. Balur had taken on a dragon head-on. And he had thought he would die that day. But he had been stronger. And ever since then, it had been harder and harder to find that thing to fling himself against. That thing that would make his death something truly spectacular.

But Barph... perhaps Barph was that thing.

"I am seeing you, Barph, kin slayer!" Balur called. "I am hearing your voice and your commands. And I am saying to you that you cannot compel me. I am saying that I will not be bending to your will. I am saying you are *a* god, but not *my* god."

"No," Barph muttered, rubbing at his temple. "No, you aren't saying that at all."

"Be hearing me!" Balur roared. "I am rejecting you! I am rejecting your divinity! I am coming to slay you! I am coming to bring your throne down around your ears! I am coming to bathe in your entrails and to be feasting upon your face. I am coming to defile your legacy and shit on your forefathers. I am coming to end you. I am being Balur of the Analesian Desert, and I am defying you with every fiber that I am."

And then he started to run. The time for words was over.

"No," Barph said again, his voice rising. "I don't want you to say that."

Balur thought of Lette as he ran. She would have understood this, he thought. She wouldn't have approved. Definitely not. But she would have understood.

Barph stretched out his hand.

Balur dived right. Lightning smashed into the ground beside him. He felt shocks run up his tail, smelled his own flesh burning. He kept running.

He thought of Cois. Would zhe understand? He thought perhaps zhe might. And he wished now that he had not asked hir to stay behind in Avarra. He wished zhe could be there now with Will and Afrit, watching this. That zhe would know how he died. That zhe would know it was glorious.

Another lightning blast. He dived and rolled. Each landing sent pain splintering through his body, his wounds and broken bones screaming their resistance. He ignored them. He silenced them. He denied them. He was not weak. He would not give in to the glass in his side or the fractures in his tail.

He was Balur. He was forged in the Analesian Desert. He was strong.

"I told you to stop!" Barph screamed. "I said no!"

Balur was laughing. He spread his arms.

"Be coming on!" he roared.

He leapt. He committed himself utterly to this. There were no course corrections now. This was his path. He bared his teeth.

"No!" Barph shrieked.

But yes. Yes. Yes.

And Barph's fist came down, blanking out the sky, on a path as firm and implacable as his own. A denial of Balur's plans and his hopes. And it struck him down, smashed him down into the floor in an explosion of organs and skin and scales. It obliterated him completely.

But yes.

71

Why We Fight

Will watched Barph's fist come down. He watched Balur disappear beneath it. He watched the fist come up.

And that was it. That was all it was.

Balur's death.

Another death. Quirk. And Lette. And now Balur too. And Barph had killed them all, but it was Will who had supplied the opportunity. Over and over again he had brought these people, his supposed friends, his loved ones... He had brought them into these situations. He had told them he had plans, and they had believed him. Over and over and over again.

"No," he said. He should have screamed it, should have howled it, but his voice was barely above a whisper. "No." He just didn't have the energy anymore.

"Look," Barph was saying to his bloody hand. "Look what you made me do."

"Move, you jackass!" Afrit seized Will's arm, hauled at him. "Now!"

Will stumbled after her.

Quirk. And Lette. And Balur.

"No!" Barph roared. "No!"

What he was denying, whom he was denying it to... Will was incapable of understanding.

Afrit hauled him through a doorway. There was a ceiling above his head again. The space felt small and choking after the ever-opening expanse of the collapsing throne room. His feet clattered on the tiles.

Through another door. Barph's howling growing more distant now, the pressure of his unexpected anguish on Will's frontal lobes less obvious. But that relief just seemed to make more space for the grief.

Quirk. And Lette. And Balur.

He was stumbling over his own feet, over the rubble that littered the place.

The palace wasn't attacking him anymore, he noticed. Maybe it was broken beyond repair.

Broken beyond repair...

Quirk. And Lette. And Balur.

They stumbled into a corridor. Or maybe it was a room that had lost its ceiling. There was the sound of water running somewhere. And Barph's screaming was getting louder.

Then Will was falling. No. Afrit was pulling him down. They were sliding behind a part of the palace. He thought there was the beginning of an arch's curve, a fragment of a carving.

Broken beyond repair...

"What do we do, Will?" Afrit had him by the shoulders. She glanced up over the edge of their makeshift cover, then back at him. She stared into his eyes. "What do we do?"

His eyes. What did she see there? What answers could she possibly hope to find?

"Will!" She was shaking him hard. "Snap the fuck out of it!"

"I..." He tried to get out words. His mouth was very dry. "I don't know, Afrit. I have tried everything I can think of, and all I have to show for it is dead friends. Why in the Hallows would you ask me what to do?"

Quirk. And Lette. And Balur.

He was broken. Broken beyond repair. But at least he finally recognized it. At least he could finally take a step back from the fractured mirror of his own vanity and see how insane he was.

He was here to try to steal the heavens. Even after the death of ten thousand. Even after Quirk's death. Even after Lette's death. The woman he loved. He had still thought that *he* had a way to redeem himself. That *his* plan could somehow undo the hurt he had caused. What sort of person considered that? What sort of twisted piece of human wreckage?

"I need you, Will," Afrit was saying. "I need you to help me figure this out."

"No," he said. "No more plans. Nothing else from me. I am an architect of misery, Afrit. That's it. That's all. And I can't cause any more harm. I can't watch you die because of my actions."

"Your inaction is going to fucking kill me in a second, you arsehole!"

"Run," he told her. "That's all I have. Run away. From me. From Barph. From here. Find your own way. Do something I wouldn't do. I'm toxic, Afrit. I'm broken. I've broken everything."

He kept waiting for a feeling like catharsis, but all he had was pain.

Afrit's fear was coalescing into something harder and sharper. She glanced up again. When she looked back at him there was something of the fire of her dead, lost love in her eyes. "Have you ever considered, Will, that maybe it's not you killing them, you self-centered shit-wit? It's the fact we're in a fight with a god. This is a fight in which people die."

"Lette died!" he screamed at her. And gods, it was the first time he'd said it out loud like that, just bald and naked and frail. And it almost broke him utterly. He felt the edges of his mind fracturing from the pressure of the grief.

"Quirk died!" She let go of him, pushed him away bodily, raised a hand, seemed to hesitate, and then come to a decision. She slapped him full across the mouth. He found the taste of his own blood almost familiar now.

She leaned in close. "Quirk died too, Will. And do not think for a second that I do not hold you at least partly responsible for that. That I do not think that it was your hasty plan that was to blame. That I do not hate you for that. Because I do."

Quirk. And Lette. And Balur.

"But—" The intensity did not die in Afrit's eyes, not even for an instant. "I remember something else as well, Will. I remember leaving the Hallows. I remember being reunited with the woman I loved. I remember the nights spent in her arms that I should never have had. I remember the months of bliss that I should never have had. But I did have them. And I remember that I had them because of you. You defied death, Will. You planned our way out of the Hallows. You gave that to me. And I love you for that too."

And somewhere, somehow, she had guided him into the eye of the storm. A moment of peace while chaos swirled all around him.

"I destroyed the Hallows," he said to her. But he wasn't on the verge of hysterics anymore. It was as close as he could get to openly begging for redemption.

"You did." Afrit had dialed down her intensity, but the passion was still there. "You did awful things, Will. But you did beautiful things as well. And sometimes they were the same things. But that's not special to you, Will. That's not exclusively your domain. You've just done things on a grander scale than most people. That's all there is to it.

"Life," she said, "will continuously beat you down. Over and over and over again it will strike you in the face and smash you to the floor. Each and every one of us. Not just you. Not just me. And all we ever get to do, Will, is decide whether to curl up into a ball and give in to the beating, or get back up and meet it standing on our own two feet."

Her palm came to his face again, not violently this time, but softly. Holding him. Supporting him.

"I really need you to get back up on your feet now, Will." She managed a small, lonely laugh. "I think the whole world does."

The ground was shaking beneath them. The air was full of the roaring of a god, the roaring of fire, the roaring of the palace as it collapsed around them.

"Please, Will," Afrit said. "Whatever you have in mind... Yes, there's a chance it will make things worse. But there's also a chance it will make things better. And whatever that chance is... Well, right now I think it's worth taking. So please. Get back up. Fight. Please."

Quirk. And Lette. And Balur.

And ten thousand more.

Ten thousand who had trust in him. And one last one, sitting before him. And she had no reason to trust him. He had given her every reason to despise him. And she did. But she was still here. She was still asking him to help.

And he could throw that back in her face. He could point out that he was a charlatan, a fraud, a cheap con man, a...

A cheap con man...

Oh gods. Oh gods, he had a plan.

And Will Fallows stood back up.

72

Going Down in Flames

Piss and fire and blood and hate—Yorrax rained it all down upon the heavens of Avarra.

A thousand wounds had been carved into her flanks. A thousand holes had been punched into her wings. Their edges hung ragged. And each mark, each mutilation, each insult just strengthened her resolve. When she controlled the heavens, the very first thing she would do would be to tear the Summer Palace to the ground.

It had killed them all. All her dragon kin. A building had. A homicidal building. These fucking gods and their madness...

Blottax had been the first to fall, trying to force his way through a window. The frame had chewed him up, crushed his skull. Chessax had actually managed to make it into one room, only for the ceiling to send a beam through her skull. Gerrax had landed on the roof and been speared by eight lunging chimneys. Flerrax had been shot out of the sky by a vast roof vomiting up its own tiles. Terrax the coward had tried to flee, and an entire wing of the building had lifted up and crushed him.

And now she was the only dragon left in all Avarra.

And what was the point of that?

Who would do her bidding now? Who would crawl craven and low before her now? Whom would she deride and berate? What was the point of dominance if there was no one to dominate?

This bastard building. She would raze it to the very ground.

But she was tired and bleeding and scared, and her throat was raw from the gouts of flame she had hawked up. And the palace still stood.

A dormer window flared open at her, shot glass planes and the content of a room in her direction. She spun away, felt a chest of drawers crack against a back leg. She bellowed in flame, breathed fire.

Her flames lapped uselessly against uncaring mortar.

And then, suddenly, unbidden, against all sense, cracks appeared in the bricks she had splashed with fire. And a great hope leapt in her heart. And she poured more and more flames onto the buildings, and the cracks grew deeper...

But then she lifted her head, hacking and coughing, and she saw that the cracks were everywhere, and her fire had no meaning here. The central arch of the central hall's ceiling was collapsing, a great shaking racking this building, and she was being denied even her desire to tear it down. And nothing, nothing was going to plan.

She screamed again, choked again.

But then, like a silent answer to her hopes, the face of her tormentor appeared in the midst of the collapsing ruins. Barph, staring wild-eyed as his home crashed to the ground around him.

Barph, the architect of all the dragons' woes.

She swept up into the sky, and then, with claws extended, plunged straight toward his face.

73

Life Punches below the Belt

Will stood. Will stared. The Summer Palace was a shattered ruin, a broken jungle of masonry and sheared columns. Walls sagged, ceilings were absent, tiles were cracked. Flames ate through the ruins, consuming corpses with a ravenous hunger.

And in the middle of this stood Barph, still massive, robe torn, hair matted, half his beard torn raggedly away. And in his eyes he looked utterly and completely lost.

He was, Will saw, holding a dragon in his hand. A small one. One with blue and yellow scales. And gods, he recognized her. Yorrax, still here at the end of things, raging and biting and breathing fire, and utterly impotent in the face of everything.

Barph raised a fist, about to smash the dragon into oblivion.

This plan, Will thought, *is stupid, and it's going to get me killed. But at least it will probably get* only *me killed.*

He hesitated. Just a moment. Just a fraction of a second to remember Lette's face one last time. Then he filled his lungs.

"Hey!" he screamed. "Hey, you sack of shit!"

Barph shouldn't have heard him. Not over the noise of it all. This collapse. This breaking. This ending.

Barph turned and looked at him.

"Hey!" Will screamed, and he grinned, a wild manic grin. The grin of a corpse. "Look at all this!" he shouted, and waved at the destruction surrounding them. "You truly are," he yelled, "the god of absolutely nothing!"

Barph was utterly frozen. Just for a moment. Just for a second. Then his face contorted with the purest, most divine rage Will could ever have imagined.

"You!" The word was a howl, a baying drawn-out wail. Barph dropped Yorrax to the ground, still whole, the killing blow never delivered. "Yoooooooooou!" Spittle flecked his beard and lips. "I deny you! I end you! I destroy you!"

"You do nothing," Will scoffed. "You are nothing. You are a shadow playing dress-up in his father's robes. You are a temper tantrum. You are meaningless. You are nothing, you mean nothing, you achieve nothing."

"Will," Afrit said, still hunkered down behind the fallen chunk of wall they had been using as cover. "What in the Hallows are you doing?"

"And that," Will finished, voice rising, "is why you will always, always be alone. Why you will always be hated. Why you will always be rejected."

And that, he saw, had done it. So Will started to run.

Barph's words no longer had meaning. It was just an outpouring of sound and anguish. A barking, braying wail. And it was the only head start Will was going to get.

The gates of the heavens. He had to get to the gates of the heavens. Through the ruins of the Summer Palace. Through the wilderness of the gardens beyond. Past any surviving guards.

At a flat run it would take him perhaps ten minutes. Perhaps longer.

Barph started to chase him. Barph—thirty feet tall, with strides that ate distance faster than the flames ate wood, with all the faith of Avarra's devout citizens powering each step.

Ten minutes to get to the exit, and Barph would be on him in thirty seconds.

This plan was stupid, and it was going to get Will killed.

74

The Lesser of Two Evils

Yorrax lay gasping on the ground. Her throat was bruised, her ribs battered.

She had been...Barph had been about to...Death had breathed its flames directly into her face.

And yet she was still here. She was still alive. Barph had let her go. Because...because...

Because of Will Fallows.

She didn't understand. She wasn't sure she cared to. But his actions had saved her.

Slowly, painfully she rolled onto all fours, spread her wings, and beat at the air. She lifted up into the sky. It was time for her to leave this place. Not to run, perhaps, but to regroup, plan, calculate a new angle of attack.

She slowly spiraled upward, trying to use the thermals from the fires sprouting everywhere to gain height and freedom.

She could see Barph beneath her, running madly across the rubble of his fallen palace, his hair and robes streaming out behind him—ragged and torn. He was chasing someone. Will, she realized. Barph was about to catch him and end him.

One of her enemies about to kill the other. And she regretted that she would not be the one to kill Will Fallows, but...

And as the thermals finally filled her wings and buffeted her away, an unexpected emotion filled her mind: doubt.

Because she had goals in mind for the life that came after this, but...how would she achieve them? How would she kill Barph? How would she seize the heavens?

She did not understand the gods. She did not understand how they lived or how they died. She did not understand how she could kill one.

But Will Fallows did.

And she did not like Will, or his plans, but there was an efficacy to them that had, as much as she hated to admit it, evaded her all her life.

And as she watched, it seemed to her that Will Fallows was not just running *away* from Barph. He was running *toward* something. He had a purpose.

Will Fallows had plans. He had ways to achieve his goals.

Would Will Fallows be easier to kill than Barph? Could she even save him? Could she delay Barph for long enough? Could Will Fallows truly defeat the god?

What did she believe?

She circled once, twice. She thought she could see her way out of here, an escape glinting past the ruins and the tangle of the overgrown gardens.

Barph was almost on Will.

What did she believe?

She let out a long frustrated howl. Then, talons outstretched, she swooped down, aiming directly for Barph's eyes.

She believed in Will Fallows.

75

The Bigger They Are...

Death, Will knew now, was a shadow. Death was a crushing fear descending just beyond the corner of your eye. Death was the knowledge of exactly how fruitless and pointless all your hopes and dreams were.

Death was Barph's foot coming to crush you into oblivion.

He felt the foot crash down behind him more than he heard it. The massive expulsion of air and dust blasting over him. The quake running through the floor.

The next footfall. That would be it.

He could see the edge of the rubble field. The end of the fallen palace. But the gardens stretched for a mile beyond. The gates of the heavens were still not in sight. And there was no way he could reach them. There was just no way.

Barph's foot rose. Will ran. Will waited for Barph's foot to descend.

And then, from nowhere: a spark.

Inside Will, a beast left forgotten and starving caught the scent of food and stirred its head.

Will felt it. He felt all of it. And he recognized it. And Will knew that somehow, somewhere, someone *believed* in him.

He felt the scrap of the Deep One that had wormed its way into his heart and mind wriggling. He felt it sucking on that scrap of belief for all it was worth. And there was fear in that, and horror, but above all there was a question: Who? Who here, and now, could possibly believe in him?

There was a roar, and a flurry of wings. Barph bellowed.

Barph's foot didn't fall.

Will needed to run. He needed to put his head down and run until his heart burst from the effort. His only focus had to be on what was ahead of him.

Still, Will turned back and looked over his shoulder.

Yorrax. Yorrax was back for more. Her talons were buried in the sides of Barph's face. She was biting, and hacking, and howling, and breathing fire and flame into his eyes.

Barph staggered, ripped at her, roared back twice as loud as the dragon.

It was a desperate, futile, foolhardy attack. But it bought Will time. It bought him time because—gods, he could feel it—she believed in him. There was a piece of her, no matter how grudging, that still thought he could be a god.

It wasn't much. It was only a scrap, a spark in an ocean of night. It would be gone in an instant. Yorrax's life would be gone in an instant. But for just a moment, it was his.

And perhaps it was all he needed.

Will folded space around him. He took hold of the gates of the heavens with his mind, and hauled himself toward them.

The spark flared in him. He felt it flicker. It was about to die. He let go. One last ember. He had to hold on to one last ember. If he didn't, this was all for naught.

He looked around. And gods, gods, gods, maybe, just maybe it had been enough. Because suddenly the palace ruins were far behind him. Suddenly the glow of the gates was startlingly close.

There was a draconic scream behind him, and the rhythm of Barph's pounding feet, but far distant now. He was closing the distance, but Will had time. Perhaps just enough time.

He ran. And he ran. And he ran. He hurdled branches, tore through brambles, left behind his skin, carried on uncaring.

Behind him Barph grew closer. The footfalls approaching like thunder.

And then he saw the gates. Still broken, still twisted, but beautiful all the same. And beyond them...not the miles of clouds they had flown through to get here. But Avarra. The whole world spread out below him. Each country and coastline clear. The whole beauty and scope of creation spread out before him. He could see everything he was trying to save.

He looked back. And gods, Barph was close. How had he gotten so close?

"No more!" Barph screamed, his eyes full of everything but sanity. "No more of you!"

Will scrambled to the edge of the gates. The ground came to a ragged end inches from his feet. Wind beckoned and billowed at him, pulled him toward that terrible fall.

He looked back again.

Barph was breaking free of the garden. Barph was twenty yards behind him. Two giant paces. "An ending of everything you are!" Barph screamed.

This plan was stupid. This plan was going to get him killed. But in the end, that was the whole point. For something to truly be worth fighting for, it had to be worth dying for. Lette had understood that. And Quirk. And Balur. And now finally Will did too. It was just a question of making his death count.

It was a question of *where* he was killed.

Will's heart was a hammer beating in his throat, and he couldn't breathe, and he had never been more scared in his life.

For Lette. For Quirk. For Balur.

Will jumped.

The wind punched him. A balled fist of it smashing into his already well-smashed face. Into his gut. His legs. His gods-hexed balls. It tore at his hair, plunged icy fingers into his eyes.

He tried to breathe. Couldn't. He tried to control his tumbling plunge. Couldn't. He caught glimpses of Barph standing on the edge of the heavens staring down at him in hatred and rage.

Come on. Come on.

The wind forced tears from his eyes, obscured his vision.

Come on.

One way or another this plan was going to kill him. Now it was just a question of how: Barph or the ground.

A gust of wind whipped the tears away. For a moment everything was clear, and Will so desperately wished he had someone to pray to.

And then Barph jumped. He dived. Hands outstretched. Fingers held like claws. His anger and madness and grief riding him all the way down. Barph jumped from the heavens and he came to kill Will.

And Will smiled, and he blew on the very last scrap of divinity that was left in his heart.

He grew. He grew, and he grew, and he grew. Larger and larger and larger, feeling the unreality of his suddenly massive body, feeling the way the wind pounded against it changing. He grew until he dwarfed even Barph.

And then, then he was finally and utterly spent. All his divine magic gone.

Barph sneered, even as he plunged through the air toward Will. And he grew as well. And then they were both vast giants tumbling toward the ground, only the wind and the clouds beneath them. But one was spent, and one had all the belief in Avarra powering him.

Then they collided in midair, and Will flailed, and with a snarl Barph closed his fingers around Will's throat.

76

The View from the Cheap Seats

Cois craned back hir head and stared.

All about hir, the populace of Essoa was doing the same. All of them shading their eyes and watching the heavens. All across Avarra, zhe was sure, everyone was doing the same. Because in all of Avarra's history, in all of its myths and legends, zhe was certain that nothing like this had ever happened before.

Two titans were tumbling through the sky. Figures vast beyond imagining. They grappled and bit and fought as they fell. And zhe knew them both.

Will and Barph were in the sky, fighting furiously. And even from here, it was obvious one of them would be dead long before they hit the ground.

77

... The Harder They Fall

"An ending," Barph said, through gritted teeth and through the howling of the wind. "A cessation of all things."

He saw it now. He saw it and it was beautiful. It had been there since before the beginning of time. It had been waiting. Waiting for him. It was the very thing Lawl had always been trying to counter, to strive against.

The Void.

The Void was chaos. The Void was anarchy. The Void was the annulment of all rules, all orders and hierarchies. It was freedom in its purest, most absolute sense.

Lawl had created life. So Barph would free all the world from life. He would send all of creation to the Void.

And the first person he would send there would be Will Fallows. Will would see. Will would understand. Will would stop fighting. Stop resisting. Stop trying to undermine him at every turn. His god. His master.

He could feel Will's neck beneath his fingers. The stringy muscles and ropy sinews, the hard bulge of his Adam's apple. He could feel the sweat and the oils of his skin. He could feel Will's increasingly weak thrashing.

"Yes," he breathed through gritted teeth. "You see now. You see how I free everyone."

Will gurgled and flopped.

And it was so easy. Finally it was so easy. It was as if with

Lawl's murder the scales had finally fallen from Barph's eyes. He had been so caught up in what other people thought. In trying to please the people. But he knew best. Everyone just needed to shut up and listen.

"Shut up, Will," he said as Will gurgled and spasmed. "Shut up. I deny your voice. I condemn it." He giggled to himself even as the wind whipped and tore at his robes and beard.

And yet, even in the purity of his certainty, something felt wrong.

He tried to put his finger on it. Below them the ground rushed toward them. Geographical features resolved out of the haze.

One of his hands slipped free of Will's neck. Will gurgled. Barph battled the wind to try to bring the hand back to bear, but suddenly his arm felt weak. He struggled. Will bucked beneath him.

Barph gave up on finesse, slammed his elbow down into Will's face. Will's nose shattered, and blood streamed up toward the heavens, a sparkling red trail through the sky. And yet Barph's elbow also sang with pain. He wanted to grab it, but his grip on Will's neck felt precarious, the strength in his fingers slipping.

He brought his hand down again, straight into Will's face. Again. Again. He felt bones giving way, the skin breaking.

His other hand flew free of Will's neck, unable to maintain its grip.

Will's jaw was moving slightly, mumbling something unintelligible.

"No!" Barph screamed. "Shut up! I compel you! I end you! An ending of speech!"

He clasped both his hands above his head, gripping Will's chest with his knees, riding him down. And his grip felt weak. His hands shaky. What was wrong with him?

He smashed his hands down into Will's face again, again, again. Will's face became a red mask, blood sheeting off it. And yet with each blow Barph felt weaker and weaker. His breathing grew ragged.

"What are you doing?" he gasped. "What are—"

But no. He was god. The one god. The only god. He didn't ask questions. He dictated. He demanded.

"No more!" he tried to scream, but his voice was little more than a wheeze. "No more."

The wind was slashing at him now. Will's blood was a violent storm, pelting him like arrows. It smeared his vision blurry red. His legs trembled as they gripped Will's chest.

He had to end this. Whatever this was. It felt like death.

He raised a hand to pull down lightning, to fire a thousand thunderbolts into Will's skull. But the skies did not respond. The clouds stayed silent, as inconstant as a lover.

His power. Where was his power?

"What are you doing?" he screamed at Will. He didn't understand. He was god, but he didn't understand. Will was dying beneath him, and somehow Will was killing him by doing it.

"No!" he screamed with the last of the strength in his chest. He wouldn't allow this. He wouldn't let Will do this. He denied it. He denied Will. He denied him his life.

He seized Will's neck again. Everything he had he poured into that grip. Will's eyes bulged wildly. His blood-wet tongue lashed the air. And as each moment passed, Barph felt the strength flowing out of him. But if he could just hold on…just hold on…Will was so close to death…

And then, with a final spasm, the end came.

78

The Illusion of Victory

Cois stared.

Cois didn't understand. Zhe didn't think anybody understood.

Two figures had fallen from the heavens. Two figures locked in battle. Will and Barph.

They had crashed into each other in the air. One astride the other. They had screamed out their hate.

And…

And zhe had seen Will sit astride Barph's chest. Zhe had seen him throttle half the life out of Barph. Zhe had seen him beat Barph's face to a bloody pulp.

It had been impossible, but zhe had seen it.

At first she hadn't believed it. Zhe couldn't have. Nobody could. Barph had survived the dragon attack outside Essoa, after all. He had survived that storm. But then, slowly at first, with growing conviction, zhe had started to believe that Will would win. All around hir, people had started to believe it.

Barph had lain limp in Will's arms. Will had placed his fingers around Barph's throat. He had squeezed.

And then Barph's body gave a final spasm.

And…

And…

Will had won.

79

The Last Temptation
of Willett Fallows

Will felt the life go out of him.

Barph's clawing fingers had crushed his windpipe utterly. His heart was spasming and stuttering in his chest. His limbs were anchors of agony tied to his torso, ripping him apart. Pain had replaced all the oxygen in his lungs. His blood was fire in his veins, scorching him from the inside out.

It was too much to bear. It was driving him out his mind.

And then, very suddenly, it stopped.

All his pain and fear and doubt. All of it stopped.

And then, a moment later, he stopped.

No more thought.

No more consciousness.

Oblivion.

How long did it last? He didn't know. He couldn't know. There was nothing of him left to know.

A sudden blast of white.

A flare of sound.

It all came rushing back. All of it. Everything. Will came back. He emerged out of oblivion. He tore out of the Void.

Willett Fallows. Remade. Re-created.

Resurrected.

And gods...gods...it had worked. It had actually fucking worked.

It had worked.

It was a stupid plan. It was a plan that would get him killed.

Except no one else would see it that way.

Will had leapt from the heavens. He had grown to a size that everyone on Avarra below could see. He had come to the end of his divine magic. And then Barph had come hurtling after him.

And it had worked.

Because Will had one other scrap of magic to his name. One piece that did not come from the Deep Ones. One piece that came from another source.

He still had illusion.

And so he had performed one last trick.

He had swapped their appearances. He had made himself look like Barph. He had made Barph look like him.

That was all.

And that was all it had needed. Because when Barph beat seven shades of shit out of him, all anyone on Avarra below had seen was him beating the shit out of Barph. And when Barph had throttled him, all anyone on Avarra below had seen was him throttling Barph. And when Barph had killed him, all anyone on Avarra below had seen was him killing Barph.

And nobody believed in a god that died.

And so they believed for just a moment—for just long enough—that Barph was dead. And grasping for something to hold on to in the world, they believed in Will. And with all the belief in Avarra behind it, that fact became the truth.

Will had lost. And in doing so he had won.

And the people below, the very people he had fought for, had died for, they brought him back. They resurrected him. They were his miracle.

A sudden blast of white.

A flare of sound.

And then power. Power that eclipsed Will. Power that burned through his nerves and set his blood aflame. Power that burst through him and undid his seams. Power that crackled in his mind.

Will no longer fell through the sky. He was the sky. And the sky was him. And the world was him. And all the energy stored in it, every scrap of power was his. Every heart that beat was his. And he was it.

It was too much, too great. It was everything. It was monumental. It was power that would crush him utterly.

But also, it was power that meant he could not be crushed.

He was god. The god. The one god.

He held Barph in one hand. He had him by the scruff of the neck, Barph's head lolling back, throat exposed for a killing blow. His body seemed sunken in, decrepit, almost deformed. His fingers were withered claws.

Barph turned sunken eyes upon Will. His lips worked. He licked at them with a dry tongue.

This was the architect of all Will's pain. The mad god who had sought to destroy the world. The god of nothing. The avatar of anarchy. The motherless fuck who had killed Lette.

Will snarled. Because he could do anything. Anything. Any revenge he wanted could be his.

Barph's eyes danced apart, came back, managed to focus for a moment. "Eight hundred years," he whispered.

Will didn't care what this whoreson had to say. He didn't have to care what anyone said anymore. What anyone thought.

There didn't have to be any more fear or embarrassment or disappointment. That was all behind him now.

"Eight hundred years planning for vengeance," Barph mumbled, "and not a moment spent planning on what I'd do once I'd had it."

Will remembered being sent to the Hallows. He remembered the feeling as Barph had torn out his throat. He remembered how close he had been in that moment to redeeming all of Avarra. How much hope had been in his heart. He remembered exactly how much Barph had hurt him.

He felt the power of an entire world sluicing through his veins. He could do anything, be anything, have anything.

And, he found, all he wanted was revenge.

Barph had closed his eyes. Had possibly stopped breathing. Will found he didn't care. He didn't have to care anymore.

His hand went down. His fingers plunged into the flesh of Barph's neck. And he tore. He slashed. And with a spray of blood, he ripped out Barph's throat.

There, he thought, and the whole of creation thought it with him. *Now you get yours.* And he raised Barph up above his head, and as Barph had done to him, he did to Barph. He drank the dead god's blood.

This is my revenge, he thought. *This unmaking of you.* And he felt all of creation cheer with him for it. Because they had to. Because he wanted them to. Because his will was theirs.

And there was more power. Gods, there was more. With each drop of Barph's blood that hit his tongue there was more. And more. And more. And he could feel his skin ripping trying to contain it. And he simply made more skin. He could be anything. Do anything.

He could remake the world. He could save it. He could finally make everything right. He could mend all ills. All woes. And nobody would complain. Nobody would make idiotic suggestions and ruin it all. None of them anymore. Not once. Finally he could just do the right thing and be left in peace.

He was god.

But in his heart he felt Lette still. That little scrap of her that could never die, that she'd left like the tip of a glass blade in his guts.

Well, she said, *look at you now. Hanging in the sky and covered in a god's blood. And to think I found you in a cave. My farm boy. What sort of mess are you going to get yourself into this time?*

He could do anything.

He could make the world perfect.

He could make the world fair. And good. And kind. He could make people happy. He could end disease, famine, war. All of it. It was in his hands. He could make everyone live perfect lives.

Eight hundred years planning for vengeance, and not a moment spent planning on what I'd do once I'd had it.

There was another voice too, urging him, crying out for him to make the world kneel. For him to make them shout his name. For him to demand love and worship and prayers and hymns, forever and for always.

Make them pay obeisance, said the piece of the Deep One still lodged inside him. *Make them beg for your mercy.*

How many other injustices had been heaped on his head for him to get here? How many others were there left whom he could punish? Whose wrongs against him could he right...?

What sort of mess...?

Gods...gods...

Except there weren't any gods. There was only him. Only him to decide the fate of everyone.

And gods, gods, gods, he did not want it. He didn't want that. He was terrified of that. Of the power inside him. It was going to fucking kill him. And if it didn't, then he was going to kill everyone else.

"I don't want this," he said. But there was no one to answer him. No one else left.

He could do anything…

Could he…could he give it away?

And so he tried.

CODA: GOOD TIMES

80

The End of the Beginning

Lette gasped.

Air rushed into her lungs. It came with pain. Searing pain. This was the air for a scream. For the last rattle of life. This was agony. This was—

This was...?

It was nothing. A breath. An inhalation of bright morning air as she sat on the edge of a hill, looking out at a field of flowers.

What was this?

She tried to remember where she'd been, what she'd been doing.

"What happened?" she asked Will. He was sitting next to her on the hill. "What's going on?"

He turned to her, and he bit his lip. "You're going to be mad at me," he said.

"I am?" Then she nodded. That seemed likely.

"You died," Will said.

She tried that on for size. Given where her head was at, she thought maybe it wasn't the most outlandish thing she'd heard.

"Was it your fault?" she checked.

To his credit, Will only hesitated a second. "Yes," he said.

Lette nodded. "Is that what I'm going to be pissed about?" She didn't feel pissed yet. She felt... What was it?

Content?

When was the last time she'd felt content? She wasn't sure she was going to let Will spoil that for her just yet.

"A little bit," Will said. "But probably not mostly why."

That also made some sense. "Go on," she told him.

He shifted his weight. He was wearing a rough work shirt and pair of trousers. His hair was tousled and his skin was suntanned. There were more lines around his eyes than she remembered.

"Do you remember fighting Barph?"

A flash. A glimpse like lightning in a summer sky. Standing in a field of the dead. Hope and horror mixing in her in equal parts. Essoa below her. Barph towering above...

Then gone. Then sitting here with the blue sky above her and the green fields below. With a lone seagull arcing in the sky. With the scent of wildflowers on the breeze.

"Where are we, Will?" she asked.

He bit his lip. "Do you mind if I get to that in a bit?"

"Am I going to be pissed about where we are?"

"So," he said. "We were fighting Barph—"

She decided to let it go for now.

"—and I made a terrible plan. And you were killed."

She nodded. Pieces of it were coming back to her now. Ugly pieces. But she had borne ugly before.

"I don't seem to be dead anymore," she said. "That does a lot to get you off the hook." She tried to smile even as the memories undid her feelings of ease.

"Please, I'm sorry," he said. "I'm trying to tell you all this while I still think it's a good idea."

"Get it out," she said. Maybe she was going to be pissed at him because of how he told stories.

"So you were killed because of my shitty plan," he said. "But then I came up with another plan."

She cocked an eyebrow. "A shitty plan?"

"We went to the heavens. We took on Barph there."

An eye roll this time. Because there were few plans that could have been shittier.

"Seriously, Will?"

He chewed his lip again. Then licked it. In Lette's opinion he was overestimating how attractive hesitating made him. "I won, Lette," he said. "I actually won."

Lette put a hand to the side of her head. "I think there's something wrong with my hearing...," she started.

"No," he said. "I'm serious. I killed Barph. Or...I tricked all of Avarra into killing him. And letting me win."

Her mouth hung open just a little bit. "It's...it's over?" she asked. "Barph's dead?"

He tried out a tentative smile. "We won, Lette. We had our revenge."

She couldn't quite believe it. She looked around. She'd missed it—the final fight.

She'd been dead.

Another lightning flash of memory. Of searing pain. Of unending agony. Of lying on the grass, feeling her breathing die. All of her die. And then...then...?

"Will?" she said. "There weren't any Hallows left. When I died, I went to the Void."

"Yes," he said.

"I was unmade." She said it before she became afraid of the idea. When it was still nebulous and not quite real. And her sense of contentment was halfway down the hill now, fleeing from her for all it was worth.

"I replaced him," Will said. He said the words flatly. As if it were nothing.

"Replaced?"

"When they killed Barph," he said. "They made me a god, Lette. The god. The only god. All of the power of divinity. All the power of the Deep One inside of me. They made me all-powerful. They gave me the power to do anything I wanted."

She blinked at him. It was too much to really take in. *They made me a god.* As if he were telling her the sky was blue. What did he expect her to do with that information?

And then a revelation.

"You brought me back," she said. "You brought me out of the Void."

"Yes," he said. And he did smile at that. And it was like the sun breaking through clouds. It was like being alive again on a sunlit hill, with seagulls in the air and flowers all around.

"Holy shit, Will." She kissed him. She held him. She leaned back and stared at him. He was grinning like a fool. "You can do *anything*?" she asked.

And he said, "Ah."

"Ah?"

"You know how I said you were going to be mad?" he checked.

And gods...every time with him. Every time.

"What did you do, Will?"

Another hesitation dragged out beyond the point of charm. "I, erm...," he said, working his hands furiously. "I gave it away, Lette," he said.

"What?" She didn't understand. She heard the words, but they didn't carry meaning.

"It was too much, you see," he said. "Only a little bit of it had been too much...That was how I got you killed. By thinking only my way mattered. Only my will and my plans. That killed you. And it drove Barph mad. He wanted to unmake the world, I think. At the end, anyway. And this was so much more. So much worse. This was everything. I could pull you out of the Void. I could fundamentally break the rules of the world, Lette. No one should have that sort of power, Lette. It corrupts absolutely."

She stared at him. "The power...," she managed. "You gave it away?"

Gods, the things she could have done. The world she could have made. The jackasses she could have silenced. The injustices she could have ended. The world...

And surely Will could have made that better world too. But... but...

"You gave it fucking away?" she shouted at him.

Birds, wheeled away, squawking.

"I knew you were going to be pissed," he said.

She was very close to hitting him.

"Who the fuck did you give it to?" she demanded.

"Everyone."

"Everyone?"

"Everyone."

"Who the fuck do you mean, everyone?" She wanted him to be very specific here.

"I..." He took a deep breath. "I split it. I split it between every sentient being on Avarra. I gave it out equally. To humans and dwarves and elves and centaurs and giants and...everyone."

"Literally everyone?" she asked. She tried to think it through, tried to be the rational one here. "You made everyone on Avarra a fucking mage?"

"I gave Avarra back to her people," he said. And he was so gods-hexedly earnest. So...passionate. "I made it fair. Maybe not right. And maybe not good. And maybe not what it should have been. But I made it fair. That's the best I think I could do."

And gods piss on him. From a great height. How did he always make a believer out of her?

"So wait...," she said, still trying to understand. "Who are the gods now?"

"There are no gods." He smiled helplessly.

"You got rid of the gods?" And she knew they hadn't been in their heavens when she'd died, but this seemed bold even for Will.

"No," he said. "They're still...just here. With the rest of us in Avarra. They're mortal. But I gave them some divinity too. I gave it to everyone."

"Everyone?" She was still having some trouble with that. She had met a lot of people in her life, and some of them were arseholes.

"It was the only way to be fair," he said. And then another hesitation, which she knew was the prelude to some truly monumental stupidity. She arched an eyebrow until finally he said, "Even Barph."

She almost choked on her own tongue. "You said you killed him!"

"I did," Will nodded. "I did. Or the people did. Or...it's complicated. But...well, see...before I gave the power away, I did do a few other things."

"Like bringing fucking Barph back to life?" She was patting herself down for knives. Will seemed to have brought her back to life without any knives on her person. Which was apparently the only rational thing he'd bothered to do recently.

"Yes," he said. "There were quite a lot of people to bring back, actually. You. And Quirk. And Balur..."

"You killed Balur?" What the fuck...? How long had she been dead for that he'd managed to do that?

"Well, technically Barph—"

"Barph, who you brought back to life?" she checked.

He looked sheepish. "I knew you would be mad," he said.

"Of course I'm fucking mad," she snapped. "You tell me you achieve victory, and then you tell me you bring back our enemy from the dead!"

"I think he's a lot better now," Will said. "I don't think he wanted to be the only god. He just wanted his family to know how much they'd hurt him, and be sorry for it. And I think they really are. And he knows it. And really, it's only a scrap of divinity. The same amount you and I have."

And that...that was..."I?" she said.

"Everyone, Lette."

She was divine. At least...a tiny part of her. She reached out, tried to feel it. And perhaps there was something different there. Perhaps a bare flicker of possibility.

"You can meet him in a bit," Will said.

"Who?" She felt Will was being purposely unclear.

"Barph," he said.

"What?"

"He's back over that rise," Will said. "They all are."

She looked back at the hill, the flowers reaching up to its peak, the sky and the future beyond that.

"Who is?" she asked.

"Oh," he said. "Balur and Quirk and Afrit and Cois and Lawl and Klink and Toil and Knole and Betra and Barph. All of them."

"You said Balur died...," she managed.

"I brought him back," Will said. He tried out a smile. "Everyone sent to the Void, I brought them back. And I put the Hallows back. And I put Gratt and his army back. I just...I put everything back together. I did use it for that. And then I gave it up. I gave it to you, and to all our friends, and to everybody."

She just...she just...

He put the world back together.

The whole fucking world.

And she'd been dead.

And he'd gone into the Void and brought her back...

"Oh, and the dragons too," he said. And she could have sworn that he ducked.

"What?" Her voice screeched at the blue sky.

"I put them back on Natan, though," he said. "Which is where most of them were. But...I...I made it nicer for them. So there's lots of food. And gold. I thought perhaps if they were happy there, and not here, then perhaps they'd leave us alone. And, well...Barph had wiped them out. And that seemed like a lot. And Quirk would have been sad. So...I did do that too."

He gave her a nervous smile.

And...and...gods. "Will...," she said. But she wasn't sure what words came after that.

He winced a little. "How mad are you?" he asked.

"I...," she said. And still...What did you say? What did she say? Here, now, confronted with this? "I...," she said again.

"I couldn't think of a better way." He shrugged.

"It's just..." She tried to formulate it as best she knew how. "You put the world back together," she said, "and it didn't even occur to you to maybe just set aside one single barn full of gold bullion for us?"

"Oh," he said. And he licked his lips.

She shook her head. "An island of gold for the dragons, but for you and me..."

"Well." He held up his hand, like a polite schoolboy.

"This," she told him, "better be fucking good."

"You remember," he said, "how I told you everyone was waiting for us over the crest of the hill."

And she supposed that somewhere in the slew of madness, that had been communicated.

"Yes," she allowed.

"They're on a farm," he said.

"A farm?" she checked.

"A pig farm." He nodded eagerly.

And that...that took a moment. "You were a god," she checked. "And you were so powerful that you could go into the Void and save my life. So powerful you could re-create the Hallows. So powerful you brought the dragons back from extinction and gave them an island of gold."

"Yes," he said.

"And then," she checked. "You gave us a fucking pig farm, Will Fallows? A pig farm?" She wouldn't need a blade for this, she decided. Her bare hands would be just the thing.

"Verran war pigs!" he shouted. "They're Verran war pigs!"

And something about those words...She hesitated, inches short of wringing the life from his neck.

"They're Verran war pigs," he said. "You remember?"

And then she did. Standing with him, laughing and loving and planning for an impossible future that could never come.

And now it had.

Because of him. Because of Will. He had made them a future together.

Hands that were poised for violence embraced. Lips that were poised to spill angry curses kissed. Bodies that were about to collide entwined.

Lettera Therren kissed Willett Fallows. She gave him a kiss fit to serve as the ending to all things.

But for them, it was just the beginning.

Acknowledgments

Ever since I was a little kid, I have loved epic fantasy. I have read so many trilogies, I honestly can't count them. And now I have my own. It's crazy to me. It's humbling and incredible. And there are so many people to thank, but first off, I want to thank you, whoever you are, wherever you are. Thank you for coming on this journey with me. Thank you for letting me take you on this journey. None of this would exist without you. Not Will, not Lette, not Barph, not Avarra. Instead there would just be the Void. So in a way, you are the hero of this book. Thank you for that.

There are other people to thank too, so I shall do a quick roll call. Will Hinton, the editor of this series and the man who has made it so much better than I would have done on my own. If you have enjoyed this book, you owe him a debt of gratitude. Everyone else at Orbit. Much like a child, a book takes a village, and I have been incredibly fortunate in the team that has supported me. Howard Morhaim, my agent and (I am convinced) some sort of literary-oriented wizard. John Banks for bringing these books to life in the most incredible way for everyone on the audio (and who is now being forced to read this aloud on the audiobook, hopefully much to his embarrassment). The Broken Circles writing group for all the support, advice, and inspiration. And finally, my wife, Tami. If I have ever been successful at putting goodness, and hope, and love at the heart of these books, it is because of her and what she has taught me.

Thank you all.

extras

www.orbitbooks.net

about the author

Jon Hollins is a pseudonym.

Find out more about Jon Hollins and other Orbit authors by registering for the free monthly newsletter at www.orbitbooks.net.

if you enjoyed
THE DRAGON LORDS: BAD FAITH

look out for

YOU DIE WHEN YOU DIE

West of West: Book One

by

Angus Watson

YOU DIE WHEN YOU DIE . . .

You can't change your fate — so throw yourself into battle, because you'll either end the day a hero or drinking mead in the halls of the gods. That's what Finn's people believe. But Finn wants to live. When his settlement is massacred by a hostile nation, Finn plus several friends and rivals must make their escape across a brutal, unfamiliar landscape, and to survive, Finn will fight harder than he's ever fought before.

Chapter 1

Finnbogi Is in Love

Two weeks before everyone died and the world changed for ever, Finnbogi the Boggy was fantasising about Thyri Treelegs.

He was picking his way between water-stripped logs with a tree stump on one shoulder, heading home along the shore of Olaf's Fresh Sea. No doubt, he reasoned, Thyri would fall in love with him the moment he presented her with the wonderful artwork he was going to carve from the tree stump. But what would he make? Maybe a racoon. But how would you go about . . .

His planning was interrupted by a wasp the size of a chipmunk launching from the shingle and making a beeline for his face.

The young Hardworker yelped, ducked, dropped the stump and spun to face his foe. Man and insect circled each other crabwise. The hefty wasp bobbed impossibly in the air. Finnbogi fumbled his sax from its sheath. He flailed with the short sword, but the wasp danced clear of every inept swipe, floating closer and louder. Finnbogi threw his blade aside and squatted, flapping his hands above his head. Through his terror he realised that this manoeuvre was exactly the same as his rabbit-in-a-tornado impression that could make his young adoptive siblings giggle so much they fell over. Then he noticed he could no longer hear the wasp.

He stood. The great lake of Olaf's Fresh Sea glimmered

calmly and expansively to the east. To the west a stand of trees whispered like gossips who'd witnessed his cowardice in the face of an insect. Behind them, great clouds floated indifferently above lands he'd never seen. The beast itself – surely "wasp" was insufficient a word for such a creature – was flying southwards like a hurled wooden toy that had forgotten to land, along the beach towards Hardwork.

He watched until he could see it no longer, then followed.

Finnbogi had overheard Thyri Treelegs say she'd be training in the woods to the north of Hardwork that morning, so he'd donned his best blue tunic and stripy trousers and headed there in order to accidentally bump into her. All he'd found was the tree stump that he would carve into something wonderful for her, and, of course, the sort of wasp that Tor would have battled in a saga. He'd never seen its like before, and guessed it had been blown north by the warm winds from the south which were the latest and most pleasant phenomenon in the recent extraordinary weather.

If any of the others – Wulf the Fat, Garth Anvilchin or, worst of all, Thyri herself – had seen him throw away his sax and cower like Loakie before Oaden's wrath, they'd have mocked him mercilessly.

Maybe, he thought, he could tell Thyri that he'd killed the wasp? But she'd never believe how big it had been. What he needed to do was kill an animal known for its size and violence . . . That was it! That's how he'd win her love! He would break the Scraylings' confinement, venture west and track down one of the ferocious dagger-tooth cats that the Scraylings banged on about. It would be like Tor and Loakie's quest into the land of the giants, except that Finnbogi would be brawny Tor and brainy Loakie all rolled into one unstoppable hero.

The Scraylings were basically their captors, not that any Hardworker apart from Finnbogi would ever admit that.

Olaf the Worldfinder and the Hardworkers' other ancestors had arrived from the old world five generations before at the beginning of winter. Within a week the lake had frozen and the unrelenting snow was drifted higher than a longboat's mast. The Hardworkers had been unable to find food, walk anywhere or sail on the frozen lake, so they'd dug into the snow drifts and waited to die.

The local tribe of Scraylings, the Goachica, had come to their rescue, but only on two big conditions. One, that the Hardworkers learn to speak the universal Scrayling tongue and forsake their own language, and, two, that no Hardworker, nor their descendants, would ever stray further than ten miles in any direction from their landing spot.

It had been meant as a temporary fix, but some Scrayling god had decreed that Goachica continue to venerate and feed the Hardworkers, and the Hardworkers were happy to avoid foraging and farming and devote their days to sport, fighting practice, fishing, dancing, art or whatever else took their fancy.

Five generations later, still the Goachica gave them everything they needed, and still no Hardworker strayed more than ten miles from Olaf's landing spot. Why would they? Ten miles up and down the coast and inland from Olaf's Fresh Sea gave them more than enough space to do whatever they wanted to do. Few ever went more than a mile from the town.

But Finnbogi was a hero and an adventurer, and he was going to travel. If he were to break the confinement and track down a dagger-tooth cat . . . He'd be the first Hardworker to see one, let alone kill one, so if he dragged the monster home and made Thyri a necklace from its oversized fangs surely she'd see that he was the man for her? Actually, she'd prefer a knife to a necklace. And it would be easier to make.

A few minutes later Finnbogi started to feel as though he was being followed. He slowed and turned. There was nothing on the beach, but there was a dark cloud far to the north. For an alarming moment he thought there was another great storm on the way – there'd been a few groundshakers recently that had washed away the fishing nets and had people talking about Ragnarok ending the world – but then realised the cloud was a flock of crowd pigeons. One of the insanely huge flocks had flown over Hardwork before, millions upon millions of birds that had taken days to pass and left everything coated with pigeon shit. Finnbogi quickened his pace – he did not want to return to Hardwork covered in bird crap – and resumed his musings on Thyri.

He climbed over a bark-stripped log obstructing a narrow, sandy headland and heard voices and laughter ahead. Finnbogi knew who it was before he trudged up the rise in the beach and saw them. It was the gang of friends a few years older than he was.

Wulf the Fat ran into the sea, naked, waving his arms and yelling, and dived with a mighty splash. Sassa Lipchewer smiled at her husband's antics and Bodil Gooseface screeched. Bjarni Chickenhead laughed. Garth Anvilchin splashed Bodil and she screeched all the more.

Keef the Berserker stood further out in Olaf's Fresh Sea, his wet, waist-length blond hair and beard covering his torso like a sleeveless shirt. He swung his long axe, Arse Splitter, from side to side above the waves, blocking imaginary blows and felling imaginary foes.

Finnbogi twisted his face into a friendly smile in case they caught him looking. Up ahead their clothes and weapons were laid out on the shingle. Bodil and Sassa's neatly embroidered dresses were hanging on poles. Both garments would have been Sassa Lipchewer creations; she spent painstaking hours sewing, knitting and weaving the most stylish clothes in Hardwork. She'd made the blue tunic and stripy trousers that Finnbogi was wearing, for example, and very nice they were too.

The four men's clothes, tossed with manly abandon on the shingle, were leathers, plus Garth Anvilchin's oiled chainmail. Garth's metal shirt weighed as much as a fat child, yet Garth wore it all day, every day. He said that it would rust if the rings didn't move against each other regularly so he had to wear it, and also he wanted to be totally comfortable when he was in battle.

In battle! Ha! The Hird's only battles were play fights with each other. The likelihood of them seeing real action was about the same as Finnbogi travelling west and taking on a dagger-tooth cat. He knew the real reason Garth wore the mail shirt all the time. It was because he was a prick.

Despite the pointlessness of it, many of the hundred or so Hardworkers spent much time learning to fight with the weapons brought over from the old world. All four of the bathing men were in the Hird, the elite fighting group comprising Hardwork's ten best fighters.

Finnbogi *had* expected to be asked to join the Hird last summer when someone had become too old and left, but Jarl Brodir had chosen Thyri Treelegs. That had smarted somewhat, given that she was a girl and only sixteen at the time − two years younger than him. It was true that she had been making weapons, practising moves and generally training to be a warrior every waking hour since she was about two, so she probably wouldn't be a terrible Hird member. And he supposed it was good to see a woman included.

All Hardwork's children learnt the reasons that Olaf the Worldfinder and Hardwork's other founders had left the east, sailed a salty sea more vast than anyone of Finnbogi's generation could supposedly imagine, then travelled up rivers and across great lakes to establish the settlement of Hardwork. Unfair treatment of women was one of those reasons. So it was good that they were finally putting a woman in the Hird, but it was a shame that it had robbed Finnbogi of what he felt was his rightful place. Not that he wanted to be in the stupid Hird anyway, leaping about and waving weapons around all day. He had better things to do.

Out to sea, Wulf the Fat dived under – he could stay down for an age – and Garth Anvilchin caught sight of Finnbogi on the beach. "Hey, Boggy!" he shouted, "Don't even think about touching our weapons or I'll get one of the girls to beat you up!"

Finnbogi felt himself flush and he looked down at the weapons – Garth's over-elaborately inlaid hand axes the Biter Twins, Bjarni's beautiful sword Lion Slayer, Wulf's thuggish hammer Thunderbolt and Sassa's bow which wasn't an old world weapon so it didn't have a name.

"And nice outfit!" yelled Garth. "How lovely that you dress up when you go wanking in the woods. You have to treat your hand well when it's your only sexual partner, don't you, you curly-haired cocksucker?"

Finnbogi tried to think of a clever comeback based on the idea that if he sucked cocks then he clearly had more sexual partners than just his hand, but he didn't want to accept and develop the him-sucking-cocks theme.

"Fuck off then, Boggy, you're spoiling the view," Garth added before any pithy reply came to Finnbogi, curse him to Hel. Garth might be stupid but he had all the smart lines.

"Leave him alone," said Sassa Lipchewer. Finnbogi reddened further. Sassa was lovely.

"Yes, Garth," Bodil piped up. "Come for a wash, Finnbogi!"

"Yes, Boggy boy! Clean yourself off after all that wanking!" Garth laughed.

Wulf surfaced and smiled warmly at Finnbogi, the sun glinting off his huge round shoulders. "Come on in, Finn!" he called. Finally, somebody was calling him by the name he liked.

"Come in, Finn!" Bodil called. "Come in, Finn! Come in, Finn!" she chanted.

Sassa beckoned and smiled, which made Finnbogi gibber a little.

Behind them, Keef, who hadn't acknowledged Finnbogi's presence, continued to split the arses of imaginary enemies with his axe Arse Splitter.

"I can't swim now, I've got to . . . um . . ." Finnbogi nodded at the stump on his shoulder.

"Sure thing, man, do what you've got to do, see you later!" Wulf leapt like a salmon and disappeared underwater.

"Bye, Finn!" shouted Bodil. Sassa and Bjarni waved. Garth, towering out of the water, muscular chest shining, smiled and looked Finnbogi up and down as if he knew all about the wasp, why he was wearing his best clothes and what he had planned for the stump.

"I don't know why you give that guy any time . . ." he heard Garth say as he walked away.

He didn't know why the others gave any time to Garth Anvilchin. He was *such* a dick. They were okay, the rest of them. Wulf the Fat had never said a mean word to anyone. Bjarni Chickenhead was friendly and happy, Sassa Lipchewer was lovely. And Bodil Gooseface . . . Bodil was Bodil, called Gooseface not because she looked like a goose, but because Finnbogi had once announced that she had the same facial expressions as a clever goose, which she did, and the name had stuck. Finnbogi felt a bit bad about that, but it wasn't his fault that he was so incisively observant.

He walked on, composing cutting replies to Garth's cock-sucking comments. The best two were "Why don't you swim out to sea and keep on swimming?" and "Spoiling the view am I? You're the only person here with a good view because you're not in it!"

He wished he'd thought of them at the time.

Chapter 2

A Scrayling City

Three hundred and fifty miles to the south of Hardwork, Chamberlain Hatho marched through the main western gateway of Calnia, capital of the Calnian empire and greatest city in the world. After almost a year away, the teeming industry of his home town was such a joyful shock that he stopped and shook his head. Had he been one of Calnia's uncouth Low, he would have gawped and possibly cursed.

He inhaled slowly through his nose to calm himself, swelling his chest with sweet Calnian air. By Innowak the Sun God and the Swan Empress herself, Calnia was an impressive sight.

As the Swan Empress Ayanna's ambassador to the other empires, Chamberlain Hatho had travelled thousands of miles. Some of the cities he'd seen did in fact rival Calnia in size and splendour, but for the last few weeks he'd been travelling by dog-drawn travois and boat through less sophisticated lands. The greatest settlements he'd seen for a good while had been casual collections of crooked cabins, tents and other meagre dwellings. Staying in those village's finest lodgings had made Chamberlain Hatho itch all over. How did the Low live like such animals?

"Chippaminka, does Calnia not rise above every other town and city like an elk towering over a herd of deermice?"

His young alchemical bundle carrier and bed mate Chippaminka gripped his arm and pressed her oiled torso against his flank.

"It is truly amazing," she replied, her bright eyes satisfyingly widened.

He held the girl at arm's length. She was wearing a breechcloth embroidered with an exquisite porcupine-quill swan, the gold swan necklace that he'd given her to reflect light and her new allegiance to Innowak the Sun God, and nothing else. She held his gaze with a coquettish smile then licked her top lip.

He had to look away.

He was pleased with his new alchemical bundle carrier. Very pleased. The woman who'd fulfilled the role previously had disappeared early on his embassy, in the great port town at the mouth of the Water Mother. Walking along, he'd turned to ask her something and she hadn't been there. He'd never seen her again.

That evening a serving girl had seen he was morose and claimed her dancing would cheer him up. He'd told her to clear off and protested as she'd started to dance anyway, but his angry words had turned to dry squeaks as her sinuous slinkiness, smouldering smile and sparkling eyes had stunned him like a snake spellbinding a squirrel.

At the end of her dance he'd asked Chippaminka to be his new alchemical bundle carrier. She'd been at his side ever since. She was the perfect companion. She knew when he needed to eat, when he wanted time on his own, when to let him sleep, when to talk, when to stay silent and, most joyfully of all, when to make love and how to leave him smiling for hours.

Chamberlain Hatho was forty-five years old. He'd always thought that love was at best a delusion, at worst an affectation. But now he knew what love was. Chippaminka had shown him. At least once every waking hour and often in his dreams, he thanked Innowak that he'd met her.

She gripped his hand. "It is a wonderful city. But what are all these people *doing*?"

He pointed out the various stations of industry that lined the road running into the city from the western gate. "Those are knappers knapping flint, then there are metalworkers heating and hammering copper, lead and iron nuggets dug from soil to the north. Next are tanners curing skins with brains, marrow and liver, then there are artisans working with shells, clay, marble, feathers, chert, porcupine quills, turquoise and all manner of other materials to create tools, pipes, baskets, carvings, beads, pottery and more. That next group are tailors who sew, knit, twine, plait and weave cotton, bark fibres and wool from every furry animal in the Swan Empress's domain."

"They seem so *diligent*. They must be very intelligent."

"On the contrary," smiled Chamberlain Hatho. "These are the Low, the simple people who perform mundane but skilled roles so that people like me – and you, dear Chippaminka – might soar higher than our fellow men and women."

The girl nodded. "What are those Low doing?" She pointed at a team of women spraying white clay paint from their mouths in ritualistic unison onto leather shields.

"They are using paint and saliva as alchemy to create magic shields."

"Magic! Whatever next?"

Chamberlain Hatho surveyed the wondrous, teeming array of sophisticated industry and nodded proudly. "Yes, you must find it simply amazing; like something from one of your tribe's legends, I should imagine. And this is just the artisan quarter. As you'll see when we explore, there are thousands of others beavering away throughout Calnia, all dedicated to the tasks essential for keeping a city of twenty-five thousand people clothed, fed and ruling over the empire."

"So many?"

"The empire stretches north and south from Calnia for hundreds of miles along the eastern side of the Water Mother, so, yes, that many are needed."

"And what are those mountains, Chamberlain Hatho?"

Chippaminka nodded at the dozens of flat-topped pyramids rising from the Low's pole and thatch dwellings like lush islands in a muddy sea. The flanks of the largest were coated with a solid-hued black clay and topped with gold-roofed buildings blazing bright in the sun.

"They are pyramids, constructions of great magic that house Calnia's finest. The highest is the Mountain of the Sun, where we are headed now to see the Swan Empress Ayanna herself. You see that pyramid behind it?"

"The little one on the right? The much less impressive one?"

"Yes . . . That is my pyramid. It is not as high as the Mountain of the Sun, but broad enough that its summit holds my own house, slave dormitory and sweat lodge. It is where we will live."

"*We?*"

"If you will consent to live with me?" He felt the surge of fear, that terrible fear that had grown with his love, as if Innowak could not allow love without fear. The terror that Chippaminka might leave him dizzied him and loosened his bowels.

"I would *love* to live with you," she said and he resisted the urge to jump and clap. That would not look good in front of the Low. He'd never known such a swing of emotions was possible. He'd been terrified. Now, because of a few words from a girl, he had never been happier. Had humans always been so complicated, he wondered, or had the Calnians reached a pinnacle of cultural sophistication which was necessarily accompanied by such conflicting and high emotion?

"Come, let us report to the empress, then you will see your new home."

He headed off along the road with Chippaminka half walking, half dancing to keep up. Her dancing walk was one of the thousand things he loved about her.

He wrinkled his nose at the acrid whiff from the tanners and turned to Chippaminka. She'd already delved into the alchemical bundle and was holding out a wad of tobacco to render the stench bearable. He opened his mouth and she popped it in, fingers lingering on his lips for an exquisite moment. He squashed the tobacco ball between his molars, then pressed it into his cheek with his tongue. Its sharp taste banished the foul smell immediately.

Industry banged, chimed and scraped around them like a serenading orchestra and the joy in his heart soared to harmonise with its euphoric tune.

Ahead on the broad road children who'd been playing with bean shooters, pipestone animals, wooden boats and other toys cleared the way and watched open-mouthed as he passed. As well they might. It was not every day that the Chamberlain, the second equal most important person in Calnia, walked among them. Moreover, his demeanour, outfit and coiffure were enough to strike awe into any that saw him.

Chippaminka had plucked the hair from his face and the back of his head with fish-bone tweezers that morning. Tweezers gave a much fresher look than the barbaric shell-scraping method of the Low. Long hair fanned out like a downward pointing turkey tail from the nape of his neck, stiffened with bear fat and red dye. The hair on the top of his head was set into a spiked crown with elk fat and black dye, enhanced by the clever positioning of the black feathers plucked from living magnificent split tail birds. He could have used ravens' feathers, but those were for the Low. Magnificent split tail birds were long-winged creatures that soared on the tropical airs in the sea to the south. Young men and women would prove their skill and bravery by collecting feathers from the adult birds without harming them. It was nigh on impossible, so the feathers were fearfully valuable;

the six in Chamberlain Hatho's hair were worth more than the collected baubles of every Low in Calnia.

His breechcloth was the supplest fawn leather, his shoes the toughest buffalo. The crowning garment was as wonderful as any of Empress Ayanna's robes, commissioned in a fit of joy the day after he'd met Chippaminka. Six artisans had worked on it for months while he'd travelled south. It was a cape in the shape of swans' wings, inlaid with twenty-five thousand tiny conch beads. The whole was to honour the Swan Empress, with each bead representing one citizen in her capital city. He hoped it would impress her.

Despite his splendid cape, his most subtle adornment was his favourite. It was his strangulation cord. He hoped that he would die before Empress Ayanna. However, if she were to die before him, he would be strangled with the cord of buffalo leather that he'd tanned himself, cut and worn around his neck ever since. He might love Chippaminka with all his heart, but that did not dim his devotion to Ayanna, Swan Empress and worldly embodiment of the Sun God Innowak who flew across the sky every day, bathing the world in warmth and light.

"Will we be safe from the weather now that we are here, Chamberlain Hatho?" Chippaminka asked. Their journey had been plagued by mighty storms. They'd seen two tornados larger than any he'd heard of and passed through a coastal town which had been destroyed by a great wave two days before. The root of the astonishing weather was the chief finding of Chamberlain Hatho's mission. He hoped that Empress Ayanna already knew about it and, more importantly, had laid plans to deal with it.

"Yes," he said. "You will always be safe with me."

They passed from the industrial zone into the musicians' quarter, where the air vibrated and shook with the music of reed trumpets, deer-hoof and tortoise-shell rattles, clappers, flutes and a variety of drums. A choir started up. The singers held a high note then stepped progressively lower, in a sophisticated, well-practised harmony so beautiful that every hair that Chippaminka hadn't plucked from Chamberlain Hatho's body stood on end.

Two other voices rang out, sounding almost exactly like screams of terror. Hatho looked about for the source, intending to admonish them and to have them executed if they did not apologise to a satisfactorily fawning degree.

Instead, his mouth dropped open.

Several of the choir had stone axes in their hands and were attacking other singers. It was no musicians' squabble over a muddled melody; these were full-strength, killer blows to the head. Blood was spraying. Time slowed as a chunk of brain the size and colour of a heartberry arced through the air and splatted onto Chamberlain Hath's eye-wateringly valuable cape.

Further along the road, more men and women were producing weapons and setting about unarmed musicians and other Low. By their look, the attackers were Goachica.

Chamberlain Hatho guessed what was happening. This was the Goachica strike that he'd warned about for years. The northern province of Goachica had been part of the Calnian empire for two hundred years. Many Goachica lived and worked in Calnia. One of Hatho's direct underlings – which made her one of the highest ranking people in Calnia – was Goachica.

Five years before, a few Goachica had stopped paying tribute. This happened every now and then in the empire and it was simple to deal with. You either flattered the rebels into restarting their payments with a visit from a high official such as himself, or you found the ringleader or ring-leaders and tortured him, her or them to death in front of the rest.

However, the previous emperor, Zaltan, had overreacted with the Goachica. He'd sent an army with the orders to kill all who'd withheld taxes. Dozens of Goachica had failed to give tribute only because Goachica's leaders had told their tax collectors not to collect it. To any objective eye these people were as near to innocent as makes no difference; many even had the bags of wild rice that was Goachica's main contribution stacked and ready to go to Calnia.

The Calnian army had killed the lot of them.

Many relatives and friends of the slain Goachica lived in Calnia and many more had moved there since. Chamberlain Hatho had warned that these people would make trouble and advocated either apologising and giving reparations, or slaughtering them. Other issues, however, had taken precedence, not least Ayanna slaying Zaltan and becoming empress herself.

Because the massacre was entirely Zaltan's doing, and because actions like that one had been the chief reason for his assassination, people had thought the Goachica would have forgiven Calnia. Chamberlain Hatho's had warned that this was unlikely. He was less happy than usual to be proven correct.

To his right, several of the choir were fighting back with their instruments as weapons and the attackers were held.

Up ahead, he saw to his relief, three of the Owsla – Malilla Leaper, Sitsi Kestrel and the Owsla's captain, Sofi Tornado – had appeared. They were making short work of the attackers.

Malilla Leaper leapt over a man, braining him with her heavy kill staff as she flew. Sitsi Kestrel was standing on a roof, legs planted wide, her huge eyes picking targets, her bow alive in her hands as she loosed arrow after arrow. Sofi Tornado was dancing like a leaf in a gale, dodging attacks and felling Goachica with forehand and backhand blows from her hand axe. They said that Sofi could see a second into the future, which made her impossible to kill. Certainly none of the attacking Goachica came close to landing a blow on her.

Chamberlain Hatho felt a thrill to see the Owsla again. He had been ashamed when Emperor Zaltan created an elite squad based on his perverted desire for seeing attractive young women hurting and killing people in varied, often grim ways. However, the Owsla had proven to be a fearsomely effective squad of killers. More than that, the unbeatable ten had come to symbolise the success, power and beauty of Calnia.

Just as their chief god Innowak had tricked Wangobok and stolen the sun, so Calnia's rise to power had begun with alchemy-charged warriors rising up and freeing the ancient Calnians from imperial tyrants. Now Calnia ruled its own, much larger empire and the Owsla were its cultural and martial pinnacle; the beautiful, skilful, magical deterrent that kept peace across the empire. No chief dared antagonise Ayanna, knowing that a visit from the Calnian Owsla could follow.

There was a roar as a crowd of Goachica warriors rushed from a side street and charged the three Owsla.

Chamberlain Hatho gulped. Surely even Sofi Tornado, Malilla Leaper and Sitsi Kestrel would be overwhelmed by such a number? This was a much larger attack than he'd imagined the Goachica capable of.

He turned to Chippaminka, determined to save her. Their escape lay back the way they had come, surely, into the industrial sector where the Low craftspeople would be better armed and more inclined to fight than the musicians.

Chippaminka smiled at him sweetly, the same look she gave him before they made love. Had she not seen what was happening?

Her arm flashed upwards and he felt something strike his neck. A gout of blood splashed onto Chippaminka's bare chest.

What was this?

A second pump of hot blood soaked his smiling love. He

saw that she was holding a bloodied blade. No, not a blade. It was her gold Innowak swan necklace.

She'd slit his throat! His love had slit his throat! With the necklace he'd given her!

She winked then nodded, as if to say *yes, that's right.*

The world swirled. He collapsed to his knees. He reached up to Chippaminka. This was wrong, it must be a dream, she wouldn't have, she couldn't have . . .

He felt her small hand grip his wonderfully coiffed hair – coiffed by her with such love and attention. She pulled his head back, then wrenched it downwards as she brought up her hard little knee to meet it. He felt his nose pop. Blood blinded him.

Then he felt her arms around him.

"No!" she cried. "They've killed Chamberlain Hatho!"

But I'm still alive, he thought. But oh he was tired. So tired. But he was warm in her arms. As good a place as any to sleep, he thought, drifting away.